# PRAISE FOR DAVID RICCIARDI

"Starts with a bang and then gets better and better. . . .
One of the best thrillers you'll read this year."
—#1 *New York Times* bestselling
author Lee Child

"*Rogue Strike* doesn't let up for a moment. There's no
time to sit back and catch your breath, because each chap-
ter explodes with action."    —*New York Journal of Books*

"This is a fun and heady combination of suspense and
intrigue. Believable and provocative, it's a tough-as-nails
tug-of-war definitely worth your time."
—Steve Berry, *New York Times* bestselling
author of *The Lost Order*

"[A] blazing thriller with relentless pace and impressive
detail. An engaging combination of intrigue and action,
along with a breakneck cadence that will keep readers
flipping pages to the end. *Warning Light* is a winner."
—Mark Greaney, #1 *New York Times* bestselling
author of *Agent in Place*

"Over-the-top action, a deadly conspiracy, and several
well-timed twists make *Rogue Strike* another winner
from David Ricciardi, who delivers two back-to-back
fun, hard-hitting thrillers out of the gate."
—The Real Book Spy

*Berkley titles by David Ricciardi*

WARNING LIGHT
ROGUE STRIKE

# *ROGUE*
# *STRIKE*

DAVID RICCIARDI

BERKLEY
New York

**BERKLEY**
An imprint of Penguin Random House LLC
penguinrandomhouse.com

Copyright © 2019 by David Ricciardi
Excerpt from *Black Flag* © 2020 by David Ricciardi
Penguin Random House supports copyright. Copyright fuels creativity, encourages
diverse voices, promotes free speech, and creates a vibrant culture. Thank you for buying
an authorized edition of this book and for complying with copyright laws by not
reproducing, scanning, or distributing any part of it in any form without permission.
You are supporting writers and allowing Penguin Random House to continue to
publish books for every reader.

BERKLEY and the BERKLEY & B colophon are registered trademarks of
Penguin Random House LLC.

ISBN: 9780399585784

Berkley hardcover edition / June 2019
Berkley premium edition / March 2020

Printed in the United States of America
1   3   5   7   9   10   8   6   4   2

Cover art: *Man holding gun* by Stephen Mulcahey / Arcangel images
Cover design by Pete Garceau

*For my parents, who've never stopped inspiring me*

**ACKNOWLEDGMENTS**

# *ACKNOWLEDGMENTS*

Many people made significant contributions to the creation of *Rogue Strike*. All have chosen to remain anonymous. The individuals' motives for pitching in are as diverse as their reasons for serving their country: fellowship, a desire to see their respective fields portrayed correctly in the public eye, and a wish for their comrades to receive recognition for the selfless and often dangerous work they do on behalf of the rest of us.

To a man, OPSEC issues were paramount. Methods, procedures, call signs, and a variety of other details were intentionally changed or omitted so that only those who should know, do. Technical details of certain events ensured that they were believable, but not executable. On top of all that, I'm sure I made a few mistakes. Probably more than a few, if history is any guide.

On the publishing side, I owe debts of gratitude to my agent Rick Richter at Aevitas Creative Management and the team at Berkley: my editor/alchemist, Tom Colgan; the marketing duo of Fareeda Bullert and Jin Yu; my publicists, Loren Jaggers and Tara O'Connor;

and president and fellow sailor, Ivan Held. Thank you all for your hard work and support! I couldn't ask for a better team.

Most importantly, I'd like to thank my family for their unwavering enthusiasm.

*The best way out is always through.*

ROBERT FROST, 1874–1963

T HE TWO MEN in the bed of the old pickup told the driver to step on it—they could survive a rough ride.

They might not survive being late.

Two days earlier, a communications intercept had revealed an upcoming meeting involving the number one target on the U.S. government's disposition matrix. Known as Mullah Muktar, he was a quasi-religious leader who'd helped plan the September 11th attacks, then risen to become the leader of a violent extremist organization known as al-Qaeda in the Arabian Peninsula.

And it was time to send him to Paradise.

A wake of dust rose behind the pickup truck as it pounded over the dirt road. The monsoon rains usually turned the Wadi Bana into a flowing river that made life in southern Yemen almost tolerable for a few months each year, but the rains had been light this season. The land was hard and dry.

The driver switched on his lights as he turned onto a paved road. The town of Zinjibar loomed in the cracked windshield. Most of its buildings had been destroyed in the war, and the air smelled of smoke and a fine dust that never quite settled to the ground.

The senior CIA officer slapped the roof twice as they passed an open-air market. The pickup turned into an alley and slowed. He threw a goatskin satchel over his shoulder and jumped down to the street.

Two blocks away, the second officer hopped out. He was dressed in a mishmash of loose-fitting pants and a faded wool coat that was popular with the locals. He stooped over and feigned a slight limp, hoping that darkness and distance would make him look like one of the many old men who carried their wares to the market each morning.

*Game time, Zac,* he thought to himself.

Then he grimaced.

*Zac's gone.*

He was known as Jake Keller now and on his first mission as part of the Agency's elite Special Activities Center. He walked back to the main boulevard and climbed a pile of rubble to enter an abandoned apartment building. His partner was already there, standing in the dark with a scruffy beard, a scarf wrapped around his head, and a stubby AKS-74U rifle in his hands.

Curt Roach, a thirty-eight-year-old former special operations marine, was nine years older than Jake and had worked in the military or CIA his entire adult life. He hid a battery-powered motion detector in the lobby and motioned to the stairway. Jake unclipped his own rifle from a harness under his jacket and unfolded the wire stock. The two men ascended the concrete stairs in silence and cleared each room in the five-story building.

"Let's get set up," Roach said. "This thing could go down any minute."

Jake hung camouflage netting from the ceiling, five feet back from the outside wall. Roach set up a tripod behind the net.

"Pass me the designator."

Jake handed him what looked like a high-tech pair of binoculars. The device would bounce a beam of invisible infrared light off whatever it was pointed at. It could determine the target's coordinates or guide a missile onto it from an aircraft circling above.

"Run the antennas?" Jake said as he scratched his beard.

Roach nodded. "Just be sure they can't be seen from the ground."

Jake disappeared up the stairs, trailing a thin cable behind him. He returned a few minutes later.

"SATCOM and GPS are up. I'll check in," he said.

*"Mustang, Mustang, this is Cobra."*

From a top secret facility halfway across the Arabian Peninsula, the CIA mission control element responded.

*"Cobra, go for Mustang."*

*"Mustang, Cobra at position Alpha."*

*"Copy position Alpha. Strike package is two ships. Drifter-71 and Drifter-72 are hard altitude eighteen thousand feet and orbiting your position with fifteen hours till bingo."*

High overhead, two unmanned combat aerial vehicles flew racetrack patterns around the city. From a distance, the stealthy, bat-winged UCAVs resembled miniature B-2 bombers. They each carried fifteen hours of fuel and a pair of air-to-ground missiles in an internal weapons bay.

The two CIA officers watched the streets for hours until a battered Nissan pickup truck arrived spewing black smoke from its diesel engine. Six men with rifles hopped down. After suffering through decades of a multiparty civil war, nearly everyone in Yemen had a gun, but these men positioned themselves around the intersection with overlapping fields of fire on all of the approaches.

Curt reached for the SATCOM. He whispered despite being two hundred meters away.

*"Mustang, we have six military-age males in the open at Alpha. Definite weapons and tactical movement."*

*"Roger that, Cobra,"* said the radio. *"Be advised we are tracking three vehicles westbound to your position."*

A heavily muscled man in fatigue pants and a black T-shirt stared up at the nearby buildings. His gaze shifted methodically, right to left, top to bottom, looking for anything out of the ordinary. Despite having the early morning sun in his eyes, he paused at the floor where Jake and Curt were holed up. He started walking toward the Americans' building, when three identical SUVs stopped in the intersection.

Mullah Muktar emerged from the third vehicle.

*"Mustang, we have Jupiter at Alpha,"* Roach said. *"He's linking up with the six dismounts."*

*"Roger, Cobra,"* said mission control. *"Facial recognition confirms positive ID on Jupiter. Drifter-72 in range. Ten hours till bingo. Mustang standing by."*

The man in the fatigue pants escorted Muktar into the building across the street.

Twenty minutes later, a tan Yemeni government Land

Rover arrived and four soldiers climbed out. A civilian wearing an open-necked suit emerged from the passenger seat.

"There goes our operation," Jake said.

Roach scowled. The Agency's rules of engagement prohibited any action that jeopardized the safety of Yemeni government personnel. He picked up the radio.

*"Mustang, we have Saturn in a tan government truck with a four-man security detail."*

"Why would government forces drive that truck into al-Qaeda territory?" Jake said. "Those two have been at each other's throats for years."

"Because those aren't government forces," Roach said. "These guys know our ROE and they're using them against us. Look at Saturn's security detail. They're looking for external threats. Legitimate government forces would be watching Muktar's men. The truck is a hoax."

Roach looked through the laser designator's magnified optics as the man in the open-necked suit entered the building.

*"Jupiter and Saturn are inside the target,"* Roach said.

*"Cobra, government personnel are outside the ROE. Drifter-71 will target Jupiter's vehicle once he clears the area."*

*"Negative, Mustang. The truck is a ruse,"* Roach said. *"These bastards killed three thousand Americans and now it's payback time. Spin up your missiles."*

The man in the fatigue pants returned to the street and linked up with another man. They started walking toward Jake and Roach's building.

"You see this?" Jake said as he picked up his rifle.

Roach nodded.

"Why don't you want to hit Muktar's truck after he leaves?" Jake asked. "Just in case."

"First, there's zero chance that those are government troops. They'd never make it past the al-Qaeda checkpoints. Second, the mullah has been dodging drone strikes for years. As soon as those vehicles start rolling, his goons will play a shell game with them. The odds of a successful mission go down by two-thirds the second he gets in that truck."

The radio chirped again. *"Roger, Cobra. Drifter-72 is in range and holding on station. Prepare to provide terminal guidance."*

*"Negative on the terminal guidance,"* Roach said. *"We've got hostiles inbound. We're going to transmit co-ordinates instead."*

In terminal guidance mode, the designator would send coded pulses of laser light that would guide the drone's missiles to the target, but Roach and Jake would have to stay in position for the duration of the operation, and Roach was worried about the man in the camo pants.

Roach pressed several buttons on the designator and keyed the SATCOM.

*"Cobra transmitting coordinates now,"* he said. *"You are cleared hot."*

*"Good copy on coordinates, Cobra. Missile launch in three . . . two . . . one . . ."*

Roach's watch vibrated. "Somebody just triggered the motion detector in the lobby."

Jake took his rifle to the stairs and listened for the intruders. He glanced at Roach.

*Shouldn't the missiles have hit by now?*

Roach was thinking the same thing.

*"Mustang, repeat, cleared hot. Execute."*

*"Stand by, Cobra,"* said the voice on the SATCOM. *"We are, uh, negative contact with Drifter-72 at this time. Drifter-71 is being retargeted now."*

"What the hell just happened?" Jake said.

Roach shrugged.

*"Cobra, be advised Drifter-71 will be in range in one-six minutes. Maintain position."*

Down in the street below, the two principals exited the meeting.

Roach keyed the SATCOM. *"Mustang, we're about to lose both targets."*

The radio was silent as Jupiter and Saturn spoke on the street.

Jake heard footsteps a few floors below them. He put his rifle to his shoulder and aimed down the stairway.

Jupiter and Saturn looked like old friends as they exchanged hugs and kisses on both cheeks.

Jake heard men speaking one floor down and Roach cupped the microphone in his hand.

*"Mustang, Mustang . . . Repeat, we are losing both targets."*

The voices stopped. Roach picked up his rifle.

Two minutes later, the man in the fatigue pants and his partner appeared on the street next to Mullah Muktar.

"We've been chasing that sonofabitch for almost twenty years and he's going to walk again," Roach said.

He practically shouted into the mic. *"Mustang, this is Cobra. Jupiter and Saturn are bugging out. Does Drifter-71 have eyes on target yet?"*

The men on the street entered their vehicles. Roach hammered the SATCOM with his fist.

*"Mustang, this is Cobra, how copy?"* he said as the terrorists drove away.

He switched off the designator and sat back against the wall. He kicked the SATCOM across the floor and looked at Jake.

"We'll call for extraction once it's dark."

## TWO

THE CAMERAMAN USUALLY covered soccer matches for the Al-Arabiya television network, but the equipment today was the same, the best that money could buy. He could capture a million people in the frame or zoom in on a single face. Ultra-high-definition sensors rendered flawless images of whatever he'd selected. The control booth would occasionally tell him to take an artistic shot, and on a clear night he would zoom in on the moon and fill viewers' screens with images of craters, ridges, and shadows that most people never knew existed. It was an awesome piece of technology.

From high atop one of the hotels, he panned right to catch the buses, cars, and pedestrians that were clogging the highway from Mina. They were latecomers making their way back to the Masjid al-Haram, the enormous outdoor mosque in the holy city of Mecca, Saudi Arabia. It was the last day of the Hajj, and they were obligated to enter the mosque and complete the final *tawaf*, seven laps around the black building in the center known as the Kaaba. Only then would Allah erase their sins and their pilgrimage be complete.

Covering the Hajj was easy work for the cameraman, except for the heat, which could run to 130 or 140 degrees Fahrenheit on the roof. He downed another bottle of water and zoomed in on the profile of a single pilgrim, prostrate before the Kaaba with his hands pressed up against its stone side. Tears of joy streamed down the man's face as the song of the muezzin appeared to be directed only to him. It was one of the cameraman's favorite shots. He focused on the individual for several seconds.

The tearful man raised his head and the cameraman began to zoom out. He widened the frame until it included the dozen or so people closest to the pilgrim, symbolizing the man's family. He kept widening the picture until perhaps a hundred people were in the shot, representing the pilgrim's community. The cameraman kept zooming out until viewers could see the *tawaf,* rotating counterclockwise like a great galaxy of Islam. The final shot encompassed the entire Grand Mosque with the Kaaba drawing the viewer's eyes to the center. It was breathtaking. The booth usually held it for twenty or thirty seconds before cutting to a different angle. The cameraman lifted his eyes from his viewfinder and looked out over the scene, savoring the moment.

There was an explosion in the crowd, followed by a cloud of smoke rising into the air near the Kaaba. The crying man was gone, vaporized along with at least a thousand people around him.

*Oh, no,* thought the cameraman. *Some madman snuck in a bomb. Is nowhere sacred?*

There was a second explosion and more smoke on the other side of the Kaaba. And then he heard the sound, the whoosh of two objects flying rapidly through the air, followed by the noise of the explosions.

*Delayed by the speed of sound,* he realized. *Not a madman on the ground, but a madman in the air . . .*

The cameraman instinctively spun the camera toward the action. Its powerful lens picked up faint trails of smoke. He followed them into the sky and zoomed in until he spotted a dot in the distance. He zoomed as fast and as far as he could until the dot took form, the form of an aircraft turning away. The image was grainy on the hot and hazy summer day, but the cameraman had no doubts about what it was. The distinctive, bat-winged aircraft was possessed by only one nation on earth, and millions of people had just seen it attack the holiest site in all of Islam.

## THREE

W HAT THE HELL does 'negative contact' mean?
Did the UCAV crash?" Jake said.

Roach just scowled. He'd been wondering the same thing and the CIA mission control element wasn't responding.

"I'm going to check the east side of the building," Jake said, more out of frustration than anything else. He took his rifle.

It was early afternoon, the Yemeni equivalent of a siesta, when much of the male population was out on the street. Despite the heat, most were dressed in baggy trousers, blousy shirts, and camel hair coats, often with loose turbans wrapped around their heads. Many carried a curved dagger, known locally as a *jambiya*, tucked in their waists. Once a fearsome weapon, the *jambiya* had become largely ceremonial over the last few decades. For serious work, nearly everyone had a Kalashnikov in his hand, on his shoulder, or leaning against a nearby wall.

Most of the idlers were chewing a locally grown stimulant called qat and visiting with their neighbors, but there were others, groups of men with long beards and unblinking eyes. They were al-Qaeda soldiers, and the locals usually gave them a wide berth.

But something was different today. The qat chewers were agitated. Jake raised his binoculars. A quarter mile away, a group of men were walking down the street, shouting and waving weapons around. Someone fired into the air.

"Curt, check this out," Jake said across the hallway. He didn't bother whispering.

Roach had heard the gunfire.

"Sounds like a Middle Eastern wedding," he said as he walked over. The two men stood back from the window to stay in the shadows.

"They don't look very happy."

"Sounds like my wedding," Roach said. "Let's stick with the plan and exfil after dark."

Jake shook his head. "I don't like it. When was the last time you saw the locals walking arm in arm with al-Qaeda?"

Roach watched the action on the street for a few minutes before he walked to the other room and tried the SATCOM again.

*"Mustang, this is Cobra. Come in, Mustang . . . Mustang, Mustang, this is Cobra. How copy?"*

Jake stared through the binoculars. The mob was maybe seventy-five men now. There was more gunfire.

Roach came back scowling. "Comms are still down. This is starting to feel like a Ted Graves Special."

"What's a Ted Graves Special?" Jake asked, although he already had a pretty good idea.

"Just an expression . . ."

"Well, something is bringing the two groups together," Jake said. "Maybe a common enemy?"

"If it's the Saudis, they'll soften up the target with airstrikes before any ground offensive. We don't want to be in the tallest building around if we're looking at Saudi airstrikes. They aren't known for precision bombing."

Jake packed up the rest of their gear while Roach used a cell phone to text their driver. The gunfire on the street grew closer. Individual voices could be heard among the din. Chants of "Death to America" and "Allah is the greatest" echoed through the streets.

Gunshots rang out just below the windows and the two Americans prepared to defend the stairs. Roach thumbed his rifle's selector switch. Jake closed his eyes and listened. The shouting and the gunfire shifted around the building and began to move away. A car drove past on the boulevard.

"Our ride should have been here by now," Jake said. He wiped the sweat from his brow.

The plan was for their driver to stay inside the city limits to avoid any issues at the checkpoints.

Curt's watch started vibrating again.

"Motion detector . . ." he said.

"Maybe it's our driver."

Roach grimaced. "Maybe."

He slung his satchel over his back and put the rifle to his shoulder. He descended the stairs silently, his head and rifle moving as one, methodically clearing the open space as a series of arcs. Jake followed behind, covering the opposing doorways and hallways, until the two men reached the second floor. A diesel truck passed by in low gear. Roach shook his wrist in the air to signal that the watch was still vibrating. Whoever had entered the lobby was still there.

Roach descended the next step, his rifle moving left. The arc was clear. He continued down several more stairs, scrutinizing everything, with Jake right behind him. An old Bongo truck backfired at the intersection, but their trained minds filtered it out.

They continued down the steps with the muzzles of their rifles probing the air for trouble. Sunlight streamed in through the doorway to the street, flooding the ground floor with light. They were five stairs from the bottom when Jake saw a shadow move against the back wall.

He reached down and squeezed Roach's shoulder. The two Americans began to back up the stairs, but the man in the lobby was walking toward the doorway. He had a thick beard and a well-used Kalashnikov at his side.

He spotted the two men on the stairs.

Roach instantly realized what had transpired. The man was part of the street mob. He was using the abandoned building as a toilet, a common practice in the war-ravaged city. Roach lowered his rifle and continued down the last few steps to the lobby floor.

The man spoke to Roach and he responded, but the Yemeni dialect of Arabic was nearly impossible for a foreigner to master.

The man went for his gun.

*FOUR*
_____

I N A LUSH, mountainous region of eastern Mexico, a
group of men in their twenties ran up a steep dirt
trail. Each had thought himself a specimen of fitness
before he'd arrived six weeks earlier, but despite the
shade provided by the thick forest canopy, the summer
heat and thin mountain air had humbled them all. In
the first week, groans and the sound of vomiting were
common as they jogged up the mountainside in long
pants and hiking boots, but their times had declined
steadily for the daily ten-kilometer run. Now, they leapt
over fallen trees and dodged boulders underfoot. The
only sounds were of steady breathing and boots pounding out a brutal pace.

As usual, the one known as Señor Paraíso was the
last man in the line, but he was far from the slowest
runner. It was his leadership style. He would run alongside those who were struggling, speaking words of encouragement. In their runs and in their training, he
pushed his men to accomplish what they'd never
thought possible. At the finish line, only the slowest
man's time went onto the board. In case anyone missed

the implication, the message was written in Spanish and English over the entrance to the dining facility.

*The success of each of us depends on the success of all of us.*

After the morning run, the men spent the first half of the day refining their Spanish and English skills. The speaking of other languages was strictly forbidden, for it could betray their true identities once their mission had begun.

There were no buildings in the compound and classes were held in underground rooms. The men found it cooler, but more importantly, the federal police aircraft and the American satellites couldn't find it at all. A regional drug cartel had given Señor Paraíso's sponsor use of the camp. The three-month lease and assorted other arrangements had been provided in exchange for the one thing the drug producers valued above all else: cash.

Afternoons were divided between mission planning, cultural instruction, and weapons training. All were important, but it was the weapons training that the men most enjoyed. Russian RPG-7 rocket-propelled grenades were fired with dummy warheads until the men had become proficient with the deadly weapon. Inert 81mm mortar rounds were launched until the team developed a feel for the effects of the heat and wind on their trajectories. Underground laboratories, normally used to process drugs, became workrooms where common chemicals were made into high explosives. Finally, marksmanship training, done with the ubiquitous and reliable Kalashnikov AK-47, was done with suppressors—for despite the size and seclusion of the facility, the time for the world to note their skills was not yet upon them.

It was at the end of a particularly long and hot day that one of the men turned his ankle and cursed in his native tongue. He was a star student, with language and weapon skills among the best in the group, yet a chill spread throughout the camp. Señor Paraíso dealt sharply with transgressors, and the man had been warned twice before.

The man limped over to Paraíso and said in Spanish, "Señor, please forgive my temper. Know that I will always do what is best for the mission."

Paraíso loved his men, but there was no room for mistakes. As quick as lightning and as loud as thunder, he drew his pistol and fired a single shot into the man's face.

"*That* is what is best for the mission."

# FIVE

ROACH LUNGED FORWARD and smashed the muzzle of his rifle into the man's sternum. He cried out in pain and fell backward onto the ground. When he looked up, Roach's weapon was still pointed at his chest.

A man who'd been out on the street heard the scream and looked inside. He saw Roach holding his friend at gunpoint and raised his own rifle, but Jake dropped him with three shots to the chest. A third man, six-foot-five and at least two hundred fifty pounds, stepped into the entryway, blocking it entirely. He held his rifle at his waist and began to rake the lobby on full auto. Jake put three rounds into his torso and two more into his head before the giant fell backward onto the street.

The man lying on the floor lunged for Roach's rifle but the former marine special-operations sergeant anchored him with two 5.45mm bullets in his heart.

Roach motioned Jake toward the door. They moved along opposite walls, weapons up, looking through the doorway to clear as much of the exterior as they could from the relative safety of the interior. Roach signaled that he would go through first and clear right, and that Jake should follow and clear left.

Roach stepped through the doorway with Jake barely a second behind. A man with an AK-47 was hidden across the street behind the hood of a burned-out car. He fired wildly, stitching a line of bullet holes over Jake's head and up the side of the building. Roach skipped half a dozen rounds under the old car and dropped the shooter.

The two Americans scanned the boulevard with their weapons up. The man behind the car was out of commission, but their ride was nowhere to be seen and they'd just made a hell of a lot of noise, even for Zinjibar. They folded the wire stocks on their stubby rifles, tucked them under their jackets, and hustled around the street corner.

Roach dialed their driver. "No answer."

They took a circuitous route to their alternate extraction point, watching carefully for any surveillance they might have picked up. The driver wasn't there either.

"First Drifter-72 disappears, then the SATCOM goes down, now this," Jake said. "It feels like this op just got rolled up."

Three teenage boys with guns rode by on a motor scooter, eyeing the two Americans as they passed.

"We need to boost some wheels and get out of here," said Roach. "Let's try the old taxi lot."

Roach gripped his Glock 19 pistol in his pocket while Jake held his rifle under his jacket. The two men spoke to each other in Arabic and gestured with their free hands as they walked down the sidewalk carrying their satchels and trying their hardest to look utterly unremarkable. Both had deep tans and had dyed their hair black. They would never pass for Yemenis, but the disguises gave them some breathing room, and they needed every inch of it. Several times, they crossed the street to avoid contact with the locals.

"There's the lot," Roach said.

Most of the taxis had been abandoned because few people in Zinjibar had anywhere to go and even fewer could afford a taxi. Roach took a multitool from his belt and started one of the old vans. Jake tossed their satchels in back and jumped in the passenger seat with his rifle across his lap.

The streets were empty as they drove through town. Jake tuned the AM radio until he picked up an Arabic-language station in Aden, forty miles away. The broadcaster spoke of an American airstrike, but that was not uncommon in Yemen. CIA and the U.S. military had made it the epicenter of U.S. drone strikes over the last five years.

Roach turned north over the broken pavement, toward the dirt road they'd taken into the city that morning. The radio announcer mentioned thousands of civilian casualties. As with any military action, the death of non-combatants was a tragic by-product of the drone campaign, but one that was often exaggerated or fabricated by the enemy to generate ill will toward America.

*But thousands?*

Not even the harshest critic of the drone program had suggested civilian deaths in the thousands.

Jake and Roach glanced at each other.

"Did he say where?" Jake asked. There was static on the airwaves and Roach's Arabic was better than his.

Roach shook his head slowly.

A minute later the announcer solved the mystery.

*Thousands dead at the Grand Mosque in Mecca. The distinctive shape of an American B-2 bomber was filmed turning away.*

Roach coasted to a stop in the middle of the road. The two CIA officers felt as if they'd had the wind knocked out of them.

Jake stared at the radio. "Drifter-72?"

The math worked. There had been enough time for the drone to fly from Zinjibar to Mecca. Two missiles had struck the mosque, one on either side of the Kaaba. To an amateur observer, Drifter-72 would have looked like a B-2, and the big bomber had the capability to launch missiles, not the kind that were used in the strike, but that didn't matter. It was a U.S. aircraft and the court of world opinion had already rendered its verdict.

Roach shook his head again. "I uploaded the right coordinates."

"This is what you meant by a 'Ted Graves Special,' isn't it?" Jake asked.

"First Drifter-72 disappears, then we lose the SAT-COM, then our exfil goes dark. I'm a big believer in Murphy's Law, but I don't believe in coincidences."

"I have my issues with Ted. He's a cold, calculating sonofabitch, but he's not a madman."

Roach started driving again, keeping his eyes on a sedan with faded black paint and mirrored windows all around. He'd seen it twice since they'd taken the van and it was behind them again.

"Ted isn't crazy," he said, "but he is aggressive. He was an operations trainee the first time the U.S. missed bin Laden. The president had authorized a cruise missile strike, but there was a high probability of civilian casualties, so they aborted the strike and UBL went into the wind for another three years."

"Until he and Muktar launched the 9/11 attacks," Jake said.

"Ted felt we weren't aggressive enough, early enough. Think about how many lives have been lost and how many trillions of dollars have been spent because of 9/11. What if we'd sent a special operations team into Kandahar in the middle of the night or launched the missiles anyway?"

The sedan with the mirrored windows pulled around them and kept driving. Roach checked for a backup car, but the road was deserted as sunset approached.

"You really think Ted would attack the Hajj to take out one guy?" Jake said.

"This isn't about one guy. This is about driving a wedge between the Muslim world and the U.S., a wedge that can't be removed. It's about shattering all hope for reconciliation. There will be retaliations against the U.S., which will convince people back home to transform the war on terror into a war on Islam. And who takes the fall? A couple of CIA pukes from Ground Branch. We're just collateral damage."

"They can't blame us for this," Jake said. "We never had control of the drone."

"Graves has been chief of Special Activities for less than a year. He's not going to take the fall for this if he can find someone else to pin it on."

A dusty pickup truck approached with four men and a box-fed light machine gun in its bed. The four fighters stared at Jake and Roach as they passed.

"We need to get out of Zinjibar," Roach said as he turned down a side street, "and we can't go back to the safe house in case our driver was compromised. Let's hit Tall Mohammed's shop. He'll know where the checkpoints are."

With his commanding height and hooded eyes, Tall Mohammed bore more than a passing likeness to the late Osama bin Laden, whose family had also been from Yemen. The resemblance had been an asset in establishing Mohammed's arms dealing business, until it had become a liability, and it was how he'd initially come to the attention of CIA.

"You think we can trust him?" Jake said.

"Definitely not, but we can buy him."

They drove west toward the city's commercial center. The surviving entrepreneurs in Zinjibar were mostly drug dealers and weapons smugglers, classes of people that rarely let ideology interfere with business.

They passed an old man leading a donkey cart filled with all of his possessions and turned down another side street. Two guards with AK-47s and bandoliers across their chests were outside Mohammed's building. Roach pulled to the curb a hundred feet from the entrance. He took a short stack of euros from a pouch strapped to his waist while Jake press-checked his pistol to confirm that a round was chambered.

They stepped out of the van and slung their rifles across their backs. Entering the shop unarmed would be seen as a sign of weakness. The two Americans traded hostile stares with the guards as they approached the front door, but entered without incident.

Mohammed was sitting sidesaddle on cushions on the floor, watching the television coverage from Mecca and smoking a hookah with three other men. A cloud of sweet shisha tobacco smoke hung in the air. Along the walls were well over a thousand well-used weapons: Kalashnikovs in a dozen configurations, American M-4s and M-16s, light and heavy machine guns, close to a hundred Makarov and Glock pistols, and a stack of RPG-7s propped in a corner. Mohammed grimaced when he saw the two Americans and motioned them to a back room. They spoke in English across a wooden table.

"You are either very arrogant or very foolish to come here today," he said.

"It wasn't us, Mohammed," Roach said.

"The television shows otherwise. There is no stepping back from the line America has just crossed. There were many in the Muslim world who hated the armed men more than the Americans, but that time has passed. Blood was literally spilled on the Black Stone today. There could be no greater affront to the memory of the Prophet, peace be unto him, and to mankind. Even the moderates will turn against you."

"That's why we need to get out of Zinjibar and straighten this out," Roach said. He pulled the bills from his pocket. "Which of your trading routes are still open?"

"We have done much business together," said Mohammed. "I am a merchant, and the conflict has been good for me, but I am also a Muslim. If you prove to me that the United States was not responsible for this horror, then I will once again embrace you like brothers, but until then, take your money and leave. You are not welcome in my shop, in my city, or in my country."

Mohammed drew the dagger from his belt and thrust it an inch deep into the hardwood table.

## SIX

PRESIDENT J. WILLIAM Day entered the White House Situation Room. The video monitors recessed into the walls were dark, the mood somber. Seated around the table were a dozen principals from the military, intelligence, diplomatic, and law enforcement communities. The president had already reamed out the CIA director in private, but this was the first meeting of the national security power players since the disaster in Mecca.

The president spoke to FBI director Ed Kerr. "Walk me through some scenarios, Ed."

"There are three possibilities, Mr. President," said the director. "First, there was a technical failure. The UCAV flew where it wasn't supposed to and launched its weapons due to some bug in the code, but we can dismiss that for obvious reasons. The odds against it flying to Mecca and striking the Grand Mosque during the Hajj are astronomical. Unfortunately, the other two possibilities entail malicious tampering with a special-access-program weapons system. Either someone hijacked it or the operators went rogue."

"Let's not engage in speculation," said Director David Feinman of CIA.

"I asked him to speculate," the president said. "The police treat every death as a murder until they prove otherwise, and right now everyone is a suspect until we prove otherwise. The United States has never been this isolated. This attack puts our economic prosperity and our physical safety at risk. I want the Bureau investigating it over at Langley immediately."

"Yes, sir, but we also need to pursue the possibility that this was a cyber attack. Based on recent intrusions and attempted intrusions into our networks, there are several countries that make the suspect list for something like this. In terms of capability and motive, I'd say Russia, China, and North Korea are at the top. India and Taiwan might have the capability but probably not the motive. Iran and Pakistan are at the bottom because they likely don't have the ability and it's improbable that another Muslim nation would attack Mecca. We're already coordinating with the director of national intelligence."

"This is one more reason why DoD should be running *all* of these operations," said the secretary of defense. "CENTCOM prosecuted over one hundred twenty strikes in Yemen last year and we never had anything like this happen."

The CIA director knew the dig was more about budget dollars than anything else, but he'd worked closely with the defense secretary over the past two years and didn't appreciate being kicked while he was down.

"Where is the aircraft now?" said the president.

"It crashed," said Feinman, "but it was equipped with a onetime, burst-encrypted emergency landing transmitter. We received a signal that it impacted the Red Sea, west of Mecca."

"We're in for a world of hurt if the Saudis pull it out of the water," said the president. "Is there any indication they know where it crashed?"

General Jay Landgraf, an army four-star general and chairman of the Joint Chiefs of Staff, answered. "There's been no mobilization of Saudi search assets, Mr. President."

"What about on our end?"

"We have a special operations submarine en route at flank speed, but it won't be on station for another twelve hours. It has orders to hold in international waters outside the Bab-el-Mandeb Strait pending your authorization to enter the Red Sea."

"Send it," said the president. "What about increasing our military readiness? We should be ready for the next act if this was a foreign state executing a false-flag operation."

"We've already moved all U.S. forces to Force Protection Condition Charlie," said General Landgraf.

"I'm not talking about a terrorist attack. I'm talking about war. What if this was done to justify an attack on the United States?"

"Sir, our overseas forces are already at a high state of readiness. I would caution that the Russians, the Chinese, and everyone within a hundred miles of our bases will notice any escalation in our posture. The rest of the world views what happened in Mecca as a U.S. attack on a longtime ally. If our adversaries see us ramping up, they might misunderstand our intentions and perceive it as a precursor to 'additional' offensive operations."

The president shifted in his chair. "The bottom line is that it was an American aircraft that killed those people and we should expect some sort of retribution. My job now is to minimize further loss of life, so while I appreciate your concern, General, as of this moment I'm ordering you to take all U.S. forces up to DEFCON-4."

# SEVEN

A DOZEN MEN IN spotless green and gold uniforms stood on either side of the palace steps. Each had a sword on his belt and a red-and-white-checked *ghutra* on his head.

*The Royal Guards . . . all show and no substance,* thought Deputy Crown Prince Faisal bin Farah-Aziz al Saud as his motorcade of armored Mercedes-Maybach sedans arrived. As head of the Saudi Arabian National Guard, it was Faisal and his men who provided the *real* security for the country, and they were exceedingly busy right now. He had spent most of the day in Mecca before flying back to Riyadh for the emergency cabinet meeting.

"Your Highness, the regional commander in Mecca has asked for permission to notify the victims' families," said Hakim al-Shezza, the prince's chief of staff.

"Tell him to wait until the rest of the bodies are identified," said the prince as he waited for someone to open his door.

"That could be days, sir, if not longer."

The prince turned his massive head. He added a single raised eyebrow to his perpetual scowl.

"Yes, of course, Your Highness," said al-Shezza. "The families can wait."

The prince gazed out the side window. "This could be catastrophic for the monarchy."

A member of the prince's security detail opened the car door and Faisal stepped into the hot night air, ascending the steps with al-Shezza in tow. The smell of incense drifted through the air as the two men entered a square receiving room that was sixty feet across and almost as high. Like an ornate tent, thick panels of blue and gold silk hung down from the center of the ceiling and were bunched along the walls. A crystal chandelier provided subdued light.

A palace usher led them to an enormous meeting room. With blond wood walls and golden pilasters, it was an elegant and imposing blend of the modern and the classic. The thirty members of the Council of Ministers were arrayed around a massive ring-shaped desk. They were the military and diplomatic leaders of the country. Many were also members of the kingdom's large royal family.

His Majesty King Ali bin Abdul-Aziz al Saud entered the room with a dozen aides in tow. He took his seat at the desk and led the group in prayer.

"We have suffered a great tragedy today," he said, "and I have failed in my duties as Custodian of the Two Holy Mosques. There are many calling for blood, and I too feel rage at such violence in a place whose very name forbids it, but as the kingdom's leaders, we must rise above our emotions and wait until the facts are known. It is premature to conclude that the United States was responsible for—"

Gasps of disbelief cut off the king in midsentence. Murmurs and angry words ripped through the room.

"Your Majesty," cried the minister of Hajj and Umrah. "What of the television footage? Is it not proof enough?"

"The sky in Mecca was hazy this morning, as it often is. The footage is of poor quality and inconclusive."

"But it was a stealth aircraft! Nothing was picked up on radar," called out the defense minister.

"Many nations now possess stealth aircraft," said the king. "My friends, I do not know that America is innocent, but neither do I know that it is guilty, and the consequences are far too significant to rush to judgment on our long-standing ally."

"But have they not backed away since increasing their domestic supply of oil?" asked the minister of energy.

"This is an attack on Allah Himself," said the minister for Islamic affairs. "The United States has declared war on Islam!"

"Enough!" the king bellowed, loud enough that several Royal Guards burst through the double doors. A chill descended over the room as the king's soldiers surveyed the proceedings.

*That couldn't have gone better if it was choreographed,* thought Prince Faisal. *I wonder if it was.*

The council discussed events related to the attack. Faisal remained silent until he was asked about widespread reports of unrest within Saudi Arabia's minority Shia community and a rising number of gatherings in the streets. In his role as head of the Saudi Arabian National Guard, he was known for ruthlessly quelling even the slightest dissent.

"You are all aware of my position on order and discipline," he said, "but this is a time for compassion. These gatherings are but peaceful expressions of grief. All of Saudi Arabia is suffering today."

Heads nodded around the table. It was a tragedy on a national level and on a personal level. Everyone in the room knew someone at Hajj that day. Many had been there themselves. Not in the square, of course, but they had witnessed the bloodshed from opulent hotels and royal apartments overlooking the mosque.

The king adjourned the meeting. Most of the participants left, but Faisal walked to the king, who greeted him with a hug. The two spoke privately.

"Thank you, Prince Faisal, for your measured words and actions."

"You are right to stand firm with the Americans, Your Majesty. They have come to our defense against many foes. We must not be precipitous in our judgment of such a powerful and long-standing ally."

"Indeed." The king motioned around the room. "These jackals are quick to judge, but few have ever felt the responsibility of true leadership."

# EIGHT

THE TWO CIA officers left Tall Mohammed's shop and walked to the van in silence, listening for the sound of footsteps behind them. Jake sat in the passenger seat with the door open and his rifle in his hands while Roach manipulated the ignition wires.

"Who are the 'armed men' Mohammed was talking about?" Jake asked.

"Allegiances here are fluid," Roach said. "One day a guy might be an AQAP fighter and the next day he'll be working for Daesh or even the government, so 'armed men' just covers all the guns for hire."

Jake shook his head. "Dangerous place."

"You can't let your guard down for a second," Roach said. He looked over his shoulder as the engine turned over. Tall Mohammed was on the street, talking with the two guards in front of his shop. They were watching the van.

"Should we head back up the Wadi Bana?" Jake asked.

"No," Roach said as he pulled away from the curb.

"Mohammed brings a lot of guns down the wadi. We'd better try the mud pits."

The two men drove a quick surveillance-detection route before heading south through Zinjibar. Control of the area had passed between the warring parties several times in the past few years. There was the government, which had overthrown the prior government, then allied itself with the Iran-backed Houthi rebels for a while. There were the local al-Qaeda and Daesh franchises, and there was the Saudi-led military coalition. Heavy weapons were in play on all sides: rockets, artillery, missiles, even rumors of a black-market nuclear warhead. The buildings that were still standing were pockmarked with rifle and artillery fire. Others had collapsed walls and caved-in roofs. Broken concrete and twisted rebar tumbled into the streets like landslides.

Roach slowed the van as they exited a roundabout and turned onto a dirt road. Land mines and unexploded cluster munitions littered the area and he was careful to stay in the tracks of other vehicles.

It was dark by the time they reached the mud pits. Though mud bricks were once used in most of the buildings in Zinjibar, concrete had replaced mud, and apathy had replaced concrete. Even with all of the destruction, there was simply no need to build anything in a city that had seen its population fall from one hundred thousand to fifteen thousand in the past decade. The football-field-sized pits had dried up.

Jake took out the laser designator and switched the viewfinder to thermal mode.

"There are two light pickup trucks on the far side,"

he said. "Both engines are hot and one of them looks like it has a cannon mounted in back."

Roach looked through the designator. "That's a Dishka 12.7mm heavy machine gun. The Afghan mujahideen used them to shoot down Soviet helicopters. Mohammed probably dropped a dime on us."

"We should get the van off the road before they recognize it," Jake said.

Roach made a U-turn and drove back into Zinjibar, careful to avoid the neighborhood around the arms dealer's shop. Jake pointed to a three-story structure whose facade had been destroyed, leaving a cutaway view of the empty rooms on each floor.

"What happened to this one?" he said. Odd shapes and shadows from the moon played tricks on his eyes.

"IED," Roach said. "The Houthis daisy-chain old artillery shells together in the bed of a pickup truck and cover them with palm fronds. Then they drive around until they see enemy fighters and detonate a blasting cap among the shells."

"So they kill a couple fighters and send an entire block back to the Stone Age?"

"Yup," Roach said, "but the back side of this building is intact. We can hole up there and figure out a plan."

They parked the van around the street corner and crossed a field of rubble into the abandoned building. The two CIA men shouldered their weapons, cleared the building, and set up camp on an upper floor—just as they had done across town eighteen hours earlier.

"We need to check in with Graves," said Roach.

"You trust him again?"

"I'm not sure I ever trusted him, but we'll be able to see which way the wind is blowing. If he calls us back to HQ, we're screwed."

They tried to get a linkup with the satellite, but were denied. They had mobile phones that they'd acquired in-country, but neither had the capability to dial internationally.

Jake stared through an empty window frame and into the night sky. "How hard do you think it is to hijack a UCAV?"

"There are different levels of encryption: commercial, tactical, etcetera. UCAVs are right up there with ICBMs. Almost impossible."

Jake grunted. "'Almost impossible' means 'possible.'"

"I suppose, but we're talking about world-class talent and hardware. There's no way it's Daesh or AQAP."

"Drifter-72 didn't fly to Mecca on its own."

Roach nodded. "No, it didn't. Which means that everyone back in Washington and Langley is doing exactly what we're doing right now, trying to figure out how this happened and who is responsible. I know I entered the right coordinates."

"You really think they'll try to pin it on us?"

"You have a natural talent for this work, Jake, but let me explain to you how Washington works. Politicians and bureaucrats take credit for things they didn't do and blame others for things they did do. Right now, everyone inside the Beltway is jockeying to save their own asses. They want to be able to show their constituents that they *took action*. That they were *decisive* and held those responsible *accountable*. So, it doesn't matter if you and I were in the middle of a wheat field in Kansas when those missiles were launched because nothing would get more media coverage for a politician than throwing a CIA special operations team into prison for the rest of eternity."

# *NINE*

SEÑOR PARAÍSO'S REMAINING men were in the middle of their daily cultural education training. Seated on logs in an underground classroom, they discussed U.S. current events. The groups had been formed weeks earlier, with language skills playing a significant role in the selection process. Though all the men had worked hard, some were simply more adept at subtleties of accent and vocabulary. The best speakers would be covered as businessmen, the worst as migrant workers.

Señor Paraíso wandered between the groups, listening with pride as thoughtful arguments could be heard on topics ranging from immigration and politics to telecommunications and American football teams. The debaters switched effortlessly between English and Spanish.

An aide walked to Paraíso's side.

"Señor," said the man known as Carlos. "We received a message that you are to call headquarters at once."

Paraíso cocked his head. It was one p.m. in Mexico.

At headquarters, it would be nearly twelve hours later. "When was the message sent?" he asked.

"Ten minutes ago."

To avoid detection by the authorities, the men were to receive signals only—no electronic emissions could come from the camp. Paraíso and his aide walked a mile down a mountain trail to reach an old Chevy pickup truck. They headed for town and drove randomly through the streets. Paraíso dialed a satellite phone and punched in a code that routed the call directly to his superior.

"There has been a change of plans," said the distant voice. "I cannot wait until next month for my avocados. I need them this week."

"Did you say this *week*?"

"If they are ready . . ."

Paraíso thought for a moment. "They are ready."

"Send them immediately."

"I will try for tomorrow, but it may be the day after."

"No later . . . And the pottery?"

"The pottery may take more time. Just arranging the transportation took weeks."

"Is it ready?"

"It is, but—"

"Send it tomorrow or the day after."

"There is great risk in accelerating the process. I would not want it to be lost in transit."

"Tomorrow or the day after," said the voice.

The line went dead.

## TEN

JAKE AND ROACH had been forced to change hiding places twice before midnight. Groups of armed men were patrolling the city, searching for the two Americans. They'd come to the inevitable conclusion that Tall Mohammed had put a bounty on their heads as soon as they'd left his shop.

Jake was deep in thought, staring at the sky through a hole in the ceiling.

"Everyone knows our m.o. here is to use drone strikes to eliminate targets, right?"

"It isn't a secret," Roach said.

"So what if this wasn't an accident?"

"It definitely wasn't an accident."

"Not just the attack," Jake said, "but the whole operation . . . We've been after Muktar forever, right? Suddenly we get a lead on this meeting, a couple of hours from Mecca, during the Hajj. Everybody knows we'll put up a drone to take him out. What if someone engineered the entire thing just so we would put a drone in the air exactly then and there?"

"So they fed us intel we couldn't pass up?" Roach said. "You think Muktar played us?"

"Somebody played us. Maybe it was Muktar, maybe it was Saturn, maybe it was someone else, but right now, Muktar is the only lead we've got, so we might as well run it down."

Most of the players in the civil war had stopped making voice calls years earlier when the government had acquired voice-recognition software, so Jake and Curt used their burner phones to text-message their various contacts. The Agency had cultivated many sources in Zinjibar over the years. Some were trustworthy, most were not. Allegiances in the Mideast were often subject to self-interest and the almighty dollar, and Yemen, despite the outsized influences of its clans, was no different. A man who had risked his life to save someone yesterday might turn around and kill him today.

The Americans received several death threats in return, but also a response from one of Roach's contacts who was willing to meet immediately.

Jake and Curt returned to the stolen van.

"This guy can be dodgy," Roach said as he started the motor, "but he's plugged into AQAP. He's never been able to give us Muktar, but he knows things. Maybe he'll have a lead. We can work him, but watch your six."

"What's his background?" Jake asked as he climbed into the backseat with his rifle.

"He was in the Saleh government for a few years doing low-level counterterror work, but after Sanaa fell, he joined up with AQAP."

"That's a hard one-eighty."

"Not here it isn't," Roach said. He kept the van's lights off as he pulled away from the curb. "Yemen has been the breeding ground and the graveyard for scores of militant Islamic groups, so he keeps his options open."

"Sounds slippery," said Jake.

"He's a survivor," Roach said. "Shifting loyalties are the norm here, not the exception. Everyone wants to be on the winning team because it means the difference between being dead and being alive when the music stops. Hell, a bunch of Daesh fighters switched over to AQAP just because the caliphate cut their pay. We'd be out of our jobs if everyone was trustworthy and loyal."

Jake shook his head in dismay.

"Get your head around the fact that we're going to be skating real close to the edge," Roach said. "The good people of Yemen can't help us. The parents who work hard to raise their kids, the people who wake up every morning hoping to survive until the next day— they don't know Mullah Muktar. They don't want to even hear his name because nothing good ever follows. You want to find out who bombed Mecca, right?"

"Right."

"Then we have to roll up our pants and start wading through the shit because that's where those people live."

A fifty-ton main battle tank was abandoned on the side of the road with one track blown off.

"This is what we train for," Roach continued. "I've got your back, brother."

Jake nodded. "So what's the plan with Mahmoud?"

"He asked us to drive through the alley behind the market so he could get in without being spotted."

"Ambush?" Jake said.

Roach drove past the market and did a U-turn behind a delivery truck with a mangy goat in its bed and a dozen cases of water strapped to its roof. He stopped on the side of the wide boulevard and took out his phone.

"Maybe," he said. "I just sent him a text message and told him to cross the street. If he's not there in thirty seconds, we're out of here."

A lone man emerged from the darkness and walked across the street. Roach started rolling.

"Looks clear," Jake said as he scanned the nearby windows and rooftops.

Roach stopped the van and looked at Jake. "I'll go at him hard, then you give him the soft sell. Flatter him and use your Scharff training."

Named after a Luftwaffe interrogator from World War II, the Scharff technique used bluffs, indirect questioning, and misplaced trust to gain information. Jake and Roach were augmenting it with a more sophisticated version of the good cop/bad cop routine.

Mahmoud climbed into the passenger seat.

"God bless," he said in English.

He was short, with dark, greasy hair and shifty eyes. He glanced at Jake before slouching in his seat and facing forward. Jake slouched in the backseat. Mimicking a subject's body language had been proven to increase trust.

Roach pulled away from the curb and turned down a side street. "It wasn't us," he said.

"Do not insult me," said Mahmoud. "Only the United States sees fit to deliver hell from heaven."

"I give you my word," Roach said. "We didn't kill those people."

Mahmoud scoffed. "I have seen the television. No other nation has such a plane."

"What would we stand to gain?" Roach asked.

"Revenge," said Mahmoud. "Revenge for the 11th of September attacks. Revenge for your soldiers that were killed in Afghanistan and Iraq. Revenge for Saudi support of jihad. There is long list. America pretends it is above revenge, but it is not."

"So why are you here, if we're so evil?" continued Roach.

"I did not say you are evil. Everyone likes revenge." Mahmoud ran his hands through his hair. "What do you want?"

"Where is the mullah now?" Roach asked.

Mahmoud sneered. "Please stop this pretending. Muktar is in Paradise with his seventy-two virgins. Between the mosque and the mullah, your flying death machines created many martyrs today."

Roach glanced at Jake in the rearview mirror.

*Good news about Muktar.*

"What about the government official Muktar was meeting with?" Jake asked. "Were they starting peace talks?"

"You are misinformed," said Mahmoud.

"But there were soldiers and a government vehicle—"

"That truck was purchased two days ago."

"I don't understand."

"There are no peace talks!" said Mahmoud. "The truck and the uniforms were disguises to get past the stupid Sudanese soldiers at the coalition checkpoints."

"So they weren't government officials?"

"No!" said Mahmoud, exasperated. "They're not even Yemeni. They're security for the Iranian."

*Iranian?* Jake and Roach made eye contact in the rearview mirror again.

Iran had been financing and supplying terrorists for decades. Its dependents were a Who's Who of trouble-makers: Hezbollah, Islamic Jihad, Hamas, drug runners in South and Central America, insurgent groups in Iraq and Libya, even the Assad dictatorship in Syria. In Yemen, Iranian operatives were working closely with Houthi tribesmen against the Saudis and al-Qaeda. If Iran was also supporting al-Qaeda, then it was playing both sides of the field.

"How often does the Iranian come?" Jake asked.

"I have seen him three times," said Mahmoud. "The first time he came, our soldiers had not been paid in months. After his second visit, we were awash in weapons and U.S. dollars. He must have given us millions."

"And his third visit was just now," Roach said. "Do you know his name?"

"They call him 'the colonel,'" said Mahmoud.

"You were obviously right about peace talks," Jake said, flattering his source while downplaying the Iranian bombshell. "You are very knowledgeable, and we were misinformed."

"That's right," said Mahmoud.

Jake reached forward and passed five hundred dollars to Mahmoud. The Yemeni counted it twice.

"I will contact Mr. Curt if I hear of any peace talks," he said.

The three men drove in silence until they were a quarter mile from the place where they'd picked up Mahmoud.

"Stop here," he said. "Then you must turn around and leave."

Roach pulled over.

Mahmoud opened the door and stepped into the street. "God bless."

Jake climbed in the front seat and they pulled away.

"That guy puts the 'I' in 'IED,'" he said.

"At least we got Muktar," Roach said as he turned down a side street.

"That's great," Jake said, "but al-Qaeda and Iran have been at each other's throats in Yemen since the civil war started. If they're working together now, then Mecca might just be the start of our problems."

# ELEVEN

**I**NCORPORATING STEALTH TECHNOLOGY and high maneuverability, the Chengdu J-20 Mighty Dragon was China's new fifth-generation fighter jet. With a sleek fuselage and canard wings, it was both beautiful and fearsome to behold.

A flight of four J-20s flew in a tight formation at four hundred knots, with no plane more than twenty feet from any other. From three hundred feet below, those on the ground saw the formation as a single object coming over the horizon. Only as it neared could discriminating eyes discern the four aircraft.

When they were directly overhead, a fifth fighter, approaching from the opposite direction, flew through the middle of the formation at a closing speed of eight hundred knots, leaving just feet to spare on all sides.

Like a magician's audience, the spectators had been watching the four fighters approach. None had seen the fifth plane until its dramatic maneuver. The crowd cheered as the five aircraft lit their afterburners and climbed vertically to five thousand feet.

The fighters looped over backward and headed

straight down, their nose cones pointed directly at the spectators. Feet shifted and eyes darted as the planes loomed larger. The crowd was on the verge of panic until the fighters pulled up sharply and spread apart like petals on a flower, thundering over the spectators just one hundred feet above the ground.

The crowd roared its approval.

"Very impressive, General. Very impressive, indeed," said President Chéng Minsheng as the five aircraft departed Beijing's Nanyuan Airport.

"Thank you, Mr. President," said the commanding general of the air force. "The J-20 is a formidable threat to any naval or air asset. Truly, it is the most advanced interceptor in the world."

"But perhaps not the most reliable?" asked the president. "Why was it unable to perform last week as scheduled?"

"I must apologize. I will see to it that the officer responsible is disciplined," said the air force general.

A third voice, strong and calm, joined the conversation. "What did this officer do, General Zhang?"

"He wished to perform additional tests on the engines, sir."

"So this officer was concerned about safety?"

"Yes, General Wǔ-Dīng, but the engines worked flawlessly."

"And if they had not?" asked China's top military commander and member of the Standing Committee of the Politburo. Then with a smile he added, "How would that last maneuver have ended for us? I see no reason to derail this man's career. I am sure that in wartime he would take appropriate risks, but there is no need for these pilots to trade their cockpits for coffins for our entertainment."

"Yes, General Wǔ-Dīng." The air force general snapped off a crisp salute.

A small crowd of Communist Party members, senior military officers, and provincial government officials were milling about. Conversations about budgets, policy, and domestic and foreign affairs mixed together into the normal business of government. General Wǔ-Dīng was speaking with a fellow member of the Central Military Commission when he spotted the president's security detail moving purposefully through the crowd.

The general excused himself and headed toward the president, whose security team had surrounded him in a diamond formation.

"Is everything all right, General Secretary?" asked Wǔ-Dīng, using another of Chéng's titles.

"The Americans have attacked Saudi Arabia. One of their B-2 bombers struck the city of Mecca during the Muslim Hajj. There may be several thousand fatalities, but there is much confusion. I am convening the Standing Committee now. Come, General."

Two olive-drab helicopters of the People's Liberation Army landed on the tarmac. The president's aides rounded up other members of the nine-man Standing Committee and ushered them onto the waiting aircraft. Most of the passengers were civilians in suits, clearly uncomfortable as they strapped into the side-facing plastic benches. Only General Wǔ-Dīng stood. There was something about a helicopter that made the stocky former infantryman's heart race. It was rough and purposeful. It smelled of jet fuel and gunpowder.

It foreshadowed action.

Many of the passengers covered their ears as they lifted off and turned toward central Beijing. It was only a five-minute flight, but the Z-20 helicopters were considerably less luxurious than the handmade Hongqi limousines in which they'd arrived.

The first aircraft touched down on the helipad atop the Ministry for State Security. President Chéng and an aide stepped out amid heavy security and headed downstairs to his motorcade. General Wǔ-Dīng waited outside the helicopter for the older man who occupied China's second highest office.

Premier Mèng-Fù Ru moved carefully, lowering one foot, then the other. He nodded his gratitude as General Wǔ-Dīng handed him his cane and helped him down. They walked to a waiting car.

"You cannot help yourself, can you?" asked Mèng-Fù in his sharp, high-pitched voice. "Grinning like an idiot up in that death machine."

The general laughed. "I confess that I cannot, respected one. The president is in a great hurry to convene so we can again decide to do nothing. At least in the helicopter I can imagine that we are going to *act*."

"You still disapprove of our policy of 'active defense'?"

"It is no more your policy than mine. It is simply another name for the path of least resistance."

Dozens of PLA soldiers stood at attention as the car passed through the gate to committee headquarters in

Zhongnanhai, a lakeside enclave just west of the Forbidden City.

"Let us listen to what the president has to say before we render judgment," Mèng-Fù said to his protégé.

Though just sixty-seven years of age, the premier was in poor health. At the meetinghouse, he shuffled across the thick red carpet and took his seat next to the president at a large rosewood table.

The general, the first military man in twenty years to ascend to the Standing Committee, sat opposite the president. Before his selection, some had questioned Wǔ-Dīng's lack of party or provincial government experience, but his leadership of the 2.5-million-man People's Liberation Army during a difficult period of modernization and de-commercialization had been enough to secure his elevation.

Wǔ-Dīng had transformed a third world army into a modern and well-equipped fighting force with an annual budget of over $200 billion while also reducing corruption and disposing of nonmilitary business interests. They were monumental tasks, fraught with political and execution risk, but not only had the general succeeded, he had earned the admiration of the men above and below him in the process.

An aide passed him a note as he took his seat.

A briefer from the Ministry of Defense stood at the far end of the room. "Distinguished gentlemen," he began. "It appears that the United States has attacked the Saudi Arabian city of Mecca. Hours ago, an American aircraft launched two air-to-ground missiles into the crowd at the Masjid al-Haram mosque. Casualties are estimated to be between five and ten thousand . . ."

Several men looked around the room.

"There are several significant aspects to this operation," the briefer continued. "First, the U.S. attacked the Grand Mosque, in Mecca, during the Muslim holy pilgrimage. Second, the bomber flew low and launched missiles, when it could have dropped precision bombs from high altitude. Third, the aircraft was likely a B-2 Spirit bomber, an unmistakable design owned by no other nation on earth. Fourth, the weapons used were overpressure devices meant to kill as many people as possible in the open-air mosque. America was not attempting to hide this attack, but rather to take credit for it. This was not a 'warning shot.' This was a psychological operation."

The Standing Committee of the Politburo was the highest governing body in China. Its members managed one of the largest and fastest-growing economies in the world. They put down domestic dissent and gathered intelligence on their enemies. They were the political elite, accustomed to the difficult decisions that accompanied great power, but as they digested the news of the attack, they were silent.

Considered by many insiders to be the wisest of China's political leaders, Mèng-Fù was a man who operated behind the scenes. Practically unknown in the West until he was named premier, he and his network of *guanxi* had been responsible for the ascension of many of the Standing Committee's members to their present positions. While the president and Mèng-Fù were not of the same party faction, the two men respected each other greatly. It was Mèng-Fù who spoke first.

"Thank you, Colonel. Why did you say it was 'likely' an American B-2 bomber carried out the attack? You said yourself that no other nation possesses such a distinctive aircraft."

"The television footage was quite grainy due to thick haze over the city, but the outline of the aircraft was clear enough to make a reasonable assessment. Image analysts are working now to enhance the footage."

"And because it was a stealth aircraft, there were no radar tracks," added Mèng-Fù. "So we do not know where it came from or where it returned to?"

"That is correct, sir."

"There is some recent news," added Wǔ-Dīng, looking up from his note. "The Saudi news media is reporting that an aircraft crashed into the Red Sea shortly after the attack. A local fisherman has identified a photograph of an American B-2 as the same type of aircraft."

"My apologies, General. I—"

"It was a thorough briefing, Colonel. I received this update just moments ago. The Saudis are likely scrambling ships and sonar-dipping helicopters to scour the seabed as we speak."

"General Wǔ-Dīng," asked another committee member, "do you think there is a possibility that this attack by the Americans might lead to a larger conflict?"

"They have just moved to a higher readiness level," said General Wǔ-Dīng, again glancing at the note. "As far as their next actions or repercussions from the attack, those are political questions, and I will defer to the rest of the committee, whose experience in such areas exceeds my own. However, I would recommend that we increase our Combat Readiness Condition from Level Four to Level Three, given the unpredictable nature of this American action."

"Might increased mobilization aggravate a situation which does not presently concern us?" asked President Chéng.

"Sun Tzu would tell us not to rely on the likelihood of the enemy not coming, but on our own readiness to receive him," said Wǔ-Dīng.

"And Napoleon said to never interrupt your enemy when he is making a mistake." The president smiled. "General Wǔ-Dīng, your expertise in military matters exceeds my own, yet we must consider the implications of a move that the Americans will be quick to notice."

"Of course, Mr. President. Yet I am troubled by a powerful nation that launches an unprovoked attack on the civilian population of an ally. Such unpredictability will be hard to defend against if China is not ready."

"Perhaps," said Mèng-Fù, glancing around the table, "we should be considering *why* the Americans conducted this operation before we devise a response."

"As always, Mèng-Fù," said the president, "you see the heart of the matter."

The nine men discussed several theories about the motive for the attack, from an accident to revenge to intentionally provoking a response that would justify a U.S. nuclear response. No consensus was reached and, as the only man in uniform among eight dark suits, the eyes around the table eventually drifted back to Wǔ-Dīng.

"Out of an abundance of caution, I once again recommend elevating our Combat Readiness Condition," said the general.

"I think 'an abundance of caution' dictates that we not provoke an already anxious adversary when we have no stake in the quarrel," said the president. "We will publicly condemn the attack, but our military posture shall remain unchanged."

The president bowed his head slightly toward Wǔ-Dīng. "But, mindful of the general's expertise and concerns, I will convene the Central Military Commission to further discuss the matter."

The meeting adjourned and General Wǔ-Dīng walked the premier to his waiting limousine.

"The president *is* chairman of the Central Military Commission," noted Mèng-Fù. "Though he is not a soldier, it is his decision to make."

Wǔ-Dīng opened the car door. "Let me ask you a question, respected one. Do you guard your own home?"

"Of course not." The premier shook his head as he entered the car. "I have loyal men who are trained to protect me."

"So does China," said Wǔ-Dīng.

## *TWELVE*

PRIOR LEADERSHIP CHANGES within al-Qaeda had brought considerable bloodshed to the organization, and Muktar's death would be no different. Some would see it as an opportunity to move up, while the group's enemies would use the confusion to probe its defenses, infiltrate forces, or emplace IEDs deep in the heart of al-Qaeda territory.

It was an especially dangerous time for two CIA officers to be driving through the predawn streets of Zinjibar.

"Why would Iran give millions of dollars to al-Qaeda?" Jake said. "They were barely operational at the time."

"I can't figure it out," Roach said. "AQAP used to get the lion's share of their financing from the Saudis and Pakistan's Inter-Services Intelligence Agency, but the U.S. cut off most of it. That Iranian cash saved al-Qaeda."

The van's headlights washed over four armed men standing on a street corner. It was impossible to tell if they were AQAP, Tall Mohammed's goons, or one of the local militias that was operating on its own agenda, but it really didn't matter.

"We're missing a piece of the puzzle," Roach said. "We need to talk to Graves."

Jake checked the SATCOM again. "Still no link."

"It has VoIP capability. Let's try Tall Mohammed's Wi-Fi."

"Seriously?"

"We've hacked his network before."

"Before he threatened to kill us . . ."

"He's never there before sunrise prayers."

The two Americans received hard stares as they drove past the men on the corner a second time. Roach killed the headlights and pulled into the alley behind the arms dealer's shop, driving no faster than a man's walk. Neither of them wanted to be one inch closer than necessary to pick up the signal.

"I'm in," Jake said.

Roach stopped the van, but left the motor running.

Jake dialed Graves's number and put the call on speakerphone.

"Tell me about Drifter-72," Graves said.

"We lost comms while we were still at observation post Alpha," Roach said. "We're unclear what happened after."

"Well, for starters, your aircraft missed its target by six hundred miles and struck Mecca," said Christine Kirby. The former helicopter pilot was one of Graves's lieutenants. "It's the largest loss of civilian life since 9/11, but I'm sure you knew that . . ."

"What's that supposed to mean?" Roach said. He could hear papers shuffling through the SATCOM.

"The mission controller asked you if you wanted to call off Drifter-72," Kirby said, "and you responded, 'Negative, Mustang. The truck is a ruse. These bastards killed three thousand Americans and now it's payback time. Spin up your missiles.'"

"Curt was talking about Muktar's role in the 9/11 attacks," Jake said. "We didn't want him to slip through the Agency's fingers again."

"I must have missed that part of the transcript," Graves said. "But I did notice that you were able to upload the target coordinates for Mecca before you 'lost comms.' The Gang of Eight has been knocking down my door, Curt. They want answers."

Roach scowled. *Here it comes.*

"I need you to tell me something that I can tell Congress that explains how a targeted strike in Yemen turned into wholesale slaughter in Saudi Arabia."

"Listen, Ted. We're trying to figure this out too," Jake said. "We just met with an AQAP source who identified Saturn as an Iranian national. Iran is supporting the Houthis and al-Qaeda. They're playing both sides of the field."

Roach pointed out the windshield as the four men with Kalashnikovs entered the alley, maybe seventy-five yards from the van. He put it in gear and started backing up.

"Look, we've got a situation here," Jake said. "We're going to have to call you back."

Graves began to protest but the connection was already lost.

Roach backed out of the alley and made a half-hearted surveillance-detection run. With only two other cars and a donkey cart on the road, they would have quickly spotted a tail if they'd had one. The real threat was from the foot patrols that seemed to be everywhere.

They turned onto a dark street and abandoned the van on the side of the road. With their satchels over their shoulders and their rifles tucked under their jackets, they walked several blocks in silence. Most of Zinjibar had been without electricity for over a year, leaving only a hint of morning twilight to light their way.

The two Americans made their way to the top level of yet another decrepit building. Jake slumped on the concrete floor, leaned against the concrete wall, and finished the last of his food and water.

Roach started pacing. "I don't trust those two," he said.

"The mission record will be our defense," Jake said. "They can't ignore that."

"If Congress wants scalps, do you think Graves is going to give them his or ours? He'll suppress that record on the grounds of national security."

Jake had had another run-in with Graves the prior year. The man played for keeps.

"There will be people who believe we went rogue," Roach said. "They'll argue that we were trying to provoke the Muslim nations into retaliating so the United States will finally take the gloves off. No more counterinsurgency operations. We just go in and level the place."

"The whole Middle East?"

"And half of Africa," Roach said. "Look, I'm not saying it's rational, but neither was attacking Mecca, and that just happened. You and I need to get out of Yemen. Too many people are looking for us here, including Graves. Let's drive to Saudi. I know two Arab American operations officers in Riyadh we can trust and we're going to need some support to get ourselves unfucked."

Roach stopped pacing as the plan coalesced in his mind. He ran Jake through the particulars of how they would make contact. Though Roach knew the two men well, he'd let Jake make the initial approach. It would be good training.

And it would be good to be on offense again.

## THIRTEEN

**M**OST VISITORS TO the jagged mountains and snowcapped peaks of the Alborz mountain range came for the scenic vistas, but there were others for whom the decision to visit the northern foothills of Tehran was not their own. Their views were blocked by thirty-foot-high concrete walls and endless coils of concertina wire.

Section 209 of Iran's Evin Prison was filled with political prisoners, alleged spies, and other perceived enemies of the state. Few knew for certain what happened inside, for few left alive. Rumors of torture and betrayal were common. Inmates found themselves pitted against one another to reveal information. To those who remained quiet, came death. To those who spoke, came more pain. Most eventually "committed suicide."

Lashed naked to a chair and sitting in his own filth, the man in the interview room had been awake for fifty-one hours. It was a critical point in his interrogation. Behind a thick panel of one-way glass stood a man whose uniform identified him as a major general in the Republican Guards. With salt-and-pepper hair and a predator's eyes, he watched intently. Though domestic operations were not normally within his purview, the circumstances surrounding the prisoner's apprehension had required his presence.

The interrogator had a well-used wooden baton in his hand.

"Again, I must ask, who sent you?"

Bright red blood dripped down the prisoner's face and onto his teeth.

"I . . . I was only looking for my goats."

The interrogator struck him with the baton.

"Who are you working for? MEK? The Zionists?"

"We are Bedouin." The man's head fell forward. "Food . . . for family," he mumbled.

An aide entered the observation room and whispered to the general. He rapped on the glass with his knuckles, summoning the interrogator to the observation room.

"Yes, General Shirizani?" said the interrogator.

"I must go," said the commander of Iran's Qods Force.

"Of course, General. What should we do with the prisoner?"

"Do you think he knows anything?"

"I do not. I think he is a nomad who wandered into the restricted area."

"Did you ask him about the nuclear facility?"

"Several times."

"Then he knows something. Kill him."

Shirizani walked out with his aide holding the door. Though his main office was in the western city of Ahvaz, the general also maintained an office in the former U.S. embassy in Tehran. He answered his encrypted cell phone as he rode in his armored Toyota Land Cruiser.

"Sir! I have not had a chance to speak with you since the attack on the Masjid al-Haram," said the caller. "I am beside myself with fury. Thousands of pilgrims, hundreds of our Iranian brothers among them, were slaughtered at the mosque of the Prophet. To attack such a place during the Hajj is—"

"Yes, it's terrible," said Shirizani impatiently. "Why have you called?"

The man took a deep breath to calm himself. "After our meeting, Muktar was killed by a second American drone strike. Their external operations planner, a man named al-Quereshi, has temporarily assumed command."

"This may be a blessing in disguise. The mullah had lost his effectiveness. He was too well known, too focused on simply staying alive. It is time to topple the Saudi monarchy, time to crush their spirit and their bodies. Tell al-Quereshi that he must attack the Saudi southern border within twenty-four hours."

"That's an aggressive timetable, General."

"Have him attack Al-Wadiah, just inside the Saudi border. I want them to slaughter the men, the women, the children, the animals in the village. I want blood flowing down the streets. Then he is to do the same farther north in Sharorah."

"What if al-Quereshi resists? He is a Saudi national."

"Convince him that this is the opportunity for him

to secure his position as Muktar's successor. Show him that it is the only way forward."

"Yes, General."

"There is a ship, already through the blockade and about to berth at the Port of Salif, which will resupply Hakim Walid al-Houthi and his fighters with Katyusha rockets, heavy weapons, and high explosives. After al-Quereshi—"

"Forgive me, General, but al-Qaeda and the Houthis will never coordinate operations."

"No, but we can coordinate them without their knowledge. After al-Quereshi moves on Al-Wadiah, the Saudi National Guard will saturate the area with troops, thinning their ranks along the rest of the border. The moment this happens, we will direct the Houthis to mount an incursion in the west, and the Saudis will be forced to divert domestic security forces to reinforce their southern border. I do not understand the attack on Mecca, but it presents us with a unique opportunity. It has driven a wedge between the Americans and the Saudis, and we are going to be the sledgehammer that splits it open."

# FOURTEEN

SOMEONE PINGED ROACH'S mobile phone.

"Mahmoud wants to meet again. He says he has new information."

The two Americans hid their gear under a pile of rubble and slipped out the back with only their weapons. They walked two blocks with their rifles under their jackets and their eyes scanning the streets. It was just past sunrise and the city was quiet. The foot patrols were gone.

Jake approached a twenty-year-old Toyota sedan and popped the door lock and the ignition switch. They drove one block west of the agreed-upon meeting place and texted Mahmoud the new address.

A lone figure emerged from a doorway up ahead and walked toward them with the sun at his back.

A delivery truck pulled behind Jake and honked its horn, shattering the early morning quiet. Jake looked in his rearview mirror. The driver was gesturing with one hand and holding down the horn with the other.

"This guy is going to wake up the whole neighborhood," Roach muttered as he looked over his shoulder. "Pull up to the intersection."

Mahmoud crossed the intersection ahead and was fifty yards away.

Jake pulled forward, but the delivery truck kept honking.

"I don't like this," Jake said.

"Let's get out of here," Roach said. He lifted his rifle onto his lap.

Jake sped up, but the delivery truck stayed right on his tail. He floored it as they approached the intersection.

"That's not Mahmoud!" Roach said. He raised his rifle and pointed it out the window.

A pickup truck appeared from a side street and screeched to a halt, blocking the intersection. Jake jumped the curb and smashed into the rear of the pickup, knocking it sideways. Metal screeched against metal as the sedan scraped by.

The man they'd thought was Mahmoud raised a pistol and fired several rounds at the car. Roach fired back and the man dove for the street. Jake floored it again once he reached the intersection, but the old Toyota sputtered to a halt with fluids leaking from its engine compartment.

Jake and Roach stepped out with their rifles up, but they were surrounded by half a dozen men with AK-47s, and one with an RPG.

## FIFTEEN

THE CALL FROM General Shirizani had accelerated everything. Paraíso had been issuing orders and reviewing his mission checklist from the moment he returned to camp. The new schedule had disrupted their carefully laid plans.

But the general was right about the timing.

The attack on Mecca had turned world opinion sharply against America. This time there would be no international outpouring of sympathy and cooperation as there had been after 9/11. Paraíso's attacks on the U.S. homeland would be seen for what they really were. Justice.

He used a flashlight as he walked through a dirt-walled tunnel to the underground team room. Several men in tailored suits and silk ties stood around a table. They were filling their carry-on bags with binders and presentations from a conference on wind energy that had ended the day before in Mexico City. If questioned, each man could speak intelligently on the topic for a few minutes.

A dozen others sat around a table dressed in khakis and matching polo shirts with the name of a technology company embroidered on the chest. They worked on laptops and spoke about sales software.

There were other men dressed as tourists, and a pair of backpackers, but it was Ibrahim and Kahlil, two men dressed in straw cowboy hats and stained T-shirts, who lightened the mood as they wandered around the room. The would-be migrant workers approached each of the other groups and shrugged as they pulled the empty pocket liners out of their faded blue jeans.

Paraíso's men were not the first to attempt terror attacks from Latin America. Operatives had infiltrated the United States from Mexico before. Most had snuck across the border or arrived as visitors with foreign passports. In the majority of cases, their plans had been foiled by the American security services, either by intercepting the "coyotes" who ran the men across the border or by analysis of the digital trail that started when they crossed into the United States with foreign passports. Those who aroused suspicion found their movements and contacts prone to surveillance and eventual arrest.

Paraíso's plans could not be subject to such random chance.

The brilliance of his strategy was that the men would appear to be returning home to the United States. It had been an expensive precaution, but in addition to unfreezing billions of dollars in foreign assets, Iran had literally received planeloads of hard currency from the United States in 2015 after agreeing to the nuclear deal known as the Joint Comprehensive Plan of Action. The $500,000 it had cost to secure authentic U.S. passports from a corrupt American consular officer was no more than a rounding error. The chips implanted in the passport covers would corroborate the dates, the photos, and the travel history stamped inside, and the men's light brown skin and dark hair would match border officials' expectations of naturalized citizens from Mexico.

Paraíso's greatest regret was that he would not be accompanying his men across the border, but the long scar running down the left side of his head made it impossible. It was a souvenir from an Israeli airstrike in southern Lebanon, and he wore it as a badge of honor, but in an era of facial recognition software, it made him far too identifiable to cross into the United States.

The two men covered as farmhands departed in the old pickup truck for their nineteen-hour drive to Texas. They needed to be across the border before the first shots were fired and security was elevated. Other vehicles took the rest of the team to the airport in Mexico City.

Only Paraíso and Carlos remained behind. Though they would not be going to America, the change in plans affected them too. They had to drive to the docks at Veracruz and figure out how to get a shipping container into the United States four weeks ahead of schedule.

## SIXTEEN

JAKE AND ROACH were stripped of their money and weapons, hooded, bound, and thrown into the back of the delivery truck. It drove straight for four blocks, turned left and then right. It was poor tradecraft on the part of their captors, unless they had no intention of ever releasing the Americans.

They were led to a ground-floor room and shoved into heavy wooden chairs. The air smelled of human suffering: vomit, blood, excrement. The terrorists retied the Americans' hands behind the seat backs. An hour later they removed the hoods.

There was a single window in the cinder-block room and no furniture aside from the chairs and a rickety table with a few dirty dishes and a dozen flies. An old woolen blanket covered the doorway. Mahmoud was already there, seated in a triangle with Jake and Roach. One of the Yemeni's eyes was bruised and grotesquely swollen, and his chin rested on his chest, but it was the blood covering his face and shirt that was most telling. It was brown and crusty. It had left his heart hours before and not been replaced.

The man who'd impersonated Mahmoud during the ambush entered the room with a bandage on one arm.

*Gotcha,* Roach thought. At least one of the rounds he'd fired had found its mark.

The man recognized Roach as well. He drew his pistol, a heavy, steel-framed CZ-75, and smashed it across Roach's face, shattering his nose and unleashing a steady flow of blood into his mouth and onto his clothes.

"You have known Mahmoud a long time?" the man asked in Arabic.

Roach spit out a mouthful of blood. "Who's Mahmoud?"

The man struck Roach again. Jake opened his mouth to speak, but Roach shook his head a few degrees.

The man gestured to Mahmoud. "During your meeting yesterday," the man said, "you discussed what?"

"We've never met," Roach said.

The man held up Mahmoud's mobile phone and grimaced as he used his injured arm to type. A moment later Roach's cell phone pinged.

"You killed Mullah Muktar on the same day you attacked the holiest site in all of Islam," said the man, "so let us dispense with this fiction. You are never going to leave this room alive. If you cooperate, you will suffer little and die quickly." The man smiled. "If you do not cooperate, you will wish that you had."

He turned his attention to Jake. "And how do you wish to die?"

"I've never seen that man before," Jake said, gesturing toward Mahmoud.

One of the guards smashed the muzzle of his rifle into Jake's ribs. It felt like a dagger in his side.

"Tell me what you know of the deal with Turani," said the interrogator.

Jake hesitated, and the guard hit him in the side of the head with the butt of his rifle stock. Jake's world started spinning.

"Tall Mohammed told us who you are, so there is no longer any secret for you to keep. What does the United States know about the deal?"

The questions continued for more than an hour. Each denial, each bout of silence, was met with another savage blow. It was not long before Roach lapsed into unconsciousness and the interrogator's anger turned into rage.

"How did you find Muktar?" he shouted. "Did Turani betray him?"

He punched Jake so hard that it knocked him off the chair.

"What about Riyadh? What did Mahmoud say about the embassy?"

The two guards lifted Jake up and shoved him back into the chair. Roach's eyes opened.

The interrogator returned his attention to Roach. "Again I ask, what does the United States know about the package?"

Roach mumbled something unintelligible. The interrogator bent over, inches from Roach's face, and began shouting. Spittle flew from his mouth. Veins bulged in his face and neck, but Roach's unfocused gaze saw none of it. His bloodied ears heard none of it.

The interrogator pistol-whipped Roach several more times. Blood splattered across the walls as Curt's head whipped from side to side, but the interrogator did not relent. Blows to the head, strikes to the body. He beat Roach mercilessly for refusing to answer his questions, but Roach had long since lost consciousness. The interrogator could stand it no more.

He took a single step backward, raised the pistol, and fired.

# SEVENTEEN

PRESIDENT J. WILLIAM Day was in the Oval Office speaking with the chairman of the Joint Chiefs of Staff. Though it was nearly midnight, General Landgraf was clean shaven and in full uniform. The theory around the Pentagon was that the chairman didn't sleep, ever. Subordinates, peers, and night watch officers all swore that whenever they'd needed the general, whether it was three p.m. or three a.m., he was lucid, decisive, and invariably in the middle of something else.

"Sir, the Saudis have located a local fisherman who saw Drifter-72 crash into the Red Sea. They've mobilized an extensive search for the aircraft."

The president frowned. "How is our search coming along?"

"Approximately six hours ago, the USS *Michigan* passed through the Bab-el-Mandeb Strait and into the Red Sea. It's now on station and conducting a contour search with a remotely operated vehicle. Based on the drone's ELT transmission and the probable drift of the wreckage, the aircraft likely struck bottom in the deepest part of the Red Sea."

"That's the first piece of good news we've gotten," said the president.

"It would be, sir, but the Russians have offered a deep-submergence rescue vehicle to the Saudis. It's already airborne on an AN-124 cargo aircraft to King Faisal Naval Base in Jeddah. It could be in the water in as little as twelve hours."

"Bring in more assets if you need them, just don't get caught or the Saudis will think we're planning 'another' offensive operation."

"We should be in good shape, sir. The *Michigan* will have to be cautious, but the Saudis are scouring the area with active sonar and that announces itself pretty far out."

A Secret Service agent opened the door and CIA director David Feinman entered. The president gestured to the sofas in the center of the room and the three men sat down.

"We're catching a lot of flak this morning, David. Last night eight people died in Detroit after a protest and a counterprotest turned violent, and the Bureau thinks we're going to see more of the same, especially with the heat wave we've been having. The House Select Committee on Intelligence is talking about cutting all funding for HUMINT and operations—"

"They want NSA leading the effort," added General Landgraf. "To take humans out of collection altogether."

"The international situation is even worse," continued the president. "Nearly every ambassador in D.C. has asked to meet with the secretary of state. The EU is hitting us with punitive economic sanctions and suspending purchases of U.S. capital goods. NATO has said they won't invoke Article 5 if we're attacked as a result of this, and there is a movement inside the organization to kick us out altogether. I'm not saying it's rational, but people feel as if they have to do something. King Ali won't return my calls, and you know as well as I do, despite all this talk of energy independence, if they stop shipping crude here, we'll be short of gasoline, jet fuel, and diesel. In another three months the heating season will start, and cold, stranded voters make for angry voters."

Director Feinman had been a U.S. attorney specializing in intelligence matters for over two decades before accepting the top job at CIA. He wasn't a politician, but he knew how politics worked. He opened his briefcase and placed a piece of paper on the coffee table.

"Mr. President," he said, "the Agency is not culpable in this, but I understand your position, and I am tendering my resignation as director of Central Intelligence. I'm sorry, sir."

The president looked at the document for several seconds, but left it where it lay.

"To paraphrase Abraham Lincoln, it's not wise to switch horses in midstream. We're in a tough spot, David, but I'd like you to see this through, whatever the outcome."

"Of course, Mr. President. Thank you, sir."

"But heads are going to roll," said the president. "I want that drone team back here ASAP."

"But those men—"

The president picked up the letter of resignation and began to read it. "Someone has to be held accountable."

"I'll have them here forthwith, Mr. President."

## EIGHTEEN

ROACH WAS DEAD.

Jake cursed at the interrogator in Arabic, referencing his mother, a dog, and the act of his conception in the same sentence. The interrogator pointed the pistol at Jake.

Jake screamed another curse and spat in his face.

A guard struck Jake in the head with a wooden rifle stock. He tumbled from the chair and crashed into the table. The dirty dishes tumbled to the floor.

The flies followed, circling Jake's bloody wounds as he lost consciousness. The interrogator kicked Jake in the ribs, but there was no reaction. The interrogator kicked him a second time. It was like hitting a sack of potatoes.

"A fitting end for an American spy," said the interrogator. "Covered in yesterday's garbage."

The guards laughed.

"Get rid of the bodies," the interrogator said as he left the building.

The two goons lifted Mahmoud from the chair and hauled him outside. They returned a few minutes later and grabbed Roach.

Jake regained consciousness in time to see his friend and teammate being dragged across the floor like a piece of trash. Jake trembled with rage, but he fought it down; for while the terrorists had found humor in the broken dishes, he had found a knife.

It was a steak knife, with a serrated blade, and Jake held it in his fingertips, sawing fervently at the rope that bound his hands behind his back. He cut himself twice, but the pain didn't even register. He just kept sawing until the rope dropped from his wrists.

The blanket covering the doorway swung open and Jake played dead, lying motionless on his back. The two terrorists each grabbed a leg and dragged him toward the door. Jake switched his grip on the knife.

The terrorist on the left pulled the blanket back and the bright sunlight blinded him for an instant.

It was all Jake needed.

He lunged, driving the knife into the ankle of the man on his right. Jake yanked the knife backward, slicing the man's Achilles tendon. The terrorist screamed in pain as he fell to the ground.

The man on the left went for his gun, but Jake swept his legs before he could bring it to bear. The guard fell to the ground and Jake scrambled on top of him, trapping the pistol with his left arm. The man fired, sending a round ricocheting through the small concrete room. He fired a second time and Jake lost his grip on the weapon.

Jake raked the knife across the man's neck, severing his arteries, his windpipe, and his jugular vein. The terrorist dropped the gun and brought his hands up to his gurgling throat, but his strength had already left him. In just a few seconds, he was dead.

The man with the severed Achilles reached for the loose pistol. Jake kicked him in the face with his heel. The man's head snapped backward into the concrete wall and he stopped moving.

Jake's heart was racing. He grabbed the gun and dropped the magazine. It was an all-steel CZ-75, just like the interrogator's. There were five rounds left, plus one in the chamber. He reinserted the magazine and stood over the man with the sliced Achilles. He was losing a lot of blood.

"Who's Turani?" Jake asked, but the man was in shock.

Jake repeated himself, louder.

The man opened his eyes. His hand quivered as he slowly wiped the blood from his face.

"Tell me about Turani," Jake said slowly.

"I don't know," the man whispered. He clutched his ankle, struggling to comprehend the pain.

Jake pointed the gun toward the man's face and pulled the trigger. The bullet struck the floor three inches from his head.

"He gave us money . . . and weapons," the man said weakly. His voice sounded like two pieces of sandpaper being rubbed together.

"Did he die with Muktar?" Jake asked.

The man shook his head once.

"Where is he now?"

The man hesitated. Jake raised the pistol again.

"Riyadh. Al-Quereshi is meeting him at the American embassy."

"Who the fuck is al-Quereshi?" Jake shouted.

The man pointed toward the door. Al-Quereshi was the interrogator.

Jake stepped outside. The sonofabitch had left in the delivery truck—and his henchmen had thrown Mahmoud and Roach into a shallow trench.

Jake burst back inside. "When? When are they supposed to meet?"

The man's eyes were open but unfocused. He looked dead . . .

Jake yelled at him again.

. . . Or maybe he was playing dead. It had worked for Jake.

Jake fired a single bullet in the terrorist's forehead; then went outside and buried Roach and Mahmoud.

# NINETEEN

Wǔ-Dīng's vast responsibilities dictated that he be constantly on the move. The general had been in the Pudong district of Shanghai, visiting a special PLA unit that took its orders directly from him.

As vice chairman of the Central Military Commission and the most senior officer in the People's Liberation Army, Wǔ-Dīng rated an aircraft; in his case, a brand-new Y-20 transport. The huge four-engine jet was capable of carrying helicopters or even a tank, but in its role as the general's mobile command center it was outfitted for communications and passengers. Today it carried only the general, a few aides, his security detail, and his wife.

Now that their only son had grown to become a career army officer himself, Wǔ-Dīng's wife frequently accompanied her husband on trips. Their time aloft was often their only time together. She was not like many of the party bosses' spouses—infamous for lavish spending and mercurial temperaments. She would usually visit with soldiers and their families while he attended to official duties. Like her husband, she was loved by the troops, often bestowing hugs on enlisted men and women after meeting them. To her, they were all her children.

General Wǔ-Dīng finished a phone call as they flew over the lights of Nanking. President Chéng had convened the CMC in the general's absence, knowing that no one present would advocate elevating China's military readiness against Chéng's wishes.

Though his face was a mask of stone, Wǔ-Dīng's wife could tell something was bothering him.

"You are unhappy?" she asked.

"It is nothing."

His wife stared at him with a rare frown across her own face. "Well, I am unhappy too, unhappy with these pilots."

"They cannot control the turbulence, my dear. The hot summer air is unstable, so we bounce around, even in this giant plane."

"I am not complaining about the ride . . . Do you know what I heard the pilot call me earlier?"

"'Old mother'? They have been calling you that for years. You know they mean it only as a term of endearment."

"No," she said sharply. "I like 'old mother,' but today, before we left Shanghai, I heard one of the pilots say to the other that they needed to get the 'chubby girl' back to Beijing tonight so she could get 'serviced.'"

The general chuckled. Then he began to laugh. Soon he was laughing so hard that his thickset frame was doubled over upon itself.

"It is not funny," his wife shouted, slapping his arm with the back of her hand. "I know I have put on a few pounds, but if you think you are 'servicing' me after mocking my body, you are very much mistaken!"

Tears streamed down the general's face.

"Chubby Girl . . ." he said, struggling to catch his breath.

She hit him again.

"Chubby Girl is what they call the *airplane*," he said, wiping the tears from his cheeks. "It's the widest of all our aircraft."

The general's wife glanced at the cavernous interior before bursting into laughter herself.

"Maybe we can discuss that service appointment after all," she said.

# *TWENTY*

JAKE STAGGERED THROUGH Zinjibar under the
midday sun. Several times, he ducked into abandoned buildings or behind piles of rubble. While
not every car and truck on the road was driven by al-
Qaeda gunmen, he couldn't afford to make a single
mistake. He stumbled across town for hours, clutching
the pistol in his pocket, until he finally reached the
hideout that he and Roach had left that morning. Jake
climbed to the upper floor and slumped in a corner
with the pistol held tight.

He woke to the sound of a passing truck's horn and
the smell of a wood fire blowing through the open
walls. Jake sat up and brushed the concrete dust out of
his hair. It was just after sunset. He ran his fingertips
through the debris on the floor, thinking of the countless lives that had been destroyed by the civil war.

Yemen had always been a land of weak government
and strong tribes, and the country's decentralized power
base had allowed the formation of many radical, but
fleeting, militant Islamic groups. Time, the government,
and the groups' own missteps led to the eventual extinc-

tion of all them—until February 2006, when Mullah Muktar and twenty-three other inmates escaped from prison and formed the core of what became al-Qaeda in the Arabian Peninsula. The terrorist organization grew rapidly in the lawless regions of Yemen, outliving its predecessors by carefully targeting its messages at home and its attacks abroad. Its members were some of the most experienced murderers in the world.

And Jake was fighting them on his own.

He'd been in Special Activities for less than a year. He was to be the apprentice, learning at Roach's side for at least another year. Curt was a legend in the organization, a master of low-visibility, denied-area operations. It was why Graves had paired them up.

But now, after four weeks, Roach was dead and Jake was alone and engulfed by a cloud of suspicion.

He dusted off the SATCOM. It had been the first domino to fall, back when they'd ordered Drifter-72 to fire its missiles, but he aimed the antenna through a hole in the ceiling and tried it anyway. Much to his surprise, the little satellite icon turned green. Graves picked up after a few rings.

"Curt is dead," Jake said.

"How?"

"We set up a meet, but the source was compromised. We were ambushed by a guy named al-Quereshi who seems to have taken over for Muktar. It got rough. He kept asking about an Iranian who I think is Saturn. Curt died during the interrogation."

"This isn't good."

The two men were half a world apart. Their conversation was being scrambled, then bounced off ground stations and relay satellites and who-knows-what-else before being unscrambled, but Jake knew Graves, and there was something in his tone that made Jake nervous. He wasn't saddened by Roach's death or concerned for Jake's safety. There was something else.

"Keller," Graves said, "I need you back here. Get to your primary extraction point at 04:00. I'll have a Sealion semisubmersible waiting for you just off the beach."

Jake thought back to what Roach had said after their last conversation with Graves.

*Ted's not going to take the fall for this if he can find someone else to pin it on.*

Graves had lost his fall guy . . . but he'd found another.

## TWENTY-ONE

A FLATBED TRUCK PULLED into a line of tractor trailers at the entrance to the Port of Veracruz. In the cab were Señor Paraíso and his aide, Carlos. They were clean shaven and dressed in khakis and button-down shirts.

"Good morning," said a guard in Spanish as the truck reached the gate.

"Good morning," Carlos said from behind the wheel. He removed the top sheet from a clipboard of dog-eared papers and handed it to the guard. "This container is supposed to go out today, but the shipping company sent us a bill of lading for four weeks from now. We only discovered the mix-up yesterday."

The guard pulled up the record on his own computer.

*One twenty-foot-equivalent container, Talavera pottery, scheduled to go out on a major carrier, one month from now, just like the man said.*

"Did the shipping company issue a new bill of lading?"

"They told us to come back in four weeks, 'like it says on the paper,' but we'll be fired before then if this stuff isn't already in Houston. We're going to see if we can get somebody to do a physical inspection and get it out today or tomorrow."

"The whole port is jammed up," the guard said as he handed back the sheet of paper. "You're going to have to beg somebody to take it."

Paraíso leaned over and made eye contact with the guard. "Hey, man, I've been married eight years. I'm used to begging!"

The guard hit a button on the console in front of him and the red and white gate pivoted into the air.

"Good luck, guys," he said with a laugh. "You're going to need it."

They drove to the shipping company's office and climbed an exterior staircase to the second floor. A woman with heavy makeup and a dozen silver bracelets on each arm was working on a computer in the reception area.

Paraíso explained their predicament.

"Did you call yesterday?" she asked without looking up.

"Yes, I—"

"What did I tell you yesterday?"

"That we would have to wait for our original shipping date."

"And what do you think has changed in the past eighteen hours? As I told you on the phone, U.S. Customs requires preclearance at the port of embarkation, and that will take at least a week to schedule."

"We were hoping someone could do a physical inspection. We need to get it to Houston this week," said Paraíso.

The woman looked up from her computer for the first time. "They haven't done physical clearance checks in ten years. Besides, there's a storm out over the Yucatán now and it's headed for Tampico. We're trying to move freight out of the port. We're not looking for extra work."

Paraíso knew, of course, that a physical inspection would not be done. Opening every box and examining each piece of pottery would be far too time-consuming given the 130 million containers that crossed the ocean each year. Physical inspections were only done when customs agents were already suspicious.

The two men left the office. They could see the entire port from the second-floor landing. Hundred-foot-high gantry cranes and rows of heavy trucks were loading brightly colored containers onto the nearest vessel.

"What storm is she talking about?" asked Carlos, looking at the clear blue skies.

"No idea," said Paraíso.

He looked over the two dozen ships that were tied up in port.

*We only need one of them to say yes.*

"Let's take a walk."

The two men stopped at a small outbuilding where a video monitor listed the ships' departure times and destinations. A second monitor displayed the local weather channel.

*Tropical Storm Beulah.*

It had spent the prior day as a tropical depression over Cuba before picking up additional heat and moisture as it blew over the open sea. The weather system was now over the Yucatán Peninsula, lashing the area with high winds and drenching rain as it moved west, directly across the route to Houston.

The two men exchanged a look and kept walking. They passed tankers and smaller cargo ships until they reached the low-rent district of the port where coastal barges and regional freight boats lined the quay. There were no crewmen about except for a lone figure aboard a small tramp freighter.

*El Nuevo Constante.*

No more than eighty feet long, streaks of rust ran down her black sides. Higher in the bow and in the stern, her midsection was long, low, and flat, with a built-in crane that could lift the twenty-foot-long container, assuming the bolts holding it to the deck weren't rusted out.

"What a piece of junk," said Carlos. "You think it could make it to Houston?"

"It's only twelve hundred kilometers. It's perfect," Paraíso said as he approached. "Hello!" he called out.

The ship's captain walked to the railing. He had a large knife on his belt.

"We're interested in hiring your ship," said Paraíso. "Is it available?"

The captain waved them up what passed for a gangway, three old boards nailed together, bleached nearly white by the sun and salt. Carlos waited until his boss was aboard before walking across himself, lest their combined weight break the wood and plunge them into the sea.

The captain stared at them.

"We have a twenty-foot container that needs to go to Houston," said Paraíso.

"Today," added Carlos.

Deeply tanned, with salt-and-pepper hair and an unkempt beard, the captain said nothing. He had survived many years by keeping his business away from the drug trade. It hadn't been easy, but it had been the right thing to do for him and for his family. He would rather be poor and proud than another rich slave to the drug lords.

"What's in the container, señor?" he asked.

"Talavera pottery," said Paraíso. "It was supposed to go out on one of the big MSC ships in four weeks, but our client needs it in Houston now or I'm going to lose my contract." He handed over the bill of lading from the reputable shipping company.

The captain was reading it over when a man in his early twenties appeared from belowdecks.

"It's the raw water pump again, Papa."

The captain's shoulders sank. "Can it be fixed?"

The son shook his head.

"See if Gutiérrez can get us a rebuilt one."

The son nodded and walked down the gangway. He drove away in a thirty-year-old pickup truck with a cloud of light-blue smoke trailing behind it.

The captain returned his attention to Paraíso and his aide.

"Even if I wanted to, I couldn't leave until the engine is fixed."

"How long would that be?" asked Paraíso.

"At least a day," said the captain.

"That might be too late," said Paraíso. "Isn't there a storm coming this way?"

"We would be north of the storm before it crossed our route. But even if we get the pump fixed in time, I am still short of crew. We need at least one more deck-hand, and everyone has been hired to prepare for the storm. I am sorry, señor."

Paraíso spied another empty freighter down the quay. "We'll keep looking," he said. He and his aide walked to the gangway.

Carlos took him by the arm. "I'll go. I'll be the extra crewman."

"It would mean your martyrdom," Paraíso whispered. "You know the ship will never dock in Houston."

"I am prepared."

Paraíso took a long look at the loyal soldier. "You always wanted to be part of the teams, but you were too valuable to me. And now, Allah has revealed to us why He saved you, for the most important mission of all."

The two men embraced and walked back to where the captain was standing.

"Captain," Paraíso said, "my cousin has volunteered to accompany your ship to Houston and back. He will be the extra deckhand you need."

The captain took stock of him. He was young and fit.

"What do you know of the sea?" asked the captain.

"Nothing, sir, but I am a good mechanic and I don't drink or do drugs. I follow orders."

The captain sighed heavily and looked out over the rail. The sun was low over the western Gulf of Mexico.

"I'll offer you ten thousand dollars U.S., on top of your normal rate, to help with the engine repairs," said Paraíso.

The voice in the captain's head that had kept him away from drug money was back, but though these men were desperate, they weren't like the thugs who'd approached him previously.

Paraíso sensed the hesitation. "If I don't get this shipment there in time, I will be out of business. Ten thousand dollars is almost half my profit for the year."

The captain looked at his ship. Replacing the water pump was going to leave him nearly broke. One more repair and his business would be ruined. The bank would sell *El Nuevo Constante* for scrap and he and his son would be unemployed. In a few months, there would be no money to feed his new granddaughter.

"Fifteen thousand, up-front," said the captain.

Paraíso nodded.

The captain pointed to a spot on the docks. "Leave the container there. We leave tomorrow at sunrise."

## TWENTY-TWO

JAKE SMASHED THE SATCOM with a piece of concrete. It was his only link to the outside world, but Graves could track it, and he didn't trust Graves. The laser-target designator met the same end.

Jake was on his own now, cut off from Agency oversight, but also Agency support. He needed a plan.

His earlier theory that Muktar had fed the United States details of his meeting to lure a drone into a place where it could be hijacked made sense operationally, but anyone sophisticated enough to hijack a drone would have known that standard procedure was to launch multiple UCAVs for such a mission, so hijacking only one drone would have still left the al-Qaeda leader exposed. And like most terrorist leaders, the mullah was the type of man who was happy to order suicide missions, but not to execute one himself. The infinite glory of martyrdom and the immediate ascension into Paradise were rewards best left to others . . .

*No*, Jake decided, *al-Qaeda wasn't the source of the intelligence*.

But the al-Qaeda men had still known more than

Jake, and they'd shown little concern over the death of Mullah Muktar. They'd been more interested in "the deal," "the package," and Turani.

Muktar was history, but Turani was the future.

Jake looked down from the bombed-out building as evening twilight faded from the sky. Four men with Kalashnikovs were at the end of the street. They were focused and alert. Three of them stepped into an abandoned building, while the fourth watched the door. They were searching for something.

Or someone.

It was time to leave.

He limped down the stairs, traveling light, with only the knife in his pocket and the gun in his hand. The wooden door to the street had long ago been scavenged and turned into firewood. Jake raised the pistol and peered through the open doorway. The sentry was fifty yards away, on the same side of the street. Jake walked through what had once been the building's narrow lobby, to the side that had been hit by the IED, and stepped outside. He moved in the shadows as he made his way toward a parked car, a four-door Datsun with faded paint and bald tires.

On the side of the road, a seven- or eight-year-old boy was picking through the rubble of a bombed-out home.

Jake smashed the passenger-side window with the butt of the pistol and used the knife to pop the steering column and start the motor. The little four-cylinder engine idled roughly.

The little boy was holding a stuffed animal covered

in concrete dust and watching Jake from the side of the road.

Jake gunned the engine and switched on the one working headlight as he pulled away from the curb. He drove through Zinjibar, avoiding Tall Mohammed's shop and the other AQAP hangouts, until he reached the eastern edge of the city. He was stopped at a coalition checkpoint, but the soldiers were on the lookout for truckloads of heavily armed fighters, not a lone man in a tiny car. With none of the high-tech gear he and Roach had been using, he was allowed to pass after a brief search for explosives.

He followed the coastal highway east along the Gulf of Aden for nearly an hour before turning north. The car's small engine began to strain as the road snaked its way through a mountain range. He passed several slow-moving trucks laden with drinking water—a precious commodity in a country rocked by cholera and famine.

The Saudi border was nine hours away, and Jake had only moonlight and a memory of a map to guide his way, but despite the long drive and his extreme exhaustion, the rough road and his burning anger kept him alert. The terrorists liked to label their actions as a global jihad, a struggle to rid the world of those that had corrupted it. Left in barren lands without economic opportunity, impressionable young men were taught to blame others for their situations. It was an easy out, adopted by people everywhere, but as it was in most cases, they should have been looking closer to home.

Since birth, Muslim men had been taught to respect the mullahs. Many of the religious leaders were good, decent men, men who interpreted texts written 1,400 years ago, when people still believed that the earth was the center of the universe and bloodletting was considered advanced medicine, and adapted the texts to civilization.

But there were always the corrupt few. As it was with any profession, be they congressmen, cops, CEOs, clergy, computer scientists, or community organizers, there would always be some who would abuse the trust that others had put in them. On a macro level, it was Middle Eastern dictators who'd stolen natural resources and squandered economic opportunities for personal gain. On a micro level, it was leaders of local schools and mosques who'd encouraged young men to commit violence against innocent people in the name of God.

Jake became angrier as he drove, angry at the men who were co-opting their faith and corrupting the minds of those in their care. It was the Muktars and the al-Quereshis of the world who were responsible for the hateful ideology that was masquerading as a religious obligation. Such men needed to be stopped.

Stopped dead.

After a few hours, the steep mountains and rocky plateaus gave way to gravel plains and sand dunes. The change became more dramatic the farther north he traveled. Eventually there was no traffic on the road and even the tenacious sagebrush seemed to die out. There was no life at all.

Jake had entered the Hadhramout. The largest of Yemen's twenty-one governorates, it was a lawless region where AQAP and Daesh ran training camps, built

IEDs, and planned operations against common enemies and one another. With the government on the verge of extinction, and the Saudi coalition more concerned about eradicating extremists from the nation's urban centers, it was a land that had been left to its own devices, a land where truly anything could happen.

Jake drove in the moonlight for another ninety minutes without seeing another vehicle. Eventually he needed to take a bathroom break. He was standing on the side of the road when a van approached from the south, illuminating him in its headlights as it passed.

The sound of screeching tires pierced the night air. Jake saw the van's brake lights, then watched as it made a hasty three-point turn back toward his location.

Jake ran back to his car, killed the lights, and floored the accelerator. He didn't know who was in the van, but in the ungoverned Hadhramout, in the middle of the night, it probably wasn't a Good Samaritan.

The little Datsun and the van passed each other heading in opposite directions. The van turned again and gave chase. Jake looked for a turnoff, but the road had been cut through the middle of the desert. There were no crossroads and there was nowhere to hide. The old car reached sixty, then seventy miles per hour over the broken pavement. It was unsteady at the higher speeds, swaying dangerously across the lanes. He aimed for the middle of the road simply to keep the tires on the pavement.

Jake could see the van behind him only intermittently in the hills, but he knew it was there, and the memory of Roach's mutilated corpse left no doubt in Jake's mind about his own fate were he to be captured.

The car reached eighty miles per hour over the cracked blacktop.

Jake crested a small hill and hit a patch of wind-blown sand. The Datsun began to drift to the left. Jake turned into the slide, but the bald tires lost contact with the pavement and the forty-year-old car bounced off the road and stalled out. Jake heard the approaching van, its engine pushed to the redline. He opened the door and headed into the desert. Fifty yards from the car, he fell into a dry streambed and cursed.

The van sped by.

Its brake lights flashed.

The van turned around again and switched on its headlights. It spotted the stalled Datsun and pulled off the road. Two men leapt out carrying rifles. Jake couldn't tell if they were highway thieves, Daesh fighters, or al-Qaeda henchmen, but there was one thing he did know, and it was quickly becoming a core tenet of his survival.

Everyone he'd met in Yemen was trying to kill him.

## TWENTY-THREE

GRAVES SUMMONED CHRISTINE Kirby to his office.
"What's up?" she said.
"Curt Roach died a few hours ago."

Kirby sighed. "How?"

"Keller said it was an al-Qaeda ambush."

"Keller is OK?"

"He hung up on me when I told him to come in," Graves said. "He thinks he's identified Saturn, but Keller hasn't been in the field that long. Al-Qaeda might have fed him some disinformation and let him escape. He's in trouble already and he's dragging us down with him. I don't want him off on some wild-goose chase. He should be back here and strapped to a polygraph or stuck in a hole."

Kirby frowned.

"What?" Graves said. "The kid is a shit magnet."

"I think you're pulling out too soon. What if he's right about Saturn? What if Saturn was responsible for the attack on Mecca and not Roach and Keller? It doesn't hurt to leave Keller in the field."

Graves cracked his knuckles.

"You ordered him back and he disobeyed the order," Kirby said. "So put the word out that you're looking for him, but don't look too hard. Leave him in play and maybe he'll find something . . . Either way, your ass is covered."

# TWENTY-FOUR

THE OLD PICKUP truck approached the U.S. border just past seven in the morning. Los Indios, Texas, was a gateway for many of the two to three million migrant workers who made their way legally into the U.S. to work each year, but there were many others who tried to enter the country under false pretenses. National security threats, those with counterfeit documents, and various other criminals were the most common offenders.

The U.S. Customs and Border Protection officer working the pickup's lane had seen every trick imaginable in his sixteen years on the job: hidden compartments containing people twisted like pretzels, tires and seat cushions filled with drugs, door panels stuffed with weapons.

And those were just the vehicles. It was amazing what people would do to their bodies to smuggle pills and cocaine into America.

Ironically, it wasn't the truck's battered condition that had raised the warning flag. Dented sheet metal and faded paint were common at Los Indios. It was the fact that most of the migrant workers arrived in cramped buses and vans that were barely roadworthy. Pickup trucks occasionally made the trip, but they carried at least eight passengers to defray the expense, and they never had Texas license plates.

Two men traveling alone didn't fit the profile. Of course, the officer didn't call it a profile because that would get him fired, even though all of his experience and training had taught him to spot subtle deviations from the norm. No, these two were too well off to be migrants, but he'd hear what they had to say.

He waved them up to the checkpoint and was moderately surprised when they handed over two U.S. passports. The officer handicapped the probability that they were fake at about eighty percent as he scanned them into his computer.

Then he started in with questions.

Lots of questions. Unusual questions. He was fluent in English and Spanish and alternated between the two, asking about departure points and arrival destinations, travel histories, employment information, and favorite football teams.

The internet had been a blessing for the officer, allowing him to verify simple details about places he'd never visited, but the technology worked both ways. Ibrahim and Kahlil had done their homework too, using satellite and street map photographs to memorize key details of the small Texas town of Nacogdoches.

The two men were not very talkative, and their answers to his questions were simple declarative statements in basic Spanish and English, but that was not uncommon. Many of the migrant workers were intimidated by the border crossing process.

But there was something the border officer couldn't quite place. Something that didn't add up.

He directed the pickup to a separate area for secondary inspection. A dog was brought in to search for drugs. The men were swabbed for explosives. The truck was x-rayed for hidden weapons.

Nothing.

The border guard returned with the two men's passports. They were legal American citizens with no criminal history or outstanding warrants. Everything checked out. Without reason to hold them any longer, he waved them through.

But as the old pickup truck drove onto U.S. soil, the veteran officer couldn't shake the feeling that he'd just made a terrible mistake.

## TWENTY-FIVE

THE GUNMEN LEFT the van's headlights on. Jake was partially hidden in the dry streambed, but it would be only a matter of time before they found him. The single most valuable lesson he'd learned during his time in the field was that it was better to be the aggressor, to dictate the terms of an engagement, than to be a victim of events.

He drew his pistol and crawled through the streambed. He peered above the bank and saw a third man emerge from the van.

Al-Quereshi.

The three al-Qaeda men searched around the Datsun with their rifles up. It was dark, and Jake could barely see the sights on his weapon, but he pointed it at the closest man. When the others were on the far side of the car, Jake pulled the trigger.

The shot missed. The man spun toward the sound and Jake fired again, hitting his target center-mass. The man sat down and mumbled something.

Jake scrambled ten yards through the streambed and looked up. Al-Quereshi was crouched behind the

Datsun, his rifle pointed over the hood at the area where Jake had just been. The mutterings from the first man stopped. The second fighter was nowhere to be seen.

Jake fired at al-Quereshi and immediately scrambled another ten yards through the streambed. An AK-47 clattered and muzzle flashes lit the area as bullets tore up the ground around him. The AK ran dry and Jake heard the shooter changing magazines.

Jake sat up and fired.

And missed.

Al-Quereshi saw the flash and dialed in Jake's position, unleashing another burst. The rounds hit the earth just inches from his head, spraying sand into his face. He scrambled backward ten feet through the dry streambed. His heart was pounding. He was flat on his back and holding the pistol in tight. In the silence of the desert night, he heard footsteps coming closer.

Jake had one round left.

The al-Qaeda fighter peered over the edge of the streambed.

Jake shot him in the face. He died instantly, tumbling forward and landing on top of Jake.

But it wasn't al-Quereshi.

Jake rolled the dead man off and took his rifle before scrambling through the streambed and peering above the bank. He scanned the area with the gun up. He was sure that he'd at least wounded the terrorist leader.

Nothing.

Jake ran to the Datsun and slid behind the engine block, but he didn't draw any fire. He didn't hear any movement. He crouched behind the car and scanned the area again. Nothing. He ran to the van and searched under it, around it, and inside of it.

Still nothing.

Jake fired a few times into the desert. The ex–Delta Force operators he'd trained with upon joining the Special Activities Center had called it "recon by fire," and Jake hoped it would draw out al-Quereshi, but the terrorist didn't take the bait.

Jake searched the area, wondering how the al-Qaeda thugs had tracked him. He thought of the little boy with the stuffed animal who'd watched Jake steal the car. Having lost his own parents at a young age, Jake had felt empathy for the kid, but the terrorists had probably told him that the American he'd seen was responsible for bombing his house and killing his family, further spreading their dogma of hateful intolerance and gaining a future recruit through the propagation of more lies.

Jake searched for half an hour, but there was no body, no blood trail, and no sign of al-Quereshi.

Jake glanced at the Datsun. With a little luck, he could still make the Saudi border before sunrise.

But the only luck in Jake's future was bad luck.

The car's left front wheel was slanted forty-five degrees. It had broken an axle when it veered off the road. He decided to take the van.

As he walked toward it, the van's headlights revealed a bullet hole in the loose fabric of his jacket.

*Close . . .*

# TWENTY-SIX

THE REST OF Señor Paraíso's men departed on U.S. and Mexican air carriers, taking various flights to various cities. The Hezbollah militants had used satellite photos from the internet and advance-team reconnaissance to scout their targets while their equipment had been shipped ahead weeks earlier in a miniature narco-submarine provided by their Mexican hosts. Each of them could close his eyes and visualize his entire mission, but none had actually been to the United States until his aircraft crossed into American airspace.

Several team members spotted their objectives through their plane windows.

The groups that landed in San Diego and Los Angeles used their American passports to pass swiftly through immigration. They took rental cars and taxis to several Los Angeles–area hotels, then another set of taxis to their rendezvous point, a warehouse in East Los Angeles.

The men ate. They prayed. They checked and re-checked their equipment. Some had lingering doubts about their ascension into Paradise as martyrs, but Paraíso had told them that such feelings were to be expected, and they should not doubt themselves. One could never know Paradise until he had achieved it, but faith and action would get him there.

Theirs would be the opening salvo in a new war, and while the teams' tactical objective was to destroy the targets, Iran's strategic rationale for the attacks was a complex and often contradictory mix of theology and economics.

Most Iranians were Shia Muslim who believed in a messianic figure who would one day reappear. Similar to the Christian concept of Judgment, the return of the Islamic Mahdi was to bring universal justice to the world. Iran's theocrats took the belief to an extreme, reasoning that the further mankind ventured from universal justice, the greater would be the need for the Mahdi, thus accelerating his return. This twisted logic was their justification for supporting anarchism and terrorism around the globe, despite the fact that the underlying prophecy included the prophet Jesus working hand in hand with the imam.

Though Iran's antagonistic foreign policy was usually attributed to religious extremism, its leaders' other goal in attacking the United States was much more pragmatic. Despite having $100 billion in assets unfrozen after the Joint Comprehensive Plan of Action was concluded, the country still had a cash flow problem. It was spending so much on graft, its military, and its nuclear programs that the basic necessities of many of its people were going unmet. With the government openly hostile to foreigners and the region continually rocked by sectarian violence, the only commercial asset the country had was oil.

It was Iran's only reliable source of hard currency.

But the United States had drastically reduced its dependence on foreign sources of energy by forcing fluids into the earth to loosen enormous deposits of oil and natural gas trapped amid underground formations of shale rock. The American government supported the hydrofracking, as the technique was called, partially to reduce the nation's dependency on the Middle East, and while many Muslim nations also looked forward to reduced U.S. involvement in the region, the new supply sent the price of oil plummeting.

Economies that had grown dependent on ever-increasing oil prices were caught short, struggling to pay their bills and keep their economies solvent. For Iran to prosper at home and project its disruptive policies abroad, oil prices needed to be higher. The attack on Mecca had already sent them up by 30 percent as investors speculated about yet another war in the Middle East.

By the next morning they'd be higher by another 50 percent, and the economic powerhouse that was Southern California, an automobile-centric region with little mass transit, would grind to a standstill.

## *TWENTY-SEVEN*

SIX BLACK MERCEDES Geländewagens sped down the highway in close formation. In the back of the second vehicle, Prince Faisal rode with his chief of staff.

"There has been small-scale violence outside Briman Prison in Jeddah," said al-Shezza, "and the typical unrest in the Shia regions in the east, but the demonstrations in Riyadh have been peaceful so far. The only concern is a growing crowd outside the U.S. embassy."

The prince admired the magnificent Kingdom Center skyscraper through the window. Lit in the green and gold Saudi national colors, its oval-shaped base tapered into two peaks like a giant letter U. A skybridge spanned the peaks, nearly a thousand feet in the air.

"Sir," said al-Shezza, "our inaction is being noted by both sides. Our commanders are asking for their orders . . . Perhaps it is time for the troops to send the troublemakers home?"

"Not yet."

Al-Shezza paused for a moment. "Yes, Your Highness."

The motorcade slowed as it turned through a pair of wrought-iron gates. Uniformed soldiers watched the vehicles leave the urban desert and enter a lushly landscaped oasis. Rows of date trees, planted forty deep on each side, lined the perfectly straight driveway. Fountains, ponds, and towering palm trees adorned the car park in front of Al-Yamamah Palace.

The prince and his chief of staff joined other royals and government officials inside a mammoth octagonal meeting room. The aides stood behind their principals, against the blond wood walls. Everyone rose when a pair of eighteen-foot-tall bronze doors opened.

King Ali crossed the room at a pace befitting a man of his age and unhealthy lifestyle. His black camel-hair robes trailed over the marble floor. Upon reaching his chair he gave a barely perceptible nod, and the others took their seats.

Greetings were exchanged and prayers were said. Most of the men in the room looked to their religion for strength and guidance, and those who didn't had long ago learned to fake it, for there was no greater crime in the kingdom than the abandonment of one's faith. Apostates swiftly found themselves separated from their heads at the hands of a sword-wielding executioner in Riyadh's Deera Square.

"What is the most recent number?" the king asked his minister of the interior.

"It appears that three thousand pilgrims were martyred, Your Majesty. The wounded number several thousand more."

"Three thousand . . ."

"Yes, Your Majesty, three thousand," added one of the younger princes. "The same number that were killed in the 11th of September attacks in the United States. An unlikely coincidence."

"You think the attackers planned to kill exactly three thousand Muslims as revenge?" asked the king, his hands folded in his lap.

"Your Majesty," continued the young prince, "fifteen of the hijackers were Saudis. Osama bin Laden was Saudi. Saudi support for Daesh and Wahhabi madrassas is well known. This is the United States affecting Qisas. The Americans call it 'an eye for an eye,' but it is the same principle."

"But Qisas does not apply to the deaths of non-Muslims."

"So you say," countered the prince, "but there are elements in the United States who are celebrating this as the beginning of a greater war against Islam. Their own president has not denied responsibility. We must condemn—"

The king raised a single hand above the table. The young prince stopped in midsentence.

"I am sorry, Your Majesty," said the prince. "I beg a thousand pardons for my outburst."

"This is a difficult time for the kingdom," said King Ali, "and also for the United States. There are indeed factions that celebrate the attack, that are calling for all-out war on Islam, but the majority of Americans are horrified." The king looked at Prince Faisal, repeating his earlier advice verbatim. "The United States has been a long-standing and powerful ally—"

"Only because they want our oil," said the young prince.

King Ali's thick eyebrows tightened and his mouth pursed as he glared at the young man. With his left hand, he pointed to the door and a moment later two uniformed guards manhandled the young prince out of the room. His life was now in jeopardy, but the meeting continued.

"The United States has been a long-standing and powerful ally," the king repeated. "It would be foolish to turn them into a long-standing and powerful enemy before we have proof that they were responsible."

Many in the room seethed at the king's refusal to face reality, but their desire to remain among the living kept them silent. The royal family viewed themselves as not just the leaders of the kingdom, but also its owners. As its head, the monarch's power was nearly absolute.

"There are pressing domestic issues that require our attention," the king said, turning to Prince Faisal. "What of the public unrest? The National Guard has traditionally dispersed such gatherings swiftly."

"The people are mourning, Your Majesty," said Faisal. "On this tragic occasion, and with your blessing, of course, I feel that it will not compromise security to allow them to express their grief in public."

The king moved to other business. When the meeting had adjourned, he summoned Prince Faisal to his office.

"You do not seem yourself, Faisal. Is there something you would like to say privately? You know I value your counsel and support. Please, speak freely."

"As always, Your Majesty sees through my facade. I fear that our reluctance to address the American role in the attack is creating a void, a breeding ground for instigators and agitators. Like you, I do not believe that President Day would order such a thing. The Americans have a 'moral compass,' as they say, and while it often wavers and is often weak, it values human life to a fault."

"You think I should make a public statement in support of America?" the king said. "I would prefer to wait until we know more."

"The people need to mourn, Your Highness, but they also need to be led. The middle ground satisfies no one. If you stand by the United States, the people will follow, as they always have."

# TWENTY-EIGHT

L NUEVO CONSTANTE slipped her lines at day-
break and motored away from the dock. The
twenty-foot-long container sat amidships. The
captain's son had lashed it into place with heavy chains
after Carlos had returned with the $15,000 in cash.

Up in the deckhouse, the captain shaded his eyes
from the rising sun as he headed out of the Port of
Veracruz. Miguel and Carlos were on the foredeck, inspecting the thick anchor chain and coiling the rough
dock lines. Miguel was teaching the new hand how to
turn the lines so they wouldn't kink, and Carlos was
working hard, moving the heavy ropes with ease.

The ship turned north-northeast in the calm seas
and soon reached her cruising speed of twelve knots.
Carlos and Miguel spent a few hours preparing for the
voyage, and they were laughing and talking loudly
when they joined the captain on the bridge for lunch.
The space was utilitarian. Its walls were adorned with
loose lines, rain slickers, and even an old longshoreman's hook, a relic from the days before containerized
cargo.

"I was thinking we could repair the hole in the fore-deck today," said Miguel. "The steel plate is too heavy for you and me, but Carlos is as strong as an ox."

"And I know how to weld," volunteered Carlos. "Miguel showed me the rusted section and I think we could replace it in five or six hours."

"Please do," said the captain. "That sheet of plywood will snap in two if we take any green water aboard. Lunch will be ready in half an hour."

The captain smiled as the two young men headed below to check out the job. Perhaps his concerns about the cargo were unfounded. After all, this young Carlos wasn't anything like the thugs from the cartels. They'd never volunteered for anything except shooting up the local towns.

Miguel and Carlos unbolted the plywood from the deck to reveal a large hole in the badly corroded steel. The captain joined the younger men to celebrate completion of the easiest part of the job. He handed out beef burritos and bottles of water.

"Thank you," said Carlos, dripping in sweat from the midday sun. He took several bites of the burrito. "This is fantastic," he said, ignoring the fact that the meat was undoubtedly not halal.

"It's the *queso fresco* that makes it special," said the captain.

"No microwave for Papa," said Miguel. "He cooks fresh every day."

"This afternoon lunch is usually our main meal aboard ship," said the captain, "but the way you two are working, we might have to have two main meals on this trip." He drew the bowie knife from the scabbard on his hip and sliced his own burrito in two, giving the second half to Carlos.

The men ate together on deck, enjoying the light breeze, calm seas, and clear skies. The captain made his way back to the wheelhouse while the younger men resumed work on the deck plate. Miguel used an oxy-acetylene torch to cut away the rusted metal. It fell into the empty hold, clanging loudly as it hit the hull.

The men moved the new steel plate into place and lap-welded the corners. The final welds would take a few more hours and likely be finished at night under the ship's deck lights. Miguel and Carlos were taking a short break when the captain yelled down, summoning them to the bridge.

"What is it, Papa?" asked Miguel.

"The engine is overheating again," he said.

"I'll have a look," said Miguel.

The captain pulled the throttle back to neutral and shut off the old diesel. *El Nuevo Constante* began to slow.

Carlos looked out the window at the setting sun. "Will this affect our arrival?"

"It depends how soon we get it fixed," said the captain. "If it's the—"

Carlos did not hear the rest, for he was already racing after Miguel.

# TWENTY-NINE

BRAHIM AND KAHLIL had been on the road for twenty hours by the time they pulled away from the border checkpoint. They obeyed the speed limit and signaled every lane change, anxious that whatever had triggered such intense scrutiny at the border might betray them again and prevent them from accomplishing their mission.

Upon reaching San Antonio they turned off the highway and into the parking lot of a big-box store. The two men donned their straw cowboy hats and stretched briefly as they exited the old pickup truck and walked toward the store.

Kahlil bent down to adjust his work boots next to a compact white SUV and removed a magnetic key holder from its left front wheel well. He rejoined Ibrahim and entered the store. They emerged fifteen minutes later with food and supplies.

The two men drove away in the white SUV. Neither imposing nor memorable, it was a style that could have come from half a dozen Asian manufacturers. Its com-

mon color and tinted windows made it utterly forgetta-
ble as they headed north toward Dallas.

They were just inside the city limits when the evening rush hour began to bite. Kahlil climbed into the
backseat and opened a large black duffel bag that had
been left on the floor. Inside, wrapped in a blanket, was
a precision hunting rifle from Finland. He threaded an
eight-inch sound suppressor onto the end of the short-
barreled gun. Far from making the weapon silent, as
was often shown in the movies, it would only reduce
the noise to a less painful level. He loaded seven rounds
into the bolt-action rifle, engaged the safety, and held
it in his lap.

Ibrahim exited onto the Dallas Parkway, an elevated
local road that crossed over the massive Lyndon B. John-
son Freeway. The LBJ was part of a beltway around the
city on which a quarter of a million vehicles passed each
day. The two men drove until a red light brought traffic
to a stop. To their left and sixty feet down, ten lanes of
rush hour traffic were moving slowly along the LBJ.

Warm air and traffic noise flowed into the SUV's
interior as Kahlil lowered the window. He raised the
rifle to his shoulder, placed the stock against his cheek,
and looked through the three-power scope. To the west
was a bridge running parallel to the elevated road. A
blue minivan emerged from underneath the bridge, and
Kahlil tracked it with the scope's reticle as it approached.

The minivan passed safely under the elevated road.

"The light is about to turn," Ibrahim said calmly.

A yellow convertible sports car came into view. The

bleach blond driver was riding with the top down, undoubtedly seeking to corrupt passing men with her brazen sexuality.

*The opportunity for her to carry herself modestly has passed,* thought Kahlil.

Weeks prior, he'd used an online map to determine that the distance between the bridge and the elevated road on which they were stopped was 124 yards. He estimated that traffic was moving around fifty miles per hour, which would cause the car to travel about ten feet from when he pulled the trigger until the bullet reached it. He placed the crosshairs on the ground three feet in front of the bumper and tracked the car as it came closer. He waited until she was halfway to him and fired.

The woman's head exploded an eighth of a second later, with only a small hole in the windshield.

He heard the sports car crash into a guardrail.

His cheek never left the stock as he worked the bolt and chambered another round. Two lanes over, he acquired a bright red pickup truck and started leading the target.

"The light is green," said Ibrahim.

Kahlil fired, hitting the pickup truck's driver in the torso. Thinking he was having another heart attack, the fifty-six-year-old plant manager clutched his chest as he plowed full speed into the car in front of him, which had stopped behind the wrecked sports car.

"Five seconds," Ibrahim said as the line of cars in front of them slowly began to move. The heavily tinted windows in the SUV shielded their activities from view.

A pileup ensued on the LBJ as tailgating drivers

joined the wreckage. No longer needing to lead his targets, Kahlil fired off four quick shots at the stopped cars, killing three office workers and a woman in a minivan.

A similar scene had unfolded in Phoenix, Arizona, just minutes earlier, with a second team killing six motorists in four cars. In a quarter of an hour, a third team, waiting on an overpass in New Jersey, would end the lives of half a dozen commuters on their drive home from New York City.

Kahlil raised the tinted rear window as Ibrahim pulled to the intersection and turned down a side road.

The three children in the back of the minivan were crying, wondering what was wrong with their mother.

# THIRTY

JAKE STOPPED THE van. Off in the distance, maybe five miles away, was a cluster of bright lights. The towns he'd driven through on the ten-hour journey from Zinjibar had been mostly dark—more victims of the war. The basic necessities for civilization had been stripped away: food, water, education, electricity. Only pockets of the country had any of them, and the northern Hadhramout had none. It was a humanitarian tragedy to be sure, but the lights in the distance also meant that Jake had finally found the Saudi border.

Crossing it would not be easy. He had no documents, no money, and no disclosable purpose in Saudi Arabia. He wasn't Muslim, he was carrying weapons, and he was driving a van that belonged to al-Qaeda terrorists.

His only chance was a clandestine penetration on foot.

Jake killed the headlights and put the van in gear. A mile down the road he discovered a gravel path leading into the desert. He knew that Bedouins and traders had crisscrossed the area for centuries, and he suspected that something as fleeting as national boundaries hadn't stopped them from continuing their travels. He turned onto the gravel and wound his way through a series of low hills for half an hour. Dunes took shape around him as he drew closer to the border. Sand spilled onto the path. Jake let some air out of the tires and was able to continue on until a sand drift blocked the road completely.

He stood atop the drift. The lights of the border checkpoint were off to the southeast now, and it was probably seven or eight miles through the desert to Al-Wadiah—the nearest town on the Saudi side.

He looked back the way he'd come, but there was nothing good waiting for him in Yemen.

*Better to keep pushing forward.*

He returned to the van and found some food and a half-empty case of water in the back. He reloaded the pistol he'd taken in Zinjibar and stuffed everything into a knapsack except the gun, which he kept close at hand.

A blazing-red sun was barely over the horizon, looming large in the eastern sky. Jake climbed over the drift and slid down the soft, cool sand as he set off for the border. He made good time for the first half mile as he followed the trail, but the shifting dunes soon covered the path completely. Each step became a full-body exercise as the fine, dry sand swallowed his feet up to his ankles.

By the time he reached the border, he was already exhausted, and he still had to contend with a fifteen-foot-high chain-link fence, topped with a foot of barbed wire.

He cursed as he put his sandals and the gun in the knapsack, then took off his jacket and folded it over one arm. He climbed barefoot up the chain link and draped the jacket over the barbed wire to protect himself from the sharp metal spikes.

Off in the distance, maybe two miles away, a Saudi Humvee was patrolling the fence line. Jake stepped over the barbed wire and jumped onto the soft sand. His legs ached, he was exhausted, and his ribs still hurt from where he'd been beaten, but he didn't waste time taking pity on himself.

He had a new problem to deal with.

The Saudi side of the border had been graded flat for maybe a hundred yards. It looked like a minefield, but there weren't any signs. The Saudis wouldn't leave a minefield unmarked, but their patrol would undoubtedly see his footsteps in the soft sand.

The patrol was close. They'd be able to see him in a minute or two. Jake dropped to his knees and dug frantically with his hands. The sand yielded easily, as if he were digging through baby powder, until he'd dug a shallow trench. He climbed in with the knapsack and covered himself, wriggling his arms down into the sand until only his nose was exposed.

He tried to relax, to slow his breathing and his heart rate, but that plan went to hell the moment he heard the Humvee's big diesel engine pulling it through the soft sand in low gear. A moment later he smelled its oily exhaust, but it was only when Jake felt small vibrations in the earth from the four-ton truck that he was truly afraid. He'd covered his head and chest with less than an inch of sand, and the vibrations were causing it to shift and settle to lower ground.

He felt the warmth of the sun on his face as it penetrated the rapidly thinning layer of sand.

The mechanical noises grew louder too, and it wasn't just the engine. Jake could hear other sounds. Something was squeaking; something else was grinding.

He held his breath.

He tried to press himself deeper into the sand.

But everything went black.

## THIRTY-ONE

I T HAD BEEN several months after the end of the 1979 Iranian revolution when government-sanctioned rioters had overpowered the skeleton staff of the U.S. embassy and taken fifty-two American citizens as hostages. For most of the next 444 days, the Americans remained inside the embassy walls as prisoners of the new theocracy. The docile American response would forever after serve as a model for Iran's relations with the United States.

The new government, led by Ayatollah Ruhollah Khomeini, created a new army to ensure that his revolution would be the last. Called the Islamic Revolutionary Guards Corps, it spread like an aggressive cancer, taking over business and military interests until it became the most powerful entity in the nation, and one of the most profitable. In the early 1980s, the IRGC began to project its growing power abroad when it founded the Qods Force. The name literally meant "the Jerusalem Force," and the brigade's reason for being was to drive the Zionists from Palestine, but Israel was far too powerful for Iran to confront directly, so Qods began to support a broad base of nefarious actors. It became a fifteen-thousand-man special operations force dedicated to supplying men, training, money, and weapons to those who could weaken the position of Iran's rivals and hasten the return of the messianic Mahdi.

Qods had a decentralized command structure, with headquarters in several cities around Iran. Thus, the U.S. embassy in Tehran, which hadn't served as a diplomatic outpost of the United States since 1979, was remarkably well kept.

A MAN EMERGED from the nearby Taleghani metro station. He was tanned and fit, with hard eyes and a long scar on the left side of his head. He entered the embassy compound through a discreet side entrance and made his way to a small suite of offices. The receptionist informed him that General Shirizani was running late.

The man with the scar had been waiting less than five minutes when a man in an open-necked suit emerged from the office. The man with the scar jumped from his seat.

"Turani!" he said. "How long has it been?"

"Almost four years," said the man in the suit as he hugged his friend.

"Yes, of course! We celebrated the Eid al-Adha together in Isfahan! How have you been?"

"Busy, my brother. Do you have time for a cup of tea?"

"I would like nothing better, but I have an appointment with the general in a few minutes."

"It is a shame, but I understand. I must soon catch a flight myself."

The receptionist looked at the man with the scar. "The general is at least half an hour behind."

He hesitated. One did not make General Shirizani wait.

"Give me your number," she said. "I'll call you if anything changes."

The man with the scar left with his old friend, stopping in the outer office for tea. The two men wandered along a deserted pathway inside the twenty-six-acre compound.

"How is Farima?"

The man in the suit grinned as he gestured to the scar on his friend's face. "I pull you from a collapsed building in southern Lebanon, your head half blown off by a Zionist airstrike, and you introduce me to my wife. How's that for gratitude?"

"She is the most beautiful woman in Tehran," said his friend. "Divorce her now and she'll be remarried before sunset."

"She was your wife's old-maid cousin!" said Turani. "But she has given me two wondrous daughters."

"Nilou and Leili? They don't look much like you."

"Don't make me hurt you."

"I'd like to see you try. I've been training hard, my friend. My body is like a piece of steel."

"You've been in the sun as well," said Turani.

"I transferred to Unit 400," said the man with the scar. "They call me 'Señor Paraíso.'"

Turani smiled. "Are you in Paraguay, señor?"

"A bit farther north . . ."

"Striking the Great Satan?" asked Turani.

"I am afraid I cannot be more specific," said Paraíso, feeling guilty about holding out on his old friend.

Turani nodded as the two men walked. "Your commitment to operational security is commendable, but I believe you will find that we have been working different parts of the same mission. It was I who obtained the package you are about to deliver."

Paraíso stopped. "Go on."

Turani took his friend's arm and spoke softly as they continued walking. "A few months after the Saudi coalition invaded Yemen, an al-Qaeda commander contacted us to see if we could broker a cease-fire with the Houthis so both sides could focus on the threat from the Saudis. General Shirizani asked me to meet with Mullah Muktar, and we de-escalated hostilities between AQAP and the Houthis, but al-Qaeda was still taking heavy losses from the coalition."

"And now that filthy Daesh is there too," said Paraíso.

"And now Daesh," said Turani. "Another front in the war, which further weakened AQAP."

"But al-Qaeda has recently inflicted much pain on the Saudis and Daesh," said Paraíso. "What changed?"

"Six months ago, the mullah approached me again. He was desperate. They were out of money and out of weapons."

"But the Houthis are fellow Shiites," said Paraíso. "Why would we provide salvation to their sworn enemy?"

"I asked Muktar the same question," said Turani, "but he had something to trade for our support. Something priceless."

Paraíso looked into Turani's eyes. "Where did he obtain this 'something'?"

"From a sympathetic source inside Pakistan's Inter-Services Intelligence Agency," Turani said. He smiled as he saw the recognition in his friend's face.

"Since its first day, al-Qaeda has strived to acquire such a capability," said Paraíso. "I cannot believe they would give it up."

"They had no choice. Their very existence was at stake. We gave them arms and three million U.S. dollars."

"Why did we not give the weapon to Hezbollah?" Paraíso said. "To use against the Zionists."

"It was a condition from ISI. The Pakistanis have already reported the weapon stolen, and the U.S., unsure of itself as always, will fire a few cruise missiles and nothing will change. But the Israelis . . . they would bomb Pakistan back to the time of the prophets."

Paraíso walked on, realizing that his friend knew more than he. "I am relieved to hear it is a Pakistani weapon. My greatest fear was that the device was one of our own. I agree that the Americans have grown soft, but they could flatten *our* cities if they so chose."

"The United States would never do such a thing," said Turani. "America has lost the will to make hard choices."

The two men walked in silence for a few minutes until Paraíso's phone vibrated in his pocket. He glanced at the screen.

"I must return to meet the general," he said.

"So many years later and here we are, together again on the path of destiny," said Turani. "I am off to Riyadh. Tell me . . . when does it begin?"

Paraíso looked his friend in the eyes. "Now."

## THIRTY-TWO

THREE BLACK FORD Expeditions with tinted windows and livery license plates left the garage and turned south onto the 710 freeway. A keen observer would have noted the heavy-duty skid plates and run-flat tires on each of the trucks, but at night the three SUVs looked as if they belonged to one of the hundreds of limousine companies in Los Angeles.

Each of the Expeditions drove at a steady seventy miles per hour, staying in the flow of traffic to avoid unwanted attention. There was no turning back now. They had too many weapons and too much ordnance to hide. If they were stopped by the police, the war would simply begin early.

Two of the SUVs continued south on the 710, but the third turned west on the 105, toward the Pacific Ocean. Thirty minutes later, it approached the massive El Segundo Refinery near Los Angeles International Airport and smashed through a chain-link gate. A warning Klaxon began to sound as the truck bounced over the uneven road that led to the heart of the thousand-acre facility. Distillation towers for processing crude oil loomed 120 feet tall in the windshield as the driver skidded to a halt. Two of the Hezbollah gunmen leapt from the rear seat and fanned out with automatic weapons while two others climbed out of the rear gate carrying a rocket-propelled grenade launcher and extra ammunition.

Abdul bin Fatah braced himself against the side of the SUV, sighted in the first objective, and fired.

The rocket-propelled grenade smashed into a massive reactor vessel at near-supersonic speed. The shaped-explosive warhead sent a jet of molten copper through the thick steel before exploding inside. Superheated steam erupted from the container, causing it to collapse violently upon itself.

Two of the other terrorists fired relentlessly with their AK-47s as a plant security vehicle approached, filling the white Jeep Cherokee with dozens of 7.62mm bullets. The security guards inside were already dead when the Jeep crashed into a concrete containment trench.

Police sirens wailed in the distance as another terrorist passed Abdul a second warhead. He lined up on the next target, a gasoline reformer the size of a small townhouse.

Two more security guards arrived in a full-sized pickup truck and took cover behind their vehicle. Abdul fired again, hitting the reformer broadside. The armor-piercing warhead sliced through the steel and exploded inside a tank of pressurized hydrogen heated to 1,300 degrees Fahrenheit. The rush of outside air caused the hydrogen to vaporize for a fraction of a second before it ignited. The ensuing explosion launched twisted metal and burning fuel in every direction. One of the terrorist gunmen died instantly when a forty-ton steel plate landed on him. A secondary explosion and fire killed the two security guards and another terrorist. A dense black cloud of smoke swirled into the air.

The shock wave knocked Abdul to the ground with blood dripping from his ears and nose. He staggered to the back of the SUV, retrieved more warheads, and lowered himself to one knee. He fired into the refinery's three-hundred-ton coker vessel, then again into a distillation tower. Both exploded spectacularly, shaking the ground and sending more clouds of noxious black smoke billowing into the sky.

Two El Segundo police cruisers bottomed out briefly as they sped through the main gate at eighty miles per hour.

Abdul and the surviving gunman returned to the SUV to find the driver's head shredded by fragments of auto glass. He looked as if he'd been hit by a shotgun at close range. They pulled his body from the vehicle, kicked out the shattered front windshield, and drove deeper into the complex, for El Segundo was more than just a refinery—it was also a storage facility for half a billion gallons of highly flammable liquid hydrocarbons.

On his flight into LAX, Abdul had noted which of the enormous floating-roof tanks were full and which were empty. Though the explosions had left him deaf and suffering from a concussion, he screamed for the new driver to stop at a particular tank. Over sixty feet tall and two hundred fifty feet in diameter, it held five hundred thousand barrels of diesel fuel. The SUV skidded sideways in the gravel as the driver mashed the brake pedal to the floor. Abdul stepped out and fired at a range of five hundred feet, but he'd rushed the shot and the round missed high. The warhead landed in a residential neighborhood to the north, killing a family of three.

Abdul reloaded the RPG and fired again, hitting the diesel tank on his second attempt and blowing a hole in its side. Burning fuel spewed from the void. He and the driver jumped back into the SUV and headed for their next target.

The two police cruisers had seen the RPG flying through the air and turned toward the base of the smoke trail. Sergeant Hector Lopez, a twelve-year veteran of the El Segundo police force, pursued the SUV as it accelerated away from the flaming wreckage, gravel spitting from its tires. Lopez and his up-engined pursuit car closed quickly with the SUV and clipped its rear quarter, causing it to spin out.

The SUV's driver reached for an AK-47 he'd stashed between the seats, but Lopez was already out of his cruiser with his service pistol up. He fired seven rounds from the .40-caliber Glock through the SUV's window and door, killing the driver and wounding Abdul.

Abdul staggered onto the gravel as Sergeant Lopez walked around the SUV with his pistol up. The terrorist fell to his knees with the RPG on his shoulder and pulled the trigger. The grenade leapt from the launch tube toward an enormous kerosene tank.

Lopez fired four more rounds, killing Abdul, but

the warhead was long gone. It flew true to its target and exploded inside the tank. Flaming kerosene flooded the ground, flowing into the twenty-foot-wide containment trenches that ringed the tank farm. Ignited by the intense heat, more tanks exploded, and the trenches became burning rivers of fuels and chemicals.

The trenches quickly transformed into a vision of hell, with one-thousand-degree flames reaching ninety feet into the night sky and clouds of thick, toxic smoke blowing over the ground. The heat caused car tires to melt and windows to sag. The terrorists were already dead, but for Lopez and the other officer, despite their valiant efforts, there would be no escaping the fiery lake of burning sulfur.

## *THIRTY-THREE*

JAKE LAY MOTIONLESS in the sand as the Saudi Humvee passed directly overhead. He counted to five hundred to ensure the soldiers were out of sight and emerged from the trench he'd dug. There were tire tracks eighteen inches from where his head had been.

*Small victories.*

He climbed to the top of the nearest dune and found Al-Wadiah. It was the next patch of shade, it was eight miles away, and it wasn't coming to him.

Jake cursed as the soft sand swallowed his foot. Climbing and descending the dunes was exhausting, so he stayed low when he could, walking in the troughs between the dunes. The sun rose quickly into the cloudless sky and the heat climbed through the eighties and into the nineties in what seemed like an instant. He draped his coat over his head. Every breath felt as if he'd sucked it out of a hair dryer.

The sheer volume of sand was incomprehensible. Occasionally there were loose rocks or a scrub brush poking through, but for miles in each direction there was nothing but sand, blown into endless and elegant formations by the shifting desert wind. He was in the Empty Quarter, the Rub' al Khali. It was a quarter of a million square miles in size and the largest expanse of desert in the world.

It was land that even the nomadic Bedouin tribes refused to cross on foot during the daytime, instead preferring to use camels and travel by night.

Less than halfway to Al-Wadiah, he was stumbling over the ground. He fell to his knees, exhausted, and drank a bottle of water.

Jake had played water polo while at Boston College, and kept himself in top physical condition ever since, but the desert was relentless. Like nothing else, it found his weaknesses and ground him down. He pushed away some of the hottest sand, covered his head with his jacket, and tried to sleep.

The temperature was over 120 degrees, without a hint of breeze, when he awoke. Shimmering waves of heat rose from the desert floor. Blisters were forming on his lips and the soles of his feet.

He drank another bottle of water.

Jake staggered to the top of a tall dune and looked to Al-Wadiah, but the village had vanished, its image obscured by a mirage of reflected heat. He searched in every direction without seeing a single sign of life or distinguishing feature. Even the sun was conspiring to kill him. It was directly overhead, offering no sense of direction. His footsteps told him where he'd come from, but he could go no farther. Holding a heading over the featureless desert would be impossible.

He lay in the sand, tugging frequently at his clothes to cover his exposed skin. Every so often, he would project an imaginary line from his footsteps out to the horizon. After several tries, he finally caught a glimpse of Al-Wadiah, or at least he thought he did.

The village was right where he'd hoped it would be, northeast of his position. He knew that mirages were dangerous temptresses who led men where they had no business going, and the voice of reason in his head told him to wait for sunset, or at least a few hours until the sun started to set in the west, but Jake wasn't listening. His obsession with finding Turani overruled his common sense.

He staggered forward into the constantly changing mirage. He saw roads where he knew there were none, dark clouds on a clear horizon, and puddles of water between the parched dunes. But he kept going. In another day or two Turani might be gone, and if Jake didn't find him before al-Qaeda or Graves found Jake, he might never get another chance.

## THIRTY-FOUR

FAISAL'S HELICOPTER RATTLED the palm grove as it approached Al-Yamamah Palace. The deputy crown prince had been strategizing with his regional National Guard commanders when the king had called another meeting of the Council of Ministers. Much to his displeasure, the prince had been forced to cut short his own meetings and return to Riyadh.

He stepped down from the helicopter and into the 110-degree heat. The rotor wash from the big Black Hawk nearly blew the ghutra from his head, but the moving air felt good as it circulated through his robes. Though he was inside the highly secure palace grounds, an armored Range Rover shuttled him the five hundred feet to the palace entrance.

He and al-Shezza had barely entered the building when a dozen black-uniformed paratroopers appeared from a side hallway.

"Faisal," bellowed the king as the guards parted. "It is good to see a friendly face. The machinery of the kingdom has been running roughly since the attack. Events are beginning to acquire an inertia of their own."

"Your Majesty has always guided his subjects with wisdom and grace," said the prince. "I am confident that your judgment and faith will continue to show us the right path. We would be foolish to forsake our long partnership with the Americans without indisputable proof."

"Unfortunately, you and I may be the only ones who understand that."

"Fortunately, that's enough."

The king nodded as they reached the meeting chamber and the Royal Guards opened the eighteen-foot-high doors. Commensurate with their high offices, the thirty ministers were wearing formal black *bisht*s over their white *thobe*s. The men were speaking in knots around the room when the king entered. Looks were exchanged. Conversations ended. They took their seats at the ring-shaped desk.

The minister for Islamic affairs led the group in prayer, then quickly segued to his own agenda.

"The people are angry. If the government will not bring justice, then the faithful will be obligated to take jihad into their own hands."

The minister was from the al-Wahhab family, the religious core of the nation. Three hundred years earlier, Muhammad bin Saud and Muhammad ibn al-Wahhab had formed the partnership that led to the first Saudi state. Though many years and many marriages had mixed the bloodlines of the two families, there were still many differences. While the al-Sauds governed a modern economy in a modern world, the Wahhabi sect of Islam had not changed its interpretation of

a Muslim's duties from what was written in the Holy
Quran fourteen hundred years earlier. There were the
faithful, the infidels, and the worst of the worst, the
apostates. It was really quite simple.

The Wahhabis often supported organizations that
chose to execute their interpretations of Allah's will
with force. To maintain harmony at home and retain
their grip on power, the Sauds usually played along or
at least turned a blind eye. After the recent attack on
Mecca, the Wahhabis were out for blood, and the minister of Islamic affairs' rebuke of the king removed any
possible misconception that they were willing to be patient. The king looked to Prince Faisal for support.

"We have been conducting raids outside Jeddah
where nefarious elements have been known to gather.
The National Guard will not rest until order is restored."

"Thank you, Faisal," said the king. He recited the
prince's earlier words. "We would be foolish to forsake
our long partnership with the Americans without *indisputable* proof."

Looks of displeasure shot across the massive room.

"Have we located the aircraft that struck the Masjid
al-Haram?" asked the king.

The crown prince, who was also the minister of defense, was coordinating the search of the Red Sea. "We
have approximately forty ships, ten helicopters, and two
of our Type-209 submarines searching around the clock
with sonar. Russia has loaned us a deep-submergence
rescue vehicle, and it has investigated several promising
hits, but found nothing, or at least nothing they are
telling us about. Our sonar tells us one thing, but when

the DSRV gets there it finds nothing with its cameras, and there is no room for a KSA crew member in the control section." The defense minister scowled. "And now the sub is down for repairs. It has been running almost nonstop chasing down these leads, and of course the hits came in hundreds of kilometers apart. It is hard on the crew and the vessel . . . I think the Russians may be playing undersea games with us."

"Or the Americans," said the minister of foreign affairs. "Surely they are searching for their own aircraft."

"The submarine commanders have detected several anomalies, but nothing they could conclusively identify as a foreign vessel. We could move anti-submarine-warfare resources from the Arabian Gulf, but—"

"No," interjected the king with a wave of his hand. "Do not move a single asset from the Gulf. This is precisely the type of opportunity Iran would seek to exploit."

"They are already blaming us for the attack," said the minister of Hajj and Umrah. "They claim it is further proof that we are unfit to provide pilgrims with their most basic need for safety."

"Of course they are," said the king. His official title was "Custodian of the Two Holy Mosques," and none more than he felt the sting of failing to protect Allah's children. It made his ministers' sniping and backbiting that much more infuriating.

The minister of the interior spoke up. "There was surprisingly little physical damage to the mosque. The Americans—excuse me, Your Majesty, the *attackers*—used a special type of weapon that kills people with air pressure, not fragmentation. The marble and concrete construction of the mosque is intact. The Kiswah was covered in blood and blown into the crowd, but the Kaaba is undamaged. I do not mean to be insensitive, but the time and expense of repairs will be minimal."

"It is not crass of you to say so," said the king. "There are a few more hours left in our time of mourning, but we must still govern. To that end, the recent spike in petroleum prices is alleviating some of the pressure on revenues we have been feeling over the past few years."

"We are diversifying away from oil at exactly the wrong time," said the minister of energy.

"I seem to recall you made the same argument in 2007," said the minister of the interior. "We are not trying to time the market. Now is when we should reaffirm our commitment to the National Transformation Program, when political instability around the world is high and oil revenues are strong."

"Without the American nuclear umbrella, we are going to need that money to develop one of our own," said the crown prince.

"Enough!" said the king, rising from his desk. The paratroopers from the Royal Guard Regiment snapped to attention. "We cannot continue to assume that the United States did this without proof."

"Your Majesty," offered Prince Faisal, "solely for the purpose of discussion, perhaps we should examine an appropriate course of action if we do find proof of American involvement."

The king saw the olive branch for what it was, a dignified way to step back and regain consensus with the council. Besides, Faisal was on his side. The king took his seat and nodded to the prince.

"Of course, Faisal. We must plan for all contingencies."

The group discussed potential American motives for the attack and defense plans against any further aggression. They addressed diplomatic developments, the military coalition's progress in Yemen, and civil unrest in the mostly Shiite eastern provinces. The conversation eventually returned to the nation's external defense.

"Your Majesty," began the crown prince, "in this spirit of hypothetical discussion, it might be prudent to once again examine our decision to not develop nuclear weapons of our own. Perhaps we should reconsider the reactor deal the Russians offered us."

"We would still be a decade from having a weapon of our own," said the minister of energy.

"Ten years with a nuclear-armed Iran across the Gulf?" said the king. "The kingdom would not survive it."

"His Majesty is correct, of course," said Faisal. "If we're not going to work with Russia to develop our own nuclear capability, then perhaps it is time to invoke our treaty with Pakistan."

"That is a dangerous liaison," cautioned Prince Sahib, the minister of foreign affairs. "Can we trust the Pakistanis to honor it? I fret that if this attack escalates into war with America, Pakistan will find a way to extricate itself from its obligations."

"What about China?" asked another minister. "We have purchased arms from them in the past. Might we be able to turn our commercial relationship into something more?"

"Prince Faisal," said Sahib, "you negotiated our purchase of the DF-21 missiles. Your contact there is quite senior now, is he not?"

"He is," acknowledged Faisal.

"Perhaps you should reach out to him," said Sahib. "Nothing official, of course, but maybe broach the subject of a deeper alliance to see if there is desire on the Chinese side."

Heads around the room nodded in agreement.

Thick veins were visible on the king's forehead. Sahib, his longtime lieutenant and the head of the Allegiance Council, had backed him into a corner. Attempting to reassert his authority, but unwilling to further alienate the entire cabinet, the king looked at Faisal and said the only thing he could.

"Make it so."

# THIRTY-FIVE

H E HEARD A crow's wings flapping a hundred feet overhead. In other circumstances it would have been a magnificent experience, a demonstration of the all-encompassing silence of the desert, but the best Jake could do was shield his face from the sun, push through the pain, and keep pressing forward into the unknown. Occasionally he caught a glimpse of what he thought was Al-Wadiah, but was more likely a mirage.

He stumbled along for hours, struggling to put one foot in front of the other, until he noticed an escarpment rising up from the desert floor. He'd seen it earlier, in the general direction of Al-Wadiah, before the rising waves of heat had clouded his view. It was off to the right now, maybe a mile distant.

Jake drew on some unknown well of energy and pushed forward, never taking his eyes off the escarpment lest it vanish into another mirage. He staggered forward for another hour before falling to his knees in gratitude.

He saw Al-Wadiah.

It was no more than a small village with a dozen pedestrians, twenty or thirty single-story buildings, and a paved road along its eastern edge.

Jake rose to his feet and started moving. It was time to play car thief again. There weren't many choices. A blue sedan was closest, but its ability to complete the drive to Riyadh was questionable. A white van was in reasonable condition, but it looked like a commercial vehicle whose absence would soon be noted. A dust-covered silver hatchback seemed to be the best option. Small, unremarkable, and in fair condition, it was maybe ten or fifteen years old.

Jake started it quickly and pulled to the intersection, but he skidded to a stop as he was about to turn onto the paved road to Riyadh. An army truck passed by, headed south toward Yemen. Jake glanced to his left. There were more trucks behind it. A lot more.

For as far as he could see, a Saudi military convoy filled the road.

Armored personnel carriers, towed artillery, tanks, troop transports, and dozens of support vehicles were making their way south to join the coalition forces. Jake was forced to wait.

He drummed his fingers against the wheel as he glanced in his rearview mirror. The townspeople of Al-Wadiah were coming out to watch the spectacle, and Jake was sitting in a stolen car between them and a thousand heavily armed Saudi troops.

## THIRTY-SIX

THE OTHER TWO black Expeditions had continued south on the 710 freeway to the twin oil refineries in Carson, California. They were imposing sights—massive towers connected by miles of pipe and lit by spotlights and flashing red anticollision lights.

Security at the main entrance was tight, with thick retractable bollards blocking the gate, but like water flowing down a mountainside, the terrorists followed the path of least resistance. In this case, one that was scouted weeks earlier by an advance team. The SUVs turned into a neighboring parking lot and accelerated hard, their V8 engines straining as they smashed through a chain-link fence and into the complex. The first truck sped past the refinery, but the second SUV screeched to a halt. Abdel and Aataz, two hardened guerrillas from Hezbollah's Revolutionary Justice Organization, jumped out with Kalashnikov automatic rifles.

Two others leapt from the rear of the SUV with rocket-propelled grenade launchers. They quickly destroyed several key structures, with only superficial injuries to themselves. The men were preparing to drive to another target when a pickup truck stopped two hundred feet behind them.

The four men in the pickup were members of the plant's security team, and each had seen combat in Iraq or Afghanistan before working at the refinery. They instantly recognized the backblast from the rocket-propelled grenades.

The guards leapt from their vehicle and fanned out behind cover, unseen by the terrorists. Plant policy dictated that they were not to engage unless fired upon, but Jaquon Jackson had been a U.S. marine in western Mosul. The RPGs and hundred-foot-high flames told him that this was no robbery. These folks had come to play.

*I'd rather be tried by twelve than carried by six,* he thought.

Jackson opened fire with his 5.56mm rifle. The other guards followed suit and the two RPG gunners went down with fatal wounds. Jackson crawled behind the engine block of the pickup truck and inserted a fresh magazine into the AR-15. He took two deep breaths and rolled onto his stomach, firing a dozen quick rounds from under the pickup. The high-velocity bullets shattered glass and punctured metal as they tore through the terrorists' SUV. The driver and front seat passenger died in their seats, but Jackson was forced to roll back behind the engine block as incoming fire kicked up the gravel around him.

Abdel and Aataz, combat veterans themselves, ran behind their SUV and returned fire. The exchange soon took on a resonance familiar to both groups. The sharp crack of the American rifles on one side, and the throaty staccato of the fully automatic AK-47s on the other.

Jackson's teammates leapfrogged along an eighty-foot-long building, providing covering fire for one another as they moved, until they'd flanked Abdel and Aataz. One of the guards stepped out from behind the building and drew a bead on Aataz, but not before Abdel spotted him. The terrorist put a round in the guard's forehead and the man collapsed like a rag doll.

The other two guards came around the building, one high and one low, and unleashed a hailstorm of fire, driving Abdel and Aataz backward . . . and straight into Jackson's sights. The marine had put the terrorists in a classic L-shaped ambush, and it was time to execute.

Literally.

Jackson fired a total of eleven rounds at the two terrorists and Abdel and Aataz were dead before they hit the ground.

Jackson sounded the all clear as he rose from behind the pickup. One of the guards radioed the plant fire department that it was safe to enter and that they had one "friendly KIA." He didn't know how else to say it. The three survivors knelt down beside their dead teammate, when a brilliant flash in the distance caught Jackson's eye.

It wasn't lightning.

Half a second later he heard an explosion and saw flames lick the sky. Only then did he realize that there was a second group of terrorists at the other complex. The three guards jumped into the pickup, but the second refinery was already ablaze by the time they arrived. Geysers of burning liquids spewed into the air, setting fire to everything nearby. Thousand-degree heat and twisted steel blocked the guards' path, forcing them to take a circuitous route outside the plant to reach the terrorists.

But an L.A. County sheriff's deputy had no such problem.

The police car stormed through the facility's northern entrance with its lights and siren blazing, but nothing in Christie Alexander's decade-long career as a deputy had prepared her for what she saw: enormous clouds of thick black smoke, towers of flame reaching hundreds of feet into the sky, and thick steel torn apart like tinfoil.

It looked like the Apocalypse.

She killed the lights and siren and unlocked the Colt patrol rifle mounted between the front seats.

Deputy Alexander drove through the adjacent tank farm, searching for the cause of the destruction. When she spotted the terrorists' SUV silhouetted against a wall of flames, she grabbed the rifle and advanced on foot.

She braced herself against the side of an enormous fuel tank and opened fire. The report from her rifle was lost amid the roar of the flames, and the RPG shooters fell before they realized they were under counterattack. The remaining two terrorists saw their teammates go down and, with their night vision ruined by the fire, started spraying bullets with their AK-47s.

But the deputy had chosen her spot well. She saw the

muzzle flashes and rolled up a third terrorist with a shot that shattered his pelvis.

The last of the Hezbollah fighters picked up an RPG and aimed at a storage tank, but Deputy Alexander spotted him and put two rounds in his chest. His last act among the living was to pull the trigger as he fell to the ground. The antiarmor grenade leapt from the launch tube at almost one thousand feet per second. A trail of smoke, tinted orange by the flames around it, followed the warhead through the air.

HOURS EARLIER, THE hot summer day had caused much of the fuel inside the nearly empty tank to evaporate. Some of the vapor had settled back into liquid as the tank cooled after sunset, but what remained aloft were billions of droplets of jet fuel surrounded by air. It was the perfect explosive.

The RPG's warhead detonated inside the vapor cloud, triggering a blast more powerful than the entire conventional payload of a B-52 bomber. In a fraction of a second, the tank itself ceased to exist. A massive shock wave radiated outward, sending the terrorists' SUV flipping backward over the earth like a tumbleweed. A mushroom cloud of thick, caustic smoke billowed into the air.

The explosion knocked Deputy Alexander unconscious, but the storage tank she'd been using for support protected her from the lethal overpressure wave. Yet she was far from safe. Burning fuel from the explosion had splashed on the tank's exterior skin and caused the temperature of the ten million gallons of high-octane gasoline inside it to climb rapidly.

Jackson and the other guards reentered the plant in their pickup truck, bouncing over the ground as they raced toward the clouds of smoke rising into the sky. The truck's thermometer was pegged at 130 degrees and Jackson was about to turn back when one of the others spotted the empty sheriff's car. Jackson edged closer until they found Deputy Alexander lying on the ground. Two of the guards leapt out, shielding their faces from the heat as they ran to the fallen officer. Coughing uncontrollably from the toxic fumes, they carried her back to the truck and drove for the exit.

They were half a mile away when the gasoline tank exploded. The shock wave sent the back of the six-thousand-pound pickup briefly into the air before slamming back onto the road. Jackson gunned it back to the northern gate, where a dozen fire engines and three ambulances from the L.A. County Fire Department were already waiting. Paramedics administered oxygen and cold packs to the fallen deputy while the three guards sat on the liftgate of their pickup and watched the world burn.

They thought they'd left this shit behind them in the sandbox.

## THIRTY-SEVEN

JAKE SAT IDLING in the silver hatchback, his path to the main road blocked by the military convoy heading south into Yemen. The town of Al-Wadiah was small, seven blocks from end to end, a place where everyone undoubtedly knew everyone else. There had to be close to a hundred townsfolk making their way to the roadside, but Jake refused to make eye contact with any of them. There weren't many cars in Al-Wadiah, and the silver hatchback was the only one of its kind.

He glanced in the rearview mirror. There was a man standing on a small hill with a commanding view of the town and the convoy. Jake recognized him from somewhere, but it was not al-Quereshi or one of his thugs. More people crowded around the car, possibly even the owner, but Jake couldn't take his eyes off of the rearview mirror. He knew the face. He recognized the man's confident, relaxed posture. The subject was alert, but not obviously so.

It was the Iranian who'd been meeting with Mullah Muktar in Zinjibar.

It was Saturn.

Jake's hand reflexively went to his pistol, but he put both hands back on the wheel. He didn't want to start a gunfight with a thousand soldiers driving by. There was simply no way to apprehend the Iranian without it costing Jake his life.

When a short gap opened up between two military trucks, he gunned the engine, chirping the tires and speeding across the intersection into the northbound lane. He earned ugly stares from the soldiers in the trucks, but he was on his way to Riyadh.

The road wound its way through the Arabian desert for hours. Huge, windblown sand dunes extended to the horizon in every direction, reflecting the blistering heat back into the air. The little hatchback had neither a thermometer nor air-conditioning, but Jake didn't care; he was focused only on getting ahead of Turani and uncovering who was responsible for the attack on Mecca.

It certainly wasn't the al-Qaeda fighters who'd ambushed him in Zinjibar. Their amateurish interrogation had revealed more than it had obtained. Like most terrorist recruits, they'd probably been impressionable young men who'd fallen for the false promises of the mullahs, the hypocrites who promised eternal peace through the commission of earthly murder. They'd been nothing more than poorly trained thugs . . . but the bastards had killed Roach.

Jake shook his head. He had been in a similar predicament the year before, taken prisoner in Iran and tortured nearly to death. He'd escaped, but his freedom had come at a heavy cost. He'd been forced to assume a new identity and leave behind everything that was important to him: family, friends, girlfriend. After being Zac Miller for twenty-eight years, he still didn't think of himself as Jake Keller. It had been grueling and painful, but at least he was alive.

Curt had been divorced, with no children, but that didn't make it any easier. The man who was to mentor Jake, the man who had promised to watch his back, the man who had become his friend, had died violently not six feet in front of him. Jake's only solace came from the fact that he'd exacted revenge upon two of the thugs swiftly and completely.

But violence had always been a last resort for Jake. Having lost his parents at a young age, he knew that the knock-on effects of violence could be complex and unpredictable, and when it came to the science of it, most people responded better to encouragement and direction rather than abuse and intimidation. But the soft stuff didn't work on those driven by malice and evil.

Jake did not enjoy killing, but there were some people that simply needed to die.

*Like al-Quereshi and everyone he'd ever met . . .*

As Jake contemplated what he might find in Riyadh, he concluded that "Saturn," whom CIA was tracking, "the Iranian," whom Mahmoud had mentioned, and "Turani," whom al-Quereshi had been concerned about, were all the same person. It meant that Colonel Turani was the one who'd provided the millions of dollars to al-Qaeda for some unknown service. And it must have been something substantial, for the AQAP franchise did not need a great deal of money to run its operations.


NIGHT HAD FALLEN by the time Jake reached Riyadh. He drove by the safe house where Roach's two colleagues from CIA's Directorate of Operations lived. It was a small, freestanding building with a roll-up garage door for a gate and a ten-foot-high cinder-block wall around it. Jake parked two blocks away and approached on foot. There was an intercom and a camera at the gate.

He rang the bell and a voice answered in rapid-fire Arabic. Jake looked at the camera and repeated the Arabic code phrase Roach had told him back in Zinjibar.

The gate opened. To the left was a carport. The front door was to the right. A Saudi man opened the door and greeted him in Arabic. Jake repeated Roach's code phrase.

The man smiled and gestured inside. "Please, come in," he said in Arabic.

Jake stepped inside and closed the door. A second man grabbed him from behind and threw him face-down on the floor. The man who'd answered the door had a suppressed pistol pointed at Jake's head.

"Who the fuck are you?" he said.

# THIRTY-EIGHT

CARLOS AND MIGUEL worked in *El Nuevo Constante*'s engine room for several hours before heading back to the bridge. Night had fallen while they'd been below. The gentle wind had been replaced by a gusty breeze and the flat seas had grown into large swells.

The captain was at the wheel, listening to the radio and staring at the radar, when the younger men returned.

"Is the water pump fixed?"

Miguel shook his head. "The heat exchanger is corroded. We're lucky we stopped when we did. The engine would have seized up if we'd used it any longer."

"Can it be fixed?"

"We'll need to fabricate two new tubes."

"When we get home, I'm going to take the money from this voyage and replace that damn engine once and for all."

"We have the materials on board, Papa. It will just take time."

"How much?" asked the captain.

"Five or six hours, maybe a little longer."

"That's too long. The storm has picked up speed. Can Carlos finish the deck plate while you fix the engine? The last thing we need is for that plate to come loose during a heavy storm."

"We need the welding torch to make the tubes," Miguel said. "We could do the plate first—"

"Fix the engine," said the captain, "but don't waste a single second."

THE TWO YOUNG men worked furiously inside the engine room. The captain stayed topside, knowing that looking over their shoulders would be counterproductive. He policed the ship, checking hatches and fittings, stowing loose gear, and adding another set of heavy chains to secure the container.

Carlos had done a good job welding the corners of the new deck plate, but it was only temporary. The seams needed to be finished for it to hold any weight.

The two young men returned to the bridge four hours later, breathless and soaked with sweat. A streak of blood had dried on the side of Carlos's head.

"What happened to you?" asked the captain.

"It's nothing," said Carlos.

"We got knocked around pretty hard down there, Papa. These must be ten-foot seas."

"And we're taking them on the beam while we're dead in the water," said the captain. "How is the engine coming along?"

Miguel pointed to the starter switch.

The old diesel had flooded in the rough seas, but it turned over on the fourth try. The captain put it in gear and felt the prop catch. He advanced the throttle smoothly, regaining steerage and then speed. A few drops of rain splattered on the windshield.

"Now finish that deck plate. We're not going to outrun this storm."

# THIRTY-NINE

THOUGH THE WORD "riyadh" meant "garden" in Arabic, it was not the shade of the juniper trees or the mist from the many fountains that drew Colonel Turani to the extravagantly landscaped park inside the capital city's Diplomatic Quarter. While the scenery was a welcome change from the rest of the desert city, the Qods Force officer was interested only in privacy. He removed his secure mobile phone and dialed Major General Shirizani.

"What is the mood there?" asked the general.

"Volatile. The people are impatient with the king's indecision. They view the terror attacks inside the United States as legitimate retribution for the bombing of Mecca, but they see it only as a start. They want Saudi Arabia to cut all ties with America and apportion blame where it is due."

"The Saudi Arabian National Guard is still taking a hands-off approach with the protesters?"

"I do not understand it. The National Guard troops

look like dogs straining against their leashes. You can see in their eyes that their training and their instinct is telling them to attack, but their masters are holding them back. There are hundreds of demonstrators outside the American embassy, burning American flags and an effigy of President Day, yet a week ago the National Guard would have arrested someone for loitering for more than a few seconds."

"What is the government's strategy?"

"I can only assume they prefer the protesters to be focused on an external enemy rather than the difficulties at home. I saw it in Al-Qatif as well. Since the 2016 crash in oil prices, the reduced government stipend and increased unemployment have left a large, angry population of young males. Idle hands are the devil's workshop."

"Are the authorities showing the same tolerance in Al-Qatif?"

"The situation in the east is more nuanced. The operational tempo of the Mabahith and General Intelligence has increased, but the National Guard is holding back. I saw someone throw a Molotov cocktail onto one of their armored vehicles and they did nothing."

"Are the protests organized?"

"Not in a meaningful way," said Turani. "The only common elements are frustration and anger. I have instructed our operatives to also focus their ire on the United States, but we will shift our attention to the regime once the unrest achieves critical mass. A few well-placed provocateurs could turn the demonstrations into full-blown riots. If the protesters get ahold of weapons, the government will be forced to act."

"Then we'll make sure they get those weapons soon. The fires of hell will burn inside Saudi Arabia once the National Guard starts shooting civilians."

# *FORTY*

I T WASN'T UNUSUAL for a vehicle to spend a night in the parking lot of the big-box store. There were several restaurants and bars in the neighborhood and their customers often used the lot when space was tight, but the store's policy was clearly posted. *No overnight parking.* Whether it was a few too many drinks, a spontaneous romance, or often a combination of the two, the store's security guard tried to give people a break, letting the cars sit as long as he could. But his boss would get to work in an hour, and if the old pickup truck was still sitting out front, it was the guard who was going to have a bad day and not the pickup's owner.

The tow truck driver reported the pickup's license plate number to the San Antonio police before he hooked up the tow bar. It was standard procedure so that when the owner returned to find his vehicle missing, the police wouldn't waste resources searching for a stolen car that wasn't, and they'd be able to give the owner the modestly better news that his vehicle had only been towed.

But the entry of the pickup's plate number triggered

a law enforcement flag. That in itself wasn't a big deal. Maybe 10 percent of his tows had expired registrations, lapsed insurance, or some other issue, but this was a federal hit. He'd never tripped one of those before, and he had no idea that it had been placed by the Customs and Border Protection officer in Los Indios who had searched the truck the day before.

The CBP officer's white and green Chevy Tahoe averaged ninety miles per hour on its way to San Antonio. He thought through all sorts of possibilities as he drove, from a simple breakdown to something much more nefarious. He called ahead to the big-box store and had them pull the parking lot surveillance tapes from the prior day. By the time he arrived, the security guard had located the two men arriving in the pickup at 11:57 a.m., but he had been unable to find them leaving. It was only when the CBP officer reviewed the tape that he realized that the two men had ditched their cowboy hats and left in a light-colored compact SUV at 12:14 p.m. Unfortunately, the low-resolution black-and-white video was unable to capture the SUV's color or plate number.

The officer did some quick math in his head. The men in the pickup could have driven from the border to San Antonio in four hours, then easily made it to Dallas in time for rush hour. It was a long shot, he told himself, laughing mirthlessly at the unintentional pun, but his gut told him that he might have just identified the men responsible for yesterday's highway shooting in Dallas.

The initial conclusion from the first responders at the

scene had been that they were looking at a high-speed pileup. Multivehicle crashes were common enough on the big expressways, where people tended to drive too fast and follow too close. It was only when a veteran crash scene investigator had examined the shattered glass and smashed sheet metal that the first bullet hole was located. She then scrutinized the entire debris field until the other windshields yielded the same telltale marks of a skilled rifleman. Postmortem analysis of the victims showed conclusively that trauma incurred during the wrecks were not the causes of death.

The CBP officer pulled the names and photos of the men in the pickup from their entry records and called the Dallas Police Department.

# FORTY-ONE

WORK THE YEMEN account with Curt Roach," Jake said in English.

"Get up," said the man with the gun. "Slowly."

Jake rose from the floor. The second man frisked him and confiscated the pistol and the knife.

"Where's Curt?" asked the first man. He was just out of arm's range, with the gun trained on Jake's chest. The second man was positioned off to the side, where he wouldn't catch a bullet if his partner fired.

"Curt's dead. We were in Zinjibar running drone ops."

The second man inspected the knife. "Is this dried blood?"

The two operatives from Riyadh shared a look. Jake explained the events leading up to his arrival.

"The Saudi Navy is looking for your drone right now in the Red Sea," said the first man. "How do we know it wasn't you that fed the coordinates for Mecca to the UCAV?"

"And then killed Curt and pinned it on him?" asked the second.

Jake reviewed it all a second time, then added, "I

only knew to make contact with you because Roach told me. We decided to come here after Ted Graves implied that we intentionally attacked Mecca."

"Graves . . ." said the first man.

"Fucking Graves," added the second.

The first man motioned toward the sitting area. Everyone sat down.

"You can call me Fadi. He's Youssef," said the first man. He kept the gun in his hand.

"Curt and I were in the same training class at the Farm," Fadi said, "and we ran a few operations together after graduation. Not in a million years would I believe that he intentionally targeted Mecca. I'd lay my life down for that guy, although I suppose that's an idle boast now."

Jake shook his head. Roach's death was still raw.

"But I don't know you," Fadi said, "and I know almost everyone in Ground Branch."

"I'm new," Jake said.

"I said I don't know you, but I've heard of you," Fadi said.

Youssef tapped his finger on the coffee table. "Graves put out a cable this morning to notify Special Activities if you're located."

"He made it sound as if you might have PTSD," Fadi said, "like you needed to see the wizard."

"It was just like you told us," added Youssef, "except without all the facts."

"Graves can be very selective with facts," Jake said, "especially when they conflict with any questionable activities he might be running."

Though the Special Activities Center was structured to support the other CIA mission centers, it had considerable leeway in how it operated. Graves was renowned for circumventing the branch chiefs underneath him and directing the men in the field himself. He was effective, but dangerous.

"What do you want from us?" Fadi said.

Jake told them more details about the interrogation where Roach had been killed, about "the package," "the deal," and about al-Quereshi.

"And Iran is involved," Jake said. "At first Roach and I thought the drone hijacking might have been an al-Qaeda setup, with them dangling Muktar in front of us, knowing we'd launch a UCAV that they could then hijack, but we had two ships orbiting and the second one got Muktar."

"Maybe they miscalculated," Youssef said.

"It wasn't AQAP, but the Iranian is a player. I've shifted my focus to him."

"Who is he?" Fadi said.

"He's known as 'Colonel Turani.' I don't know if it's his real name or a cover, but he's most likely Qods Force. I also spotted him on my way here, conducting reconnaissance in Al-Wadiah."

"Seems thin," said Youssef.

Fadi stood. "We can't help you," he said. "It's a trust issue. I knew Curt for years."

"I have nothing," Jake said. "No money, no documents, no place to stay. I'll start jacking people on the street if I have to, but that could put the Agency in a tough spot."

Youssef looked at Fadi. "The Al-Suwaidi apartment has another month on the lease."

Fadi nodded and in ten minutes they'd provided Jake with a hundred dollars' worth of Saudi riyals and the keys to a safe house in the neighboring Al-Suwaidi district.

"This is clean," Fadi said as he gave Jake a prepaid mobile phone, "but assume the Saudis are listening."

Youssef produced the knife and the gun he'd taken off Jake when he first arrived. Youssef dropped the magazine, ejected the round from the chamber, and put it all in a large manila envelope with the knife and sealed it. He handed it to Jake as he stepped through the door.

"Don't open that until you're outside the gate," Fadi said. The suppressed pistol was still in his hand. "And don't you dare cross us. If I find out you're even remotely responsible for Curt's death, I'll hunt you down and kill you myself."

# FORTY-TWO

MIST FROM AN early morning sun shower rose from the pavement as General Wǔ-Dīng walked along the garden path. The secure government complex at Zhongnanhai allowed his aides and protection detail to follow at a relaxed distance while the general spoke on his mobile phone.

"I am glad to hear you are well, little tiger. General Fang can be demanding, but he is brilliant and an imaginative tactician. As my son, you will have to work twice as hard as your fellow officers to earn his respect, but you will learn much under his command. Tell me, when is your next leave?"

The general listened as he continued along the path.

"Excellent. Come visit us. I have been shuttling between North Africa and Shanghai a great deal lately and your mother will throw me out of my own airplane if I don't spend a few weeks in Beijing soon. I must say good-bye now. I have a Standing Committee meeting to attend."

The general smiled as he listened to the phone.

"The president I can manage; it's your mother who

gives me grief," he said. "Work hard, my son. This can be the Chinese millennium if we make it so."


PRESIDENT CHÉNG MINSHENG and Premier Mèng-Fù Ru took their seats across from the general. The meeting addressed several domestic matters before turning to foreign affairs. Wǔ-Dīng steered the agenda to the U.S. attack on Saudi Arabia, but it was the president who spoke first.

"Two days ago, I convened a meeting of the Central Military Commission to review the ramifications of the American aggression in Mecca. The CMC decided—"

"*You* decided," said General Wǔ-Dīng. Though the Standing Committee spoke publicly with one voice, internal debates were often heated. Personal attacks were not uncommon.

"I am chairman of the CMC . . . and you were in Shanghai," said the president. "In this case, the political ramifications of further aggravating the Americans, and the negligible threat posed to our own interests, did not warrant changing our posture."

"I would like to remind the committee that the United States has just attacked a strategic ally and a critical supplier of natural resources," said Wǔ-Dīng. "America has become unpredictable and China cannot plan for the future by looking at the past. A two-and-a-half-million-man army does not respond immediately. Training cycles need to be altered, maintenance performed, weapons inspected, watches changed. These are not provocative measures, but if the United States does have hostile intent toward China, it will see that we are alert and prepared, and it will think twice. Advancing our threat condition will not bring us closer to war, but ensure peace."

A few heads nodded around the table.

"There is an expression I learned in America," said the president. " 'We do not have a dog in this fight.' It is predictably crude, but the meaning is simple and relevant. China has no direct stake in the outcome of a U.S. conflict with Saudi Arabia and we should not be seen as an instigator. Our intelligence services believe that the Americans are already very tense following the terror attacks and suspicious of Russian assistance to the Saudi government. Let the Americans and the Russians settle their differences to the benefit of China. Our threat condition shall remain unchanged."

General Wǔ-Dīng was about to protest, when Mèng-Fù preempted him. "And so the president has decided. We will revisit this topic as events dictate." Mèng-Fù looked to the president and the general. The president nodded his assent, but the general was not swayed so easily.

"Perhaps we should have a dog in this fight," he said as he looked around the table. "As the president has correctly pointed out, America is highly suspicious of Russia. Perhaps Russia is only looking to embarrass the U.S. by helping the Saudis find the American aircraft that crashed in the Red Sea, but what if it goes deeper than that? Those two may soon be at each other's throats."

The president started to interrupt, but the general talked over him.

"I am not advocating changing our military posture," said Wǔ-Dīng. "That is indeed your decision to make, but opportunities multiply as they are seized. What does our growing economy desperately need?"

Mèng-Fù nodded. "Natural resources," he said.

"Exactly," said Wǔ-Dīng. "Our demand for oil grew fifteen percent last year and we are putting more vehicles on the road, planes in the sky, and ships to sea every day. We are a hostage to U.S. dollar–based markets and suddenly the world's second-largest reserve of oil is in play."

"Over 270 billion barrels," noted the head of the party secretariat.

"We should be reaching out to the Saudis at this very moment, developing long-term contracts to realign them away from the United States," said the general.

"That will antagonize the Americans for certain," said the president.

"Then it must be handled tactfully," said Wǔ-Dīng.

"Don't you have a high-ranking contact there?" asked the vice premier.

"Prince Faisal runs their National Guard. He and I negotiated the construction and arming of their missile bases," said the general.

"And he is next in line for the throne, is he not?"

"He is *deputy* crown prince, so technically he is second in line."

"You should reach out to this man," said the chairman of the National People's Congress.

"Perhaps you should meet in person," said the vice

premier, "to get a more candid view of what is going on inside the kingdom."

"Yes. This is the proper course of action," said another.

The president seethed. He had significant reservations about the plan, but he was the only one. As the rest of the committee looked to him, all he could do was nod his assent.

## FORTY-THREE

J AKE TORE OPEN the manila envelope with his gun and knife and drove to the Diplomatic Quarter, whose gated entry and high fences housed all of the foreign embassies, including the American one. Youssef had told him that the National Guardsmen were there to keep the locals out, not foreigners, and suggested that Jake head over in the morning and pretend to be a French citizen, since he spoke the language.

But Jake couldn't wait until morning. Though it was two a.m., and he hadn't slept for more than an hour since Drifter-72 had hit Mecca, he needed to do reconnaissance for the next day, when his gut told him Turani's meeting would take place.

Two light-armored vehicles were parked on either side of the Diplomatic Quarter's guard shack, with several troops standing around steel vehicle barriers that had been lowered to the ground. Jake slowed the hatchback and a white taxi pulled in behind him.

A National Guard soldier carrying an M-16 rifle motioned for Jake to pull forward.

Jake hesitated, wondering if he'd made a mistake. He

was unshowered and unshaven, driving an old car without diplomatic license plates. For the past month he'd been living in Zinjibar, acquiring the look, the feel, and the smell of a Yemeni. He was everything the guards should be alert to, especially in the middle of the night.

The guard became more emphatic in his gestures, and Jake pulled forward. The guard waved him through the gate and into the Diplomatic Quarter. The lax security was a lucky break for Jake, but an inexplicable lapse for a country that had just been attacked.

Jake wound his way past landscaped traffic circles and spouting fountains until he reached a large square in front of the U.S. embassy. Under the streetlights were a few cars and maybe a hundred protesters. Jake parked on the periphery and continued on foot.

The white taxi that had been behind him stopped at the edge of the square and dropped off three young men. They were carrying hastily made signs and thanked the driver as he pulled away. Most of the other protesters had the same look: young, relatively affluent, partially pissed off, and partially having a good time. Collegiate rebels.

There were two police cars in front of the embassy, but no officers. Combined with the Diplomatic Quarter's porous front gate, it was shockingly lax security—at least on the outside. That was the host government's responsibility. Jake was confident that the Diplomatic Security officers and the U.S. marines inside the compound were on high alert.

And what a compound it was. Built after repeated attacks on Americans in Saudi Arabia, the building was a fortress. It had twenty-foot-high walls, a vehicle trap inside the front gate, and thick, bulletproof glass set far back from the perimeter walls.

The heat of summer and the late hour kept the crowd subdued. Half a dozen young men were smiling in front of the embassy gate, taking pictures of themselves to post on social media. A hundred feet away, someone burned a U.S. flag. It felt more like a carnival than a call to arms.

*That will change if the Saudis find Drifter-72,* Jake thought.

He stayed out of the streetlights as he approached the embassy. He was the only person there alone and he garnered a few stares as he scoured the crowd for Colonel Turani, for the face he'd first seen right before the whole world had changed.

Jake stopped in front of the embassy gate and pretended to adjust his sandals. He noticed two men stop fifty feet behind him. They were wearing short white thobes over baggy white pants that stopped above the ankles. It was a distinctly conservative style of Muslim dress and one that had been adopted by many radicals. Their behavior and their clothing didn't necessarily mean that they were al-Qaeda thugs, but if al-Quereshi had survived their encounter along the highway, he'd undoubtedly alerted his network that Jake was headed for Riyadh.

Jake kept walking, getting a feel for the area and scouting out likely meeting places. It didn't matter if you were an American or an Iranian intelligence operative, good spots for secret meetings looked the same.

He passed by a row of elegant townhouses on one side of the square. A few lights were on, but most of the residents seemed to be asleep or otherwise disinterested in the proceedings outside their front doors.

Jake bent down and adjusted his sandal again. The two men were still behind him, still watching. He turned toward the center of the square, where most of the people were, and picked up the pace. He glanced back as he walked through the crowd. The men were following, maybe a hundred feet back now.

Jake walked to the edge of the square, where he was away from the crowd and out of the streetlights, and ran like hell.

## FORTY-FOUR

GENERAL WǓ-DĪNG WALKED back to his office through the gardens at Zhongnanhai. Though he had found his calling in the army, his roots were in the land. Born into a family of farmers, he found the outdoors to be the ideal place to think.

The plan he'd formulated nearly a year earlier, after a meeting with his old acquaintance Prince Faisal, was nearly complete. They had first met as part of a high-level diplomatic meeting group in Beijing. Both were fluent in English, and Wǔ-Dīng spoke a little Arabic, so they had dispensed with the translators and aides to speak candidly about the state of the world. Throughout their many discussions, the recurring obstacle to the achievement of each man's long-term goals was the same: the United States of America.

Faisal felt that the Saudi king was too beholden to the Americans for national defense. He worried that, since the United States no longer needed Saudi oil to run its economy, an attack on the kingdom by Iran would be perceived by the West as just another war among the Muslim nations. With no domestic support for another Middle Eastern entanglement, the American president would not use the military force necessary to honor its treaty to defend Saudi Arabia.

Wǔ-Dīng had listened carefully. China's evolution from an agrarian economy to one focused on manufacturing and services had brought its own problems. Hundreds of millions of peasants like himself, who once rode bicycles and worked the land, now drove cars and worked on assembly lines. The nation's demand for raw materials had exploded. It consumed massive quantities of iron, copper, plastics, and of course oil. The general had crisscrossed the globe looking to extend military cooperation pacts to dozens of nations in exchange for raw materials, but Africa, the continent that should have been its most natural partner and supplier, was too politically unstable. Governmental control ranged from weak to nonexistent in Nigeria, Angola, Sudan, and of course Libya, with greater oil reserves than the other three combined.

Because of its resources and its political malleability, Libya quickly became the focal point for Wǔ-Dīng. He developed a strong relationship with a military/political leader who had the potential to end the sectarian violence that had decimated the country. General Nafusa was a natural leader of men, based in the city of Tobruk in the lawless eastern region of Libya. With the right resources at his disposal, Nafusa could turn the country into a reliable supplier of oil to China.

While Prince Faisal held no enthusiasm for returning an additional oil producer to an already oversupplied market, he worried about the self-destruction of yet another Sunni Muslim country. The will of the people was fine in theory. In practice, it had devastated every Muslim nation that had experimented with it. Faisal had no desire to let the scourge reach Saudi Arabia. He needed General Nafusa to kill it where it was.

Wŭ-Dīng and Faisal traveled to Libya several times to discuss practical considerations such as equipment and training, timelines and alliances. These early talks soon led to more philosophical conversations when the two men were alone. Desires were aired, hypothetical scenarios put forth. It was obvious that a Sino-Saudi partnership would benefit both countries, but the two men always returned to the impenetrable obstacle of the existing U.S.-Saudi relationship.

It would not end of its own accord.

Prince Faisal perceived the Saudi king to be a vassal of the United States, and though the prince was already second in line to the throne, his ascension could be twenty years off, if ever. A change in leadership needed to happen soon, before the damage became irreversible. It was Faisal who had initially theorized a false-flag operation against his homeland, suggesting that they make it look as if the Americans had done it.

But it was more than a theory to Wŭ-Dīng, for he knew things the prince did not. There was a bureau of the People's Liberation Army, spun out from its Third Department, that had more computing power, and more capable and creative minds, than almost any other agency in the world. Because of the extreme sensitivity surrounding such operations, Wǔ-Dīng had put the covert operation directly under his command.

Unit 7474–505B of the PLA had been hacking into corporate and government systems of the United States for years. Among other things, it had stolen designs for aircraft and satellites, printed circuit boards, and financial services software. The unit had proved its worth many times over before the fateful day when its commander told General Wǔ-Dīng about its successful penetration of an unmanned U.S. aircraft. Wǔ-Dīng had commended the man in charge, encouraging him to develop the capability without being detected.

The operation to hijack an American drone had been launched soon after. Wǔ-Dīng and Faisal enlisted General Nafusa to provide a deniable base of operations. He was not told the details, but that was the price for accepting Chinese weapons and Saudi cash. Hidden in a desolate area of ancient Roman ruins, the site selected by the Libyan warlord was perfect. PLA technicians visited the area several times as generators were brought in, computers were hidden, and satellite dishes were emplaced.

Faisal had wanted to target the Hajj from the outset, but the general demurred, thinking that an attack on the Muslim holy city was a step too far. Faisal pressed, however. High unemployment and a soft economy were weakening the king's standing among the royal family. With a strike on the Masjid al-Haram during the pilgrimage, the king's loyalty to the United States would be his final undoing.

Three months ago, the commander of Unit 7474–505B notified General Wǔ-Dīng that they were ready. They could control any unmanned aerial system they chose.

One week ago, they dangled the intelligence about Muktar's meeting in Zinjibar in front of the American intelligence community.

## FORTY-FIVE

THE AUTHORITIES IN Dallas, Phoenix, and New York had each thought that the sniper attacks in their cities were local incidents. It was only when all three stories hit the national news that the scope of the attacks became clear. Extra police patrols were added in each of the three municipalities, but the terrorists had driven through the night to three different cities and ambushed more than a dozen commuters during the morning rush hour.

The FBI immediately took the lead in the investigation, naming the three teams after the cities where they'd first struck. Based on time and distance calculations, it appeared that the New York team had moved west to Chicago, the Phoenix shooters had gone northwest to San Francisco, and the Dallas crew had driven east to Atlanta. Assuming the teams would roughly maintain their initial directions of travel, the Bureau advised major metropolitan areas in their projected paths to go on alert.

The Dallas team was expected to hit Washington, D.C., Miami, or Indianapolis. Federal, state, and local authorities flooded the highways with extra patrols and aerial surveillance for the evening commute. The photographs and names from the men's passports went onto the national Known and Suspected Terrorist list and specialized hardware and software capable of locating the origin of gunshots was emplaced. Extra personnel were brought in to scrutinize traffic camera video in real time.

But they were looking in the wrong places.

After killing a delivery truck driver and the occupants of a luxury sedan in Atlanta, Ibrahim and Kahlil had reversed course. The Hezbollah snipers drove west on Interstate 20, passing through the scenic southern city of Birmingham, Alabama. They slept at a rural highway rest stop for a few hours, then doubled back again. With a population of just 220,000, Birmingham wasn't on anyone's radar for an attack.

The compact white SUV attracted little attention as it pulled to the side of the I-65 overpass. It had been a scorching hot day, the kind of day where the Alabama countryside felt like a steam room. The outside air engulfed Kahlil as he lowered the window and raised the gun.

His heart leapt.

*Praise be to Allah for His bountiful blessings.*

Though they were atop a three-level interchange, the shot was to the middle level. It would be almost flat, perhaps a twenty-degree down angle at most. As before, they had measured various distances as part of their advance work and he used a road sign to calculate the proper lead and pace the target.

He pulled the trigger.

A small white circle appeared where the bullet struck the windshield, but glare on the flat pane of glass prevented Kahlil from seeing the driver's reaction.

The school bus continued on.

Kahlil quickly worked the bolt and chambered another round. He took a snap shot and placed a second hole six inches from the first just before the bus disappeared under the bridge. There was nothing more he could do. Allah's divine will was beyond the comprehension of a man.

He chambered another round and placed it squarely in the chest of a tractor trailer driver. This time the Hezbollah sniper was rewarded with an immediate response as the big rig veered off the road at sixty miles per hour.

Ibrahim was already rolling. Now that the world was aware of their mission, they limited their time on the roadside to ten seconds. He'd hit the window switch and pulled away as soon as he'd heard the third shot.

The bridge shuddered as the compact white SUV merged back into traffic. The sounds of metal twisting and glass shattering echoed through the sweet southern air as the tractor trailer plowed into a concrete bridge support. The last noise they heard before the window closed was the sound of tires screeching as drivers attempted to avoid the trailer, which had overturned across all three lanes.

Kahlil looked to his right. The school bus was gone. It was inexplicable. He had shot through tempered safety glass many times with an identical rifle and ammunition during training in Mexico. Occasionally a shallow angle of impact would deflect the round, but today he had been nearly perpendicular to the flat windshield. He had even seen the entry holes. And while he would never doubt divine will, he could not understand why his shots had failed to have the desired effect. Not even the Americans could afford to put bulletproof glass on every school bus.

Perhaps it had been too much to hope for. Their premission planning had informed them that the American schools would not be in session and their only chance of spotting such a target would be from the much less common day camps or summer schools.

The overpass took the terrorists' SUV to the south as the road returned to ground level. Kahlil had already hidden the rifle underneath the blanket when he began to climb into the front seat.

"Look!" he shouted.

"What is it?" said Ibrahim, wary of taking his eyes off the road in the heavy traffic.

"It is the greatest of blessings."

Off to the right, the school bus was flipped over on its roof, its windows broken and its sides crushed. Its driver had died with his foot on the accelerator and the bus had continued on for a hundred yards, passing under the bridge before crashing into a guardrail. The bus's high rate of speed, its high angle of impact, and its high center of gravity had caused it to roll over the guardrail and plunge forty feet to the bottom level of the interchange.

\* \* \*

THE SNIPER ATTACKS and the destruction of the west coast refineries led to a massive increase in security across the United States. Federal, state, and local authorities ramped up surveillance and questioning of suspicious persons, looking for the next homegrown radical, sleeper cell, or anything else that might help them prevent further attacks. As part of the nation's post-9/11 preparedness planning, protocols for protecting lives and critical infrastructure were implemented around the nation.

But the authorities couldn't be everywhere.

On a remote country road, one hundred miles northeast of Atlanta, Georgia, an official-looking work crew wearing hard hats and fluorescent vests had spent an hour excavating a ditch. They used the hydraulic backhoe they'd rented to expose a twenty-foot section of stainless steel pipe.

The thirty-two-inch line carried refined petroleum products from Houston to New York. According to its owner's website, in addition to transporting vital supplies of diesel and jet fuel, it provided over 40 percent of the gasoline supply to the east coast of the United States.

Paraíso's men packed over a thousand pounds of homemade explosives against the pipeline before backing their truck away and firing the detonators. The three-quarter-inch-thick pipe imploded, causing an enormous cloud of gasoline vapor to form in the vacuum outside. It ignited a fraction of a second later and the ensuing explosion was far greater than anyone had expected. It flipped the terrorists' truck into the air like a tossed coin, killing everyone inside. The pipe spewed flaming gasoline from a sixteen-foot gash in its side.

Nearly a million gallons of fuel spilled from the damaged pipe before the system stopped pumping. A river of fire flowed into the neighboring woodlands. Visible with the naked eye from the International Space Station, it would soon become the largest forest fire to ever hit the eastern United States.

## FORTY-SIX

J AKE STOPPED RUNNING at the main boulevard
and dove for the ground as a military truck approached. The al-Qaeda men were behind him,
shouting as they ran through the palm grove next to
the embassy.

A car approached from the opposite direction. Jake
pulled his scarf up around his face and drew the pistol.
He stepped into the street and leveled the gun at the
driver's-side window. The Maserati coupe screeched to
a halt and Jake motioned for the two young men inside
to get out. They did so immediately, their gaze never
leaving the ground.

Jake drove past the guard shack and pulled onto the
main road. There were a few cars behind him, but none
that were following closely or acting aggressively.
Though he hadn't picked up a tail in the car, he'd definitely had one at the embassy.

The al-Qaeda thugs might have seen Jake arrive at
the square or they might have been watching Fadi and
Youssef's safe house, but it didn't matter now. Jake

should have run a surveillance-detection route. It was the kind of mistake that Roach never would have made.

Jake glanced in the rearview mirror. There were different cars behind him now, but that only meant he wasn't being tailed by amateurs. Other drivers stared at the Maserati as he passed. Though Riyadh was littered with flashy cars, a loud Italian coupe was no way to remain in the shadows.

He stopped at a twenty-four-hour convenience store where a few night-shift workers and blue-collar expats were loitering in the parking lot. It was a good place to make a cover stop and lose any tail he might have acquired. Jake parked the car on the street and left it running, hoping that someone might take it for a joyride and break the chain of Jake's movement.

He walked through the store to a side street and hailed a cab. The taxi dropped him several blocks from the safe house in Al-Suwaidi and he spent twenty minutes walking through the neighborhood, taking random turns and doubling back on his tracks until he was certain that he wasn't being followed. He would not make the same mistake again.

The safe house turned out to be a simple studio apartment on the ground floor. The building had a single entrance from the street and an alarmed emergency exit to a back alley, making it distressingly easy to watch. Except for two sleeping bags and a case of water in the refrigerator, it was completely empty. Its only virtues were its utterly common appearance and the fact that it had recently been swept for surveillance—although the television blaring through the thin walls from the apartment next door would have defeated all but the most sophisticated listening devices.

Jake walked to the air conditioner and switched it on.

Twenty minutes later, it was blowing hot air like a convection oven.

He pulled back the window shade and checked the street. Half a block down, through the iron bars over the window, he could see a cigarette burning inside a parked car. Jake slid to the floor with his back against the wall and drank a bottle of water.

*Impossible,* he thought.

Maybe a trained surveillance team could have tracked him without being discovered, but not a group of al-Qaeda goons. He sat there wrestling with exhaustion and a dozen conflicting possibilities. Accepting that he would never know for sure what had happened, he pushed it to the back of his mind and decided to take a shower.

He stepped under the water fully dressed, washing away the dust that permeated every fiber of his clothing. When the dirt was gone and the water ran clear he stripped down and scrubbed his body. Though he had no soap, and the water pressure was a fraction of what it was in the West, he felt almost normal when he was finished. He hung his clothes up, figuring the desert air would dry them by morning.

He doused the lights and yawned as he peered behind the window shade again. The car was still there.

Jake lay naked on one of the sleeping bags and looked at the clock above the sink. With the noise of the air conditioner almost drowning out the television next door, and the loaded pistol next to him on the floor, he was asleep before the minute hand moved.

Five minutes later he bolted upright to an unfamiliar sound. Jake grabbed the gun and quickly swept the room until he realized that it was only the phone that Fadi and Youssef had given him.

*Need you back here ASAP,* said the text message.

Jake dressed in his damp clothes, wondering if the two operations officers were now taking orders from Graves.

# FORTY-SEVEN

PREMIER MÈNG-FÙ RU'S office had been decorated in the style of imperial China, with vermilion walls and hand-carved furniture. General Wǔ-Dīng helped his friend to a black-lacquered armchair with a Yinglong dragon painted on the seatback.

"The old dragon," observed the general, whose own office was stark and businesslike.

"You are referring to me or the chair?" snapped Mèng-Fù.

The general smiled. "The chair, of course, wizened one."

Mèng-Fù gazed at his protégé. "And you fancy yourself a dragon slayer, General?"

"Have I done something to offend?" asked Wǔ-Dīng with genuine concern. Mèng-Fù was like a father to him.

"Not to me, but the president felt your sword against his throat today. You left him with no way out in front of the entire Standing Committee."

"It was you who taught me many years ago that actions and ideas are useless without each other. The president has neither."

"His is a steady hand."

"Like a statue," said the general with a dismissive wave of his own hand. "Opportunities must be grasped, and a statue is incapable of doing so. President Chéng is a manager, not a leader. This can be the Chinese millennium, but it will not happen on its own. We must make it so."

Mèng-Fù grunted. "What of Saudi Arabia? Do you think you can make it work?"

"My contact there is a strategic thinker. He will see the wisdom of our proposal."

"But the king still supports the Americans. He said as much during a public statement earlier today."

"The king clings to the United States because he sees no better option. When a partnership with China is offered, he will realize that it is in the best interest of the kingdom."

"What makes you so certain?"

"My sources tell me that demonstrations across the country are undermining his authority. His grip on power grows more tenuous by the day."

"This puzzles me. The Saudis have traditionally understood the value of domestic order. This experiment of letting the protests continue is a mistake. Once unrest begins, the people do not know when to stop." Mèng-Fù tapped his index finger on the desk. "But perhaps it will help our negotiating position. Call your man. Let us see if the Saudis are ready to make a clean break from the Americans."

\* \* \*

A LIGHT RAIN fell as Wǔ-Dīng walked back to his own office. Situated just west of the Forbidden City in downtown Beijing, Zhongnanhai was both a palace and a prison. With its high walls and numerous guards, it afforded him the ability to walk without his security detail when he so chose, but it also detached him from the people that were the soul of China.

Such were the trade-offs that came with great power.

The general smiled as a few droplets landed on his face. He'd always derived strength from the warm summer rains that blew through the region. Wǔ-Dīng didn't consider himself a religious man. His parents were Taoists, and he had grown up during a time in China when religious faith would have excluded him from advancement within the Communist Party, but he harbored a suspicion that his existence was not completely transient. Though he had not put a label on his beliefs, he felt strongly that the rain brought him closer to nature, closer to whatever force had put him on the earth.

The showers intensified, but Wǔ-Dīng did not hurry. The water soaking into his uniform was cathartic. Just as rain brought growth and renewal to the land, Wǔ-Dīng would bring growth and renewal to China. The downpour was confirmation that he'd chosen the correct path. The path was not without danger—just recently he had backed the president into a corner, but Wǔ-Dīng had prevailed. The Standing Committee had seen the wisdom of bringing Saudi Arabia into China's orbit, of depriving America of one of its key suppliers of natural resources. Many believed that the United States no longer needed Saudi oil, but if U.S. reserves ran out in another twenty or thirty years, the country would be back in the market, paying prices its economy could not support. Americans thought in terms of years, or maybe decades if Wǔ-Dīng was feeling generous, but these were short time frames, no more than tactical maneuvers to the Chinese mind. They were pointless without a grand plan.

Wǔ-Dīng stepped into his outer office and handed his dripping jacket to an aide. He entered his private office and dialed a long number on a secure telephone. He looked through the windows at the rain falling outside, washing away the old and bringing forth the new. The Chinese millennium was approaching.

"I met with the Standing Committee," he said into the handset.

"And Chéng?"

"Paralyzed by inertia," said Wǔ-Dīng. "He lacks the capacity to recognize the opportunity in front of him."

"It is the same here. The Council of Ministers is losing faith in the king's ability to manage the crisis."

"Which is why we must lead them, Faisal. I appreciate your sacrifice. As a military man, I understand how painful it is to lose so many of your own people, even for a worthy objective."

"The Sudairi clan has spent too long ruling Arabia. They have sold their souls to the West on credit, and now that credit has run out. It is time for a new era."

"On the terms we discussed?" asked Wǔ-Dīng.

"Three Chinese bases and the ability to purchase

current-generation weapons in exchange for fifty percent of our oil production."

"At a ten percent discount to the spot price, with a right of first refusal on the rest at full market price."

"Of course," said the prince.

"Thank you, Faisal. This will give me the leverage I need with the Standing Committee to consummate our deal and advance our state of military readiness. Once we are on a war footing, the United States will not dare strike us."

"The committee will not view the military preparations with suspicion?"

"Some may, but with the chaos in the United States, it is rational to be cautious of the Americans. Predators are most dangerous when they are wounded. The Standing Committee will do as I suggest."

"Much has come from our early discussions in Libya," said Faisal. "I must go now. Good-bye, General."

"Good-bye, my friend."

## FORTY-EIGHT

PRESIDENT J. WILLIAM Day sat alone in the Oval Office. The country was in disarray. Previous terrorist attacks inside the United States had caused the American people to rally around their government, but the voters were already frustrated with polarized political parties, and the new attacks served to stoke that frustration with fear and anger. Combined with universal condemnation of the American strike on Mecca, the nation's leaders had lost the trust of their citizens.

It was a dangerous time.

Though many people were fearful of assembling in large numbers, domestic protests against the bombing of the Grand Mosque in Mecca had been widespread. Predictably, small numbers of agitators used the mostly peaceful assemblies to lash out, throwing Molotov cocktails and firing weapons at police forces already on edge. Detroit, with its large Muslim population, was seeing some of the fiercest rioting. Efforts by police to protect lives and property were sensationalized by unaccountable cell phone photographers and uninformed internet commentators, further fanning the discord within the country.

Several fuel tanks at the west coast refineries had exploded when the water used to fight the fires sank through the burning liquids inside the tanks. The intense heat and pressure at the bottoms of the tanks caused the water to become steam and instantaneously expand to sixteen hundred times its original volume. The explosions claimed dozens of lives and drove firefighting equipment and personnel so far back from the blaze that the fires were effectively burning themselves out. The prevailing southwest winds pushed clouds of caustic gas to the foot of the San Gabriel Mountains, forcing the Federal Emergency Management Agency to evacuate a million people from the cities of Los Angeles, Pasadena, Pomona, and Anaheim and to issue shelter-in-place orders for two million more.

Almost half of Southern California's refinery capacity had been destroyed. Early repair estimates were in the range of ten to twelve months. With jet fuel production crippled, and gasoline in limited supply along the entire east coast, gas prices spiked north of ten dollars per gallon during the peak summer driving season. Lines at filling stations that still had fuel were over ninety minutes long. The only silver lining, if one could even call it that, was that demand was lower because the sniper attacks had made most people fearful of taking to the roads.

The bombed-out pipeline and a months-long summer drought had set ablaze much of the national forest north of Atlanta and destroyed thousands of homes.

Firefighters were again forced to the sidelines, unable to make a dent in a fire whose scale was simply unfathomable.

The environmental and economic implications for the nation were catastrophic.

The president crumpled the most current casualty estimates and damage assessments and threw them in the trash. While the estimates were well-intentioned, fresh terror strikes, second-order effects, and civil unrest rendered the figures obsolete long before they arrived on his desk. The real numbers would be significantly higher.

One of his assistants ushered in several senior officials. The president joined the group in the sitting area across from his desk.

"What do you have for us, Jay?" asked the president.

"The USS *Michigan* and the USS *Jimmy Carter* are searching for Drifter-72 in the Red Sea west of Mecca," said General Landgraf. "The KSA Navy is also out in force, pinging the seabed with everything they've got, including the littoral-combat ships we sold them. Ironically, this actually provides some cover for our subs because active sonar lets us know where the enemy surface ships are, but the Saudi Navy also has a few diesel-electric subs, which they bought from Germany. Those are very good. We can track them, but they're damn quiet when they're running submerged, so our boys have to stay close to the bottom and use low-powered sonar for our own searches to avoid detection. It's a slow process."

"We need to find that aircraft first, General." The president turned to the secretary of the treasury. "How bad is it?"

"Domestic equity markets are off twenty percent. International stock markets are down even more," he said. "U.S. treasury bonds, traditionally a safe-haven investment, are seeing their values plunge as investors are fleeing all dollar-denominated assets. The Federal Reserve wants to cut rates, but our currency is already down eleven percent and they're afraid of knocking it down more. People are seeing their savings just disappear. On top of that, fuel prices are so high that people can't afford to fly or drive anywhere, even if they weren't worried about dying in a terrorist attack. It's a perfect storm."

"Worldwide boycotts of American exports are gaining traction as consumers, corporations, and governments are choosing to buy from anyone but the United States," added the secretary of state, "and I've been told our trade agreements with the European Union are being torn up."

General Landgraf spoke up. "As you'd expect, Mr. President, I have some very senior contacts throughout NATO, general officers I've known for twenty to thirty years, men I'd trust with my life. They're telling me that anything we know—from war plans to communications— they've been told to toss it in the trash. Additionally, the military forces of Russia, China, Pakistan, North Korea, and several others have significantly increased their op tempo."

The president scoffed. "How much of this is posturing? Do these governments really believe that the attack on Mecca was a tool of American foreign policy?"

"Whether it's a reaction to the attack or our elevated

DEFCON level, I can't say definitively," Landgraf said, "but the rest of the world thinks the United States just attacked a long-standing ally, and no one wants to be the next target on our list. It's a dangerous time, sir. We're one flawed assumption away from a nuclear exchange."

# FORTY-NINE

MAJOR GENERAL SHIRIZANI worked furiously inside the Qods Force operations center. Despite the predawn hour, a dozen senior staff officers and a full complement of communications personnel were on duty with him. Video monitors on the walls displayed maps and images from theaters of interest around the world. Multiple conversations filled the room as distant operatives were connected by voice and video over fiber-optic cables and satellite networks. He was surveying a table-mounted map of the Arabian Peninsula, when an aide approached.

"It's across," said the major.

"Riyadh?" asked the general.

"Midnight, local time."

Shirizani nodded. He turned to a whiteboard on the wall and crossed an item off a list, then summoned one of the communications staff. The specialist returned a few minutes later with a telephone call for the general.

"Colonel Turani," said the specialist as he handed over the secure telephone.

"The shipment just crossed the Yemeni border," said

the general. "You'll have it by midnight: two hundred pistols, half as many rifles, plus C4, RPGs, and grenades. They're hidden in sacks of rice. Have men ready to unload them."

"I have men to unload them. I need men to use them," said Turani. "Unfortunately, much of the population is still loyal to the king."

"They are not loyal to the king," said Shirizani. "They fear the king. The people are ignorant sheep. Since birth they have been raised in their madrassas to revere him and his Sunni faith, but give them the means to throw off their yoke and they will do so eagerly."

Shirizani paced around the room as he spoke.

"We must act now, while there is anger and confusion. Most of the country is sitting at home, quietly furious with the king for cutting their stipends and failing to condemn the United States. Show them a few well-staged images of revolution in the making and they'll take to the streets themselves. Arm these people, Colonel. Frighten them. Make them believe that they need to protect themselves against the king and his American colonial masters. We do not have time. You do not have time."

"I understand, General."

"Controlled chaos is what Qods does best," said Shirizani. "Distribute the weapons around Riyadh as soon as you get them. Another transshipment has already left Kuwaiti waters. The Saudi Arabian National Guard is stretched too thin to defuse the situation with a peaceful show of force. Once they start shooting civilians, the masses will take to the streets."

The general stopped pacing in front of the map and traced a line on it with his finger. "Tell al-Quereshi to advance on Al-Wadiah and Sharorah eight hours after the National Guard troops have withdrawn. Tell him to spare no one."

"He will need no encouragement. The AQAP foot soldiers are furious about King Ali's fealty to the Americans. They may go all the way to Riyadh."

The general scowled. "Then you'll need another band of murderers. The Saudis may be on the verge of political disarray, but half a dozen of their Apache gunships will fertilize the soil with the blood of al-Quereshi's men. The element of surprise is their only advantage. After they've razed Sharorah they must retreat back to Yemen and melt into the countryside while the Saudis mobilize a counterattack. The maneuver will stretch the Saudi lines and allow al-Houthi to attack in the west."

"And Saudi Arabia will soon become another failed Sunni state."

"Indeed it will, Colonel, but it will not happen by itself. The key to it all is the American embassy. It has to start there. For a hundred years, when the world looks back on the fall of Saudi Arabia, they will remember this day."

## FIFTY

JAKE HEARD THE call of the muezzin as he stepped outside. Broadcast five times each day from loudspeakers throughout the city, it summoned the faithful to prayer. Men glared at him as he walked to the main boulevard while they entered the Ibn Taymiyyah mosque for dawn prayers.

Jake took a taxi to a busy traffic circle and walked the wrong way down a one-way street before catching another cab. Ten minutes later, he announced himself at Fadi and Youssef's safe house. The roll-up gate began to retract. Fadi was at the wheel of an old van. Youssef was standing next to it with a pistol-grip shotgun held low along his leg. Both were wearing white thobes, checked red and white ghutras on their heads, and dark sunglasses.

"Let's go," Youssef said, gesturing for Jake to get in the van.

Jake hesitated, his eyes on the pump-action 12-gauge.

Fadi lowered his window. "We've got a job at the embassy."

Jake climbed in. Youssef slid the door closed and took the passenger seat.

"There's a duffel bag at your feet," he said to Jake. "Get dressed."

Jake unpacked a thobe and ghutra from the bag.

"HQ ordered us to evacuate the ambassador in case the security situation deteriorates," Youssef said. "We need a third man to do it right, and we figured you'd want to get eyes on the embassy."

"Ambassador Marek isn't some political bundler," Fadi said. "He's the architect of practically our entire Mideast strategy. Washington can't have him fall into unfriendly hands."

"He should be safe in the embassy," Jake said. "I was there last night. The place is a fortress."

"And it has a safe room for fifty people," Youssef said, "but it's designed to survive a temporary breach, not war with the host nation. The Saudis have the Egyptians, the Sudanese, the Russians, and even a French frigate helping them search the Red Sea right now. If they find that drone, the locals will lay siege to the embassy and it will be Tehran, 1979, all over again."

"There were maybe two hundred people scattered around the square last night," Jake said. "Mostly students. Getting him out shouldn't be a problem."

Jake chose not to mention the two men who'd followed him. He didn't want Fadi and Youssef to shut him out of the operation. Except for some additional traffic, the ride to the Diplomatic Quarter was much the same as it had been for Jake's first trip.

Until they reached the square.

In just a few hours, the hundreds of protesters had turned to thousands. The easygoing college kids had been replaced by men in their twenties and thirties. Angry men. Men who looked as if they were looking for a fight. Cars were parked haphazardly along the road.

"I'll park as close as I can," Fadi said, "but we're going to have to bring the ambassador across the square on foot."

The van attracted stares as it threaded its way through the crowd. Jake stared right back, searching for Colonel Turani among the throngs of people. The road soon became impassible and Fadi parked the van. The three Americans stepped out, with Jake carrying the duffel bag. It was already over ninety degrees in the shade.

Jake subconsciously ran his hand over the pistol in his waistband as he took stock of the sinister elements that had arrived during the night: men who checked 360 degrees around them when they got out of their vehicles, men who carried weapons under their untucked shirts and jackets, men with hatred in their eyes.

The three CIA officers wove through the crowd. Evidence of rage and destruction were everywhere. The police cars Jake had seen earlier had been torched. Barricades had been built from trash, scavenged construction materials, and whatever else was lying around. Smoke rose into the air from a garbage can fire where men were using American flags as fuel.

Most of the rioters stood near the embassy, with the loudest and most aggressive of the group clustered in front of the main gate, taunting the U.S. Marines and

Diplomatic Security agents inside the compound. Exterior security was supposed to be provided by the host nation, but the Saudis had pulled back, giving the rioters close access. Many covered their faces to preserve their anonymity, some carried signs and banners, and others burned flags on long poles. Chants of "Death to America" broke out occasionally, but the barrage of rocks and bottles thrown over the embassy walls was constant.

Jake and the others jostled their way through the mob. They chanted along with the protesters or spoke to each other in Arabic, doing whatever was necessary to blend in as they worked their way to the far side of the square.

Fadi turned and looked at the others as they pressed farther into the bedlam.

"Keep it tight, boys. I have a feeling this is going to be a hot evac."

# FIFTY-ONE

**M**EETINGS OF THE Politburo's Standing Committee were typically scheduled by the party secretary at the direction of the president. Though its members were the most powerful men in China, the president's ability to summon the others at will was a subtle display of power familiar to managers and leaders everywhere. Standing Committee members would occasionally skip meetings to demonstrate their independence or their displeasure. Attendance itself was often a referendum on policy.

It was noon in Beijing when the party secretary received a call from General Wǔ-Dīng. It was the general's opinion that the situation with Saudi Arabia required immediate attention and he wished to schedule an emergency session of the Standing Committee.

The secretary stared at the handset as he hung up the phone. He had observed the tension between the president and the general. Scheduling a meeting now would be interpreted by the president as support for Wǔ-Dīng and a challenge to the president's authority.

But failing to do so would be an affront to Wǔ-Dīng.

In another month, the Presidium of the National People's Congress would meet to approve the nominees for the top party offices, including the secretary's. His decision to grant or refuse the request for a meeting could have significant implications for his own career.

The president's term was also up for renewal, but the Standing Committee was clearly disappointed with his leadership during the current U.S.-Saudi spat. What would happen during a real crisis? Would President Chéng again be paralyzed by inaction? If the committee's confidence in his abilities continued to deteriorate, it was increasingly likely that Premier Mèng-Fù Ru might be elevated to general secretary of the party and president of the country. He had the respect of the highly influential party elders and had largely avoided the ugly side of factional politics, having helped guide the ship of state with wisdom and conscience over his lifetime of service—and General Wǔ-Dīng was the premier's protégé.

The secretary was being forced to cast his ballot early and for all to see.

He scheduled an emergency session of the Standing Committee for two p.m. and stared out the window. All of the committee members were in Beijing. Attendance at the meeting would render judgment not only on the president's standing but on the secretary's decision as well. If the committee members declined to attend, it would mean the end of not only Wǔ-Dīng's career but the secretary's too.

\* \* \*

GENERAL WŬ-DĪNG ARRIVED outside the meeting room a few minutes before two o'clock. He spied Mèng-Fù by the door, standing uncomfortably on his bad hip.

"They are waiting for you, General," he said. "All of them."

The general started to enter when Mèng-Fù's bony fingers grabbed his arm.

"I don't know what you're up to," hissed Mèng-Fù, "but Chéng is not happy. I won't be able to save you if you fuck it up."

Wŭ-Dīng nodded. He'd purposely kept Mèng-Fù in the dark to protect him. The man was likely to be the next leader of China, and he would be a good one. There was no reason to drag him down if events did not go as planned.

The premier released Wŭ-Dīng's arm and walked into the conference room. President Chéng was seated in his customary spot, having a discreet conversation with the head of the Central Commission for Discipline Inspection. The president stopped speaking and fixed Wŭ-Dīng with a cold stare.

"Mr. President," said the general before he took his seat, "I must apologize for the breach of protocol. Given the urgency of the matter, I thought it best to act quickly, before Mèng-Fù retired for the evening."

A few people chuckled around the table, including Mèng-Fù. He did not mind the jab at his age. It had defused the tension in the room and he was pleased that

Wǔ-Dīng had finally learned to let the vanquished save face.

The general bowed his head deferentially to the president, who took a minute to remind those present of Wǔ-Dīng's diplomatic outreach to Saudi Arabia, but the others already knew that, for they had been the ones who'd encouraged it over the president's objections. Chéng's attempt to reassert his authority was seen as the transparent ploy that it was.

"General, the floor is yours."

"Thank you, Comrade Chairman," said Wǔ-Dīng. In modern China, the title "comrade" had fallen into ambiguity. While officially still a sign of respect and party unity, younger generations had come to use it derisively. President Chéng and the others were still contemplating Wǔ-Dīng's intent when he began to speak.

"Saudi Arabia wishes to partner with China," he said.

"You received an answer so soon?" asked the head of the Central Commission for Discipline Inspection, one of Chéng's staunch factional allies.

"Indeed. My contact is deputy crown prince and head of the Saudi Arabian National Guard. He speaks with authority."

"What do they want?" asked the deputy party secretary. "The terms . . . are they acceptable?"

"That, of course, is for the committee to decide," said Wǔ-Dīng. "I serve merely as a messenger."

Premier Mèng-Fù nodded slowly. The general's diplomatic skills were developing nicely.

"The Saudis desire three things. First, they would like China to replace the U.S. mutual-defense treaty. This is no small request in such a turbulent area of the world. Second, they desire that China provide a guaranteed off-take of fifty percent of Saudi oil. Recent price fluctuations have wreaked havoc with their economy and led to much civil discontentment. Third, they would like China to join the military coalition operating in Yemen. They do not require a significant role, but they believe that a few Chinese bombers over Sanaa would prove to the world that we are serious about our support for the kingdom."

The president began to speak, when the party secretary cut him off. "What is your opinion of the deal, General?"

"I believe it is just. Our annual oil imports already exceed fifty percent of current Saudi output. Perhaps we could structure pricing at a discount to the forward curve. We should get something in exchange for our guarantee, should we not?"

"A five percent discount would offset most of our costs," said the minister of the interior.

A few heads around the table nodded their assent.

"Then I will press for ten percent," said Wǔ-Dīng.

"What about our military commitment?" asked the head of the chairman of the National People's Congress. "Does it benefit China or are we simply providing protection for the Saudis?"

A tight smile formed on General Wǔ-Dīng's face. "Of course, President Chéng, as chairman of the Central Military Commission, would have to review the particulars, but forward-deployed aircraft on the Arabian Peninsula would add critical redundancy to our base in Djibouti and enable us to project power over the entire Mideast, including the Suez Canal. It would be a sound strategic move."

"The optics of joining the coalition make sense," said the deputy premier. "Flying a few sorties over Yemen now might avert a regional conflict later. Iran and the rest of the world will see that Chinese action will back up Chinese words."

"Indeed, Minister," said Wǔ-Dīng. "The terms appear to be beneficial to both sides."

"And King Ali has agreed to this?" asked President Chéng. "He has traditionally been a staunch ally of America."

Wǔ-Dīng leaned forward and looked the president in the eyes. "The king's indecisiveness during the current crisis has undermined his authority considerably. The ministers who run the government on a daily basis are eager to take concrete steps to protect the nation. Prince Faisal is quite certain that either the king will see the wisdom of partnership with China, or the Allegiance Council will act on a succession plan."

"But the Allegiance Council swears an oath of loyalty to the king," said the foreign minister.

"They do," said Wǔ-Dīng before returning his gaze to the president, "but there are provisions for the failure to exercise the responsibilities of the office. There are consequences for inaction."

The president held Wǔ-Dīng's stare. "Might this be seen simply as a power grab by an ambitious lieutenant?"

"Removal of an ineffective leader would put him closer to the seat of power, but not in it," said Wǔ-Dīng. "Hopefully, those in power will see the opportunity in front of them and more drastic steps will not be required."

The room was quiet for several seconds until Premier Mèng-Fù Ru spoke up.

"Let us discuss the merits and perils of the proposal from China's perspective," he said.

"China can buy all the oil it wants on the open market," said the president.

"But a partner would reduce price volatility," said the chairman of the National People's Congress. "And a five percent discount would be well worth our while. At ten percent, we would be foolish not to agree."

"Guaranteed supply would be a strategic asset in times of military conflict," added the party secretary. "As would additional bases in such an unpredictable region."

"What if we decide to wait on this opportunity?" asked the president. "The U.S.-Saudi relationship is already fractured. We could then negotiate a treaty in the future without provoking the United States."

"I doubt we will have the chance," said the foreign minister. "The Europeans are probably considering the same partnership. They need energy independence from Russia and they don't want another refugee crisis like they had with Syria if the Saudi monarchy should collapse."

"And there are powerful elements within the United States that are displeased with Saudi support for al-Qaeda and Daesh," said Wǔ-Dīng. "The strike on Mecca may have been intended as a parting shot."

"Perhaps the Americans have not acted as rashly as we initially thought," said Mèng-Fù. "They have long wished for the Saudis to end their support of terrorism and encouraged Europe to shoulder more of its own defense. Striking Mecca may have accomplished two goals at once."

"Without subjecting them to debate inside the U.S. government," added the foreign minister.

"General Wǔ-Dīng is correct," said the head of the Central Commission for Discipline Inspection. "This is a very different United States. We must take action to secure our supply of natural resources before America makes another unpredictable move."

"Or the Europeans beat us to the prize," said the party secretary.

"General Wǔ-Dīng," said the deputy premier, "do you think the Saudis might decide to remain independent after their betrayal by the Americans?"

"Saudi weapons are excellent, but their training and discipline are poor. An unaligned kingdom would be highly vulnerable," said Wǔ-Dīng. "The external menace from Iran, and possibly now the United States, requires a credible defense, and the high concentration of wealth makes the nation susceptible to internal strife as well. They cannot manage both threats alone."

"General, what second-order effects might we see from a Saudi realignment to China?" asked the party secretary.

"Saudi advisers and Chinese weapons could once again make Africa a stable and productive supplier of petroleum products," said Wǔ-Dīng. "Such a development would further lower oil prices and eliminate a major breeding ground for religious extremists."

"We should advance negotiations with the Saudis," said the deputy premier as he looked around the table. The other members of the Standing Committee nodded their assent, except President Chéng.

"Mr. President?" asked General Wǔ-Dīng.

President Chéng knew he had been outflanked. Another time, he would have struck down Wǔ-Dīng and put him in his place, but the nominations for the National People's Congress were soon to be decided. The president was up for a second term as general secretary of the Communist Party, and the only men who could grant it were in the room and supporting Wǔ-Dīng.

"News of this proposed initiative will undoubtedly raise the risk of conflict with the United States," said the president, "so continue your work with the Saudis, General, but you have left me no choice but to move PLA forces to Combat Readiness Condition Three. Let us hope they won't be needed."

## FIFTY-TWO

A DETACHMENT OF SAUDI National Guard troops had blocked off the embassy square with troop carriers. The soldiers watched intently as Jake and the others approached one of the townhouses, but lost interest when Fadi produced a key and the men stepped inside.

He led the others to the basement and entered an elaborate home gym with floor-to-ceiling mirrors. He lifted a phone on the wall and dialed an eight-digit number. One of the mirrors popped open on hidden hinges. Beyond it was a steel door with an electronic lock. Fadi punched in another code and the three-inch-thick door opened to a tunnel. Dim red lighting lit the way.

"Do the Saudis know about this?" Jake said.

"Maybe," said Youssef. He pulled the short-barreled shotgun from under his thobe. "Keep your head on a swivel."

The three men reached the end of the ninety-meter tunnel but a second steel door barred the way. Fadi was about to knock when it swung open. Four U.S. marines stood on the other side with M-4 rifles aimed into the tunnel. Brilliant white weapon lights blinded the CIA officers.

"Hands! Get your hands up, now!" shouted one of the marines.

The three CIA officers complied immediately. Youssef carefully placed the shotgun on the ground.

"We're U.S. government," said Fadi. "Where's your regional security officer?"

An athletic-looking woman in her late thirties appeared.

"I'm the RSO," she said.

"We're Sabre Shield," Fadi said. It was the code phrase each side had been given.

"I was told to expect two of you."

"We brought an extra man," Fadi said. "It's getting nasty up top."

"It's OK, guys," she said to the marines. "They're on our side."

The marines lowered their weapons and the group headed into the embassy. Youssef tucked the shotgun back under his thobe.

The RSO spoke as she led the way. "I don't have much time. I have three hundred eighty-four staff and dependents upstairs who are counting on me to keep them alive while every other person in Saudi Arabia would like to see them dead."

"We'll be out of here quickly, ma'am," Fadi said.

The RSO stopped and turned around. "Good luck with that. The ambassador isn't planning on leaving."

She turned to the marine sergeant. "Escort these men to a conference room and notify the ambassador."

The marine guards led Jake and the others upstairs. No foreign workers were allowed past the security hardline and the appearance of the Arab-looking CIA officers with their marine escort generated stares from the rest of the staff.

"Sergeant," Fadi said to the senior marine, "I need you to talk to the ambassador. Not one of his assistants, not the deputy head of mission, directly to the man. Tell him there are three CIA officers here and we need to speak with him in the next five minutes."

"Copy that, sir." The marine left the room.

Ambassador Marek arrived an hour later, wearing a suit and tie.

"Leave it to CIA to make a bad situation worse," he said. "What if they find that aircraft out in the Red Sea? Then what? What's going to happen when that mob outside overruns the embassy?"

"I'm sorry, sir," Fadi said, "but unfortunately your safety takes precedence. We need to get you out of here immediately."

"I'm afraid not," said Marek. "I'm not leaving my people. The captain goes down with the ship."

"I respect that, sir, I really do," said Fadi, "but if you would just call the DDO at Langley—"

"He already called me, and I'll tell you the same thing I told him. I don't work for CIA and I'm needed here. You guys can pack up and leave, or you can stick around and help with security. The DS team can use all the help they can get. Good day, gentlemen."

\* \* \*

AN HOUR LATER, Ambassador Marek stormed into the conference room a second time.

"I just got off the phone with the secretary of state. I've been ordered out of Saudi," he said. "You sons of bitches went over my head."

The ambassador shoved a chair against the wall.

"Goddamned CIA!" he shouted. "This mess is your fault, and now I'm being recalled in the middle of a crisis. I'll be back in two hours!"

He slammed the conference room door as he left. The three men watched through the glass walls as the ambassador began shouting at the RSO and the marine guards who'd been ordered by State Department headquarters not to let him back into his office. The RSO walked the ambassador back to the conference room.

No one commented on the abrupt U-turn.

"Given the elevated threat level outside, we have a disguise for you, sir," Youssef said as he opened the duffel bag.

With pale skin and thinning gray hair, the ambassador said nothing as he changed out of his suit and into white pants and a thobe. He stared bitterly at Youssef as the CIA officer applied skin-darkening makeup and a fake mustache to his face, then added a wig and ghutra.

"You look good, sir," said the RSO. "You'll be fine out there."

"I know you're just following orders, Shelley. Take care of these people. They're our family."

"Count on it, sir," she said. "The secretary's office said you're scheduled to be shown meeting with him and the president shortly after you arrive back in Washington. They feel it will take some of the heat off us here without rubbing the Saudis' noses in it."

The ambassador nodded. It was a good plan.


THE TEAM TOOK the tunnel back to the townhouse. Probably five thousand people were in the square now, and the Americans could hear them through the concrete walls and double-paned glass.

Youssef left to get the van.

Twenty minutes later Fadi got a text message. "He's idling on the eastern edge of the square."

Jake looked at Marek. "Mr. Ambassador, do you speak Arabic?"

"I do, but my accent is terrible."

"Chant with the crowd while we're walking," said Jake. "And yell if you need us—your accent will be harder to pick out if you're shouting. Don't look nervous. Look angry. Everyone out there is angry."

"Jake and I are armed," said Fadi, "but drawing a weapon will be an absolute last resort, so don't take any unnecessary chances. Our best outcome is a quick, boring walk to the van."

The ambassador took a deep breath. "I'm ready."

The three men walked out of the villa with the ambassador in the middle. They were jostled by the crowd the moment they entered the square. There was constant physical contact. Coming, going, side to side. Rioters shoved their way through the mob.

The ambassador pulled the ghutra tight around his face and walked with his head down, practically holding the back of Fadi's thobe. Jake grabbed a discarded sign off the ground and handed it to the ambassador. He stared at the crudely drawn picture of a bomb falling on the White House and nodded.

"Death to America!" he shouted in Arabic.

The midday heat and the dense crowd pushed the temperature on the blacktop to 120 degrees. Tempers were short. Sporadic fights broke out among the protesters. A group of five men shoved their way forward. One of them collided with the ambassador and the two men fell to the ground. The man dropped his satchel and yelled at the ambassador, but Jake stepped between them and picked up the bag. It was heavy and shapeless, like it was filled with rocks. Jake handed it over, noticing several Iranian-made hand grenades through the open top.

The man stood.

"Death to America," Jake said.

"Death to America," said the man before shoving his way toward the embassy.

Jake turned around, but Fadi and the ambassador were gone. Jake pushed forward, scanning the area between the ambassador's last position and the rendezvous point. An abandoned city bus at the far end of the square was ablaze. Flames spilled through its melted windows, sending thick black smoke climbing into the air. Gunfire echoed from the direction of the embassy gate. There was action everywhere, but no sign of the ambassador.

The crowd thinned as Jake walked and he soon spotted the van parked just off the square on a side street. Youssef was standing next to it, watching everything from behind dark sunglasses, the shotgun concealed under his thobe. Jake was a hundred feet away, surveying the crowd for Fadi and the ambassador, when his eyes came to rest on a lone man under a palm tree, standing back from the fray. Jake thought it might be one of the men who had followed him the night before, but the shade from the palm fronds mottled the light on his face.

Jake walked to the van.

"Where're the others?" Youssef said.

"We had a little scuffle in the crowd and got separated."

"Should we backtrack to the villa?"

"It ended OK. They'll be along."

Youssef gave a curt nod and resumed watching the square. Jake walked fifty feet into the mob, searching for Fadi and the ambassador. They emerged a few minutes later, dripping with sweat, but none the worse for wear. They headed for the van and Jake resumed his prior role as rear guard.

He glanced toward the man under the tree, but the man had moved. Jake walked into the daylight for a better view of the action.

"That's Turani," Jake said.

Fadi put his hand on Jake's arm. "Our job is to get the ambassador out of here."

Jake rolled his arm over Fadi's, breaking his grip.

"One way or another, that sonofabitch is responsible for this." Jake gestured to the pandemonium in the square.

"Don't do it," Fadi said, but Jake was already shoving his way through the mob.

He removed his pistol from his waistband as he approached Turani from behind.

"We need to talk," Jake said.

"Who are you?" Turani said. He moved slowly, trying to buy himself some time, but Jake shoved the pistol into the Iranian's back and manhandled him through the crowd until they were a hundred feet from the van.

A second later they were on the ground and disoriented. Everyone was shouting and screaming. A car bomb had detonated and sent a massive shock wave through the square.

Jake felt as if his chest had exploded. He was on his hands and knees, shaking his head as he tried to regain his composure. He saw his pistol on the ground and was reaching for it when a heavy boot kicked him in the side of the head. He tumbled onto his side and Turani kicked him again, this time in the rib cage. The blow to Jake's already bruised ribs felt like a knife in his side.

Turani kicked a third time, but Jake rolled out of the way. He caught Turani's foot and wrenched it ninety degrees. The Iranian screamed and fell to the ground, holding his knee. Jake dove on top of him and punched him several times in the side of the head before yanking the Iranian to his feet. The pistol was nowhere to be seen.

*"AMRIKI! AMRIKI!"* Turani yelled to the mob.

The rioters surged forward, hoping to tear a real American limb from limb and not just an effigy. Jake shoved Turani toward the van.

Youssef saw the scene unfold from the passenger seat.

"Back it up! Back it up!" he shouted.

Pedestrians dove for safety as Fadi reversed through the crowd. The mob had Jake surrounded when the van screeched to a halt and Youssef jumped out. He raised the pump-action shotgun and fired three rounds into the air. The mob scattered, but Turani had escaped in the melee.

Youssef climbed back into the passenger seat while Ambassador Marek opened the van's side door and Jake dove inside. Fadi stomped on the accelerator and sped out of the square. The second they'd reached a side road, he looked in the rearview mirror and screamed at Jake.

"What the fuck was that?"

## FIFTY-THREE

HURRICANE BEULAH MOVED slowly as it passed the Yucatán Peninsula, her winds roiling the southern Gulf of Mexico for days on end. Though dangerous to mariners, the churning seas acted like a safety valve on the Category Two storm, pulling cold water from the depths to the surface and keeping its power in check. But Beulah sped up as it moved into the western gulf, pulling more heat and more moisture in from the warmer surface. The vortex grew quickly, multiplying its destructive force until it had become a Category Five storm with wind gusts of 180 miles per hour.

*EL NUEVO CONSTANTE* had restarted her broken engine, thanks to the skill and determination of her two young crewmen, but the captain's original plan to be north of the storm track was no longer realistic. He now made best speed to the southwest, hoping to diverge as much as possible from the northwest-moving eye.

The heavy seas had arrived a full day before the

storm. Driven over miles of open ocean by Beulah's winds, their power grew until fifteen- and twenty-foot waves were not uncommon. The rain followed. At first just a few drops splattered against the windows, but soon a mass of steel-gray clouds darkened the entire eastern horizon. *El Nuevo Constante* would not receive a glancing blow. The ship would be in a fight for its life.

"Let me take the wheel, Papa," Miguel said. "It's almost midnight. You need to rest."

The captain hesitated. His place was at the helm, especially in a storm.

"He's right, señor," added Carlos, holding an overhead rail for stability. "We need your mind sharp. Miguel can steer the ship."

"OK," the captain said, "but promise me one thing . . . fetch me the first time you wonder if you should."

Miguel took the wheel as his father staggered to his bunk. The ship was pitching and rolling in the building seas. A rain squall lashed the wheelhouse.

"I'm worried about the deck plate," Miguel said. The heavy weather had made further welding impossible. "I'm not sure it will hold if we take a big wave aboard."

"The sea is not my specialty," said Carlos, "but that steel plate is better than the piece of plywood you had on there before."

Miguel laughed. The two young men had developed a pleasant camaraderie during their time aboard ship. Successfully repairing the engine and getting the steel plate into position over the rusted hole in the deck had earned Carlos the respect of father and son.

"What is your specialty?" Miguel asked, his eyes fixed firmly on the horizon. "I would not have made you for a laborer from Veracruz-Llave."

It was not said as a challenge or a test, but Carlos's legend had not been meant to survive multiple days in close proximity to native Mexicans. Miguel had picked up on something.

"My family left Mexico when I was little," Carlos said. "I was raised in Texas mostly, but work there was hard to come by, and my cousin's business was doing well, so I came back to work for him." Then he added truthfully, "I've never been to sea before, but I love the adventure, the oneness with God."

Miguel glanced at the radar. With his right hand, he held a railing. His left hand gripped the wheel. His legs were braced for stability and his rear end was pressed against the seat. He looked through the window, past the ancient windshield wiper, and into the windswept seas of the raging storm. He chuckled as a torrent of spray cascaded over the bridge.

He turned to Carlos and said, "I don't know if you're brave or just crazy, but I'm not ready to meet God just yet, so why don't you say a prayer to get us through this storm."

Carlos nodded and thought, *I am not ready either, but soon* . . . He glanced at the compass and turned to face Mecca, but Miguel had returned his attention to the storm.

Two hours later, Miguel asked Carlos to retrieve the captain. The wind had become deafening and white veins of turbulent water ran through the surface of the sea. The three men were assembled on the bridge and braced for stability as the ship was tossed about.

"Papa, I know you wanted to run before the hurricane, but the storm has overtaken us. We can't hold this heading any longer."

A fast-moving wave struck the ship's starboard side and crashed over the gunwale, flooding the deck. *El Nuevo Constante* rolled hard to port. The ship leveled out slowly as the water returned to the sea. It was becoming dangerously unstable on its current heading.

"It is time to face our demons," said the captain. "Come into the wind, my son."

Miguel turned the wheel and they were soon heading into the southwestern corner of a Category Five hurricane.

The swirling winds inside the storm and its track over the earth made for a confused sea. Sets of huge waves would occasionally come at right angles from the prevailing ones, sending the eighty-foot-long ship pitching up and down and rolling from side to side. The captain was especially concerned about the rolling. Between the sheets of rain, he looked at the container amidship and scowled.

"We're riding heavy," he said. "Miguel, you and Carlos take two flashlights and go below to check for leaks."

The two young men did as they were told and returned to the wheelhouse five minutes later.

"There's a lot of water in the bilge," said Miguel, "and the pumps are running flat out."

The captain frowned again. "It's as if that box is full of lead," he said, gesturing toward the container.

Carlos looked at the captain's face and decided that it was a harmless exaggeration, not an informed accusation.

Two hours later, the men were still in the deckhouse, taking turns at the wheel and watching the ship for signs of stress in what had become seventy-knot winds and thirty-foot seas. The old diesel engine, which had failed twice in the last few days, was chugging away steadily, providing *El Nuevo Constante* with just enough power to steer, run her pumps, and power her electronics.

A gust of wind blew across the sea, a ghastly howl that the three men feared might rip the steel deckhouse from the ship. A crash of metal over their heads and warnings on their instruments told them that the radio mast had broken.

Carlos looked through the rain-splattered windshield. The turquoise waters and puffy clouds of their departure were a distant memory, replaced by a sea and sky blended together into an infinite blackness. Water exploded over the bow as the ship was struck by a relentless onslaught of waves. Carlos glanced down at the container as he'd done a hundred times before, but this time he leapt forward and pressed his hands to the glass.

"What is it?" asked Miguel, who had taken the wheel back from his father.

"One of the chains has broken," said Carlos. His face was a mask of terror. It was the first sign of fear they'd seen in a man who'd never been to sea, much less faced a hurricane.

"There are five more," said the captain calmly. "It's not going anywhere."

Carlos said nothing as he leaned back from the

windshield. Twenty minutes later a second chain snapped on the same side. The container was rocking every time the ship rolled. The remaining chain on the starboard side wouldn't hold for long.

"I must fix it," Carlos said. "I'm going down there."

"No, you're not," said the captain in a reasonable tone of voice. "Any one of these waves could wash you overboard, and we can't turn around in this storm or we'll capsize. Losing that thing over the side might be the best thing for us." He put his hand on Carlos's shoulder. "Your cousin will understand."

"I promised him I would get it to America," Carlos said.

"Your cousin wouldn't want you trading your life for whatever's in that damn box," said the captain.

*I already have,* thought Carlos as he ran from the deckhouse.

## FIFTY-FOUR

KAHLIL WAS BEHIND the wheel when they pulled into a truck stop just after two a.m. The two men had taken mostly rural roads out of Alabama before taking I-75 south through Georgia and into Florida. They'd been driving for six hours straight. They needed gas, bathrooms, and food.

Ibrahim filled the SUV's tank, noting with satisfaction that they'd had to wait forty minutes and pay three times as much as they had just a few days earlier. Kahlil returned from the toilets and the two men walked to the convenience store, discussing how few cars were on the road. Whether it was a function of the late hour or the terror attacks, they did not know. They had never seen America before.

Nor had they seen the unmarked Florida Highway Patrol car parked outside.

State Trooper Shelby Turner was sitting in his blacked-out Dodge Charger, watching the two men leave the white SUV, when he noticed the Texas plates.

*Nothing unusual about that, although I-10 is only nine miles south of the truck stop and a whole lot faster.*

Still, the highway sniper attacks were on everyone's mind, and the last one had happened just six hours before.

*The I-75 truck stop is about six hours from Birmingham.*

The consensus among law enforcement was that the Dallas shooters were probably responsible.

Turner used his cruiser's computer system to search for a roll-call bulletin he'd received about two suspicious men who'd crossed the border, then abandoned their truck in San Antonio. Apparently the feds thought the men might be involved with the Dallas team, if not the shooters themselves. The bulletin came up in a few seconds.

*Two men, Hispanic appearance.* Check.

*Light-colored compact SUV.* Check.

The black-and-white surveillance pictures from the big-box store weren't any good, but the photos from Border Patrol were pretty damn close. The two fellas at the rest stop were clean shaven and better dressed, but it was worth another look.

Turner drove past the white SUV, careful not to stop and risk alerting the subjects. The license plate reader on the right side of his car automatically ran the Texas plate.

*Clean tags. Vehicle is leased to a Pablo Valle of Nacogdoches, Texas.*

It didn't match the names on the men's passports, but he still had probable cause for a stop. He pulled closer to the exit, backed into a parking space with his lights off, and called for backup.

The white SUV passed by two minutes later. Turner let the men reach the entrance ramp to the highway before he pulled out and turned on his headlights. He got on the radio and updated the dispatcher, who informed him that the closest unit was still nine minutes away.

There weren't a lot of cars on the road at that hour, mostly just semis making the overnight run from Atlanta to Jacksonville, so Turner kept a couple of tractor trailers between him and the suspects to avoid spooking them.

He almost missed the white SUV when it exited the highway a few minutes later.

Turner slammed on his brakes and cut across the grass to the off-ramp. The SUV was gone. It was a busy interchange, with a fast-food restaurant, a gas station, and a ramp back onto the highway, but the men had just left food, gas, and the highway. The trooper's instincts told him that they'd gone south on Route 129.

He stomped on the gas and blew through the intersection, calling for more assistance and telling the original backup car to stay on I-75 and look for the white SUV in case he was wrong.

But he wasn't.

Two miles south of the highway, Trooper Turner was doing almost one hundred miles per hour when he spotted the sidelights of a vehicle stopped at a crossroads up ahead. The vehicle moved forward a few feet into the intersection and Turner lit up his warning lights.

A fraction of a second later, he realized it was the white SUV.

His windshield erupted into spider cracks as the .308 rifle round caught him in the shoulder. Turner's subconscious reaction was to jerk the steering wheel to the left, away from the danger, but it was the wrong move.

The highway patrol car skidded off the road and its airbags deployed, but the paramedics on scene would later determine that Trooper Turner had died instantly when his cruiser impacted a stand of pine trees at close to eighty miles per hour.

## FIFTY-FIVE

"WE'VE GOT COMPANY on our six," Fadi shouted. "A red SUV and a white sedan."

The van's tires squealed as he took a sharp right turn followed by a quick left. The SUV and the sedan followed. The van sped up, but, with four passengers, it wouldn't be outrunning anyone.

"Are they after me?" Marek asked.

"Don't know," Jake said. "What've we got for weapons? I lost mine in the square."

Youssef raised the shotgun and Fadi pulled a Glock 19 pistol from his hip. He passed it back to Jake.

Jake addressed the ambassador. "You should move to the front of the van, sir, in case we take any incoming fire."

"Won't the sheet metal stop the bullets?"

Jake shook his head, and the ambassador understood. The CIA man, the man he'd disparaged as a renegade and a cowboy, was willing to stop bullets with his own body to save the ambassador.

"I'm fine where I am," said the ambassador.

"It would be better if you moved forward," said Jake.

"I said I'm fine where I am," snapped Marek, then he added, "Thank you."

The SUV and the sedan were twenty yards behind the van as they approached the Diplomatic Quarter exit. Dozens of heavily armed Saudi Arabian National Guard troops were at the gate.

"Weapons down," Fadi said. "Soldiers up ahead."

"The Delta barrier is up!" Youssef shouted. "No-go on the exit."

"I see it!" Fadi said as he sped up. "Brace yourselves—this is going to be close."

A pair of ambulances raced through the entrance, sirens wailing and strobe lights flashing as they sped to the scene of the car bombing. Fadi swerved behind the second ambulance and floored the accelerator into the oncoming lane of traffic. Two National Guardsmen leapt out of the way as the van raced the wrong way through the entrance. An enormous yellow fire engine blasting its air horns filled the front windshield as it came speeding toward the van. Fadi veered away at the last second and sped down a side street.

Jake looked out the rear window. "SUV just made it through!" he shouted. "The car too."

Fadi turned onto another side street, tires screeching as he cut the corner at high speed, but the overweight and underpowered van was no match for the red SUV and the pursuers quickly closed the distance.

"RPG!" Jake shouted as a man leaned out of the passenger window of the SUV. Fadi immediately swung left, forcing the RPG shooter to hold on as the SUV followed.

"Hold straight five seconds!" Youssef shouted. "Jake, take the driver's side."

The two CIA men fired out the side windows. The 12-gauge shotgun boomed twice as Youssef blasted the RPG shooter. Jake stitched half a dozen bullet holes across the SUV's windshield and it smashed into a parked car. Tires squealed as the sedan swerved around the crash. Fadi made two quick turns and accelerated through the gears as he pushed the van to its limits on a long straightaway.

One of the sedan's passengers held an AK-47 out a window and fired on full auto. Most of the rounds went wild, but a few struck the back of the van. Jake returned fire, but Fadi was weaving through traffic and the shots went wide. The SUV's passengers dumped the dead driver on the side of the road and rejoined the chase.

Jake glanced at the ambassador. He was grimacing.

"You all right?" Jake asked.

"Fine." His gritted teeth said otherwise.

Jake looked down. Marek was holding his right calf and blood was leaking from between his fingers.

"It's a scratch," said the ambassador. "Do your job."

"My job is to get you home alive," Jake said.

He knelt down inside the swaying van, pulled the ambassador's hand away, and lifted his pant leg up over the calf. The ambassador yelled in pain. It was definitely more than a scratch. Jake could see the hole in the back of the van where the bullet had entered.

"I need a med kit!" Jake shouted. "Do we have any—"

"We're losing fuel," Fadi yelled.

The ambassador looked out the rear window and saw gasoline blowing wildly in the van's slipstream.

"No fire," he said between shallow breaths, "but the tank's leaking."

"Down to half a tank!" Fadi called out.

There was no medical kit in the van.

"Give me your ghutra," Jake said to the ambassador.

Jake tore the cotton headscarf in two and pressed one piece into the wound. The ambassador nearly fainted from the pain, but Jake held the compress tight against the tissue and tied the second piece around the calf to hold it in place.

"You're going to be fine," Jake said.

The ambassador nodded curtly.

"Quarter tank!" Fadi yelled. "Start thinking about evacuating to cover."

The gunman in the sedan fired again. Two rounds shattered the van's rear window, but no one was hurt. Jake kicked out the glass and emptied his pistol at the shooter, sending hot brass ricocheting through the van, but causing only cosmetic damage to the car. He took another magazine from Fadi and reloaded, but heavy incoming fire forced everyone to the floor.

The road in the rural Al-Mahdiyah district was straight for as far as the eye could see. The red SUV accelerated in front of the white sedan and a new shooter leaned out of the window with the RPG.

A quarter mile ahead, two black Chevy Suburbans were parked on either side of the road.

"This is it," yelled Fadi. The van could go no faster.

The RPG gunner fired. The rocket-propelled warhead exploded on the road behind the van, briefly lifting its back wheels into the air and peppering it with shrapnel. The van slammed to the ground, fishtailing wildly as Fadi fought to keep it from spinning out of control. One of the rear tires started losing air.

Red and blue warning lights started flashing on the black Suburbans. The RPG shooter reloaded and Jake emptied another magazine into the red SUV, but it kept coming. The van was fifty yards from the Suburbans when blinding streaks of light flashed by the side windows.

The ambassador was mesmerized as he stared out the rear window. The streaks of light converged on the pursuing SUV and tore it to pieces. In just a few seconds it was in flames and nearly unrecognizable.

"What are those lights?" asked Ambassador Marek as they passed the black Suburbans.

"Tracers," Jake said.

The tracer fire moved to the white sedan. Thousands of rounds of armor-piercing 7.62mm ammunition tore through the glass and metal, shredding everything and everyone inside. The sedan caught fire.

The ambassador looked at the two black SUVs. Atop each one was an electrically powered minigun turret and a gunner. A fountain of spent brass cascaded through the air as the rotating barrels spit out three thousand rounds per minute.

"Are those Saudi police?" the ambassador asked as one of the SUVs fell in behind the van.

"Not exactly, sir," Jake said.

The Suburban followed the van for several seconds until both vehicles stopped.

Jake jumped out and slid open the side door. He helped the ambassador out on his wounded leg. Twenty yards down the road, a white Gulfstream G500 was idling on the road with its stairs lowered.

A CIA paramilitary operations officer jogged over from the plane wearing khakis and a black polo shirt. The former Army Special Forces sergeant had a pistol holstered on his belt.

He looked at Jake. "Who're you?"

Jake's ghutra and dark sunglasses covered most of his face.

Jake began to answer, but Fadi interrupted. "He's Diplomatic Security from the embassy."

"Are you coming with us?" asked the PMOO.

It was a no-questions-asked trip back to the States, but Jake still had to clear his name, and he still needed to find Turani.

"I'm staying."

"All right," said the PMOO. He turned to the others. "Let's hustle up, folks. As far as air traffic control knows, the aircraft is having 'transponder issues.' If it's off radar for more than a few minutes, the Saudis are going to come looking for it."

"We're going to need a vehicle," Fadi said. "The van's gas tank is shot to hell."

"Looks like you've got a flat too," said the PMOO.

Jake looked up at the black SUVs. The gunners were

slewing the turrets back and forth, methodically scanning the horizon for threats.

"Can we take one of those?" Jake asked.

The PMOO laughed. "No chance. Those are going to disappear into a warehouse ten minutes after we take off, but you can take that sweet Crown Vic over there." He pointed to a beige sedan on the side of the road. "We were going to torch it with the van and make it look like an accident. Keys are in it."

The PMOO headed for the airplane. "And one more thing. If you guys run into a Ground Branch officer named Jake Keller, call it in. HQ is looking for him."

"Will do," Fadi said. Youssef just nodded.

The PMOO was at the base of the stairs when the ambassador looked at Jake.

"Help me to the plane," said the ambassador. "Thank you for what you did back there, *Jake*. I was wrong to bad-mouth the Agency earlier. Our country needs men like you."

"Thank you, sir. Unfortunately, there's more bad news coming for the Saudis. You might want to pass a message to them if you can."

"Something specific?"

"There's an Iranian colonel who's been working with al-Qaeda. I spotted him in Al-Wadiah yesterday doing reconnaissance for an attack on the town. I don't know the timing, but my guess is very soon."

"I'll mention it," Marek said. "Maybe it will buy us some goodwill. In the meantime, a man called for me a few hours before we left the embassy. He claimed to be a senior official in the KSA government, but he wouldn't give his name. He said he had 'critical information' about the crisis."

The PMOO was waiting at the bottom of the stairs. Marek pulled something from his pocket and handed it to Jake. It was a telephone number.

"Check it out."

# FIFTY-SIX

THE RESIDENTS OF Minot, North Dakota, were used to living a moment away from death. With nuclear missile silos on three sides and an air force base to the north, they knew that their hometown might one day become the front line in a war.

But no one expected it to be the war on terror.

A train of tank cars headed east through the Souris River valley in the predawn light. Many years earlier, oil had been discovered in the enormous Bakken shale formation in the western part of the state. With a rapid increase in crude production and not enough pipelines to carry it, the trains had become a common sight in Minot as they transported oil to refineries elsewhere. Two locomotives pulled from the front, and one pushed from the rear, as the eighty-five tank cars in the middle carried two and a half million gallons of light sweet crude oil.

The oil train rode onto a trestle that crossed the valley just outside of town. The first locomotive was near the end of the 1,800-foot-long bridge when it jumped the tracks. The two-hundred-ton diesel-electric engine plunged ninety feet to the ground and burst into flames. Inertia and a strong coupling caused the second engine to follow. In total, thirty-two railcars crashed to the valley floor, spilling nearly a million gallons of oil.

Thirteen miles to the north, sensor operators at the 91st Missile Wing registered the explosion and the base went on alert for several minutes until an enlisted airman standing guard duty noticed thick plumes of decidedly nonnuclear black smoke darkening the sky.

Burning oil flowed through the valley and flames lapped at the railroad trestle until the metal beams could no longer support the weight of the remaining train cars. The trestle buckled a few feet, then gave way completely, crashing to the valley floor. The rest of the train followed.

Parked atop a ridge one mile away, Paraíso's men watched the dense black smoke and smelled the sulfur-laden stench of the burning oil. What had once been a beautiful valley was now an earthly manifestation of hell.

They looked on with satisfaction and drove off to find some breakfast.

## FIFTY-SEVEN

THE GEOGRAPHICAL DISPERSION of the terrorist attacks had put the entire United States on alert. National Guard troops were deployed to protect sensitive infrastructure. Highly visible police units cruised the highways and roads. Armed citizens patrolled their neighborhoods. Everyone was looking for something, anything, that might prevent another attack.

It was barely seven a.m. when two BearCat armored personnel carriers from the Sacramento Police Department SWAT team rolled up on a semidetached home in the Northgate neighborhood. Sixteen heavily armed officers stepped off the boxy trucks while patrolmen cleared bystanders from the area.

Forty minutes earlier, the cops had received a tip from a neighbor who'd been out walking his dog. As happened many mornings, the four-year-old coonhound had spied a squirrel and maniacally chased it into a neighbor's backyard and up a tree. The dog's owner had followed it into the yard and noticed, through an open curtain, a group of six or seven men inside the house, on their knees, praying.

The 911 operator, frustrated by days of well-intentioned but unproductive calls, testily pointed out to the dog owner that freedom of religion was not only protected by the First Amendment to the Constitution, but also one of the reasons for the settlement of the United States. The caller mentioned that he'd seen a few of the men around while he'd been walking his dog. They all spoke Spanish, but never socialized with the rest of the largely Hispanic neighborhood. The operator was unimpressed. The caller commented that the men looked Hispanic but didn't really act Hispanic. The operator was about to disconnect the call when the dog owner finally mentioned that the house had been vacant for months until the men had moved in . . . one day before the first terror attack.

HALF OF THE SWAT team hugged the outside of the building as they made their way toward the back of the house. The lead officer spied an old wooden deck and warned the others. An average team member weighed 240 pounds with all of his gear, and experience told him that the dry wood was going to creak, if not break, the moment they stepped on it.

The other half of the team stacked up on the front door and waited.

The site commander told the rear team to advance, and the old boards squealed right on cue. A second-floor window shade opened.

A police sniper covering the rear of the house spotted the movement but did not fire. Though the circumstances were suspicious, no crime had been committed by the men inside. The sniper relayed the information to the site commander, who ordered both teams to enter at once.

The rear team crashed the back door immediately, but the team in front needed three swings of a battering ram to open the steel-framed door. A pair of flash-bangs followed, and the last man in the stack was still outside when the gunfire started. The site commander called for ambulances.

Two minutes later the house was clear. Nine police officers had been hit, but only three had sustained injuries thanks to the Level-IV body armor they'd been wearing. Six terrorists were dead, with two more cuffed and clinging to life as police officers carried them outside and attempted to save the men who'd just tried to kill them.

## FIFTY-EIGHT

THE AGENCY PILOT pushed the throttles to the firewall and twenty seconds later the Gulfstream G500 lifted into the air above Riyadh. The men on the ground watched the plane climb steeply, the sun glinting off its white wings.

Jake turned around. The SUVs with the miniguns were already gone and smoke from the burning wrecks was rising into the afternoon sky.

"Thanks for covering for me."

Fadi glared at him. "I was protecting us, not you. You nearly got the ambassador killed."

"You knew I was looking for Turani. What did you think I was going to do, give him a business card and ask him to call me?"

"I thought you were going to help us with our mission and conduct reconnaissance. We're supposed to operate as a team."

"We already had Marek, and Turani might be the solution to this whole riddle."

"We'll give you a ride back into town, but after that, you're on your own. And I'll take my weapon back now."

Jake returned the pistol and the three men climbed into the big Ford sedan. Jake got out once they reached the Al-Suwaidi neighborhood. He stopped at a market to pick up supplies, then walked to his apartment and called the telephone number Ambassador Marek had given him.

The man who answered was cryptic, offered no details, and insisted that Jake meet him alone.

Jake picked at a bag of dried dates and stared at the clock over the sink until it was time to leave.

Though he didn't see anyone on the street, he assumed that the apartment was still under surveillance, so Jake left the lights on and walked to the fire escape door to the back alley. He used a magnet that he'd bought at the market to defeat the alarm's simple reed switch, then placed a strip of duct tape along the open jamb to prevent the lock from reengaging.

He slipped out of the apartment building just before sunset and made his way through the narrow alley and onto the main street.

Jake took a cab to the Al-Wazarat district, a rundown area of Riyadh that had been developed in the 1970s and not touched since. The district was a microcosm of Saudi Arabia's shortcomings and its strengths. Lured by its affluence, and benefiting from its citizens' historic aversion to labor, the neighborhood had become a place where immigrant workers could afford to live and save enough to support their families back home. Bengali, Pakistani, and Indian accents could be heard on the streets.

Jake was on his way to meet a man who'd refused to

give his name, his occupation, or any details of who he was or what he wanted. He might be a productive walk-in agent or a nefarious dangle, a "too good to be true" source intent on feeding bad intel to the United States or flushing out American spies. If Ambassador Marek hadn't asked, Jake never would have taken the meet.

He walked through a dimly lit convenience store and exited out back, checking for surveillance, but the only tail he'd spotted belonged to a feral cat that was scavenging for scraps. Jake kept the knife tucked inside his sleeve as he walked through a dead-end alley where clotheslines were strung between the buildings and trash was scattered over the pavement.

He moved into the shadows and waited until a car with its headlights off drove toward him in the alley.

The large sedan stopped and the driver lowered his window.

"Is there a petrol station nearby?" he asked in Arabic.

"There is one in Al-Murabba," Jake said, "by the Historical Center."

"But I'm going to Az-Zahra."

The code complete, Jake climbed into the passenger seat and the late-model Lexus sped backward out of the alley. The driver was in his early fifties and dressed in a tailored suit. He switched on his headlights when he reached the main road, then headed west, away from the city center.

"My name is Hakim al-Shezza," he said. "I am chief of staff to His Highness Deputy Crown Prince Faisal bin Farah-Aziz al Saud."

"He runs the National Guard," Jake said.

"And is second in line to the throne," said al-Shezza.

"The United States was not behind the attack on Mecca," Jake said.

Al-Shezza carefully followed the speed limit and signaled every turn. Unlike most of the Middle East, where driving was an exercise in natural selection, Saudi drivers were routinely thrown in jail for minor traffic offenses, and tonight would be a particularly inopportune time for a visit from the police.

"How can I help you?" Jake said as they stopped at a red light.

"For many years the king has treated the Saudi people like his children," said al-Shezza. "He has been a stern father, but a good one—raising living standards, improving education, and protecting them from harm."

"It's been a challenging time," Jake said, attempting to build rapport, without yet knowing which way al-Shezza was leaning.

The Saudi nodded. "And now the prince is betraying him. Faisal encourages the king to publicly support the United States, then undermines him with the other ministers. He tells the king to let the people grieve in the streets, but only to weaken his control. The prince's actions are tearing the kingdom apart."

Al-Shezza was about to add something, but the light turned green and he pulled across the intersection.

"Those are serious charges," Jake said. "Why didn't you take this information to the king? Meeting with an American official at a time like this might end with you being tried for treason instead of the prince."

"A man like myself is never alone with His Majesty, and telling anyone else would be fraught with peril. It would put my life, and the lives of my family, at risk. The prince is a very powerful man."

"And his actions are deplorable, but I'm not sure this concerns the United States. You understand that in the current environment, the king is unlikely to believe anything we say."

Al-Shezza pulled to the side of the road.

"You do not care about treason?" asked al-Shezza.

"It's not enough to go to my superiors and ask that we intervene in an internal power struggle. We're trying to salvage the relationship we have."

*Besides, my superiors are out for my head right now,* Jake thought.

Al-Shezza opened his mouth, but closed it without speaking.

"Go on," Jake said.

"Do you not see how this will end? The United States will lose its most important partner in the Middle East when Faisal negotiates another mutual-defense pact for Saudi Arabia."

"I appreciate your concern, Mr. al-Shezza, and the United States wants to keep the kingdom as an ally," Jake said, "but I also understand Saudi Arabia's need for security. With a struggling economy at home and a resurgent Iran to its north, it would be a dangerous time for the kingdom to be unaligned."

Al-Shezza pulled back onto the road.

"Saudi Arabia will not be unaligned. The prince is not

foolish enough to deal with the Russians, but his lies will push the kingdom into the arms of the Chinese."

"That's foreign affairs, not treason."

"It is treason when you do it against the wishes of your sovereign," said al-Shezza. "The prince has been conspiring with the Chinese for years, holding secret meetings in Libya to hide their treachery."

Al-Shezza seemed to be an intelligent man with an important job, yet he was acting irrationally. He'd surely seen power struggles before. Ambitious princes were hardly a novelty, and realigning the kingdom to China when the Saudis believed they'd been attacked by the United States seemed perfectly logical.

"Is there something you're not telling me?" Jake asked.

The Saudi checked his watch as they passed the State Security building. Every light was on.

"I do not fear for my own life," said al-Shezza, "for truth leads to piety and piety leads to Paradise, but I cannot put my family at risk."

Now Jake was interested.

"What if we could protect your family?"

Al-Shezza formed a tight smile. "In Saudi Arabia? Impossible. The prince is far too powerful."

"What if we could get all of you out of the country?" Jake said. "Would you honor your king and the kingdom you swore to protect?"

Al-Shezza stopped the car. "Get out," he said.

Jake stepped out of the car. Al-Shezza pulled forward ten feet, then slammed on the brakes. Jake walked up to the car as the Saudi lowered the window.

"What you propose is far more difficult than you think, for Saudi intelligence has penetrated every facet of our society," he said, "but if you can ensure the safety of my family, then I will unveil before your eyes the most heinous treachery in the history of Islam."

## FIFTY-NINE

"STAY HERE!" THE captain shouted to Miguel. "If that fool wants to risk his life, that's his own business, but I won't lose you too."

The relentless violence of Hurricane Beulah continued as Carlos raced to secure the container. Flashes of lightning were visible in the distance as winds swirled in a deafening concert and rain fell as if from a waterfall.

Yet the greatest danger to *El Nuevo Constante* was not from the wind, the rain, or the bolts of lightning. It was from the sea. The tramp freighter was stressed in ways she'd never been designed for. Often half her length was out of the water as she rose and fell with the waves. The captain worried that the old ship might break her back.

Carlos appeared under the deck lights holding the end of a rope that was tied around his waist. He tied the loose end to the railing and began to make his way forward along the starboard side. Coiled over his shoulder was a long length of heavy chain. He'd taken just a few steps when *El Nuevo Constante* plunged down the face of a steep swell, sending the ship crashing into the next wave. The two men in the deckhouse held their breath as a twenty-foot-high tower of water broke over the bow.

Carlos grabbed the railing with both hands as the water raced down the deck and lifted him off his feet.

"He must be made of steel," whispered Miguel.

The captain nodded. Any normal person would have been washed from the deck and plunged into the sea.

Carlos resumed pulling himself forward as soon as the wave flowed overboard. He showed no sign of fatigue or weakened resolve. Smaller waves and countless gallons of spray washed over him as he approached the container, repeatedly sliding his safety tether forward on the railing and retying it on the other side of the vertical stanchions.

The twenty-foot-long steel box was rocking violently, its right side repeatedly lifting a few feet into the air before crashing back onto the deck.

"He's committing suicide," said the captain.

Carlos attached the new chain to a hard point at the top of the container and ran it down to the deck. The chain whipped wildly in the winds and heavy seas, striking him twice as he worked. He secured the loose end to a thick steel pad eye on the deck and tightened it. The container's rocking began to subside as he cranked the chain tighter. He watched for a minute as the ship crashed through another set of waves, but the container didn't budge. Satisfied, he began to make his way aft, untying and retying his makeshift safety tether as he went.

Though they were still in the teeth of the hurricane, Miguel and the captain looked at each other with wide smiles as their new friend made his way back toward the raised deckhouse. His strength and determination had been inspirational.

But the hair on the back of the captain's neck stood up as he returned his gaze to the sea.

Straight ahead, at the farthest reach of the deck lights, a fast-approaching rogue wave towered fifty feet over the ship. Carlos was timing his moves carefully, retying his tether between the wave sets, but the rogue was out of sync with the others, and Carlos had just untied his safety line.

"Mother of God," muttered the captain.

Miguel pounded on the glass with his open palms, but Carlos was watching his every step as he staggered aft with the loose tether in his hand. The captain sounded several quick blasts on the ship's horn.

Carlos turned and immediately recognized the danger. He dropped to his knees and began knotting the tether around the steel railing, but the wave was unlike any other *El Nuevo Constante* had encountered. The tramp freighter crashed into the wall of water and cut it in half. A thousand tons of seawater crashed down on top of the ship, submerging the deck under ten feet of water.

The seawater raced aft and smashed into the deckhouse, shattering the front windowpanes and flooding the room with hundreds of gallons of green water. The ship's lights flickered and the instruments went dark as Miguel and the captain were swept off their feet. Miguel dragged himself upright. His father was bleeding from his forehead and dazed, but alive. Miguel looked out the windows. Most of the ship was underwater, forced down by the immense weight of the rogue wave.

Yet the old diesel kept turning, the lights stayed on, and the instruments came up. Miguel helped his father to his feet and the two men watched the remainder of the wave wash over the side.

But Carlos was gone.

"There!" shouted Miguel, pointing to the rope tether dragging through the water. It was rigid, like a bar of steel.

Miguel turned toward the door.

"Stop," said his father, putting a hand on his arm. "I don't want to lose you over some stupid pottery."

"This isn't about pottery, Papa. This is about a man."

Miguel raced down the companionway and made his way to the rail. Carlos was facedown in the water, dragging against the steel hull. Miguel grabbed the rope and pulled. The rough line burned his palms as he hauled it in, hand over hand. His shoulders and back felt as if they might explode, but Carlos came forward, one foot at a time. His face dragged through the sea and his body crashed into the hull, but Miguel kept pulling until his friend was halfway out of the water.

Miguel pulled again, but he couldn't get the unconscious man over the side of the ship. Miguel's strength began to leave him and the rough line began to slip through his bloody hands. Carlos was sliding back into the sea when a second pair of hands reached over the side and heaved him onto the deck. The captain used his knife to cut the line from the younger man's waist and raced back to the wheel. *El Nuevo Constante*'s autopilot couldn't be trusted for long in these conditions.

Miguel dragged Carlos into the deckhouse and rolled him onto his side. He coughed several times and vomited the seawater he'd swallowed. After a few minutes, he lifted himself up to a sitting position, wincing as he did.

Carlos looked at Miguel kneeling over him, panting and with blood dripping from his hands.

"Thank you, brother."

## SIXTY

P RESIDENT DAY TOOK his seat in the White House Situation Room. Assembled were most of his counterterrorism experts and a few cabinet secretaries. Not a person in the room had slept for more than three hours in a row since the first terrorist attack.

"Director Kerr and I were just discussing a cooperating suspect from the Sacramento raid," said the secretary of homeland security.

The head of the FBI chimed in. "One of the eight men survived the shootout with the local police. We've determined that more than half a dozen teams were training in Mexico, practicing language and weapon skills, and they all crossed into the United States on the day of the Southern California attacks."

"What's their affiliation?" asked the attorney general.

"They're not Mexican. The suspect indicated that they were part of 'the caliphate.' That would imply Daesh, but our experts think he's either speaking metaphorically, meaning they're simply part of the Muslim world, or it's a red herring. We're leaning toward the metaphorical explanation, as the high level of coordination and sophistication is inconsistent with other Daesh operations. At this point, the suspect is speaking freely and we didn't want the discussion to become adversarial, so we tabled it until follow-up interviews."

"Either way, the attacks have been in the works for months," said the secretary of homeland security. "This was not retribution for Mecca unless the two events were coordinated ahead of time."

"Right now, the evidence suggests that they were not coordinated," the FBI director said. "Our suspect said their timetable was accelerated after the attack on Mecca, and their commander was furious when he heard about the drone strike. They certainly didn't have advance knowledge of it."

"That could just be good operational security," said the secretary of defense. "We don't tell every boot every aspect of every operation for just this reason. What about additional attacks? Is it over?"

"It's not over," said Director Kerr.

"Do we know specific targets?" said the president.

"No specifics," said the director. "As the secretary said, their operational security was good. They all trained together, but only the team leaders knew the missions, and our guy wasn't a team leader. It was tightly compartmented."

"So how do you know it's not over?"

"Headcount and weapons. They were training on rifles, RPGs, explosives, and mortars."

"Mortars?" said the president.

"I've hung a few rounds with our mortar platoons in

Iraq and Afghanistan," said General Landgraf. "They're serious weapons."

"Ed, this is informative, but none of it is actionable," said the president. "How do we track down the terrorists that are still out there?"

"We're making progress, sir. As soon as the suspect told us he crossed into the country with a U.S. passport, we involved State's Diplomatic Security arm. The passports usually cost $20,000 to $25,000 on the black market—"

"They bought counterfeit U.S. passports?" asked the president.

"Not counterfeit, sir. These are the genuine item, issued by the Department of State. Usually it's a consular officer trying to make some cash on the side, but once issued, for all intents and purposes the holder is a U.S. citizen."

"There are checks and balances," said the secretary of state, "but no system is infallible."

"I think we've learned that lesson," said the president.

The FBI director continued. "Diplomatic Security took our suspect's alias and his date of entry into the U.S. and located his passport record. They then created a data set of all the people whose passport applications were approved by the same consular officer."

"There have to be hundreds of legitimate citizens in there," said the director of national intelligence.

"One thousand nine hundred and twenty-seven, to be exact. The officer has been working there a long time. But DS refined the search to passengers who'd crossed into the U.S. from Mexico within the past week and whose passports were approved within a month, plus or minus, of our suspect's."

"And?" said the president.

"State came up with sixty-four questionable individuals. Some were immediately cleared of suspicion based on prior work visas, green cards, or family ties. These people had been in the system for years before they were naturalized. The remaining pool are our suspects, men who appeared out of thin air and immediately became citizens."

"Customs and Border Protection took the list and identified groups that traveled by air to nine cities," said the secretary of homeland security. "Another pair crossed over in a pickup truck at Los Indios, Texas."

Several organizational charts appeared on the wall-mounted video monitors around the room. Each one was titled with the city of entry, and displayed the name and two photographs of each of the suspects.

"The photos on the left are their passport pictures, on the right are from CBP at their respective ports of entry," said the FBI director. "We're running both sets through the Terrorist Identities Datamart Environment for possible facial-recognition matches."

"We think the groups from San Diego and Los Angeles hit the refineries, Sacramento was after Silicon Valley data centers, Atlanta executed the pipeline bombing, and Minneapolis derailed the oil train in North Dakota."

"And the others?" asked the president.

"Assuming we're dealing with three two-man sniper

teams, we have up to twenty-four suspects still on the loose," said the head of the FBI.

"Which foots with the number of men that were training in Mexico," said the secretary of homeland security.

A large monitor at the front of the room lit up with another group of faces.

"These are the men we believe to be at large," said Director Kerr. "Right now, we're executing basic law-enforcement investigative techniques. We're running down rental cars and public transportation from the airports. We've pushed these pictures out to local authorities and—"

"I want to focus on these highway shooters," said the president. "People are afraid to go to work. They're afraid to take vacations. It won't take long for this to strangle our economy."

"We have a lead on the Dallas snipers and are conducting a manhunt for them in Florida."

"These are the two men who shot the state trooper this morning?"

"It appears that way, sir," said the director. "The officer called in their license plate number before he was killed. Unfortunately, the shooters aren't following any obvious pattern. The first attacks were in Dallas, Phoenix, and New York, and those cities went on high alert, but the shooters had already moved on. Based on their predicted movements we saturated other large cities with law enforcement, but the shooters reversed course and hit the smaller cities of Birmingham, Alabama; Palo Alto, California; and Fort Wayne, Indiana."

"So what happened today?"

"The snipers changed their m.o. again. Instead of shooting from overpasses, where people have started watching for stopped vehicles, they parked along highways and shot approaching cars and trucks, and instead of synchronizing their attacks during the morning and evening rush hours, they struck at random times during the day and night, often more than once."

The president scowled. "We need to find these men, all of them."

"We'll get them, sir. We're monitoring CCTV footage and using machine-learning algorithms to try to predict the next attacks. We're also executing critical infrastructure protection plans for the entire country. Local emergency response teams are on a twenty-minute call-out, FBI and DHS SWAT teams and armed CBP helicopters are on alert-five status, and we've deployed manned and unmanned aircraft to conduct wide-area aerial surveillance of the National Capital Region and the highest-profile energy and transportation targets around the nation. The National Counterterrorism Center is coordinating the effort."

"What do you need from me?" asked President Day.

"We'd like to disseminate these photos to the public to enlist their help and restrict the terrorists' freedom of movement," said Kerr.

The president frowned. "The citizens are going to panic when they find out how many terrorists are on the loose."

"Some will, and some will welcome the opportunity to do something," said the FBI director. "Do you remember the mood after 9/11 or on United Flight 93? It was a citizen who discovered the Boston Marathon bomber when every cop and SWAT team in Massachusetts couldn't find him."

"I'm also worried about a backlash against Hispanics," said the president. "These men are all traveling under Hispanic names."

"Respectfully, Mr. President, I think we need to give the public credit for differentiating between terrorist elements and everyone else," said Kerr. "For what it's worth, it was a Hispanic male who turned in the men in Sacramento. From what our experts are telling us, these men are all Middle Eastern, probably Lebanese, based on their photographs and the dialect of Arabic. We're leaning toward Hezbollah because they've been trafficking drugs and weapons through Central and South America for decades."

"Do what you need to do," said the president as he stood to adjourn the meeting. "I've got your backs."

## SIXTY-ONE

A NONDESCRIPT DREDGING SHIP steamed north from the Gulf of Aden. One hundred fifty-three feet in length and sailing under a Panamanian flag, it passed into the Red Sea through the Bab-el-Mandeb Strait, which separates the Arabian Peninsula from Africa. Her crew lounged on deck in the midday heat.

Two Saudi patrol boats and an Egyptian missile boat watched her pass.

Six hundred miles to the north, more than twenty warships from the Saudi Navy, plus Egyptian, Sudanese, Russian, and French naval forces, were searching for the wreckage of the American aircraft that had attacked Mecca. The sonar sets used by the various frigates and corvettes sent pulses of sound through the water until they encountered something dense enough to reflect the sound back. The equipment timed the round trip of the echoes to determine the object's depth, creating a map of the seafloor as the ships followed a predetermined search pattern. If a ship detected something shaped like an aircraft on the seabed, it might be Drifter-72, but if the ship discovered something solid between the surface and the seafloor, it had located an enemy submarine.

A thousand feet below the waves hovered the nuclear-powered USS *Michigan*. The former ballistic missile submarine had been converted many years earlier to a special operations sub capable of carrying conventional weapons and unconventional forces. Her nuclear missiles had been replaced with antiship and land-attack missiles and, for this cruise, a pair of thirty-eight-foot-long dry-deck shelters had been mounted topside behind her sail.

Aided by an emergency-landing transmitter that had revealed Drifter-72's impact point, the *Michigan* had located the downed drone several hours earlier. Inside one of the dry-deck shelters was a remotely operated vehicle capable of recovering objects from the seafloor. Ten feet long, with four independently controlled thrusters at its corners and two powerful claws in front, the tethered ROV looked like a mechanical lobster as it dove to the seafloor.

While most submarines were vulnerable to direct hits from sonar, the *Michigan* had a sonar-masking system that could sense incoming sonar pulses and transmit inverse-phase signals back into the sea on the same frequencies. Sonar waves reflected off the bottom, the surface, temperature gradients, and everything else in the water, presenting an astonishingly complex problem, but seaborne computers had finally attained the speed necessary to continuously solve it in real time. The transmitting ship's sonar set would register nothing until the *Michigan*'s system transmitted additional pulses just fractions of a second later, fooling the surface ship's transceiver into registering clear water all the way to the seafloor.

But the system did not render the sub invisible to all who would cause her harm. The greatest danger to any submarine was from other submarines, which searched passively, listening for the mechanical noises generated by other vessels. As a former ballistic missile platform, the *Michigan* was designed to run silently. Submariners often said that you could only find one of its *Ohio*-class sister ships by locating a hole in the water where there was absolutely no sound. But the ROV tethered outside the sub was designed for research and recovery, not running silent and deep. It would be vulnerable to any direct hits from sonar when working outside the *Michigan*.

The ROV dove repeatedly to the seafloor, retrieving the smaller pieces of Drifter-72 and loading them into one of the dry-deck shelters.

The 560-foot-long *Michigan* hovered directly over the ROV to reduce its sonar signature while it worked. The *Michigan*'s crew fought back their instinct to evade the surface ships and instead trusted their training and their technology to hold position over the ROV.

Once the last fragments of Drifter-72 had been loaded aboard the *Michigan*, the ROV began its final run to the bottom to retrieve the aircraft's fuselage. Once a model of stealth and aerodynamics, the drone's airframe had been badly mangled by the impact with the sea.

The ROV's pilot cracked his knuckles as its work lights illuminated the wreck for the final time. He maneuvered the ROV until one of its mechanical claws clamped down on the drone's airframe.

The *Michigan* began to ascend to a depth of three hundred feet, where divers would exit the sub and lash the wreckage to her hull.

The small fragments carried by the ROV had been light enough for the minisub to raise using only its thrusters, but the heavy fuselage required additional buoyancy. The ROV, usually silent when running on its electric motors, hissed loudly as it vented compressed air into its ballast tanks. The sound was unlike anything from a ship, submarine, or marine mammal as it radiated out from the ROV, but it was a necessary risk. It was picked up by the sonar operators on the *Michigan*.

Ten thousand yards away, it was also heard by a Saudi Arabian attack submarine.

The ROV attempted to ascend, but the drone had settled into the muddy bottom. The ROV pilot expelled more compressed air into its tanks and the airframe began to separate from the muck.

The Saudi sub turned to investigate. The German-made diesel-electric submarine was extremely quiet when running on battery power, and the *Michigan*'s crew didn't notice her amid all the noise generated by the surface ships.

The ROV pilot worked for several minutes, using his thrusters and the buoyancy of the ROV, before eventually pulling Drifter-72 from the seafloor and starting its ascent back to the *Michigan*.

The Saudi attack sub increased speed.

The *Michigan*'s captain was monitoring the progress of the ROV when a call came over the intercom.

"Conn, sonar! New submerged contact bearing zero-six-zero degrees, range twenty-five hundred yards and closing. Probable Saudi Type-209."

"Estimate speed and depth."

"Eight knots, below the layer, maybe eight hundred feet. She's on a constant bearing, decreasing range."

The captain turned to the ROV pilot. "How fast can you move?"

"She'll make three knots and a helluva racket holding the drone."

"Come right, heading one-five-zero," said the captain to *Michigan*'s crew. "Make your depth one thousand feet, speed two knots."

The officer of the deck repeated the instructions back and issued the appropriate orders.

The captain issued the same commands to the ROV pilot. The three-dimensional hunt had begun. If the *Michigan* was no longer above the ROV, the sonar-masking device couldn't shield the ROV from the surface ships, but the Saudi submarine was closing on the spot where it had heard the hiss of the air tanks. If it found the ROV hauling the fuselage through the water, it would discover not only the ROV, but Drifter-72 and eventually the *Michigan* as well.

The two American vessels moved at a right angle to the Saudi submarine's approach. Tension on board the *Michigan* escalated as it dove deep in an attempt to interpose itself between the Saudi sub and the ROV, in case the Saudi submarine chose to explore the anomaly with active sonar.

While the Saudi sub was smaller and more maneuverable, the crew of the American sub was far better trained, and her sensors and weapons were unparalleled. It wasn't a shooting match her crew was worried about; it was what came after. If the Saudi sub found them, the *Michigan* would have to jettison the ROV and Drifter-72 to survive the engagement, and fail in her mission.

"Contact is increasing speed," said a sonar operator.

"Closest point of approach?" asked the captain.

"Four and a half minutes," said the officer of the deck. "Estimate seven hundred yards separation."

"All stop. Hold your depth at five hundred feet," ordered the captain.

There wasn't enough time to dive below the Saudi sub. At seven hundred yards, even the smallest noise would betray the *Michigan*'s existence. Her best bet was to run silent. The ROV pilot brought his vessel to a standstill as well. The tether between the two submarines hung motionless in the sea.

No one moved on board the *Michigan*. If the sub were detected, the Saudis would mine the Bab-el-Mandeb Strait and blockade the Suez Canal. There would be no escaping from the confines of the Red Sea.

Every few seconds, a sonar operator whispered the distance to the approaching Saudi submarine. "Nine hundred yards . . . Eight hundred yards . . . Seven hundred yards . . . Seven hundred yards . . . Eight hundred yards . . ."

The crew of the *Michigan* breathed a collective sigh of relief as the Saudi sub passed by. The *Michigan* and the ROV resumed maneuvering once they were in the Saudi ship's baffles, where passive-sonar listening was much more difficult. A minute later the Saudi boat turned 180 degrees and came around on a reciprocal heading, forcing the American subs to once again cease operations. The Saudi captain searched for another half hour, frequently changing course and depth, until he finally abandoned his investigation and resumed his patrol.

The *Michigan* and the ROV rendezvoused at a depth of three hundred feet. Navy divers exited the submarine and lashed the drone's fuselage between the *Michigan*'s sail and her dry-deck shelters while the ROV was secured inside the starboard shelter. The big sub dove to one thousand feet. With the mangled drone fouling her shape and generating unwelcome noise, the *Michigan* moved at a nearly silent five knots as it headed south toward the shallow strait.

The *Michigan* rose closer to the surface as she passed Farasan Island, just north of Yemen.

It was just after sunset when the dredging ship came to a halt outside the shipping lanes. A crew member took a hammer and climbed down into the hold. He banged on the hull three times. Ten minutes later the banging on the hull repeated itself, but this time it came from the outside.

Two powerful hydraulic rams opened the ship's hull like a clamshell and seawater flooded the hold. The crew lowered a steel cable through the gap and into the depths.

A hundred feet below, the divers from the *Michigan* received the cable and attached it to Drifter-72. The dredging ship winched the drone into the hold as the divers guided it between the two halves of the ship. In twenty-five minutes, the hull was closed, the drone was hidden under a tarp, and the dredging ship was steaming for open water at sixteen knots.

## SIXTY-TWO

AL-SHEZZA SPED AWAY, leaving Jake standing on the darkened roadside. Though Graves had effectively cut him off, Jake's sense of duty compelled him to pass the intel he'd gathered back to headquarters. His only option was to speak with Fadi and Youssef, and not over some burner phone that could be listened to by the Saudi Presidency of State Security. It had to be done in person.

Jake rifled through his pockets. He didn't have enough money for a cab, and the late-model cars common to Riyadh would be impossible to steal without proper tools, so he chose a bearing from the distinctive Kingdom Center skyscraper and started walking.

Though he could pass for a Lebanese or maybe a Syrian with his dark hair and beard, there were few pedestrians out on the hot summer night and Jake felt exposed, finding it difficult to blend into the cityscape. He walked with his head down, continuously evaluating escape routes. Twice he turned down dead-end streets, cursing his isolation from CIA. The detours were immaterial, but they brought his predicament into sharp relief. He was a member of one of the most elite organizations in the world, yet he was walking ten miles through a city he barely knew, in a country where his very presence might get him sentenced to death, to pass information that would be received with skepticism and suspicion.

Jake gripped the knife in his pocket as a motorcycle slowed beside him, but the motorcycle gunned its engine and disappeared down a side street.

When he finally reached Fadi and Youssef's neighborhood, he spent another twenty minutes checking for surveillance, then texted them that he was outside.

"Look at the camera," said a voice in Arabic over the tinny speaker.

Jake looked up and the gate opened. Fadi was waiting at the front door.

"You've got real balls showing up here," he said.

"Ambassador Marek gave me a walk-in before he left," Jake said. "A Saudi national named Hakim al-Shezza. He's chief of staff for Deputy Crown Prince Faisal—"

"He runs the National Guard," said Youssef.

"And he's second in line for the throne," Jake said. "I just met with al-Shezza. He said that the prince is subverting the king and trying to realign the kingdom to China. They've been having secret meetings in Libya. Apparently the—"

Fadi and Youssef glanced at each other.

"This might be important," Youssef said.

"That's why I'm here," said Jake.

"Important for reasons you're not aware of," said

Fadi. "We were briefed two hours ago that a joint task force from the NSA, Cybercom, and the National Reconnaissance Office now believes it's possible that Drifter-72 was hijacked."

"There were satellite transmissions from North Africa," Youssef said. "Specifically, Libya."

"Then Roach and I are in the clear," said Jake.

"Not by a long shot," Fadi said. "The transmissions from Libya are only one possible explanation and al-Shezza's intel is unverified."

"HQ is going to want to know more," added Youssef, "and we can't tell them that you're al-Shezza's handler. The intel would lose its credibility."

"You could be implicating Faisal and the Chinese to exonerate yourself," said Fadi. "Hand al-Shezza off to us. We've been working the Saudi account for years. We'll validate the source and bring him in."

Jake considered his options. Al-Shezza had revealed tantalizing glimpses of information, but he was already skittish, already doubting his decision to contact the United States. And Fadi and Youssef were Saudi Americans. It was part of the reason they were so effective in their current assignments, but it might also frighten al-Shezza, who would question their true loyalties. The prince's aide would be in the wind before he accepted new handlers.

And Jake would lose the only bargaining chip he had.

"That's not going to work," Jake said. "He's done talking unless we get his family out of the country."

"That's a tall order in this threat environment,"

Youssef said. "We're going to need more before we can bring it to headquarters."

"Do we have any assets in Tobruk who can ask around about a Chinese presence?" Jake said.

"None that we can call on without authorization," said Fadi. "Tobruk is a hard-target objective."

"I'll go myself if I have to," Jake said.

Youssef looked at Fadi. "We could set him up with Sharif."

Fadi raised his eyebrows.

"Who's Sharif?" Jake asked.

"Pilot," Youssef said. "He's done some trips for us in the past, mostly black stuff."

"He's also tied the record for low-altitude flight a few times," said Fadi.

"And walked away from each one of them."

"Could he get me to Tobruk?" Jake asked.

"He has an old King Air," said Youssef. "It could get you there."

"We can't have anything to do with this," Fadi said. "If it goes sideways, you're on your own."

"Story of my life," Jake said as he rose to his feet. "Set it up."

## SIXTY-THREE

M IGUEL HAD TORN the skin from his palms pulling Carlos from the sea. He'd wrapped his hands with bandages but done nothing for the pain. There simply wasn't time. His father was exhausted and the ship was handling poorly in the heavy seas and strong winds, barely making enough speed to maneuver. Miguel gritted his teeth as he turned *El Nuevo Constante*'s wheel.

Water sloshed over the deckhouse floor as the ship pitched and rolled, but a few inches of water was the least of the crew's worries. The ship had sustained severe damage from the giant wave that had taken Carlos overboard. The radar and radio had stopped working, the GPS was functioning only intermittently, and the deckhouse windows had been shattered, spraying the other electronics with rain and seawater.

Carlos sat dazed on the floor. "You better not have eaten my burrito," he said weakly. They were his first words in over an hour.

The captain looked down and smiled. The young

man had been foolish to race onto the deck in the middle of a hurricane, but the captain was proud of Miguel, and even himself, for saving Carlos's life. He was grateful for all that had gone right when so much more could have gone wrong.

"The storm is moving away," he said. "You'll get your queso fresco . . ."

"Is the container still there?" Carlos asked, still seated on the floor. Rain blew through the broken windshield.

"Yes, it's there, idiot," Miguel said with a smile. "Your cousin better give you a raise when we reach Houston."

A few rays of sunlight broke through the heavy clouds, revealing the ship's bow for the first time in hours.

"The deck plate is gone!" shouted Miguel. The young man pointed to the hole in the bow that he and Carlos had attempted to patch before the storm. "I'm sorry, Papa."

"Don't blame yourself," said the captain. "We'd already be on the bottom if you hadn't fixed the engine."

Miguel frowned.

"But we are riding low," the captain said softly. "I'll take the wheel. You check the pumps."

His son hurried below with a flashlight. He returned ten minutes later with a worried expression.

"The pumps are working," said Miguel, "but the water is waist-deep and rising."

A medium-sized wave broke over the bow. Most of the water ran harmlessly off the sides, but a hundred gallons washed through the hole in the deck and into the hold.

"We may be approaching a point from which we cannot recover," said the captain. "These waves aren't giving the pumps time to catch up."

The captain scratched the heavy growth on his face.

"We are going to have to dump the cargo overboard," he said. "I'm sorry, Carlos."

Carlos hauled himself to his feet, steadying himself with a railing.

"I risked my life to save that container," he said. "You can't just throw it away."

"And we risked our lives to save you!" the captain said sharply. "Our next stop may be the bottom of the sea with that heavy load aboard. Miguel, go up and see if you can fix the GPS and the radio mast. Once we have our position, I'll make a distress call to the American Coast Guard, then we'll dump the container."

Miguel strapped on a tool belt and left.

Carlos looked through the broken window and out over the ship. *El Nuevo Constante* was indeed riding heavy. Even small waves were lapping at her gunwales, threatening to wash aboard and push her deeper into the sea.

"I am sorry, Carlos. There is always a chance the ship could pull through, but I'm not willing to risk our lives on it."

Carlos stared at the captain, but the older man kept his eyes on the sea.

"Your pottery is probably broken anyway," he said. "Hopefully your cousin insured it."

*   *   *

IT WASN'T LONG until Carlos saw the little satellite icon on the chartplotter start to turn. Miguel had fixed the GPS antenna. The rest of the electronics would probably be back online in a few minutes.

Carlos pointed out the window.

"Is that a ship?" he said.

The captain leaned forward, squinting through the shattered windshield.

"Where?" he said. "I don't see it."

Carlos lifted the bowie knife from the older man's belt and thrust it into his spine.

"There it is," Carlos whispered. "Dead ahead."

## SIXTY-FOUR

THE AUTOPILOT WAS broken on the old Beech King Air, so the pilot asked Jake to take the controls as they cruised northwest in the dark through Saudi airspace.

"I have to make the piss," Sharif said over the intercom, miming the action with his left hand.

"I've never flown before," Jake said.

"Pull to go up, pull up more to go down," Sharif said. "Sorry, old flying joke. Stay at twelve thousand feet."

He lifted an old water bottle from the floor and proceeded to refill it.

"You do good," said the pilot. "You want to keep flying?"

"Sure," Jake said.

"Hold two-eight-zero degrees. Listen for the call sign."

Sharif pointed to a placard on the instrument panel with the plane's tail number on it, then folded his arms across his chest and closed his eyes.

*What the hell am I doing?* Jake thought, and he wasn't worried about flying the airplane. The entire trip to Libya had come together in six hours. Fadi and

Youssef had agreed to bankroll it, but nothing more. They'd wanted complete deniability if it went horribly wrong.

Jake had contacted al-Shezza again and learned that the site of Faisal's operation with the Chinese was actually a hundred miles south of Tobruk, in a land of windswept dunes and Roman ruins. Jake had boarded the plane with cash strapped to his waist, a satellite phone he'd borrowed from Sharif in his pocket, and an old Makarov 7.62mm pistol on his hip. The gun was a Soviet-era relic that was as common as sand in North Africa.

Jake held course and altitude for the better part of an hour until air traffic control called out Sharif's tail number. The pilot's eyes popped open like a mother who'd heard her child cry.

Sharif spoke with the controller and adjusted course, then spoke over the intercom to Jake.

"The flight plan to Al-Wajh? I cancel it."

The pilot turned thirty degrees to the north and began a steep descent toward the desert floor. They were barely a thousand feet above the ground when the faint outline of a dirt landing strip emerged from the sand. There was no control tower and no services. A parallel dirt road served as the taxiway.

"Now it is exciting," Sharif said as he switched on his landing lights and continued his descent.

"Shouldn't we put the landing gear down?" Jake said.

"You should be pilot!" Sharif said with a wide grin, but he left the gear up and kept his eyes on the rapidly approaching ground.

The twin-engine King Air descended within fifty feet of the earth and roared over the strip at 150 knots, leaving a billowing wake of dust in the morning twilight. Sharif killed the landing lights and climbed to one hundred feet.

"The people think we land," he said as he banked steeply to the left.

A minute later he tapped a kneeboard with a chart on it that was strapped to his thigh. "I have special route—we stay south of Egypt and fly at this altitude, we make it to Libya, God willing."

The pilot pulled back sharply on the yoke and the plane jumped. A huge dune passed by twenty feet beneath the plane.

"Close," he said.

Soon they were two hundred feet above the Red Sea, with Sharif flying the plane and Jake scanning for ships with a pair of binoculars. Several times they turned sharply to avoid being spotted by marine traffic. Sharif climbed to three hundred feet as they neared the coast of Sudan. The sun was just above the horizon.

"You make sick?" he asked.

Jake looked at him quizzically.

"You throw up in airplane?" Sharif said.

Jake shook his head.

"We see soon enough," said the pilot. "Bag in door."

The plane crossed a deserted stretch of coastline and Sharif punched something into the navigation system. He began to climb over the rising earth, staying three hundred feet above ground level. They turned gently into a valley and Sharif slowed the plane as a mountain range loomed in the windshield. Closer they flew until the ground and the sky disappeared and the windshield was filled with nothing but mountain. Jake pressed back against his seat.

Sharif banked the King Air sharply to the right and stood the plane nearly on its wing before pulling back on the yoke. Inertia pushed the two men into their seats as the plane narrowly missed rock walls on both sides.

A moment later Sharif repeated the maneuver to the left. The pilot was constantly in motion, adjusting the yoke and the pedals and the propellers. The plane jerked left, up, down, right, right again, hard left.

Jake glanced at the airsick bag.

They skirted the Egyptian border and turned north into Libya, eventually leveling out over the Great Sand Sea, an enormous section of the eastern Sahara Desert. Like the Saudi border with Yemen, it was the type of desert most Westerners envisioned when they thought of the Middle East. There were huge dunes as far as the eye could see. Sharif climbed to five hundred feet above the ground.

"The dunes and the shadows play tricks with your eyes. Is hard to tell how high they are until you hit one," he said. "Trust me."

Jake stared at the pilot.

"Dust storms here also. Impossible to fly through. Engines stop working, no telling up from down. Many crashes." Sharif shrugged. "But good weather so far."

Though barren and desolate, the scenery was still spectacular as they passed over it at 250 knots. Sculpted by the wind, the graceful curves and undulating height of the sand dunes was breathtaking. They passed a small oasis and Sharif buzzed a pair of wild camels, sending the ungainly beasts running for safety.

"In Libya now," Sharif said as they climbed to 2,500 feet. "Not so much air force to worry about. Maybe two or three old MiGs. We overfly site soon."

Twenty minutes later the pilot spotted the ruins and circled once around. Jake was disappointed. He'd hoped to find an overt Chinese or Saudi presence, but the area was empty. A long, straight road lay a mile to the east.

"Can we land on that road?" Jake said.

"Only crash landing," said Sharif. "Roads here very bad."

Half an hour later, they were on the ground with the engines shut down. It was early morning and the tarmac at the former air base was already blisteringly hot. The two men walked to the flight operations office, but Sharif's contact was nowhere to be found.

They found another man inside, sitting on a chair in front of a box fan. He was reading a magazine that was at least a year old, judging by its faded cover and dog-eared pages. He looked up as the two men approached, assessing them and their plane the way a lion might assess an antelope.

Sharif asked for a driver and bodyguard to take Jake south to the ruins. The man recommended his cousins. Sharif negotiated a price of one hundred U.S. dollars for the ride, the driver, and the bodyguard.

Jake took Sharif by the arm and walked out of earshot while the man used the phone.

"Is it smart to use this man's cousins?"

"It is not smart to come to Libya," said Sharif.

"I thought we were going to hire professionals."

"The man I was to speak with is not here. If you refuse this offer, you will have no one."

"I'm used to having no one," Jake said.

"Not here," said Sharif. "There is no government, no laws, no value on human life. Everyone is at war. There is the Libyan National Army and the army of the Government of National Accord. There are half a dozen militias and three factions of Daesh, all fighting one another. There is a difference between being brave and being foolish. Do not be foolish, Mr. Jake."

"Who's winning now?"

"There is no winning in Libya, only degrees of losing," Sharif said. "It's complicated . . . Africa is complicated."

The two men walked in the shade of the hangar. "What should happen here and what does happen here are rarely the same," he continued. "Qaddafi's reign lasted forty-two years. The West instituted one of its famous 'no-fly zones' when it was nearly over, but they didn't send any soldiers, so the country fell into chaos. The two main groups seeking power were the Islamic revolutionaries, supported by Iran, and the socialists, supported by France."

"Were they after the oil?"

Sharif shook his head. "Iran is trying to export the Islamic Revolution around the world. In Libya, they're allied with Turkey and Qatar, working mostly through Hezbollah to supply weapons, training, and intelligence to the Islamists."

"And France?" Jake said.

"France doesn't want the Islamists across the Mediterranean. They each seek to deny the other a base of operations."

"Any other foreign presence?" Jake said. "Russians? Or the Chinese, maybe?"

"The Chinese are everywhere," Sharif said. "They use Africa like an open-pit mine."

Jake nodded. "A lot of competing interests . . ."

"As I said, it is not smart to come to Libya, but you will not be disappointed if you let a single principle guide your actions here."

"What's that?" Jake said.

Sharif stopped walking and looked him in the eye. "Assume that everyone you meet wishes to kill you."

THE TWO COUSINS arrived half an hour later in an old Toyota sedan that was covered in dust. Ahmed stepped out of the driver's side. Gangly and in his late teens, he wore a purple L.A. Lakers T-shirt over faded camouflage pants and canvas sneakers. Hassan emerged from the passenger seat. He was in his mid-twenties and solidly built, with close-cropped hair and a bushy beard. He wore a tactical vest and carried an FN FAL battle rifle in his hand.

The men did not look like cousins.

Jake had asked Sharif to pay the men so they wouldn't see Jake carrying cash and simply rob him on the highway and leave him for dead. Sharif handed over fifty U.S. dollars and told the men they'd get the rest if they brought Jake back alive.

The three men climbed into the car. Hassan was in the backseat with his rifle on his lap.

Sharif leaned through the open passenger window and whispered, "I do not think they will kidnap you."

Jake stared at him as they pulled away.

## SIXTY-FIVE

THE WORD "DESERT" came from the Egyptian hieroglyph meaning "forsaken," and it was a painfully accurate description of Libya. Ten minutes out from the airport, the road was the only vestige of human existence, and not a flattering one. Forty miles per hour was the fastest they could travel over the cracked pavement without chipping a tooth or busting a kidney.

The Arabic language is exceedingly complicated, with individual countries, regions, and even towns often having their own vocabulary and slang. Jake knew nothing of the Libyan dialects, but he had told his companions that he was an amateur archaeologist from the south of France, and Ahmed spoke a little French and a little English, so the two men were able to converse passably. Hassan said nothing.

Ahmed took to calling Jake "Jakeem" and inquired about the West. Jake in turn asked about Libya, gently steering the conversation to the subject of foreign visitors. The young man said there were many foreigners in Libya. There were fighters, terrorists, and soldiers.

Someone in a different line of work might have failed to see the distinction, but Jake understood.

"Have you seen any Russians or Chinese?" Jake asked as he looked out the open side window.

"No Russians," Ahmed replied, "but the Chinese—"

Ahmed switched to Arabic and spoke sharply to Hassan. The car began to slow. Jake looked out the windshield. There was a pickup truck on the side of the road and several armed men standing in the shade of a plastic tarp. Jake drew the Makarov from his waist and checked the safety.

"Put that away," Hassan said in English.

The car stopped fifty feet from the pickup and Hassan stepped out. He left the FAL in the backseat. The men at the pickup truck were dressed in a mix of military uniforms and civilian clothes. They had their weapons angled haphazardly as Hassan approached. He spoke with them for a minute and waved the car up.

Ahmed drove to the checkpoint and passed some local currency to one of the men while Hassan returned to the backseat. The soldiers waved the men through and watched closely as Jake passed by in the little sedan.

"General Nafusa's Libyan National Army," Ahmed said as he checked his rearview mirror. "Dangerous men."

Jake and the others reached the ruins an hour later. He had seen the site from the air, but he'd been so intent on discovering a foreign presence that he'd neglected to appreciate its beauty. He stood in wonder as he looked up at the two-thousand-year-old oval amphitheater. Its exterior was ringed with three levels of intricate stone archways. Between the arches were bas-relief carvings of figures in poses of combat and theater.

"It looks like the Roman Colosseum," he said as he exited the car.

"No lions, God willing," said Ahmed as he removed a second FAL rifle from the trunk, "but there are other predators. I will stay with the car."

Hassan eyed Jake for a moment, then entered the ruins with his rifle.

Jake scouted the site. Tires tracks from heavy trucks were still visible in the powdery sand. He followed them through a long colonnade. With twenty-foot-tall columns on both sides, and paving stones underfoot, it was like a driveway to the amphitheater's main gate.

Jake walked under the grand archway and stepped inside. Two thousand years of dust storms had coated every surface and piled sand in every corner. He continued into the sand-floored arena, to the place where sporting events and circus acts had performed; where gladiators had raced chariots and fought wild animals, and each other, to the death.

He climbed a flight of stone steps at the end of the arena and surveyed the scene from the podium, where the Roman governors had once sat.

The sand floor, the three tiers of seating, the elegant arches and columns. It was magnificent.

And it was empty.

Jake kept searching. The arena would have been the perfect place to conceal a satellite transmitter, but today there was only sand. Behind and below the stadium seats were collapsed walls and columns, hidden rooms and narrow hallways, dozens of places that might have held racks of equipment, but did not.

He wondered if al-Shezza had sent him on a fool's errand.

Jake emerged from a stairway onto the second tier of seats. Hassan was above him on the uppermost level, perched atop a flight of steps with a stone wall around him, scanning the area with a pair of binoculars. It was a commanding view, one that would give him massive advantage against any intruders. Even in a large-scale assault, twenty men could easily hold off a hundred attackers.

Jake searched the seating areas. The steep steps and jagged stone made for perilous walking, but there was little evidence of any recent activity. He climbed to the third level and emerged from the stone stairs next to Hassan. The Libyan glanced at Jake and returned his attention to the binoculars. The big rifle was leaning against the wall.

Jake searched the aisles under the blazing sun, then jumped down through the floor where a set of wooden stairs had long since rotted away. He was in a wide, dark hallway. It took several minutes for his eyes to adjust to the darkness, but he searched the rooms at the north end of the amphitheater, then looped around to the south.

Something caught his eye.

A right angle.

Everything else in the ruins had been worn smooth by two thousand years of windblown sand, but on the floor, behind a crumbling stone wall, was a metal box the size of a thick laptop computer. Its matte tan paint was nearly invisible against the sandstone. There were buttons and a display up front and a metal identification plate on the back, but he couldn't read it in the dim light.

Jake heard Hassan shouting, but the thick stone walls muted his words. Jake took the box and ran to the stairwell.

"Hassan!" he said.

"Get to the car!" said the Libyan. He had the FAL's stock pulled tight to his shoulder.

Jake started jogging for the main gate.

The big battle rifle boomed behind him.

Jake started running.

The FAL fired a second time and Jake drew the Makarov, running with it in one hand and the tan box clutched to his chest like a football.

There were several bursts of automatic gunfire, then two reports from what sounded like Ahmed's rifle. It was turning into a gunfight. Jake ran to the southern end of the amphitheater and heard the little Toyota rev its engine as he took the stone steps to the lower level. He ran through the main gate, but Ahmed and the car were gone.

AK-47 rounds struck the wall a few feet from Jake's head. Stone chips flew through the air as he ran back inside. He was breathing heavily, with his pistol in one hand and the tan box in the other.

"Jakeem! Jakeem!" It was Ahmed. He was a hundred feet away, standing next to the car.

Jake ran to him.

"Where's Hassan?" he asked.

The big battle rifle answered the question. Hassan was still on the upper level, shooting at the unseen enemy. He fired again and received a barrage of automatic weapons fire in return.

"Who are they?" Jake asked Ahmed.

"Maybe Daesh, but probably kidnappers. Sometimes the LNA see a foreigner at the checkpoint and radio their friends."

"We're outgunned," Jake said. "We need to get Hassan and get the hell out of here."

Twenty feet away, Hassan's body slammed into the earth.

A cloud of dust billowed into the air around it.

# SIXTY-SIX

LAW ENFORCEMENT AND highway management authorities across the country had scoured every frame of traffic camera footage for evidence of the sniper teams in action, hoping to identify the vehicles that were being used as the shooting platforms, but the gunmen had been meticulous in their planning, carefully choosing areas without video coverage.

Until now.

An Indiana Department of Transportation traffic camera, installed just two weeks earlier on I-69 outside Fort Wayne, had spotted a black Ford Explorer parked on a highway overpass at the same time the shootings had occurred. It had stopped for only eight seconds, but the footage clearly showed the wreckage that occurred while it was there. The wide-angle traffic camera was unable to capture the Ford's license plate, but a search of surrounding toll-road transactions conducted by the Indianapolis Joint Terrorist Task Force ran the tags of every vehicle able to reach Fort Wayne by the time of the shooting and came up with eighty-three black Ford Explorers. Twenty-one additional blue Explorers were also included to account for what was a common mistake at departments of motor vehicles everywhere.

Of the 104 vehicles in the set, twenty-seven were police SUVs and eliminated immediately by the JTTF. Another sixty-one were registered in Indiana or Illinois and put at the bottom of the priority list, given that the New York shooters had started their slaughter almost six hundred miles east of Fort Wayne. The owners of the remaining sixteen vehicles had their driver's license records pulled and examined. Fourteen of those had accumulated parking tickets or moving violations over the past year, which left two that had seemingly appeared out of nowhere.

FBI and Homeland Security put on a full-court press, querying every toll road database and license plate reader across the nation until they discovered that one of the SUVs had already crossed into Ohio at the time of the shooting.

Which left a single vehicle with New Jersey plates.

Further examination of the traffic databases confirmed that the vehicle had moved along the route of prior shootings.

The authorities had their target. It took less than eighteen minutes for a cashless overhead toll collection system to locate the vehicle heading southwest on the Kansas Turnpike. Eleven minutes later, over a dozen vehicles and a twin-engine helicopter from the Kansas Highway Patrol were closing in on the black Explorer.

Keenly aware that they were dealing with skilled marksmen, and mindful of what had happened to their brother officer in Florida, the KHP units were careful to not give their target any advance warning. An unmarked Dodge Charger police car closed on the Explorer at nearly 120 miles per hour, slowing at the last minute and skillfully performing a PIT maneuver. The police car's front fender nudged the Explorer's rear quarter, causing the SUV to spin briefly out of control . . . until the vehicle's automated traction control system selectively applied the brakes and returned control to the driver.

The KHP car hit its lights and siren, but instead of stopping, the Explorer accelerated. The other police vehicles joined the chase while additional units set a roadblock farther down the highway.

Holes exploded from the Explorer's rear window as the snipers shot at the police. The pursuit vehicles backed off, but the KHP helicopter swooped down with one of its SWAT team snipers hanging his legs out of the open side door. It was something he qualified for every six months, but never in a million years thought he'd ever put to use.

The officer raised his semiautomatic .300 Winchester Magnum rifle and fired five rounds into the Ford's engine compartment. The Explorer coasted to the side of the road, leaking fluids and trailing smoke. A dozen police vehicles converged on it from behind while the helicopter orbited overhead. Twenty-one officers were soon on their feet, standing behind their cars with weapons raised, screaming for the Explorer's passengers to come out with their hands up.

Another round burst through the Ford's side window, but the SUV's safety glass deflected the bullet a few degrees and it flew over the heads of the KHP officers.

But it was the last straw.

The highway patrol officers opened fire with everything they had: 12-gauge shotguns, 5.56mm rifles, .40- and .45-caliber handguns, and another ten rounds of .300 Winchester Magnum. Hundreds of bullets tore through sheet metal and glass, rubber and plastic, flesh and bone.

## SIXTY-SEVEN

A FADED BLACK PICKUP truck spit gravel in its wake as it sped around the amphitheater toward Jake and Ahmed.

"Cover me!" Jake shouted.

Ahmed fired twice, but missed the fast-moving pickup.

Jake ran to Hassan and searched for a pulse, but there was already a large puddle of blood around the Libyan. He'd probably been dead before he hit the ground.

Ahmed fired again and managed to punch a hole in the pickup's windshield. It skidded to a halt and five men jumped out and ran for cover behind a row of thick stone columns.

Ahmed kept them pinned down while Jake lifted Hassan's body into the trunk.

"We need to move!" Jake shouted as Ahmed fired again.

"That's the only way out." Ahmed pointed toward the men.

Jake climbed into the driver's seat of the car.

"Get in."

He threw the tan box onto the seat next to him and

floored the engine just as Ahmed closed the rear door. The little sedan hugged the outside of the amphitheater as they sped over the gravel-strewn ground and away from the men who'd attacked them. Jake swerved to avoid a jagged rock and the right side of the car scraped along the amphitheater, crushing the side-view mirror in the process. Unholy noises arose from the suspension as the wheels plunged into deep holes and bounced over steep ridges. Even a flat tire could mean the difference between life and death.

Ahmed was in the backseat, staring out the windshield as the clatter of AK-47s sounded behind them. A round smashed through the rear window and exited out the windshield, narrowly missing both men. Ahmed jammed the barrel of his rifle through the bullet hole and returned fire. The concussion inside the car was earsplitting as the 7.62mm battle rifle sent bullet after bullet toward the black pickup truck.

Jake took his foot off the gas.

"What are you doing?!" Ahmed spun around. His eyes were wide, his hair disheveled by the wind.

But they could go no farther. In front of them was the colonnade. Its thick stone columns blocked their way.

Jake spun the steering wheel to the right and pulled the parking brake, sending the rear tires drifting over the gravel until he was perpendicular to the amphitheater. He mashed the accelerator, ripping off the other side-view mirror as the car squeezed through an exterior arch and onto the wide stone walkway inside the amphitheater. They reached the main gate a few seconds later and Jake turned onto the colonnade and sped away.

The pickup truck was too wide to follow them through the columns and Jake was already on the access road by the time the kidnappers turned around. He started to turn right at an intersection, when Ahmed screamed for him to turn left. None of the roads were marked and most were little more than hard-packed sand or at best a strip of sunbaked blacktop.

Jake accelerated onto the main road, swerving around broken pavement and trying to put as much distance as possible between himself and the pickup. Ahmed was sitting sidesaddle on the rear seat, his rifle at the ready. The road ahead straightened out and Jake floored it, doing seventy-five miles per hour over a road where forty had once seemed like a dangerous gamble.

"Ahmed!" Jake yelled.

The young man turned. Up ahead was the LNA checkpoint they'd passed on the way in. Jake began to slow the car.

Two of the soldiers stepped into the road and waved their arms in the air.

"Whatever you do, do not stop," Ahmed said.

"Stay down," Jake said.

Ahmed lay across the backseat, clutching his rifle across his chest.

Jake downshifted and slowed to twenty miles an hour.

The soldiers moved to the side of the road.

Jake was thirty feet away when he floored it. The battered old car accelerated slowly, but the element of surprise was in his favor. He was past the soldiers before they could get their weapons up.

But the surprise didn't last long. The LNA troops opened fire and the sound of their AK-47s echoed through the car's open windows. Jake swerved randomly across the road, hoping to deny them a target, but the sheer volume of fire ensured that a few bullets found their mark, chunking into the sheet metal and thudding through the rear window. No one was hit.

There was a pause in the incoming fire as the soldiers mounted their vehicle. A cloud of thick black smoke spewed from behind the diesel-engine pickup as the driver stomped the accelerator to the floor.

Ahmed fired downrange half a dozen times, but the dilapidated road and swerving car sent the rounds wild.

Jake glanced in the rearview mirror. The pickup was moving now, with two LNA soldiers standing in the bed and firing their rifles over the truck's roof.

More bullets smacked into the sedan.

"Left or right?" Jake shouted.

There was another intersection up ahead, and the road wasn't marked.

"Ahmed!" Jake yelled. "Which way do I turn?"

## SIXTY-EIGHT

JAKE LOOKED OVER his shoulder. Ahmed was sprawled on the backseat with a bullet hole under his left eye.

Jake punched the dashboard. Sharif had been right about the dangers of Libya. Two good men were already dead and it was increasingly likely that there would be a third.

Jake was almost at the intersection.

He thought back to when he and Sharif had flown from the ruins north to the airport. Jake had been looking out the window, wondering if they could land on the long, straight road that he was now on. From there it turned . . . *left*.

He swung the sedan hard left—half steering, half drifting over the sand-covered road. The pickup was still behind him, but Jake had opened up a lead and the battered truck with its five passengers wasn't gaining.

Jake grabbed the satphone and told Sharif to expect a hot extract. Sporadic gunfire followed him all the way to the airport.

He crashed into the chain-link gate at fifty miles per

hour. The twenty-foot section of fence smashed the windshield as it tumbled over the top of the car and fell to the ground. The King Air was on the runway, its engines already turning. Jake laid on the horn as he raced onto the taxiway and then the runway, skidding to a halt next to the plane and its open rear stairs.

Jake grabbed the tan box and ran for the plane just as the pickup from the checkpoint stormed through the broken gate.

Sharif stood on the brakes and increased power. Jake climbed up the hinged steps, holding the railing with one hand as he fought the building prop wash. The men in the back of the pickup started shooting.

The big four-blade propellers blew the box from his hands. He looked from the box to the gunmen, then back at the box. It was ten feet behind the stairs.

Jake jumped down and grabbed it. Bullets zipped through the air as he ran back to the plane.

He was barely on the steps when the pickup truck from the ruins sped through the entrance and swerved toward the runway.

The King Air shot forward as Sharif let off the brakes. The two pickup trucks chased it down the runway, firing their weapons relentlessly. Jake closed the door just as Sharif rotated into the air.

The pilot kept the plane a hundred feet above the ground and turned for home.

## SIXTY-NINE

A S SOON AS he landed in Riyadh, Jake took the
tan box straight to Fadi and Youssef's safe house.

"I can't read the characters," Youssef said as
he examined the Chinese writing, "but I recognize the
connectors on the back. It's a component from a porta-
ble satellite terminal."

"Like a satphone?" Fadi asked.

"Except a thousand times more powerful. You'd use
something like this to support a field headquarters, or
establish encrypted video, voice, and data links for a
battalion."

"Or hijack a drone?" Jake asked.

"Yeah," Youssef said. "It has that kind of bandwidth.
We should have the comms guys at the embassy check
it out just to be sure."

"Are you sure you want to be part of this?" Jake said.
"I can handle Graves."

"We don't work for that sonofabitch," Fadi said.
"He won't be able to ignore us."

The three CIA officers returned to the Diplomatic
Quarter wearing thobes, ghutras, and dark sunglasses.

They stepped out of the Crown Vic and Jake noticed a wisp of black smoke rising into the sky from the direction of the embassy.

Two companies of heavily armed Saudi Arabian National Guardsmen had loosely encircled the area with armored personnel carriers and troop trucks, but the soldiers stood idly by as the protesters ran wild. The king had followed Faisal's recommendation and made a pronouncement in support of the United States, but instead of rallying around the king as Faisal had assured him they would, the rioters went crazy. The air smelled of diesel fuel and spent ammunition. Burned-out vehicles and scattered debris littered the ground. The spot where they'd seen Turani was now occupied by a wrecked car with shattered windows and dented sheet metal. A smear of blood trailed from the driver's door to the pavement.

The three men walked among the chaos with Jake carrying the Chinese satellite equipment in a messenger bag slung across his back. Protesters shouted slogans and waved signs. Rioters threw Molotov cocktails at the embassy walls and brandished weapons in the air. Sporadic gunfire echoed through the square.

"I'm not sure the National Guard will be able to stop this without wholesale slaughter," Fadi said.

Four angry men walked by in the opposite direction. One of them clipped Jake hard in the shoulder as they passed.

Jake let it slide.

"Turani may not have started this fire," Jake said as he looked around, "but he's fanning the flames."

The fuel for the fire had actually been building since

the kingdom's inception, with its population caught in a confluence of high unemployment, authoritarian rule, and a lack of basic human rights. The triple miseries had been tolerated by the Saudi Arabian people when the price of oil was high and the nation's coffers full. Successive kings had used lavish social programs and generous stipends to buy their citizens' obedience, and a sharp sword to cut off any dissent.

But as the price of oil fell from $140 per barrel to $30, the government was no longer able to continue its largesse and the population grew restless. The barbaric attack by the United States and the king's humiliating refusal to condemn it were merely the most recent insults to the Saudi people.

And it wasn't just the square in front of the U.S. embassy. Violent outbreaks had erupted across the country, from the Shia ghettos in the eastern provinces to the economic center of Jeddah in the west.

"Where do things stand with al-Shezza?" Fadi asked.

"I need to talk to Graves about getting his family out of the country," said Jake.

"That should be an easy ask after he gave us Libya," Youssef said.

"You'd think so," Jake said.

The Americans stopped talking as they approached several protesters standing behind the skeleton of a burned-out bus. Two of the men clutched handguns under loose clothing. The distinctive front sight of an AK-47 protruded from the bottom of another man's thobe. The rest were standing in a circle, packing blocks of what looked like C-4 into a backpack.

The CIA officers pretended not to notice as they passed, but it was further confirmation that Turani was supplying the rioters. Too many weapons and too many explosives had appeared practically overnight. Sourcing such a large quantity of contraband necessitated the involvement of a state-sponsored organization.

Nearly a thousand demonstrators were in front of the embassy gate. The compound's high walls were heavily charred and pocked from small-arms fire. Further down, another car had been crashed into the wall in an attempt to break through to the embassy grounds, but the thirty-inch-thick reinforced concrete was intact.

The three men made their way through the tunnel and into a secure area of the embassy, where the communications staff examined the satellite equipment.

Jake, Fadi, and Youssef videoconferenced Ted Graves from a nearby conference room. Jake explained how Prince Faisal was subverting the Saudi king and making trips to Libya with the Chinese.

Graves stared at the screen for a few seconds, then yawned.

"Our chief of station briefed us on the DoD joint task force," Fadi said. "We heard it located a satellite that might have been controlling Drifter-72 when it struck Mecca."

"From what we understand," Youssef added, "it sounds as if it might not have been under U.S. control at the time of the attack, and successive iterations of analysis narrowed the transmission point down to North Africa, then Libya, then a five-hundred-square-mile chunk of desert south of the city of Tobruk."

"Which is where I found this," Jake said as he held the box up in front of the camera. "It's Chinese satellite equipment."

"I've got the same thing at my house," Graves said. "I use it to watch television, just like twenty million other Americans."

Fadi was about to say something, but Jake put his hand up to silence him.

"Listen to me carefully, Ted," Jake said. "You may choose to ignore the fact that Roach and I had nothing to do with the attack on Mecca, but you can't ignore all the facts. The blowback from this is pushing the Saudis into the arms of the Chinese. This isn't a coincidence, and we're running out of time to fix it because of your petty bullshit."

Fadi raised his eyebrows and Youssef turned his head. No one spoke that way to Ted Graves.

Graves sat back in his chair, staring at the monitor, with his thick forearms folded across his chest. After a long minute, he said, "We'd have to have someone back here examine the equipment before drawing any conclusions."

Jake leaned forward in his seat and glared at his boss. "We already had the communications team here at the embassy open it up. They said it's a block upconverter rack module for a Chinese Ka-wideband satellite transportable terminal. I'll give you the serial number if you've got a pen handy . . ."

Graves stared into the camera for a few seconds, then reached over and pushed a button on his keyboard. The screen went black.

SEVENTY

THE HELICOPTER BANKED gently through the morning sky as it turned toward the Pentagon. Though the airframe was over forty years old, every bolt, every gasket, and every instrument was practically new and precisely maintained. Though few people could identify it on sight as a Sikorsky VH-3D, almost everyone recognized the olive and white paint job as Marine One, the president's personal helicopter.

The secretary of defense hung up a secure communications handset. "CIA just found Chinese satellite hardware at the terrestrial origin point for the hijacking signal. It's confirmation that China was behind the Drifter-72 strike."

"The stakes are high on this one," said the president. "It needs to be incontrovertible."

"NSA tracked the serial number to a cyber-weapons team in the Chinese PLA," said the secretary. "We're sure."

The president stared out the window as they crossed the Potomac River. Within his gaze were over a million people who undertook life, liberty, and the pursuit of happiness with the belief that their leaders were looking out for their best interests. They trusted that he was managing the threats that they couldn't know about and didn't understand. It was a sobering responsibility, and when it came down to it, he wasn't omniscient and he wasn't all-powerful; he was just a man trying to make the best decisions possible with the information at hand.

"Jay, I'm thinking we should move up to DEFCON-3."

"Yes, sir," said General Landgraf, "but if you're considering military action against China, I would caution that a proportional response would not require the entire U.S. military to go on a war footing. If China sees us spinning up around the globe, and then we hit them, they're going to think that it's just the opening salvo. At that point, the probability that this will escalate out of control increases dramatically."

"You really think they'll just take their lumps if we leave our forces at normal readiness?"

"I do, sir," said Landgraf. "They knew when they started this dance that they might get their toes stepped on. I think once President Chéng realizes that we have proof, he'll accept a proportional reprisal and call it a day."

"Or you could extract a pound of flesh," said the secretary of defense. "Give them a list of demands. Tell them to get North Korea under control, give us new trade terms, back—"

"We'd need an admission of guilt," said the president.

"Of course, sir," said Landgraf. "I'd just advise that we do it without upping our force readiness level."

"I appreciate your perspective, General," said the president, "but we need to take a firmer stand. Just yesterday you told me that China had increased its own military preparedness. What if the Mecca strike was an opening feint to turn world opinion against us before they invade Taiwan or close the South China Sea? We need to let them know that the United States won't tolerate such behavior. We need to draw a line in the sand."

"Sir, we have almost two thousand nuclear weapons on high alert. They're ready for battle at a moment's notice. The Chinese leadership is well aware of the consequences of unbridled aggression."

"It didn't stop them from hijacking our UCAV," said the president, "and I seem to recall that China has a nuclear arsenal as well."

"They have three hundred operational warheads of two to three hundred kilotons each, and they're all in stockpile," said Landgraf. "It's truly a deterrent force."

"General, those three hundred weapons could destroy the United States. I'm going to call President Chéng when we land, but right now I'm ordering you to take us up to DEFCON-3."

## SEVENTY-ONE

P RESIDENT CHÉNG MINSHENG had called a second
emergency session of the Standing Committee.
He waited alone with his thoughts in a conference room where the table legs were carved with drag-
ons' heads and the walls were covered with red and
gold silk panels.

General Wǔ-Dīng was the second to arrive, wearing
a crisp uniform despite the late hour. He took his customary seat across from the president. The others trick-
led in over the next few minutes, each of them taking
note of the general and the president, who were staring
silently at each other.

Premier Mèng-Fù Ru entered last, dressed comfort-
ably in a long jacket known as a *chángshān*. He leaned
against his cane as he eased into his regular seat on the
president's right.

Chéng called the group to order. "I just received an
urgent call from President Day of the United States,"
he said, his eyes still locked on Wǔ-Dīng. "He acknowledged that it was one of their aircraft that attacked

Saudi Arabia, but he claims that it was under the control of a foreign power at the time."

A few people shifted in their seats.

"He claims," said the president, "that China was responsible."

"Ridiculous," said the head of the discipline commission. "They are trying to deflect the world's scorn."

"He claims to have proof of Chinese involvement," said the president.

"What proof?" scoffed Wǔ-Dīng, staring back at Chéng. "A digital trail that points to China? Second Bureau could conjure such an illusion in a matter of hours, and the Americans have had days to create this fiction. Ridiculous, indeed."

"Physical evidence," said the president. "Recovered from a site in North Africa."

Wǔ-Dīng blinked.

"North Africa?" said the chairman of the National People's Congress. "I do not understand how that implicates China."

"He said it is Chinese military equipment that could be used to control an unmanned aerial system."

"What kind of equipment?" asked the chairman of the discipline commission.

"One that is used to transmit high-frequency signals to a satellite."

The room was silent for several seconds.

"Then there is much he has left unsaid," said Mèng-Fù. "The United States would not make such a grave accusation solely on the discovery of a piece of Chinese technology in Africa. We have been operating there for decades. It could belong to any one of our partner governments and the Americans know that."

General Wǔ-Dīng leaned forward, placing his elbows on the eight-hundred-year-old table. "All warfare is based on deception," he said, quoting Sun Tzu. "Perhaps the Americans accuse us to deflect from their own action in Saudi Arabia, or maybe they seek to check our growing influence around the world. Either way, they want something from China."

"Is this true?" the chairman of the discipline commission asked. "Did the American president demand something of China?"

The president nodded. "A full admission of guilt, reparations to Saudi Arabia and the United States—"

Several members scoffed.

"And," continued the president, "he insisted that we back away from the Nine-Dash Line and cut all ties with the Democratic People's Republic of Korea."

"Impossible," said the party secretary. "The United States has purposely made the terms unacceptable."

"And if we refuse?" asked the chairman of the National People's Congress.

"Then they will consider this an act of war," said Chéng. "The president told me that they have once again raised their military readiness condition. They are preparing to mobilize forces."

The eight men looked around the table. Some looked angry, some concerned, but most were perplexed by the American accusation.

It was Mèng-Fù Ru who broke the silence. "It appears as if General Wǔ-Dīng's warning was correct. This is a new and unpredictable America."

"We should have increased our military readiness immediately after the attack on Saudi Arabia," added the party secretary. "Our inaction has only emboldened the Americans."

President Chéng held up his hands in an effort to calm the group. "The United States has made a serious accusation—"

"Which we know to be false!" said the chairman of the discipline commission.

"But if the United States believes it to be true, we may be entering a spiral from which there is no way out," said the vice premier.

"General Wǔ-Dīng," asked another committee member, "how should we counter the American threat?"

"We have the capacity to defend ourselves militarily, of course," said Wǔ-Dīng, "but our goal should be to avoid conflict without sacrificing that which is important to China. If the United States sees that it cannot bully us with these false accusations, it will not act. Yes, they have been emboldened by our hesitation, but we have the ability to avert a major crisis . . . if we act decisively."

"What do you suggest, General?" asked the president acidly.

"We must cement our relationship with Saudi Arabia and increase our Combat Readiness Condition to deter the Americans from doing something foolish."

"Both moves could be highly provocative to an already unstable United States," said the president. "With the terror attacks threatening their domestic security, and the foundation of their global hegemony crumbling, they may feel compelled to act."

"Not if China is prepared!" Wǔ-Dīng pounded his meaty fist on the table. "The United States is exploiting our indecision. The PLA will never be able to protect its citizens if we are afraid to use it." The general lowered his voice. "Gentlemen, my son is an officer, as are many of yours. I do not wish to see any of them die in combat, but if the United States thinks it can impose its will without consequences, it will do so. We must convince them otherwise before the first shot is fired."

*"Si vis pacem, para bellum,"* said the party secretary.

"Exactly," said Wǔ-Dīng. " 'If you want peace, prepare for war.' We must bring Saudi Arabia into China's orbit and secure our petroleum needs for the next half century. We must act instead of only reacting."

"And what 'actions' should we take, General?" said President Chéng.

"Elevate our Combat Readiness Condition once again," said Wǔ-Dīng. "Put our missile boats to sea, increase alert patrols in the air and maritime domains, and put the strategic rocket forces on high alert. Show America that we will not kowtow to them."

"Putting our nuclear forces on high alert has never been done," said Chéng. "Such a move could be threatening."

"That is not necessarily a bad thing," observed Mèng-Fù Ru. "America has lost its way. It will soon become a second Europe, afraid to offend and unworthy to lead. It has become obsessed with the soft at the expense of the hard. We are merely accelerating its inevitable decline."

"And humiliating them in the process," said the president.

Wǔ-Dīng's face turned red. "The United States lost the moral high ground the moment they attacked an ally," he said. "By aligning ourselves with Saudi Arabia, we are only aiding the victim of America's treachery."

Heads nodded around the table.

"This crisis is a chance to assert China's rightful role in the world," said Wǔ-Dīng as he turned to face the president, "but I fear that some do not see the opportunity in front of them."

## SEVENTY-TWO

GRAVES MAY HAVE refused to acknowledge Jake's innocence, but Jake had earned the respect of Fadi and Youssef. He'd also convinced them that Iran and al-Qaeda had joined forces to organize and arm the rioters at the American embassy. Iran had a well-known history of antagonizing Saudi Arabia and the United States, and it wasn't the first time that it had partnered with al-Qaeda to advance its cause. If the violence outside the embassy wasn't stopped, the U.S. would be forced to send in ground forces to ensure the safety of its staff, which would then force the Saudi king to defend his borders. More blood would be shed and the Saudi relationship with America would forever be destroyed, just as Iran intended.

The three CIA officers were in agreement—Turani needed to be stopped.

THE OFFICERS TOOK the tunnel from the embassy back to the townhouse, where they had a commanding view of the square. Finding Turani among the mayhem would be a long shot, but it was the only shot they had. Standing back from the windows in two darkened rooms on the second floor, they used binoculars to scan their respective sectors. Jake focused on the back of the square, searching among the shadows of the desert palm trees where he'd first seen the Iranian.

It was nearly four hours later when Fadi spoke up.

"I've got a possible," he said. "Twenty meters west of Smokey the Chair."

The team had established several reference points over the course of their surveillance, including a chain-smoking old man who hadn't moved an inch as anarchy reigned around him. He was relaxing in a plastic chair as if he were watching a soccer match.

The target was standing at the far edge of the square, near where the CIA team had parked. He was speaking with a man whose head was constantly in motion, scanning the crowd.

"It's him," Jake said.

He rubbed his eyes. Four hours on the glass had given him a headache.

They waited another thirty minutes to see if al-Quereshi materialized, but the al-Qaeda leader was nowhere to be seen.

"Let's do this," Jake said. He didn't want to lose Turani a second time.

Jake and Youssef forced their way through the crowd while Fadi stayed on the binoculars, never letting Turani out of his sight. Only once Jake had established visual contact with the Iranian did Fadi head for the car. Ten minutes later, he was idling at the edge of the square, a hundred feet from the target.

Jake and the others had run through several plans for apprehending Turani and the man who was probably his bodyguard, but the Americans were undermanned and decided to leave the bodyguard instead of blowing the whole operation. In the end, they chose to go with the basics: speed, surprise, and violence of action.

Youssef extended a metal baton as he walked up behind the bodyguard and smashed the man's knee. The bodyguard doubled over. Youssef kneed him in the groin and struck him again with the baton, this time in his gun hand. The guard fell to the ground, out of the fight.

Turani spun around and Jake hit him with a Taser until the two Americans were able to pin the Iranian's arms behind his back and muscle him to the Crown Victoria, out of sight of the Saudi soldiers. Youssef bound Turani's hands with a zip tie while Jake quickly frisked him and stuffed him in the trunk. Twenty seconds after initial contact, Fadi hammered the accelerator and they raced out of the square.

Though Fadi and Youssef's safe house was better equipped to hold the detainee for interrogation, they were still career operations officers in Riyadh. They weren't prepared to risk blowing the legends they'd established over years of working in-country by bringing a prisoner back to the house in broad daylight. They drove to Jake's apartment in the Al-Suwaidi neighborhood.

Three men were standing on the street corner nearest to his building. Though loitering was practically a

Middle Eastern pastime, the men took an unusual interest in the car as it passed by.

"Keep driving," Jake said to Fadi. "Go up to the main road, then turn left. There's an alley around back."

Fadi steered the Crown Vic into the alley. It was long and narrow and felt distinctly claustrophobic under the circumstances. Fadi made a three-point turn at the end and pulled to the back of Jake's building.

Jake opened the emergency exit and Youssef escorted the prisoner into Jake's apartment before departing with Fadi.

Jake stepped behind Turani and cut the zip tie.

"Strip," Jake said in Arabic.

Not only did depriving the man of his clothes ensure that there were no hidden weapons or escape tools, it was also emasculating, weakening the detainee's confidence and his resolve.

Turani didn't move. "I am a reporter for FARS News Agency."

"Is that why you had the armed bodyguard?"

"Saudi Arabia is a dangerous place."

"Thanks to you," Jake said. He pointed his pistol at the man's chest. "Strip."

The Iranian removed his clothing. "You are making a mistake," he said.

"It's you who's made the mistake," Jake said. He pointed to a folding metal chair. "Have a seat."

"A hundred people saw you kidnap me."

"Sit."

Turani sat.

"I bought this chair from a guy selling vegetables on

the side of the road," Jake said as he bound Turani's wrists and ankles with duct tape. "Business was slow because of all the unrest, so I offered him twenty-five riyals for it. He countered at seventy-five, and we settled on fifty."

Jake finished securing Turani to the chair.

"I tell you this not because I think you're interested in the price of used furniture," Jake continued, "but to show you that I'm a reasonable man, that I'm willing to negotiate."

Jake smiled.

"For example," he said, "if you give me the information I need, you can leave here alive."

The chair was directly under one of the recessed lights in the ceiling. It made the suffocating heat in the apartment even worse.

"Let me go now and *you* may live," Turani countered. "Many people saw your reckless actions today. They will find me, and they will find you."

"Like al-Quereshi?" Jake said.

"I know no one by that name."

"You don't know al-Quereshi?"

Turani shook his head.

"How about Mullah Muktar?"

"I know of him, of course, every journalist does, but we have never met."

"You're giving me no incentive to work with you, *Colonel*."

The Iranian said nothing, but his eye twitched almost imperceptibly.

"I know who you are," Jake said. "I know about your relationship with Muktar and al-Quereshi. I know you're working both sides of the war in Yemen. I know everything."

The Iranian stiffened in his seat.

Jake walked over to the window and peeled back the shade. There were more men on the street corner and they were looking in his direction. He searched Turani's clothes for a tracking device, but found none.

"Tell me about 'the deal,'" Jake said, "otherwise, there is no give-and-take here."

"You are the one doing all the taking."

"I gave you the chair and the ability to return to your prior life," Jake said.

Turani said nothing.

"Then let's talk about 'the package,'" Jake said.

Turani looked at the floor before answering. "The package was a shipment of light weapons to Muktar's men. Kalashnikovs and rocket-propelled grenades."

"And the deal?"

Turani hesitated. "Muktar's men were to attack Saudi coalition positions in Yemen in exchange for the weapons and money."

Now that his cover was blown, Turani was trying to appear cooperative, but it was all misdirection. The Iranian was stalling before each answer, crafting plausible lies that would be difficult to disprove. There might even be some half-truths woven in, but they weren't what Jake was after. He needed to know Iran's strategic plan and what it meant for the United States.

Jake folded his arms across his chest and looked Turani in the eye.

"Bullshit."

# SEVENTY-THREE

MPOUND LOTS, BODY shops, and tattoo parlors were the dominant businesses in the industrial neighborhood just off New York Avenue in northeastern Washington, D.C., but inside an otherwise empty warehouse, a very different enterprise was under way.

Workers were stripping three Mercedes-Benz Sprinter vans of all their luxuries, including the passenger seats. Only the rooftop air conditioners remained. Two other men were moving from van to van, applying gold lettering to the side and rear doors of the black vans.

The team leader said to another worker, "The air conditioner assembly is finished on van number one. Give me a hand with the baseplate."

The circular baseplate looked and felt like a forty-five-pound weightlifting plate. The two men bolted it to the floor of the van, then attached a heavy metal tube with a swivel. Finally, a bipod was fitted to the tube with its feet resting on the van's floor.

"Close it up," said the team leader.

With its doors closed, the van's heavily tinted windows concealed the assembly from view.

"Perfect," he said as he reopened the large sliding door. "Hand me the map and let's check the clearance."

The team leader slid the air conditioner housing backward and exposed a three-by-three-foot hole in the roof. Another worker, who was already on top of the van, lowered a twelve-foot length of three-inch-diameter PVC pipe through the hole. The team leader guided the pipe into the smooth metal tube.

"Where's the map?" he said.

Someone passed him a grid map of Washington, D.C., and the leader sat on the floor with the map, a ruler, and a calculator.

"We'll park this one on F Street, halfway between 18th and 19th," he said. "Give me a hand."

The two men adjusted the tube so it was angled twenty-one degrees forward, and six degrees to the right.

"How does it look?" asked one of the others.

The PVC pipe extended cleanly through the hole in the roof.

"Looks good," said the man on the roof.

"Lock it down," said the team leader, "and let's get started on the others."

## SEVENTY-FOUR

ALL THE DATA suggested that Turani was hiding something important, but Jake knew from experience that Iranians didn't respond well to direct questions from strangers, even in regular conversation. It was a cultural practice known as *taarof*, which caused them to circle around an issue instead of discussing it straightaway. Jake also didn't have enough of the picture to use the Scharff technique.

The Iranian would eventually break under interrogation; everyone did. Pain, sleep deprivation, and stress would weaken his resolve. His mind would become dull, his memory cloudy. Prior obfuscations and omissions would be forgotten. Lies would become jumbled.

But Turani had undoubtedly been trained to resist such methods, which would at least double the time that Jake would need to do it properly.

And Jake didn't have time.

He leaned against the kitchen counter and thought hard about what he'd learned. Mahmoud and al-Quereshi had each spoken of a major deal between Shia Iran and Sunni al-Qaeda. If Iran was now supporting al-Qaeda, it was doing so against its longtime Shia ally, the Houthis. But Iran wouldn't cast aside the Houthis and throw al-Qaeda a multimillion-dollar lifeline just so they could fight the Saudis in Yemen and raid a Saudi village. Those were routine activities.

There had to be something else.

Jake focused on the amount of the payment, considering the possibility that Iran had paid al-Qaeda to execute the terror attacks in the U.S., but he'd been told that those were being carried out by Iran's longtime ally, Hezbollah . . .

*What am I missing?*

He decided to attack the puzzle from a different angle. He ignored the amount of the payment and focused on its timing.

The deal had been struck when al-Qaeda was on the ropes, nearly bankrupt.

*Why were they bankrupt?* Jake wondered. *What had changed?*

It was about the same time that political pressure and terrorism-finance targeting had cut off most of AQAP's funding from the Saudis and Pakistan's ISI.

*But why would Iran step into the void? What could al-Qaeda do that one of Iran's Shia allies couldn't? AQAP's capabilities were so degraded that they were effectively shut down.*

Jake knew he was getting closer. He switched angles again to triangulate his way to the target.

*Maybe it wasn't what AQAP could do that was worth millions of dollars, but what they had.*

The organization had been nearly extinct. Government security services had put it under intense pressure, killing its leaders and its planners, cutting off its funding, and disrupting its operations. Al-Qaeda had finally gotten what it had always wanted, but it didn't have the capacity to use it. It was bankrupt.

There had been rumors circulating around the intelligence community and on the black market. In retrospect, ISI had likely started them to give themselves plausible deniability . . . So Pakistani intelligence hadn't abandoned al-Qaeda after all—they'd simply changed the form of their support. ISI had provided the terrorist organization with something in lieu of cash, something it had coveted since its first days.

But al-Qaeda was too broke to use it.

So they sold it.

To Iran.

To a country that relished confrontation with the West.

To a country that was currently prosecuting terror attacks inside the United States.

Jake felt the blood drain from his face as he realized that, before those attacks were over, the U.S. homeland was going to be struck by a nuclear weapon.

# SEVENTY-FIVE

THE SAUDI ARABIAN National Guard command center was modeled after an American one the prince had once visited in Tampa, Florida. Its thirty-foot-high walls were covered with monitors displaying news, video, maps, troop deployments, and other critical information. Rows of long desks, packed with computers and communications equipment, were fully staffed. It was ready for action.

And it was nearly silent.

The staffers were frustrated and confused. They saw Faisal pacing inside a glass-walled conference room. Three senior commanders had requested the meeting to explain to him how dire the situation inside Saudi Arabia had become and provide him with options to fix it.

They wanted permission to do their jobs.

"Your Highness," said the general responsible for border security, "we are severely undermanned. Smugglers of people and weapons are crossing the eastern border at will. Perhaps we could deploy some of the troops that are currently on training rotations?"

The prince continued pacing.

"More weapons are appearing in Riyadh every day," said the general running domestic operations. "Government buildings are being targeted. Saudi citizens are dying." He gestured to a television monitor showing an ambulance racing to the site of yet another car bombing.

"The time available to control these problems is running out," said the general in charge of intelligence. "If we do not address them soon, and address them aggressively, they may spread beyond our control."

The prince stopped pacing.

"My friends, you have said nothing to me that I have not said to the king. Our borders are porous, our streets are unsafe, and civil order is disintegrating before our eyes," he said. "I understand your frustrations because I share them, but—"

Al-Shezza entered the room. "Your Highness, we must depart for your next meeting."

The prince ignored him. "But the king is reluctant to criticize the Americans or enforce discipline at home, and that is his decision to make."

The generals rose from the conference room table to bid the prince good-bye. He was nearly at the door when he turned to face them once more.

"Understand that there is nothing in the world of which I am more proud than this force of Bedouin tribesmen and rural villagers. From the early days of the Ikhwani swordsmen mounted on camels and horseback, it has become the preeminent fighting force in the Middle East, and you men are its soul."

The generals straightened up a little, grateful for the rare compliment.

"I will present our case to the king once again," said the prince. "Thank you for your loyalty."

The three generals saluted as Prince Faisal turned on his heels and strode toward the door, his long white thobe fluttering in the air behind him.

Al-Shezza followed close behind. When the two men were outside, he asked the prince, "Shall I arrange a meeting with His Majesty, sir?"

"Shut up."

The prince's security detail was waiting outside with two black Range Rovers and a dark green Rolls-Royce Phantom sedan. Inlaid in solid gold upon the door was a palm tree above two crossed swords, the emblem of the kingdom. The motorcade sped from the National Guard headquarters.

Al-Shezza spoke again after a few minutes. "Prince Sahib is eager to hear about your conversation with the Chinese. He is waiting at Yamamah Palace."

Prince Faisal continued staring out the window.

The motorcade drove through the gates of the royal palace and past the groves of palm and date trees. A dozen Royal Guards with ceremonial swords stood at attention as the prince entered the palace with al-Shezza. The two men walked to a meeting room far from where the king and his ministers usually met.

"Faisal!" said Prince Sahib as the two distant cousins greeted each other with customary kisses on each cheek. Al-Shezza faded into the back of the room. Sahib had come alone.

"It is good to see you," said Faisal, "but you look tired, my friend."

"The crisis is wearing me down. It is a difficult situation we find ourselves in."

"Security is elusive when allies become adversaries and we are paralyzed by indecision."

Sahib put his hand over his heart. "Please, let us sit."

Faisal shook his head as he took his seat. "I am afraid a deal with the Chinese is not going to happen," he said.

Sahib looked crestfallen. "Do they not see value in our offer?"

"It is not that. In fact, they see a partnership with the kingdom as highly symbiotic—a steady supply of petroleum for their growing economy and a stable ally in the Middle East. Their expeditions for raw materials in Africa have been frustrating and they see us as professionals with whom they can work."

"Are they concerned about the American reaction?"

"They are not afraid of the United States."

"Then I do not understand their reluctance," said Sahib. "It sounds as if we have an excellent basis for a partnership."

Faisal leaned forward in his chair.

"I am afraid it is the king whom they cannot accept."

"His Majesty?" said Sahib, feigning indignation.

"They view him as . . . unreliable in a crisis," said Faisal. "They are concerned about the unrest inside the kingdom. As you know, they value domestic order quite highly."

The two men sat quietly, each reticent to take the next step. Speaking ill of the king's reign had cost men their heads, even senior princes. They had begun a dangerous dance.

"What is their view of the crown prince?" Sahib finally asked. His position atop the Allegiance Council included approving matters of royal succession.

It was Faisal's turn to act surprised.

"It did not cross my mind to ask," he said, "but the crown prince was defense minister through several of the arms deals we negotiated with the Chinese. I believe they respect him as a hard but fair negotiator." Faisal stood from his chair. "But this is a moot point, of course. We have each sworn an oath of loyalty to His Majesty. I will tell the Chinese that we are grateful for their interest but their requirement for alternative leadership is unfortunately impossible."

The two men stared at each other.

"The Allegiance Council is permitted to replace a king who is incapable of performing his duties. I think many would agree that the king is presently . . ."

" 'Incapable' of performing his duties?" Faisal said. "Such a conclusion requires some intellectual flexibility, my cousin. The other branches of the family are unlikely to accept it. They would lose their heads as well as their fortunes if the council's efforts were to fail."

"While I did not foresee the Chinese precondition for a treaty, I have had informal, exploratory discussions about convening the council," said Sahib, "to understand how the other members feel about the path the kingdom is taking."

Faisal raised a single eyebrow. "What does the crown prince know of this?" he asked.

"I have told him nothing. I do not wish His Majesty to accuse the crown prince of being ambitious. I would have kept it from you as well, given your role as deputy crown prince, but your relationship with China made this conversation a necessity."

Faisal looked down at the table. "Do you think the king will go peacefully?" he asked.

"It would be preferable," said Sahib, "but one way or another, he will go."

# SEVENTY-SIX

JAKE WAS CONVINCED that Pakistan had given the nuclear weapon to al-Qaeda, who had in turn sold it to Iran, who'd then given it to Hezbollah to use against the United States. But he couldn't expect Graves and the rest of the U.S. national security apparatus to sound the nuclear alarm based solely on his powers of deduction.

He needed confirmation.

Though he didn't have any evidence, he had deduced enough to try the Scharff technique on Turani. Jake could present a far more complete picture than he really had and hope that the Iranian would confirm questions that were presented as facts and fill in holes without realizing that he was doing so.

Jake pushed off the kitchen counter. Turani was frightened and angry and Jake needed him to calm down. There were times when stress and pain were powerful tools, but they could also impair a subject's memory and his willingness to cooperate. Jake didn't have the time or the resources to verify what Turani would tell him. He needed the man to tell the truth.

"I'm sorry about the incident outside the embassy," Jake said. "Hopefully your friend's knee will heal completely."

Turani said nothing.

"This was never supposed to be confrontational," Jake said. "We were planning to talk with you in Zinjibar, but the team that's been shadowing Muktar for the past several months finally decided to eliminate him during your meeting. I asked them to delay the strike, but it meant that I had to go to Al-Wadiah and wait for you there. Then the Saudi military convoy came through and it didn't seem like a good time for us to be seen together, so I left and came to Riyadh."

Jake ticked off the instances on his fingers as he spoke. He sounded bored, as if he were reviewing a list for the grocery store.

"Then the first time I approached you outside the embassy, the damn car bomb put everyone on edge and we got separated."

Turani was stunned. The Americans had known his every move—even before he'd made it.

"Which is why we were more aggressive today," Jake said. "There are a few things you and I need to discuss, and time is becoming a factor."

Jake gestured to the tape holding Turani's wrists and ankles. "It's never good to start a conversation under duress. I'll remove the restraints if you give me your word as a Qods Force officer that you won't attempt to harm me or leave before we're finished."

"I give you my word," Turani said.

"Thank you, Colonel."

Turani nodded. It might have been an empty promise, but Jake had scored his first victory. By focusing the Iranian's attention on his restraints, Jake had gotten him to confirm his rank and membership in the notorious IRGC brigade—without realizing what he'd revealed.

Jake removed the duct tape and handed the Iranian his clothes. Turani rubbed his wrists and ankles.

"Thank you," Turani said as he got dressed.

"It's a pleasure doing business with a professional," Jake said. Even obvious flattery had been proven to loosen tongues.

Jake looked relaxed as he leaned against the kitchen counter again, but he brushed his elbow against the gun on his hip so he knew exactly where it was in case Turani tried to escape.

"There are many places where our ideologies diverge," Jake began, "but in almost every case I can understand the Iranian perspective. I can appreciate the strategic or the religious reason supporting your actions. The one thing I just can't figure out is why Iran supports Sunni organizations that actively work against the Shia."

Turani was not inclined to cooperate, but the answer was so simple that it would reveal nothing.

"The Quran requires Muslims to eliminate infidels from holy ground," he said, "so Iran has chosen to pursue alliances of lesser evils until America is driven from the Islamic nations."

"Like the United States allying itself with the Soviet Union against the Nazis in World War II?"

"Precisely. Just as America did what was necessary to defeat the greater ideological and strategic threat, we occasionally choose to support Sunni organizations that advance the broader Muslim struggle."

Jake nodded. "I understand it in principle, but how do you justify it when it harms your fellow Shia?"

Turani shook his head. "We support the Shia against all who threaten them. They are our brethren."

Jake scratched his beard. "That's why I'm confused by the situation with AQAP. They were nearly extinct when you bought the Pakistani warhead. You had to know al-Qaeda would use that money to fight the Houthis."

Jake mentioned the nuclear weapon so matter-of-factly that it passed for a statement and not a question. Turani was speechless.

"I understand why you bought it," Jake continued. "I'm realistic about these things, but philosophically, why would you make the Houthis' fight so much more difficult? Was it simply that a weapon to use against the United States was more important than the outcome of the war in Yemen, or is it more nuanced? It's hard for a Westerner to understand."

Turani stared at the floor. All the secrecy, the money, the elaborate cutouts. None of it had worked. The Americans knew everything. He exhaled deeply. He felt as if he might explode if he didn't release the stress building up inside of him.

"It was a unique opportunity," Turani said quietly. "It required ideological flexibility."

*My God,* Jake thought. *It's true.*

"But you could have used an Iranian weapon, instead of paying millions of dollars to al-Qaeda," Jake said, "and the Houthis could have declared victory in Yemen by now."

"Deniability," Turani said. "The radiation will be traced back to Pakistani reactors, not Iranian."

Jake had figured that much out on his own, but Turani had unwittingly confirmed that Iran already had its own nuclear weapons, something explicitly prohibited under the 2015 Joint Comprehensive Plan of Action.

"Does Hakim Walid al-Houthi know you gave all that money to al-Qaeda?" Jake said, struggling to maintain his composure.

Turani hesitated.

"I'm sorry," Jake said. "That's not a fair question and I've been doing all the talking. What would you like to discuss?"

Turani asked who Jake represented and where he'd gotten his information, and Jake played up the impression that the U.S. government was an all-seeing eye that had assets everywhere. It reinforced the Iranian's conclusion that there was no point in hiding any details.

*If only it were true,* Jake thought to himself.

Jake offered Turani a sandwich and a bottle of water, which the Iranian accepted. Turani asked about his ability to leave and Jake told him only that it would happen "eventually."

"Is there anything else you'd like to tell me?" Jake said as he scratched his beard.

The Iranian shook his head.

"Then there is one more thing I need to tell you," Jake said, "about the attacks in the United States. We captured most of the Hezbollah operatives. They've told us everything: the training facility in Mexico, how they purchased the passports, the target list . . ."

Turani returned his gaze to the floor. He was defeated—emotionally, physically, and strategically.

"The United States is in a dangerous frame of mind, Colonel. People at home are sick of the war on terror. They want it to end. There was a school of thought that advocated pulling back and letting the Muslim nations fight it out among themselves, but that school lost out because of years of terror attacks in the West. Like I said, I understand the strategy—like any good army, you're taking the fight to the enemy. But things have changed. The world is about to enter a very dark time."

The Iranian looked up. "I do not understand," he said.

"Do you recall what I said earlier about time becoming a factor? Well, we may have missed the window to save your country."

Turani was sitting on the edge of his seat.

"A reprisal plan has been activated," Jake said.

"Reprisals against Iran?"

Jake nodded. "Because of the nuclear weapon."

For the first time, fear flickered in Turani's eyes.

"A flight of nuclear-armed B-2 bombers is already airborne and in a holding pattern." Jake glanced at the clock on the wall. "If that bomb goes off on U.S. soil, the first B-2 will be over Tabriz in two hours and that will be the end of Tabriz. The other bombers will destroy Tehran, Isfahan, Mashhad, and Karaj."

"The United States would never do such a thing," said Turani.

"You might have been right a few months ago," Jake said, "but there's a new way of thinking in America. If radical Islamists want war with the West, they're going to get it. Our enemies have long used asymmetric warfare to negate our military superiority: suicide bombers, lone gunmen, small boats against large ships. The U.S. was like a big dog playing with a child—patient to a fault because the little one didn't know any better—but the days of proportional responses are over. The days of reckoning are upon us."

Jake leaned forward and looked around, as if he were about to confide a great secret. "Do you know why we attacked Mecca? It was a warning. A warning to the Saudi royal family and others to stop funding radicals. But your supreme leader didn't get the message. He's willing to let twenty million of his own people die just to destroy some easily replaced infrastructure in the United States."

Turani looked ill, his face ashen.

"I'm not a fan of the ayatollah," Jake said, "but the thought of twenty million civilians dying . . . all those women and children . . . It tears me apart."

"I have a wife and two daughters in Isfahan," Turani mumbled.

*I figured you had to have family in one of those cities,* Jake thought. *That's why I made it up . . .*

"This is not a game to me, what we do, you and I," Turani said. "I believe that Iran is on the righteous path, that the infidels must be taught that Allah is the one true God. I believe in Qods's mission."

"Well, that mission is about to fail. If that nuke goes off inside the United States, American bombs are going to turn the Islamic Republic of Iran into a vision of hell. It will cease to exist as a nation. So I'm only going to say this once: If you know anything that might help us stop that weapon, you'd better tell me now."

Turani sighed again. "I cannot be complicit in the deaths of twenty million of my countrymen . . ."

Jake waited.

"There is a man in Mexico," Turani began. He told Jake about Señor Paraíso, Muktar, and the Pakistani ISI. He said that the bomb was small enough to be transported by air, land, or sea. It could be headed to the east coast, the west coast, or somewhere in the heartland of America. He did not know the specific target.

Jake didn't know where, and he didn't know when, but he had confirmation.

There was a nuclear weapon headed for the United States of America.

# SEVENTY-SEVEN

THE PHOENIX SHOOTERS had been busy. After killing six people during their first attack, they had driven the minivan through the night to the technology hub of Palo Alto, California. Parked on a bridge overlooking the Bayshore Freeway, they'd repeated the assault the next morning, ending another eight lives before continuing north on the 101.

Hours later, they had found a target of opportunity in the small city of Petaluma, California. The local radio station had reported that a multivehicle accident on the highway had brought traffic to a crawl. The men crept along in the minivan until they were able to exit the highway and onto a bridge that overlooked it.

They pulled to the side of the road and lowered the van's side window. The shooter fired calmly down the lanes of stopped cars, reloading his rifle three times. With the cars stuck behind the accident, and stereo systems and cell phones drowning out the sound of the rifle, no one realized what was happening until it was too late. In a little more than half a minute, he'd killed thirteen and wounded three. As they pulled away, the two terrorists thought it was a masterstroke.

But they were wrong.

Not only were the assumptions underpinning their hateful ideology deeply flawed, but on a tactical level, they had violated their own policy of never remaining in firing position for more than ten seconds.

They headed for Seattle. It was a critical psychological target, a chance to show the infidels that the hand of Allah could reach them anywhere in the United States. From the Pacific Northwest to the Florida peninsula and everywhere in between, there was no escaping Islamic justice. Paraíso's men had more miles to travel and more people to kill before their mission would be complete.

But U.S. law enforcement also had a mission. And now they had a lead.

Though the Phoenix snipers had successfully avoided traffic cameras on the overpass in Petaluma, the American public had become wise to the shooter's modus operandi and too many people had phoned 911 about a minivan at the scene of the shooting for it to be a coincidence. With the assistance of the FBI's Operational Technology Division, video from nearby cameras was compiled and reviewed until several clear frames were obtained from the footage. Further computer enhancement had yielded a license plate number.

There were hundreds of highways, county roads, and plain old surface streets that the shooters might take to their next destination, and the number of route permutations was astronomical, but a computer model utilized the location of available law enforcement assets and a probability-weighted analysis of the snipers' likely route of travel to design a plan that would cover 85 percent of the roads surrounding Petaluma with the resources at hand.

Less than forty-five minutes after the first shot was fired, every federal, state, and local law enforcement agency within a ninety-minute radius had been alerted. DHS and FBI SWAT teams were activated. Police squad cars, SUVs, and air units were mobilized.

The chase was on.

From urban metropolises like San Francisco and Sacramento to the tony enclave of Walnut Creek, everyone wanted in on the action. Fast-moving police cars traveled down highways and up county roads, past farmland and across towns. Helicopter units from the Sonoma County Sheriff's Office and the California Highway Patrol were scrambled. From north, south, east, and west, the cordon began to tighten around the minivan that had ended dozens of lives and shattered countless more.

The individual police units combined with others as back roads merged into county roads, county roads merged into state routes, and state routes merged into highways and freeways. Soon, packs of police cars and SUVs were traveling together with their lights flashing and sirens wailing. From the airships above, the coordinated ground attack looked like a giant bull's-eye.

Which was exactly what it was.

* * *

HAVING DEVIATED FROM their initial plan by completing two ambushes in three hours, the Phoenix shooters decided to not push their luck by continuing north on the 101 and instead chose to take an easterly detour through Sonoma Valley. Though their ignorance was vast and deep, their operational planning had accurately informed them that the scenic area was part of America's wine country, with a small police force that was more focused on apprehending drunken drivers than resolving matters of national security.

THE MINIVAN WAS twenty minutes from Santa Rosa when a helicopter from the Sonoma County Sheriff's Office first caught sight of it. Driving north on the placid two-lane Sonoma Highway, the terrorists were approaching the retirement community of Oakmont when the tactical flight officer in the Bell 407 vectored the first ground units onto the van's position.

The FBI supervisory special agent running the local joint terrorist task force ordered the police officers to keep their distance until reinforcements could arrive on scene. Though he'd like nothing better than to pull the trigger on the terrorists himself, the SSA hoped that an overwhelming show of force might persuade the "suspects" to surrender peacefully. The men could potentially be valuable sources of intelligence if they were captured alive.

The terrorists drove north at a leisurely forty miles

per hour as two patrol cars and a Chevy Tahoe from the CHP entered the highway from the north. A pair of Napa County sheriff's deputies joined the chase from the east, while a Sonoma County Sheriff's Office K-9 unit closed in from the south.

Deputy Rob Girard and his four-year-old Belgian Malinois were half a mile from the minivan and wary of spooking the suspects when he killed his lights and siren and blended into the flow of traffic.

Which was when a local news helicopter swooped in.

The news station had put the chopper in the air immediately after the highway shootings so it could provide live coverage of the gruesome aftermath to its viewers and listeners. By monitoring local police frequencies, the station had directed the Bell Jet Ranger into the valley where it had spotted the police helicopter flying high above the road.

The news chopper approached the sheriff's office helicopter from behind and followed it until it had located the minivan. The camera operator was hoping to get first-rate footage of the pursuit and the takedown from the gyro-stabilized television camera under the nose.

But the shooters had been listening to the radio, reveling in the horror they'd wrought, when the announcer said that they'd been spotted.

The news chopper descended until it was abreast of the minivan, barely three hundred feet away. Underneath the helicopter, a directional microwave antenna began beaming live footage back to the news station.

The first image viewers saw was of the van's side window being lowered.

A second later the terrorist fired his first shot. Shooting at a moving target from a moving platform was like playing the lottery, but the sniper had a lot of tickets. He fired four rounds before the first one hit the news chopper, right in the cockpit. The Jet Ranger was a tough and reliable aircraft, but the bullet hole in the polycarbonate side window got the pilot's attention. He turned immediately toward the van, thinking he'd cut off the shooter's angle. It was the right move, but the sniper put a lucky follow-up shot into the helicopter's engine intake.

The .308-caliber bullet was sucked into the turbine engine, where it shattered a compressor blade spinning at fifty thousand revolutions per minute. The broken blade triggered a domino effect, destroying more blades, which were then sucked into deeper stages of the engine, causing even greater damage. In less than a second, the engine failed.

Catastrophically.

The news chopper lost power and crashed into the Oakmont retirement community, killing the news crew and three people on the ground. Half a mile back and two thousand feet in the air, the Sonoma County Sheriff's Office helicopter crew saw the disaster unfold.

The minivan's driver floored the accelerator, swerving into the oncoming lane of traffic to pass a slower vehicle and running a compact car off the road in the process.

The sheriff's office helicopter was unarmed, but the tactical flight officer swiftly coordinated the convergence of nearly a dozen ground units onto the speeding van.

Deputy Girard hit his lights and siren and started moving traffic out of the way. He accelerated to eighty miles per hour as he overtook the remaining cars between him and the van. Fully aware of the danger, but unwilling to let more innocents die, the deputy deactivated the airbags in his cruiser and rammed the minivan, hard.

The minivan lost control and swerved off the road into a drainage ditch along the side of the road.

Girard slammed on the brakes and jumped out of his car with a Remington 870 pump-action shotgun. He could hear sirens in the distance, closing in from every direction. The sheriff's deputy took cover behind his vehicle and yelled for the van's occupants to come out with their hands up.

The minivan's driver ignored the deputy, trying instead to pull back onto the road, but the vineyard alongside the road had recently been watered, and the van's tires sank into a muddy ditch. Deputy Girard fired into the side of the van and nine tungsten-alloy shotgun pellets punched through sheet metal and glass, but elicited no reaction from the men inside the dark interior.

Knowing the men were armed and dangerous, Girard decided to wait for backup before attempting to subdue the suspects. The sirens were getting closer when a shot rang out. The deputy felt as if someone had put a blowtorch to his rib cage. He dropped the shotgun and fell to the ground.

The shooter emerged from the van with the rifle in his hand. His partner was already dead from Girard's shotgun blast. The sniper heard the sirens and knew that his time on earth was limited, but a violent death was his destiny, and it would be a pleasure to kill an American law enforcement officer as his last living act.

Girard grabbed a key fob on his tactical vest and pressed a button. His car's rear door opened automatically and his snarling Belgian Malinois jumped down from the backseat and sprinted for the man with the gun.

The terrorist saw the dog and tried to bring the rifle to bear, but the canine was too fast. The seventy-pound dog bared its teeth and leapt into the air from twelve feet away. It caught the shooter's arm and sank its teeth to the bone, yanking the man to the ground as it fell.

The terrorist was in tears, begging for the animal to release him, as other police units arrived and secured the scene. The sheriff's office helicopter airlifted Deputy Girard to Santa Rosa Memorial Hospital, where he received a hero's welcome upon his discharge.

# SEVENTY-EIGHT

W E'VE GOT A clandestine nuclear threat," Jake said as he entered Fadi and Youssef's safe house. He'd left Turani bound and gagged in the apartment.

The two men stopped what they were doing. Jake had their full attention.

"All the pieces fit and Turani confirmed it," he said. He pulled a digital audio recorder from his pocket. "It's either in or on its way to the United States."

In less than four minutes, they had Ted Graves on-screen in a secure videoconference.

"You need to send a CRITIC message," Jake said. It was a special code that would ensure the cable reached the president's National Security Council within ten minutes.

Jake briefed Graves on his theory about the Pakistani nuke and AQAP's miraculous resurgence around the same time it was sold to Iran. Jake walked through the logic and how he'd eliminated other possibilities, then filled Graves in on Turani—everything from how they'd first seen him with Muktar in Yemen to his confirmation of the nuclear weapon headed for the United States. Jake replayed a few sections of the recording.

"I know 'trust' is a term of art to you, Ted, but regardless of whatever issues you and I have had, you've always known that you can trust my analysis. We're looking at a high-probability, high-impact event. You need to move on this, now."

Graves nodded slowly. "So that loose weapon we heard rumors of wasn't really stolen?"

"It was, but it was an inside job. Turani said a radical faction of ISI's S-Wing was responsible. It wasn't a government-sanctioned transfer," Jake said.

"That makes sense, because the Pakistani government knows we'd erase their country from the map if we tied them back to the fallout," Graves said. "Tell me about the weapon. What kind of yield are we talking about?"

"Small, five kilotons," Jake said. "One of their battlefield nukes to offset India's ground forces' superiority. The warhead was built for the road-mobile Nasr missile, but it never made it onto the rocket."

"And the Nasr system isn't deployed," Graves said. "Which is probably why the warhead's theft wasn't noticed. So Iran has a deniable nuclear weapon and has decided to make it the capstone of the U.S. terror attacks . . . Do you have targeting information?"

"The trail goes cold there," Jake said. "Turani said that they trained in Mexico, but he wasn't read in on the delivery."

Graves stood up. "I'll send that CRITIC message now."

"There's one more thing," Jake said. "Hakim al-Shezza, the source who led us to the Chinese hardware in Libya, says he has something else, but we need to get his family out of KSA before he'll talk."

"I need to go," Graves said.

"Ted—"

"Jake, we're a hair trigger away from war with China and there's a loose nuke on its way to the homeland," Graves said. "Whatever the hell it is, I don't have time for it."

The screen went black.

## SEVENTY-NINE

PRINCE FAISAL TYPICALLY would have taken his smaller Gulfstream jet for the short flight between Mecca and Riyadh, but he'd wanted to bring his pet lion with him, so he took the wide-body Boeing 767 he usually flew to his vacation home on the Costa del Sol in Spain.

Al-Shezza was with the prince in his airborne office when Wǔ-Dīng called on a secure line.

"I was just about to call you," said the prince. "I met with Prince Sahib."

"Your minister of foreign affairs?"

"Correct," said Faisal. "Most of our cabinet ministers see our relationship with the United States as a mere remnant of what it once was. They are eager to reach an agreement with China."

"Excellent news, Faisal."

"But I informed Prince Sahib that such a pact was, regrettably, impossible due to Chinese concerns about King Ali's leadership."

Wǔ-Dīng's tone soured. "What would be truly regrettable would be for you and I to invest so much, at such great risk, without achieving the change we desire. Your personal ambition must not become a stumbling block for the negotiations."

"There will be no negotiations with King Ali on the throne," said Faisal. "He is still beholden to the United States. Just yesterday he ordered me to reposition troops based on intelligence he received from the American ambassador. If the Allegiance Council is not compelled to replace him, there will be no agreement with China, and Saudi Arabia will continue to orbit the United States. Your logic was correct, Wǔ-Dīng, but your perspective is too narrow, for Prince Sahib is not only the foreign minister, but chairman of the Allegiance Council as well."

"This is a dangerous bluff, Faisal. Your king and our president communicate directly from time to time."

"Indeed they do, but Ali will be gone before he learns of it."

"Is he not ruler for life?" asked Wǔ-Dīng.

"There are exceptions to every rule. The history of royal succession is one of circumvention, abdication, and assassination. While none of the senior princes would do anything to hurt the family as a whole, the internal politics can be cutthroat."

"It is much the same here," said Wǔ-Dīng. "The Standing Committee derives its power from the party. To the Chinese people, we speak with one voice, but behind closed doors those voices can be sharp. I had a serious confrontation with President Chéng today. Aversion to loss dictates his every move. He must go."

"Hypocrite!" said Faisal. "And you say I am the ambitious one."

"Perhaps," Wǔ-Dīng said with a laugh, "but I think the man was born without a spine. The Americans accused us of hijacking their unmanned aerial system and he began to shake in his shoes. He—"

Despite the luxurious accommodations of the 767, the prince suddenly became very uncomfortable.

"You said . . . You said this could not happen," Faisal stammered. "What do they know? How much have they discovered?"

"A piece of communications gear from North Africa. It proves nothing."

"How can you be certain? Do you even know what it is?"

"I do not, but you need not worry. China has been active in North Africa for decades. The equipment that was used in our operation was chosen not only for its ability but also for its deniability. We used nothing that had not been shared with our African partners. The Americans are chasing a ghost."

"The world is indeed littered with Chinese electronics," said Faisal, "but what about North Africa? Does it not concern you that the Americans are focused there? What if they have traced the command signals from the drone?"

"Impossible," said Wǔ-Dīng. "To do so would be like selecting a single drop of water in the ocean and tracing it back to the river from which it flowed, the stream from which it was fed, and the cloud in which it was formed. Such technology does not exist. The quantum computers we used to control the American aerial system are the most sophisticated in the world, literally destroying their own code if they are tampered with. Once the signals are beamed, they are lost forever."

"I do not share your confidence, General. I was continually amazed by the intelligence the Americans shared with us. There was always a trace that could be found or even inferred by the absence of something else." Faisal sighed. "I long for the times when one's dirty work was done face-to-face."

"You may still have your chance," said Wǔ-Dīng.

"What of President Chéng?" Faisal asked. "What will he do when he finishes 'shaking in his shoes'?"

"What he always does when confronted with a problem. Nothing. He stands like a Terra-Cotta Warrior, fearsome looking, but ultimately hollow."

"I worry that you are dismissing this American accusation too lightly," said Faisal.

"Do not worry about Chéng. What should be concerning you is the strife inside Saudi Arabia. I understand that the violence has spread to Riyadh and Jeddah, and now the Muslim Brotherhood is involved. Might the unrest be approaching the point of no return?"

"I have found that the number of devotees to a cause dwindles dramatically once bullets begin to fly. My men can put it down in an afternoon."

"We must not let the sentiment of the Arab Spring overtake Saudi Arabia," said Wǔ-Dīng. "Discipline must prevail."

"Everything in due time, General. The king's position must be weakened beyond recovery."

"Of course," said Wǔ-Dīng. "You are there and I am here."

"The American accusation concerns me," said Faisal.

"I understand, Faisal, but as I trust your judgment, you must trust mine. Our leaders have done nothing but watch events unfold around them. You and I are about to change the world for a thousand years. Do not worry about the Americans, they will not act without proof."

"But if they find proof, the result will be war."

"Then there will be war."

## EIGHTY

JAKE WAS IN Fadi and Youssef's safe house, furiously pinging Graves's videoconferencing system until the sonofabitch finally picked up.

"This Iranian colonel," Graves said, "is he secure?"

*He's by himself,* Jake thought, *duct-taped to a chair in a ground-floor apartment that's under surveillance by al-Qaeda operatives in the most radicalized neighborhood in Riyadh.*

"Very secure."

"Make sure he stays that way. He's our only link between Iran and this nuclear weapon. Without him, the NEST teams will trace the uranium back to the reactor where it was enriched, and Pakistan will go back to the Paleozoic era instead of Iran. That would be a tragedy on two fronts," Graves said, "unless you like your kebab microwaved."

"You need to focus for one minute on Hakim al-Shezza," Jake said. "His intel helped us link China to the hijacking of Drifter-72, and now he's got something even more significant. Getting his family out of Saudi is a small price to pay."

"I asked State, but they don't want to risk further alienating the Saudi government, so you're going to have to find another way to get the information. Why don't you blackmail him? Threaten to call the prince."

Jake's face tightened. "This guy is a patriot, Ted. He's risking his life to stay in Riyadh and do the right thing. He just wants his family safe. I'm not going to blackmail him for coming to us."

"Don't second-guess me, Keller. I'm here to give orders and you're here to follow them. Al-Shezza is just a pawn in this match. That means he's expendable to serve a greater goal." Graves leaned forward in his seat. "And so are you."

"You know we need this guy, Ted. You're just afraid to put your own ass on the line because State said no."

Graves stared at the screen.

"Listen to me, *Zac*." Graves used Jake's birth name, the name he'd given up when a disastrous mission, and Ted Graves, had forced him to assume a new identity. "There's no statute of limitations on murder, and your fingerprints and your DNA are still on file at INTERPOL . . ."

"Is blackmail your default setting? You know I was on Agency business when that went down."

"No one will believe it," Graves said. "I'll make sure of that."

"I warned you what would happen if you crossed me, Ted. Don't force me to do something neither one of us wants. Don't turn this into a zero-sum game."

The two men stared at each other for several seconds.

"What if I can get al-Shezza's family out another way?" Jake finally asked.

"The United States can't have anything to do with it."

"Don't worry. Your ass will be covered."

Graves leaned back in his chair. "Just don't screw it up, or your ass will be finished."

# EIGHTY-ONE

PRESIDENT CHÉNG MINSHENG rose from bed just after midnight, deeply troubled by the American president's accusation that China had orchestrated the drone strike on Mecca. The two leaders had worked diligently over the years to maintain a peaceful coexistence during China's coming-of-age on the world stage. President Chéng was under no illusion that the two men had become friends, but they had worked in good faith to reach compromises that were fair and just. He trusted the American president.

But had he been foolish to do so?

*What if Wú-Dīng is correct about this being a different America? Had past American cooperation been mere subterfuge to achieve strategic surprise? Did President Day pull us closer only to more easily stab us in the back?*

There were many questions he could not answer.

*What am I missing?*

The president donned a silk robe and entered his private study so as not to awaken his wife. He paced around the room as he pondered recent events.

*An American unmanned aerial system attacked a*

*crowd of civilians in Saudi Arabia, a close ally, but an ally of utility, not of ideals. China is about to enter the same entanglement.*

*The Russians assisted the Saudis after the strike. Are they just an agitator or an instigator, perhaps conducting a false-flag operation to drive a wedge between an increasingly cooperative America and China?*

His mind spun in circles until he stopped in front of a small bronze sculpture of the philosopher-warrior Sun Tzu. Engraved in its base was one of the general's legendary sayings from the fifth century BC.

*To know your enemy, you must become your enemy.*

Of course . . . The president had been thinking about events from China's perspective. What was critical to understanding the American actions was to understand the American motive. What was happening inside America that would drive it to such lengths, to employ such tactics? What was it after?

He lifted a phone on his desk.

"Yes, Mr. President?" asked the voice on the other end.

"General Xiang, please."

The president hung up the phone and resumed pacing. The head of the Ministry for State Security called back a few minutes later.

"Mr. President?" said the general.

"I'm sorry to wake you, General, but there is a matter on which we must confer immediately. I am struggling to understand the motive behind the American strike on Mecca and why they would accuse us of such a thing."

"My staff and I were discussing the same thing earlier this evening," said the general. "It is indeed puzzling."

"As you know, our relations with America have recently been quite good," said the president. "We have spent more time on commercial matters and less time on social and military issues. President Day and I have worked hard to forge a mutually beneficial relationship."

"Your efforts have proven their worth," said Xiang.

"Until now. Why would the Americans accuse us of such a thing? Might this be a pretext for some impending military action, perhaps against the DPRK or in the South China Sea?"

"Our intercepts and our operatives tell us that there is much confusion inside the American government. Their Federal Bureau of Investigation is probing the CIA. Such internal strife renders it unlikely that this was a grand strategic plan executed by the government of the United States. Perhaps we should be asking, what does someone else have to gain from dividing China and the United States? Who is affected most negatively by Sino-American cooperation?"

"Russia," said the president.

"Yes, sir, but also Japan, the DPRK, and Taiwansheng. Strong relations between China and the United States could cause angst for any one of them."

"Is it technologically feasible that one of them hijacked the American aircraft and tricked the Americans into believing it was us?"

"Years ago, Iran boasted that it had spoofed an American Sentinel drone, but it is more likely that the aircraft simply crashed on Iranian soil," said Xiang. "I can tell you that the encryption used to operate our own unmanned aerial systems is highly secure, but that does not mean it is impervious to attack. As you know, the cyber realm is a rapidly shifting battlefield."

"I need you to do two things, General. I need you to review the intelligence take from America over the past few months to see if something we once dismissed is now relevant with the benefit of hindsight. I also need you to find out if the technology exists to hijack another nation's unmanned aerial systems."

President Chéng stopped in front of the sculpture of Sun Tzu once again.

"If the Americans were not responsible for the attack," Chéng said, "then we must ensure our military is prepared; for if the United States truly believes that we attacked another nation in their name, then there will be war."

## EIGHTY-TWO

THE CAPTAIN SLID to the floor as Carlos extracted the knife. Miguel was still outside in the dark, trying to fix the ship's radio mast. He had already reattached the cables. Once he straightened the mast, the other instruments would quickly come online.

Carlos heard Miguel hammering away atop the wheelhouse.

"Try the radar, Papa," said Miguel.

Carlos looked at the radar panel, but could not make sense of the controls. Miguel called again, and Carlos hid in a dark corner of the wheelhouse.

Miguel climbed down from the roof and saw his father slumped on the floor, but the pool of blood was masked by the wet floor.

"Papa!" he shouted as he raced to his father.

Carlos lunged, but he slipped on the wet deck and only grazed Miguel with the knife. The Mexican saw the bloody blade and realized what had happened. He leapt outside the wheelhouse and disappeared into the ship.

Carlos punched the wall with his free hand. He could

not let the prey become the predator. There might be another radio on board, or perhaps a hidden weapon. He stepped out of the wheelhouse in a knife fighter's stance, with the blade up and his chin down.

Miguel peered around the container and watched Carlos in the moonlight, circling the deckhouse with the knife in his hand.

The knife that had killed his father.

Miguel lifted a ball-peen hammer from his tool belt.

Carlos approached the container as a wave broke over the bow and green water washed aft along the deck. He grimaced as he grabbed the railing. Though he'd learned many skills in the numerous Hezbollah training camps he'd attended, clearing a sinking ship with an edged weapon had somehow been omitted.

Miguel withdrew behind the container and raised the hammer over his head, his heart pounding. A moment later, Carlos stepped around the corner, but he was still holding the railing and out of range.

The two men made eye contact. Miguel backed up as Carlos began to advance.

"We saved your life!" Miguel shouted with the hammer held high. "Why did you kill my father?"

"He was going to destroy everything!" Carlos screamed.

Miguel's foot brushed against one of the chains that lashed the container to the deck. A passing cloud blocked out the moonlight, but his many years aboard *El Nuevo Constante* told him that the container's corner was just a few feet away.

He sprinted for the deckhouse.

Carlos gave chase, but the chain caught his left foot and he crashed to the deck.

Miguel was above him in an instant, swinging the heavy hammer.

Carlos raised his hands defensively and the hammer struck his wrist, shattering several small bones. He dropped the knife and screamed in pain.

Miguel raised the hammer again, but Carlos kneed him in the side and knocked him to the ground. The steel hammer clanged against the deck.

Carlos grabbed the knife with his good hand and lunged, cutting a deep gash in Miguel's calf. The Mexican scampered backward, but Carlos plunged the knife through Miguel's foot until it hit the deck of the ship.

He nearly fainted as Carlos twisted the blade.

Carlos leaned over Miguel and pulled his head backward to expose his neck.

"I'm sorry, brother," Carlos said as he raised the knife.

Miguel grabbed a screwdriver from his tool belt and thrust it into Carlos's gut. The terrorist screamed as Miguel worked the handle from side to side to maximize the pain.

Carlos's eyes went wide with rage. He drew the knife back and plunged it into Miguel's neck, severing one of his carotid arteries. The Mexican released the screwdriver as he lapsed into shock.

Carlos rolled onto his side and looked down. His instinct was to pull the screwdriver out, to try to stop the agony, but he left it where it was. He staggered back to the deckhouse. Each step sent flashes of pain through his body.

He found the ship's first aid kit and sat down, panting heavily. Though each shallow breath felt like a dagger in his side, the eight-inch-long screwdriver might have punctured something vital, and pulling it out might do more damage than leaving it where it was. Carlos packed the shaft with gauze and taped it in place, with the handle sticking out of his gut.

He managed to wrap the tape around his torso twice before he passed out.

## EIGHTY-THREE

JAKE TOOK A cab back to the Al-Suwaidi neighborhood and slowly walked the last few blocks. Though it was nearly midnight, the hundred-degree heat kept most of the residents indoors, greatly simplifying his surveillance detection routine. It was not until he reached his street that he spotted two men watching his apartment from a parked car.

Jake approached the car from behind. The front-seat passenger was reading something on his phone. Jake smiled. The bright light would ruin the man's night vision, but the smile faded as Jake noticed that the phone looked like a playing card in the man's massive hands.

Jake kept his face in the shadows as he opened the front door to his building. The air inside his apartment was hot, stale, and smelled of Turani. Jake looked at the clock over the sink, guessing that he'd slept a total of five hours in the three days since he'd left Yemen. His senses were dull, his judgment impaired. Adrenaline was the only thing keeping him going.

But he would be able to sleep soon. Now that Turani was a critical intelligence asset, Fadi and Youssef were coming to relocate him to their more secure safe house. Jake called to warn them about the close surveillance on the street and suggested that they again enter through the alley. Fadi said they were meeting with a forger and would be there at two a.m.

Much had changed in the past few hours, but not all of it was for the better.

Turani realized that he had betrayed everything and everyone that was important to him, including himself. He was horribly conflicted—though he couldn't stand the thought of his countrymen dying in an American nuclear strike, he had become what he had loathed most in the world, a traitor.

"Hands out front," Jake said. He cut the tape holding the Iranian's ankles and wrists in preparation for the transfer.

A car door slammed on the street and Jake instinctively turned toward the sound.

Turani grabbed Jake's wrists and kicked him in the groin. Jake doubled over and Turani landed an elbow strike to the back of Jake's neck, sending him sprawling on the ground.

The Makarov tumbled from Jake's waistband.

The Iranian lunged for the pistol, but Jake grabbed his foot and wrenched it sideways. The two men exchanged several blows to the body and head until the Iranian broke free and scrambled across the floor.

Jake got to his feet, but Turani had the gun up, and his finger on the trigger.

## EIGHTY-FOUR

"MR. PRESIDENT," SAID the secretary of homeland security, "we are doing everything we can to stop that weapon, but it's imperative that you leave the White House. We have intel corroborating a nuclear weapon inside of, or at least en route to, the United States, and no leads on the nine terrorists who flew into Dulles. All the data point toward D.C. being the target."

"It's not that I don't know the facts," said the president. "It's that I don't care."

"Dammit, Bill, if a nuclear weapon goes off inside the United States, you're going to need to talk the American people off the ledge. They're going to need their commander in chief to reassure them that the United States will emerge from this stronger than ever, and you can't do that if you're dead. You'd damn well better care."

The president and the secretary had been friends and colleagues for decades, but she hadn't spoken to him like that since he'd won the election.

"I'm sorry, Mr. President," she said out of respect for the office.

"It was a poor attempt on my part to defuse the pressure," he said. "I do care. Just a few minutes ago, I elevated us to DEFCON-2 worldwide, no exceptions. And even though it's absolutely prudent for the country's leadership to decamp from the most likely target, that group isn't going to include me. If I flee the White House, the terrorists have already scored a major victory. We always tell people to carry on with their daily lives in the face of terrorist threats. We say it because if we don't, people will decide to skip work, or not buy that car they were thinking about, or stay home instead of trying a new restaurant, and our economy will be finished. How many trillions of dollars have we spent on counterterrorism since 9/11? Afghanistan, Iraq, the very existence of your agency . . . It was the greatest victory of asymmetric warfare in history, but this country is resilient. Part of what makes the fabric of the United States so strong is that it's not dependent upon any one person or any one branch of government. We're all replaceable, and that's a good thing."

After a respectful pause, Director Kerr of the FBI spoke up. "Sir, FBI, Secret Service, DHS, Capitol Police, Joint Force Headquarters, and the Metro Police are all on high alert. The airports and train and bus stations are heavy with security and everyone is equipped with radiation detectors. The city is practically on lockdown, yet I still agree with the secretary about your safety. Killing a president would hand the terrorists the ultimate public relations victory. Those who'd previously seen no path to defeating the Great Satan would be emboldened. Recruitment and fund-raising would explode."

"I know, Ed. I know," said President Day. He looked at General Landgraf. "What's your experience been, Jay? Does leading from the front help the troops' morale?"

"Sir, when I was a colonel, I used to ride out on patrol from time to time to assess readiness and morale, to get a feel for the battlespace. More than once we were engaged by the enemy. The effect on the men was multidimensional. They loved seeing the old man out there in full battle rattle, with an M-4 rifle and a Kevlar helmet, just like them. It was like a shot of adrenaline for the troops."

The president nodded.

"But there were other effects as well," continued the general. "Nobody wanted to be the platoon leader that got the colonel killed, so, more often than not, they ended up taking me through grids that had already been cleared. I eventually concluded that my presence negatively affected the task at hand. The men were more worried about keeping me safe than executing their missions, and I ended up getting a watered-down view of what was happening. I still did the occasional trip to the front and it would get around that the old man 'still had it,' but I cut that out once I got my first star. There were too many decisions to be made, and I'd accumulated too much experience to risk getting killed doing an infantryman's job. Don't get me wrong, I think of every one of those soldiers like they're my own kids, but there came a point where I realized that what was between my ears was more important than my ability to lay down effective fire. I needed to be around to lead a war, not capture a street corner in Balad."

"So you think I should leave D.C.?"

"Yes, sir, I do. As the secretary said, we have CIA intel on the existence of a nuclear weapon targeting the United States, and Diplomatic Security has identified a nine-man cell of highly trained terrorists in the Washington, D.C., area. That's two unrelated sources pointing toward an imminent attack. New York has always been the terrorists' primary target, but the city has made itself the hardest target around. The bottom line, Mr. President, is that there are no higher-profile targets than the White House and the president. I think if the former were destroyed and the latter appeared on television an hour later, it would provide critical comfort and stability for a gravely wounded nation. The people would thank you for relocating."

The president looked around the room, staring into the eyes of each of his key leaders for a few seconds until he settled on the secretary of homeland security.

"You're right," he said. "You're all right. They're coming to D.C. and, given the size of the weapon, they won't be able to take out more than a single target. The White House makes sense."

"But you're not going to leave, are you?"

"No. I'm not. It's not rational, but I need to be here."

"Will you at least work from the emergency operations center?" she asked.

The president nodded. "Everyone who isn't down in

the PEOC with me relocates to Mount Weather, or at least outside of D.C."

"We'll execute the continuity-of-operations plan," she said, "but the Secret Service will still be on the surface."

"We all have our jobs to do."

## EIGHTY-FIVE

T URANI HAD THE pistol pointed at Jake's chest.

"I am going to leave," Turani said, "and you are going to live because you have treated me with respect."

Jake took a step toward the Iranian.

"Do not mistake my action for emotion," Turani said. "I will shoot you like a dog if you take another step."

He had the gun up in a two-handed shooting stance. From ten feet away, he couldn't miss.

Jake slowly raised his hands . . . and leapt at Turani.

The Iranian pulled the trigger and the weapon flinched in his hands as he anticipated the recoil.

But nothing happened.

Jake grabbed the pistol with both hands and planted a leg behind Turani. Jake twisted the weapon loose and knocked the Iranian backward to the floor.

Jake pointed the gun at Turani.

"The Makarov has a safety," Jake said, "unlike the PC-9 you probably trained on in the IRGC."

Jake flicked a small lever on the slide. "Now it will fire."

Turani grimaced, mortified by such a careless mistake.

"Turn around and get on your knees," Jake said.

"You do not need to do this," Turani pleaded. "I meant you no harm."

"Hands on the wall," Jake said.

Turani faced the wall, anticipating his imminent execution.

Jake put him in a sleeper hold and the Iranian stopped struggling after a few seconds. Jake eased him to the floor, then bound his wrists and ankles with a dozen wraps of duct tape.

Turani began to regain consciousness as the blood flow to his brain resumed.

"You OK?" Jake said in English.

Turani mumbled something, and Jake slapped him across the face, far harder than was necessary.

The Iranian shuddered as his eyes opened.

"You cannot—"

Jake shoved him back to the floor and slapped a length of duct tape over his mouth and a second one over his eyes.

"Let's get one thing straight," Jake said. "I can do whatever I want to."

He slid a thobe over Turani's head and arms and added sunglasses and a ghutra. Outside, in the darkness, the Iranian would look normal from anything more than ten feet away.

Jake doused the apartment lights and checked the street. A dark-colored sedan with its lights off had double-parked next to the first car. The men inside appeared to be talking. Jake grabbed a bottle of water from the counter and took a few sips. The dark-colored sedan stayed put for several minutes before pulling into an empty parking space. Two men stepped out wearing short thobes and carrying pistols. Two more got out of the first car, including the giant Jake had seen earlier.

The men from the cars nodded to the men who'd been standing on the street corner for hours.

*Al-Qaeda for sure,* Jake thought. *Probably al-Quereshi's henchmen coming to finish the job.*

The clock over the sink read 12:30 a.m. Fadi and Youssef wouldn't arrive for another hour and a half. Jake cursed and led Turani into the hallway. There was no light switch, and Jake didn't want anyone to see them leaving the building, so he poured some water into his hands and splashed it onto the overhead lights. The hot incandescent bulbs shattered, plunging the hallway into darkness and covering the floor with shards of glass.

Jake led Turani to the back of the building, saw the magnet in place, and opened the emergency exit without triggering the alarm. The tape around his ankles limited the Iranian to short, unsteady steps. They weren't going to be outrunning anyone. Jake turned to the deepest part of the dead-end alley and led his prisoner into the darkness.

There were several old cars parked nearby, but the al-Qaeda goons would be in the alley before Jake could get one started. He approached an old Chevrolet sedan and tried the trunk, but it was locked. He pulled out the steel-framed Makarov and smashed the driver's-side window, then reached down and popped the trunk.

"Nod if you understand me," Jake said.

The Iranian nodded.

"We're going for a ride now. You're going in the trunk. If you resist or make any noise, you're a dead man. Got it?"

The Iranian nodded again and Jake pushed him backward into the trunk and slammed the lid. He was eighty feet from the main road when the door to his building opened. Two men with flashlights stepped out and quickly found Jake in the beams.

He darted around the corner and across a vacant lot with footsteps and shouting behind him. Jake ran down the street, vaulted over a low fence, and ran through a yard to another street. He repeated the maneuver several times, moving diagonally away from the safe house. Every additional block multiplied the number of streets his pursuers would have to search and drew them farther from Turani.

Jake slid under an outside stairwell and was sheathed in darkness. He took deep, slow breaths as he attempted to slow his heart rate. The Makarov was in his hand.

He waited for several minutes, then walked to a run-down section of Al-Suwaidi where he'd seen older cars parked along the road. He smashed the window on a tiny Renault coupe and had it started in a couple of minutes. Jake drove a circuitous route back toward his safe house. Though the streets were mostly empty, his mind was processing a hundred inputs: the shape of a trailing car's lights, the body language of a pedestrian, the changing pitch of a distant siren, potential escape routes where his small car would give him an advantage. Nothing could be overlooked.

He returned to the alley from a different direction, parked fifty yards away, and watched. There were no Islamic radicals, no police cars, and no curious neighbors.

The alley seemed to close in as he entered. He drove the little Renault to the end and did a three-point turn, hoping to flush any surveillance, but there was no movement as he pulled alongside the old Chevy with Colonel Turani in its trunk.

He left the Renault's engine running and was walking to the Chevy when a deep voice called out.

"I have a gun," said the man in heavily accented English. "Put your hands on the car."

## EIGHTY-SIX

A STEADY STREAM OF helicopters, vans, and black SUVs ferried the Supreme Court justices, most of the president's cabinet, and key members of Congress to the High Point Special Facility in Bluemont, Virginia. Colloquially known as Mount Weather, the underground bunker could sustain and protect the nation's civilian leadership through an extended nuclear crisis.

Already under a state of emergency because of the ongoing terror attacks, the continuity-of-government plan had emptied Washington, D.C., of its remaining leaders. Only General Landgraf, the secretaries of state and homeland security, and a few aides and advisers remained with the president in the emergency operations center below the White House.

"Mr. President," said Director Kerr of the FBI over a video feed, "the National Counterterrorism Center identified two men in Colorado attempting to buy enough ammonium nitrate to either blow up a city block or fertilize the entire state. The local police picked them up and turned them over to us."

"Are they members of our original group or is this a cell we didn't know about?" asked the president.

"Their border-entry photos identify them as the Minneapolis team. They're most likely the perpetrators of the North Dakota train derailment who were out pursuing targets of opportunity."

"How many more of these 'opportunists' might be out there?"

"Theoretically, as many as eight," said Kerr, "but given the intensity of the refinery fires it's probable that most of those still missing were incinerated during the attacks."

"That should give them a nice preview of eternity," said the president. "Is there any evidence that Iran co-ordinated the attacks with China? The timing seems awfully convenient."

"We have no indication of it," said Director Feinman via secure video feed from CIA headquarters, "and the link between China and Saudi Arabia almost eliminates the likelihood of a third link to Iran. There's no Venn diagram we can draw where those three overlap."

"The Bureau concurs," said Director Kerr. "All the intel indicates that Iran was planning to execute the attacks several weeks from now but accelerated the time-table once Mecca was struck. They'd have coordinated the timing if they'd been working with China."

"This can't go unpunished," said the president. "We need to show the world that actions have consequences." The president directed his attention to General Land-graf. "Jay, what are our options?"

"Sir, the first page in the portfolio in front of you is

our Iran target deck. We've focused on the country's nuclear facilities and Qods Force assets to clearly define our actions as retribution for the nuclear weapon and the terrorist attacks. The uranium enrichment complexes in Arak and the training base in the northeastern . . ."

General Landgraf continued as President Day scanned the list. He closed the binder a moment later.

"We need to do more," said the president. "I want to decapitate their government."

The secretary of state spoke up. "Mr. President—"

"I want to kill the supreme leader, the cabinet, the heads of the IRGC and the Assembly of Experts, and any of the other Haghani-school hard-liners who might step into the vacuum. The president and the foreign minister are the two most moderate and most popular leaders in the country. Somehow, we have to spare them so they can take control in the aftermath."

"That's a tall order, sir," said the secretary of defense, who was airborne in an E-4B Nightwatch aircraft from which he could control the entire U.S. military. "After the first few targets go down, the rest of the group will go to ground."

"We could strike a Supreme National Security Council meeting," said the CIA director. "That would take care of most of your list. Separating the president and the foreign minister would be tricky, though."

"Let's hit them at night, right where they sleep," offered General Landgraf. "It would require intense close-target reconnaissance, but, between CIA and JSOC, we could do it."

"Do you agree, David?" asked the president.

"JSOC and the Agency conduct extensive joint operations inside the country, Mr. President. We could get it done."

"I just want to reiterate," said the president, "that as long as reformers are in a position to take charge, we go ahead. I'm not asking for a guarantee, but I don't want to give some IRGC general or another ayatollah a reason to think he can take a shot at it. I'm under no illusion that this will be easy, but a decisive show of force might deter whoever is controlling that nuke from detonating it on American soil."

Heads nodded around the room.

"Lay it out, General," said the president. "How would we do it?"

"We'd kick down the door with a flight of eight F-22 Raptors penetrating east through northern Iraq. They'll use HARM missiles and glide-wing bombs to take out the Iranian air defense system, followed by a pair of B-2 bombers with an escort flight of more F-22s. Tehran is a large city, almost one hundred twenty square miles, but with precision-guided munitions we can hit all of our targets on a single pass, before their leadership can scatter. It won't be a milk run, though. They have upgraded S-300 surface-to-air missile batteries protecting the city."

"Losses on our side?" asked the president.

"I'd expect losses to be minimal, sir," said the general.

"Why would we have *any* losses?" asked the secretary of state. "Aren't those stealth aircraft?"

"Technically, Mr. Secretary, we call them 'very low

observables,'" said Landgraf. "After the 2015 Joint Comprehensive Plan of Action was agreed to, the Iranians used some of their newly unfrozen cash to purchase L-band active-phased-array radars from Russia. They can probably detect an F-22, but they still can't target one."

"Can't they shoot it down if they can see it on radar?" said the secretary.

"The phased-array radars are large and sensitive, but they don't have the accuracy to guide a missile onto a fast-moving target. On the other hand, missile-guidance radars have very focused energy, but their seeker heads are too small to track VLO aircraft."

"That doesn't make any sense," said the secretary of state with a dismissive wave of the hand.

The general glared at him.

"Maybe this will help," said Landgraf. "Imagine it's midnight, you're all alone, and I break into your house. You hear a strange noise and grab a gun. Your ears are like the phased-array radar. You know I'm out there, but you're not exactly sure where. The sound you heard could have come from the kitchen, or possibly the living room. Maybe I'm already in your bedroom. To fire your weapon, you'll need your eyes. They're like the missile-guidance radar, but I've cut the power, so you can't see me. That's stealth. You might fire a few shots in my general direction, but you probably won't hit me. So even though you know I'm there, I'm still going to kill you, and there's not a goddamn thing you can do about it."

The secretary regarded the general warily.

Landgraf turned to the president. "We might want to consider giving Israel a last-minute heads-up on this. Iran might try to provoke a response from them once the shooting starts, like the Iraqi Scuds during the first Gulf War."

"They screwed us pretty good on the Olympic Games operation," said the president. "I'm sure they'll figure it out. Let's move on to China. Treasury has already prepared strong economic sanctions. Where are we militarily?"

"If you'll turn to page two, you'll see we've provided a number of targeting options," said the general.

The president read the list. "What's the name of the group that hijacked Drifter-72?" he asked.

"PLA Unit 7474–505B, sir. They operate under the control of the Second Bureau of the General Staff Department's Third Department. They are the PLA's most aggressive, and most effective, cyber-warfare group. They're responsible for tens of thousands of intrusions into our intelligence, commercial, industrial, and military networks. As far as we've determined, they're the only ones with the computing power and the expertise to even attempt a real-time hijacking of a UCAV platform."

"Then why don't I see them on this list? Wouldn't that send the clearest message?" asked the president.

"The unit's main offices are located in a high-rise building in the densely populated Pudong district of Shanghai. By design, it's a commercial building occupied by mostly civilian businesses. Targeting it would generate significant collateral damage and, to the untrained eye, nothing in the wreckage would appear to be military. Given the classified nature of our evidence, we'll never be able to convince the general public that we acted justly," said General Landgraf. "The Chinese will portray us as lashing out at innocent civilians, just as they have with the attack on Mecca."

The president frowned. "How many civilian casualties would we be talking about?"

"If we hit it when the offices are occupied, several hundred, and a kinetic strike may still fail to achieve the desired effect," said the chairman. "These operations are decentralized networks by design. We won't have any idea if the people walking in the front door are legitimate targets or commercial sector office workers. We could flatten the whole block and still not kill a single unit operative."

The president nodded. "OK. Let's not create more enemies than we eliminate. What are our other options?"

"We have several large-scale cyber attacks ready. We could shut down the power grid in a major city, tank their financial markets, or cause a nuclear reactor to melt down," said the chairman. "The options are almost unlimited, but any existential cyber attack comes with a significant risk of retaliation, and because most Chinese infrastructure is newer, it was designed to be online, as opposed to ours, which was adapted to be online. We may be better offensively at cyber, but we're also more vulnerable. I'm not explicitly recommending against it, but we should expect some surprising and very unpleasant retaliation if we go cyber."

"So where does that leave us?" asked the president.

"Sir, I'd recommend number seven on that list," said Landgraf, "the factory that produces their UAVs. Given that it's right on the coast, a submarine-launched cruise missile attack would have a very high probability of success and the subs would be in deep water before the PLA Navy could respond. It's proportional, with limited civilian casualties, and it sends the message that our action was direct retribution for the hijacking and false-flag operation with Drifter-72."

"It's a start," said the president, "but I want to do more."

"We could also hit number eight," said the defense secretary from the doomsday plane. "It's their primary drone-control center, like Creech Air Force Base in Nevada. It's far inland, in eastern Qinghai province, but still well within range of the Tomahawks. We—"

"Sir, forgive me," said General Landgraf, "but the Chinese drone-control facility is colocated with a launch complex for their road-mobile nuclear ICBMs. They have a small fleet of DF-31A missiles that can hit the United States, and they're constantly moved about on the back of transporter/erector/launcher trucks. If the Chinese think our cruise missiles are trying to take out their nuclear second-strike capability, they are going to escalate, quickly. I would strongly encourage us to find another target."

"Those missiles haven't been there for almost three months," said the secretary of defense. "The Chinese used one of our drones to hit Mecca. They'll know exactly why we're hitting their drone-control facility."

"Mr. President," said Landgraf, "because of their relatively small ballistic missile fleet, China is what's known as a countervalue targeter. That means if they send ICBMs our way, they won't be looking to take out military targets; they're going to wipe out our cities."

"How sure are we that those missile launchers aren't near the drone-control complex?" asked the president.

"A satellite passed overhead twelve hours ago, sir," said the defense secretary.

"That works for me. General, how long would you need to execute the most comprehensive plans against Iran and China?"

"Twenty-four hours, Mr. President."

"Get the assets into position," said the president. "I want to hit it all."

## EIGHTY-SEVEN

BRAHIM AND KAHLIL continued into the countryside, driving randomly down a series of back roads until they were twenty turns and as many miles from the intersection where they'd ambushed the Florida state trooper.

The warm glow of early evening was descending on the wooded country road when Kahlil pulled to the shoulder. He shut down the engine and activated the hazard lights. After the past few days of nonstop action, he was struck by the simple tranquility of walking through the weeds and wildflowers alongside the pavement. The high humidity and dense woods were in sharp contrast to his native land, where the climate was dry and the land was barren.

He raised the SUV's hood and felt a wave of heat rise from the engine. It had performed well, but it had been running almost nonstop for three days. The hot metal ticked slowly as it began to cool.

A car passed by a few minutes later.

Kahlil was still standing in front of the SUV when a gray pickup truck pulled to the side of the road. It was enormous, with four doors and six tires, and the mechanical roar of its eight-cylinder turbodiesel engine shattered the quiet as the driver backed toward Kahlil.

"Evening," said the man with a smile as he stepped down from the truck. He was wearing jeans, work boots, and the ubiquitous American baseball cap.

Kahlil returned the smile. "I think we have overheated."

The man nodded. *It's amazing those little four-bangers work at all,* he thought to himself. He dropped the liftgate to get a rag and a jug of water.

"Once it cools down, we'll—"

From seventy-five feet inside the woods, Ibrahim's bullet caught the Good Samaritan in the center of his back, shattering his spine and exploding his heart. The man had barely hit the ground when Kahlil grabbed him by the ankles and dragged him into the woods, before the draining blood could leave a telltale mark on the pavement.

Ibrahim climbed behind the wheel of the pickup truck while Kahlil took the white SUV. They drove in search of a convenience store or a parking lot where the SUV would not be immediately noticed. After ten minutes, Ibrahim grew tense, fearing that they would be spotted. Their pre-mission briefing had warned them about U.S. law enforcement technology such as license plate readers and dash-mounted cameras. After killing the policeman, they knew that they could no longer use the white SUV.

Kahlil swerved off the pavement and onto an overgrown dirt road. Two hundred yards into the woods, he abandoned the SUV.

Ibrahim enjoyed the novelty of driving the huge pickup truck down the wide country roads, but the new vehicle had given them the ability to once again travel along the region's highways, and that was an opportunity they could not pass up. They needed to cover a great many miles, and they could not predict whether it would be a few minutes, a few hours, or a few days before someone found the abandoned SUV or reported the pickup owner's absence.

Kahlil checked the GPS. They were back in Georgia, just southwest of the small city of Valdosta. It would be a four-hour drive to Orlando, their next target and the home of America's degenerate "amusement" parks. They headed east toward the entrance to the I-75 superhighway.

"The park visitors will have gone home for the night by the time we arrive," Kahlil said. "Perhaps we should look for a target of opportunity along the way."

"We should follow the plan," said Ibrahim as he turned onto a main road. The woods and farms gave way to suburban sprawl as they drove.

"We will be waiting for nine hours for the parks to open. It is a long time to sit in a stolen vehicle."

"What should we do, abandon the plan that has worked so well for us?"

"Not abandon, but modify," said Kahlil. "We could pursue an intermediate objective." He checked the GPS again. "We could be in Miami in seven hours. We would have many targets among the fornicators seeking the delights reserved for men in Paradise."

"Paraíso isn't here," said Ibrahim, focused on a six-way intersection up ahead. "You don't need to spout that garbage to me. We're here to kill people."

Kahlil scowled. "Your lack of faith has always been—"

There were traffic lights on the near and far sides of the wide intersection, on poles coming up from the ground, and on arms reaching across the road. Ibrahim was confused.

"What am I supposed to do here?" he said as a car horn sounded behind him.

"You must follow the teachings—"

"No, you unwashed ass. Can I make the right turn or must I stop?"

"The light is green, so go!" Kahlil said, pointing to the wrong stoplight.

Ibrahim sneered at his teammate as they pulled into the intersection.

An open-top Jeep appeared out of nowhere and collided with the pickup's rear quarter.

"I hope you die like a dog," Ibrahim said to Kahlil as they pulled to the side of the road. "What now?"

"Have faith."

Ibrahim rolled his eyes.

The Jeep pulled over. Its driver was already out of his vehicle and inspecting the damage.

Ibrahim stepped out. "I am sorry. I was confused by the many lights."

"You're not from these parts, are you?" said the Jeep driver, noting Ibrahim's accent. "Don't worry about it.

This has got to be the worst intersection in the state of Georgia. My sister did the same thing a couple of months ago. You and me should exchange information. I'll grab my insurance."

Ibrahim relaxed a little as the man walked back to his Jeep. At least he hadn't wanted to call the police.

"What are you going to do now?" Kahlil hissed. "Your license and the insurance information will not match. He will—"

The Jeep's driver walked to the front of the giant pickup and laid his information on the hood.

"Here you go," he said. "We can just shoot pictures with our phones and we should be good. Can't be more than a couple hundred bucks' worth of work there."

Ibrahim stared at the man.

The man looked back at Ibrahim, then glanced at Kahlil, looking nervous in the passenger seat.

"Maybe we should call the cops," said the Jeep driver, "just to, uh, get an accident report."

Ibrahim took a step toward him.

Kahlil reached for something on the floor.

"Hey, I don't want any trouble," the man said. He raised his open palms.

Ibrahim took another step.

The man snapped his left hand to his stomach and his right hand behind his hip. Half a second later the two hands came together and he was pointing a handgun at Ibrahim.

"Back off!" the Jeep driver shouted, but Ibrahim did not move.

The man caught sight of Kahlil struggling with something in the front seat of the pickup.

The Jeep driver swung his weapon toward the passenger seat just as the deer rifle came up. He fired three rounds through the windshield with his .40-caliber Smith & Wesson. Two of the bullets went wild, but one caught Kahlil in the forehead.

The Jeep driver aimed his weapon back at Ibrahim, but instead of backing away, Ibrahim charged. The Jeep driver pulled the trigger two more times.

From five feet away, he couldn't miss.

# EIGHTY-EIGHT

THE MAN IN the alley stripped Jake of his pistol and the knife, then led him back into the building at gunpoint. The shattered lightbulbs crunched underfoot as they walked to Jake's apartment. The man closed the door and turned on the lights. The clock over the sink said 1:45 a.m.

"Sit."

Jake turned the folding chair to face the man. It was the giant who'd been pulling surveillance earlier. He was nearly three hundred pounds and solidly built, with thick hair, a dense beard, and a wide, dish-shaped face.

*He looks like a grizzly bear,* Jake thought.

The grizzly retrieved a roll of duct tape from the kitchen counter. He wrapped Jake's wrists, ankles, and his entire torso to the metal chair. Jake felt as if he were being smothered by a boa constrictor.

The man pulled out his mobile phone, carefully dialing the numbers with his thick fingers.

*"Tell al-Quereshi I have him . . . In the apartment . . . Twenty minutes? We'll be ready."*

The man dropped the phone back in his pocket and leaned against the counter with the gun in his hand. He stared at Jake.

Jake watched the clock over the sink tick by, unable to move much besides his head. After ten minutes, he looked up at the man. He was drinking a bottle of water from the fridge.

"Hey," Jake said. "You speak English, right?"

The man finished the bottle of water.

"I do," he said.

"Why are you covered in fur?" Jake said.

Still holding the pistol, the man folded his arms across his chest and smirked.

"Seriously, you are the hairiest man I've ever seen. You're like a dog."

The smirk faded. Comparing an Arab to a canine was one of the most insulting things a person could do.

"Was your father a dog?"

The man did not react.

"Or was it your mother? I'll bet it was your mother."

The man holstered the pistol and stepped away from the counter.

"Are you married? I wouldn't think so, but maybe you found some other dog to—"

The first blow was a right cross that caught Jake in the cheek and nearly toppled the chair. He saw stars twinkling in front of his eyes.

"You and the bitch have any puppies?"

The second punch came from the left and connected even harder than the first.

Jake spit out a mouthful of blood and looked up at the clock. It was 2:00 a.m. on the dot.

"Big dog—"

A giant fist knocked the wind out of him. He gasped for breath and swallowed blood as the grizzly pounded his ribs.

Jake looked up and smiled. Blood covered his teeth.

"Dog—"

The man punched Jake in the chest so hard that he thought his heart would stop. Blood sprayed from his mouth as he began to cough uncontrollably. The next few minutes faded into a blur as the giant al-Qaeda operative pummeled Jake with his fists. At one point the chair fell over but the man lifted it back onto its legs with one hand. The beating resumed. He pounded Jake relentlessly. Consciousness came and went with the blows.

"HEY!" SAID A voice. "Hey! Are you with me?"

Jake looked up. Youssef had the shotgun trained on the giant Saudi, who was lying facedown on the floor. Youssef cut the tape holding Jake to the chair and he tumbled to the ground.

"You're late," Jake mumbled. He pointed at the clock. It was 2:10.

Youssef smiled. "The car is in the alley. Where's the prisoner?"

"Outside. More al-Qaeda coming any second."

"Shit," Youssef said. He poured a bottle of water

over Jake's face and gave him some paper towels. "Clean yourself up."

Jake got to his knees, hunched over and in pain, and wiped his face. Everything hurt. "We need to go."

"What we do with this guy?" Youssef asked.

Jake spit out a mouthful of blood. "Stuff him and put a salmon in his mouth."

With Youssef holding the shotgun, Jake duct-taped the man's wrists and ankles together. Jake grabbed another roll and wrapped the man's whole head except for his nose.

"He can barely breathe," Youssef said.

"You think I should cover the nose?"

The two Americans took the weapons and entered the hallway. Hunched over and bleeding, Jake cleared forward as they crunched the broken glass underfoot.

"How long was he working you?" Youssef said.

"I timed it to only take a punch or two so he wouldn't hear you coming in."

"It looks as if you took more than a couple of punches."

Jake looked over. "You were supposed to be here at two o'clock."

"It took us a while to find a parking space . . ."

Youssef smirked as he opened the emergency exit and scanned the alley with the pistol-grip shotgun.

Jake removed the magnet from the alarm sensor as he closed the door, then walked to the car where he'd hidden Turani. Fadi pulled up and he and Youssef quickly transferred the Iranian to the trunk of the Crown Victoria.

They'd barely closed the lid when the emergency exit

alarm started screeching. Three Saudis came out of the building with guns drawn. They started shooting as soon as they spotted the Americans. Gunfire ricocheted off the concrete buildings, shattering glass and piercing metal. In only a few seconds, the alley turned into a war zone. Nowhere was safe.

Jake ran toward the main road to draw the Saudis' fire away from Turani and the Crown Vic. He shot the Makarov until it was dry, then switched to the pistol he'd taken off the grizzly. Muzzle flashes exploded around the dark alley like fireworks.

Bullets were everywhere.

## EIGHTY-NINE

SEVERAL OBSTACLES HAD nearly scuttled the proposed treaty, but the willingness of Saudi Arabia to sell its crude oil at a 10 percent discount to market price would save China almost $20 billion annually, more than offsetting the projected cost of providing military support, with the unquantifiable benefit of denying a Saudi reconciliation with the United States.

Premier Mèng-Fù summoned General Wǔ-Dīng to his office. The high-ranking head of the Central Commission for Discipline Inspection was waiting with him. A staunch factional ally of President Chéng Minsheng, the CCDI leader confided to the two men that, given the president's clumsy handling of recent events, the other members of the Standing Committee, in consultation with party elders, had decided that the president would not be selected for another term.

"Why were we not consulted as well?" asked Mèng-Fù sharply. "We are both members of the Standing Committee."

The head of the CCDI bowed slightly. "Because you

have been chosen as the next general secretary of the Communist Party and president of China, and General Wǔ-Dīng is to become premier."

"What of President Chéng?" asked Mèng-Fù.

"In light of his many years of loyal service to the party, President Chéng will be allowed to retire quietly."

The three men spoke about details and plans for nearly an hour. When the head of the CCDI left, Mèng-Fù Ru sat silently at his desk for several minutes, twirling a small jade monkey in his hand.

"I believe the committee has acted prematurely," he said eventually.

"You are going to refuse the appointment?" asked Wǔ-Dīng.

"But I could be wrong . . ." said Mèng-Fù. The corners of his mouth turned up slightly. It was the nearest thing to a smile that he could manage.

Wǔ-Dīng nodded. It was the first time he'd seen Mèng-Fù allow ambition to eclipse his sense of fairness, but he had just been offered the highest office in the nation.

"You will have to work quickly to hone your diplomatic and political skills, General. It will not be long until you take my place as head of state."

"Please, respected one, the People's Republic has much to gain from your stewardship."

"Men such as ourselves deal in facts. There is no disputing the fact that I am not well. I am too old to run for a second term, and even a single term may be too much for my withering body." Mèng-Fù pointed a bony finger at the general's sturdy frame. "I will not die a soldier's death, but I will still die in service to my country."

It was nearly nine o'clock in the evening when Wŭ-Dīng took a walk through the lakeside gardens at Zhongnanhai. The day had been the culmination of six months of intense effort and he needed time to clear his mind. Events were moving swiftly.

He rounded a corner and stopped. Across the lake was the Forbidden City, the seat of Chinese dynastic power for five hundred years. Behind its lighted walls, the red and gold towers stirred his heart.

*Long live the People's Republic of China.*

Wŭ-Dīng used his secure mobile phone to call Faisal.

"The treaty framework has been approved," said Wŭ-Dīng. "I know the ten percent discount was a difficult concession, but it was crucial to the Standing Committee, and this partnership will benefit both of our great nations. Who will be signing for Saudi Arabia? Has the king finally come around or will it be Crown Prince Mohammad?"

"Most likely the crown prince," said Faisal, "for now."

"What do you mean, 'for now'?"

"Fear not, Wŭ-Dīng. The king will cede the throne to the crown prince, but Mohammad's health is far too precarious for such a taxing job. He will retire within six months."

"I did not know he was ill."

"Neither does he," said Faisal.

"And if he does not retire?"

"Then his condition will rapidly become terminal."

"I am grateful that we are allies, Faisal."

"Indeed, General. How is President Chéng dealing with the treaty? I would imagine this defeat has weakened him."

"In several weeks, the Presidium of the National People's Congress will nominate the next officers of the Communist Party of China. Do not be surprised if Mèng-Fù Ru is elevated to general secretary. The slate must be approved by the National People's Congress, but the party leadership has made its choice. The approvals are mere formalities."

"And how does he feel about the agreement with the kingdom?"

"He is supportive."

"Well done, General. And who will fill the role of premier?"

"Mèng-Fù is a strategic thinker. His time will be occupied with planning for the next century," said Wǔ-Dīng. "He will need someone with leadership, logistical, and budgeting experience to run the country."

"That automaton from the Ministry of the Interior?"

Wǔ-Dīng laughed. "No, Faisal. I will be the next premier."

"That is an unexpected promotion."

"We should hold a joint press conference," said Wǔ-Dīng. "Come to Beijing! We will give you a state dinner to celebrate our diplomatic achievement."

Faisal sat at his desk, drumming his fingers against the green leather blotter.

"Faisal, are you there?" asked Wǔ-Dīng.

"Yes, yes," said the prince. "I am afraid that I must stay here and keep an eye on Mohammad lest he do something foolish. The visit to Beijing will have to wait."

"Of course," said Wǔ-Dīng. "I will come to you."

"That is most gracious of you," said the prince, "but not necessary."

"If I am going to be a politician, then I must start acting like one," said Wǔ-Dīng. "I will see you in Riyadh in two days. Have the cameras ready."

## NINETY

BULLETS RICOCHETED AND gunfire echoed off of every hard surface. One of the terrorists popped his head out from behind a car and Youssef fired the shotgun. The short-barreled 12-gauge sounded like an airstrike inside the narrow alley. The terrorist went down.

"Get in the car!" Fadi shouted.

Jake and Youssef fired out the windows as they sped out of the alley.

The Crown Victoria had turned into a bullet sponge during the gunfight, with a dozen holes in its sheet metal and three shattered windows. It was a miracle that no one on the American side was injured, especially Turani, but the old Ford was a rolling invitation to trouble. They couldn't risk being stopped by the police, especially with the prisoner in the trunk.

Fadi drove to a parking garage on the south side of Riyadh and stopped next to a dusty Kia sedan. Youssef unlocked the door and the two men transferred Turani to the Kia's trunk. They drove an hour-long surveillance-detection route before returning to their safe house with the prisoner.

Jake stayed with the Crown Vic, scrubbing dried blood from his face and changing his clothes before busting open the steering column and wiping the car for fingerprints. The car's owner, a friendly Saudi citizen living in Riyadh, would report that it had been stolen sometime last night after he'd gone to bed.

Jake pulled his ghutra tight around his face and flagged down a taxi. The sun would be up in another hour, and he had another meeting.

The cab drove to the enormous Ritz-Carlton Hotel in Riyadh, where Jake passed through security at the front gate and texted al-Shezza. The Saudi met him in front of the hotel in the blue Lexus. Jake climbed into the passenger seat with a package in hand.

The prince's chief of staff pulled to a distant section of the parking lot and backed into a space. He left the engine running.

"Do you have them?" he said, gesturing to the package.

Jake tore open the package and fanned seven passports across his lap like a card dealer. "For you and your family."

Al-Shezza had provided photos of his wife and children to Fadi and Youssef, who had worked with a local forger to create the Omani passports. They'd been picking up the documents when Jake had had his run-in with the grizzly bear at his apartment.

"How will my family get to the West?" asked al-Shezza.

"A private plane is waiting to take them to Dubai," Jake said. Sharif and the Beech King Air were standing by at a local airport.

"Tell them nothing until they are ready to leave," Jake added. "A driver will collect them at 09:00 and—"

"My wife insists on driving everywhere since she has obtained her license."

"Fine. They must bring only money and clothes for a few days, to keep up appearances, but in all likelihood, they will never return to Saudi Arabia."

Al-Shezza shifted in his seat. "My wife is a very intelligent woman. She will quickly deduce that something is wrong. What am I to tell her?"

"Tell her there may be war with the United States and you will join them as soon as possible. Will she give you trouble?"

"She will ask a great many questions, but she will go for the safety of the children."

Jake nodded. He picked up the passports and put them in his pocket.

"I'm prepared to uphold my end of our deal," Jake said. "Now you need to convince me that I should."

## NINETY-ONE

*E*L NUEVO CONSTANTE swayed gently in the open seas, a ghost ship but for the invisible hand of the autopilot upon the wheel. To port and starboard it turned, keeping the course the captain had set before he'd been attacked.

The man known as Carlos regained consciousness just before sunset. He was lying on his side inside the wheelhouse, his heart racing. He braced himself against the navigation station and unleashed a horrific scream as he rose to his feet with the screwdriver still protruding from his gut.

The chartplotter showed that the ship had been steering for a holding area outside the Houston ship channel. Carlos pushed a few buttons and added a waypoint to the end of the trip. Even if he succumbed to his injuries, *El Nuevo Constante* would now continue north for another ten hours to the city of Houston. The GPS-enabled trigger inside the container would do the rest, but Carlos had also brought a remote detonator in case the Americans attempted to stop him before his mission was complete.

Either way, it would be a magnificent martyr's death.

Carlos looked at the screwdriver in his abdomen, wrapped in blood-soaked gauze. He'd been afraid to remove it earlier, fearful that the void might cause fresh internal damage, but the pain of each movement, each breath of air, was unbearable. The contents of the ship's first-aid kit were still scattered across the nav station.

He choked down several painkillers and unpacked the bloody gauze. Miguel had buried the screwdriver almost to the handle, leaving seven inches of the metal shaft inside Carlos's gut. He twisted it a few degrees, triggering another scream—a long, unholy wail from the depths of his soul. There was no way to ease it out. His only option would be to yank it free in one savage motion, but he would probably go into shock and die.

He left it where it was.

Carlos staggered down to Miguel's body. A swarm of flies circled the corpse, feasting on the blood and flesh.

*Flies . . . even two hundred miles offshore. The birds will come next.*

Motion in the distance caught his eye. The anticollision lights of a large airplane blinked against the darkening sky. It was flying low but would pass well in front of *El Nuevo Constante*. It was a four-engine propeller plane, a type he had seen many times before, but this one was not painted with the tan and green camouflage of the Israel Defense Forces. This one was white with a diagonal red stripe on its fuselage.

*The U.S. Coast Guard,* he thought. *Probably looking for survivors of the hurricane.*

Carlos doubted that they had seen Miguel's corpse on deck. It was too dark and the plane was too far away, but he had to dispose of the two bodies before someone did notice them.

He stumbled back to the deckhouse and used his good hand to drag the captain a few feet toward the main deck, but Carlos again felt faint, and his grip was too weak to go any farther.

He leaned against the wall to catch his breath and noticed the old longshoreman's hook hanging next to him. He raised the worn wooden handle and swung it into the captain's shoulder, burying the stainless steel hook deep into the flesh and muscle. He dragged the captain across the steel deck until father and son lay side by side under the night sky.

It was only then, under the deck lights of *El Nuevo Constante*, that he noticed the captain's eyes flickering between Miguel and himself.

*He's only paralyzed,* Carlos thought. *But it changes nothing . . .*

He walked to the bow and returned several minutes later with a long, thick chain. He wrapped it around both men's necks, then their torsos, then between their legs. When he was satisfied that it would not come loose, he secured it back upon itself with a shackle.

The captain's eyes darted from the starry sky, to the black water lapping against the ship, to Carlos, pulling a tall lever on the bow.

There was a mechanical rumble and then a splash as the anchor dropped from the ship. The chain banged violently against the deck as it uncoiled, the 250-pound anchor pulling it deep into the storm-addled sea.

Carlos had detached the anchor chain from the ship. He and the captain made eye contact just as the chain went taut. In an instant, the father and son were yanked overboard to begin their furious descent to the bottom of the ocean.

Carlos heard the engines of the big C-130 once again. The Coast Guard aircraft had looped around, back toward *El Nuevo Constante*. This time, it would pass much closer. He watched it approach, with its lights flashing and its propellers turning, until it flew by just five hundred feet overhead.

He waved.

## NINETY-TWO

HAVE THOUGHT VERY seriously about my decision since our last conversation," said al-Shezza as he looked out the windshield.

To the northeast was the spectacular Kingdom Center, towering nearly a thousand feet into the air. To the southeast were the elegantly geometric Yamamah Palace and Shura Council buildings with their lighted domes and extensive gardens. Palm fronds swayed in the gentle breeze. It was a stirring vision of modern Saudi Arabia. Al-Shezza sighed.

"In the next twenty-four hours, the Allegiance Council is going to depose King Ali. Crown Prince Mohammad will take the throne, but not for long. He suffers from a debilitating condition."

"What sort of condition?"

"The kind that will lead to a knife in the back," said al-Shezza, "or perhaps a bullet to the head. Faisal's diagnosis was not specific."

"That's interesting," Jake said, "but you already told us Faisal was ambitious. This doesn't justify the risk we'd be taking to get your family out of the country."

Al-Shezza folded his hands in front of him. "It was Faisal who stole your aircraft and attacked Mecca."

"We know otherwise," said Jake.

"China?" said al-Shezza. "You must understand the context to understand the operation. Faisal does not respect King Ali. He detests the king's alliance with the United States, so the prince conspired with China to murder three thousand pilgrims in America's name and shatter that alliance."

"How do you know this?"

"I accompany the prince almost everywhere, yet to a man like Faisal, I am inconsequential and therefore invisible. It would never occur to him that I would betray him."

"Even though he betrayed the kingdom?" Jake said.

"The royal family view the kingdom as their property, not their responsibility. Faisal feels that the king is doing a disservice to the family, so he has taken matters into his own hands. He sees himself not as a traitor, but as a savior."

"Tell me more about the relationship with China," Jake said.

"Faisal's coconspirator is General Wǔ-Dīng Yǒng," said al-Shezza, "vice chairman of the Central Military Commission and a member of the Politburo's Standing Committee. There is a well-documented history between the two men: weapons deals, military exchanges, and of course the trips to Libya. This episode with your drone is only their most recent partnership."

Jake leaned forward. "What about General Wǔ-Dīng—is he acting on behalf of the Communist Party?"

"Like the prince, the general has acted alone and for personal gain. At the next National People's Congress, Premier Mèng-Fù Ru will be named as the next general secretary of the Communist Party and president of China."

"And Wǔ-Dīng?"

"Mèng-Fù is Wǔ-Dīng's patron. The general will become premier, the second-highest office in China."

"But the new Politburo won't be sworn in for months," Jake said. "If the current president won't sign the treaty with Saudi Arabia, Iran may decide to act during the gap."

Al-Shezza scowled at the mention of Saudi Arabia's longtime rival.

"Iran," he scoffed. "They are nothing but apostates masquerading as theocrats. You need not worry about Iran."

He faced the window and gazed once again at the Kingdom Center skyscraper. The arch was lit with the green and gold national colors as the sun rose behind it.

"The Center tugs at my heart when it looks like that," said al-Shezza. "Leaving Saudi Arabia will leave an irreparable tear inside me."

"So why are you doing this?"

"I have everything to lose and nothing to gain, except peace in my soul."

"You're doing the right thing," Jake said, "but I'm surprised by your lack of concern about Iran. Without a nuclear deterrent, nothing will stand between them and Middle Eastern hegemony."

"Saudi Arabia will have its own deterrent," said al-

Shezza. "Prince Faisal is planning to purchase nuclear weapons from Pakistan."

Jake had been a strategic weapons analyst at CIA before transitioning to operations. He was a subject-matter expert in the field, and the thought of a nuclear-armed Saudi Arabia sent a chill through his body.

"That would start a regional nuclear arms race," Jake said, "if not outright nuclear war."

"You admit that we need to keep Iran at bay, yes?"

"I'm not worried about Iran attacking Saudi Arabia with nuclear weapons. Their leadership would be content to see Saudi Arabia implode under its own weight, allowing Iran to dominate the region."

"So how would our weapons start a war?"

"Arab countries used water rights as a pretext for attacking Israel in 1967. How do you think the Israelis would feel today about those same countries having stockpiles of nuclear weapons? Most of Israel's neighbors still refuse to acknowledge its right to exist and the rest are actively seeking its destruction. Israel has restrained itself because its forces are sufficient to deter any attack, but a nuclear arms race in the Middle East would force them to act preemptively, and that would start a nuclear war that would inevitably draw in Russia, China, and the United States." Jake looked al-Shezza in the eyes. "It could mean the end of civilization."

# NINETY-THREE

ISPLAYED ON HALF a dozen video monitors in the emergency operations center below the White House were the faces of President Day's de facto war cabinet. The continuity-of-government plan that was part of DEFCON-2 was in full effect, aiming to mitigate the effects of the terrorists' nuclear weapon if it were detonated in the nation's capital. Only General Landgraf, the secretary of homeland security, and a few aides and advisers remained with the president.

They were exhausted, stressed, and struggling to piece together the puzzle in front of them. Dressed in khakis and a blue oxford shirt, President Day took his seat at the head of the table and ran his hand over the stubble on his face.

The secretary of homeland security spoke first. "Ninety minutes ago, a Coast Guard C-130 was patrolling the western Gulf of Mexico when its radiation detector got a hit twenty miles south of Galveston, Texas. It was immediately classified as a high-interest vessel and the Coast Guard notified Customs and Border Protection, which deployed air assets to investigate."

"What kind of ship are we talking about?" asked the president.

"A tramp freighter. The Coast Guard gets hits on a lot of ship traffic, but their sensors are designed for long range and can't differentiate between different types of radiation."

"So they can't tell if they're detecting medical equipment or a nuclear weapon?"

"That's right, sir, but it's rare for this type of ship to be emissive, and given our current threat condition, we scrambled a Black Hawk and a Dash 8 to investigate. Both have radioisotope identification detectors that can discriminate the source. The aircraft should make contact within the next ten minutes and let us know exactly what the threat, if any, is."

"Where is the ship now?"

"About thirty miles south of Houston, Mr. President."

"Are either one of your aircraft armed?"

"They're not equipped to resolve this type of threat. We'll coordinate military assets for the takedown. We don't want to sink the ship, just disable it quickly at standoff distance from the coast. The concern with any nuclear threat is that, if the subject becomes aware that he is about to be arrested—"

"He detonates the weapon," said the president. "OK, be aggressive. We might not get a second chance on this one."

"We're on it, sir."

"Tell me about this Saudi prince."

CIA director Feinman spoke via one of the video

monitors. "Deputy Crown Prince Faisal bin Farah-Aziz al Saud is the head of the Saudi Arabian National Guard and second in line for the throne. He conspired with the Chinese in the attack on Mecca, and now he's using discontentment inside the country to prod the Allegiance Council to align the KSA with China and depose the king."

"In which case Crown Prince Mohammad will take over," said the secretary of state.

"How do we feel about the crown prince?" asked the president.

"Favorable, but we expect his reign to be short," said the CIA director. "He's likely to come down with lead poisoning . . . high-velocity lead poisoning, to be specific. Faisal already has plans to push him aside."

"So Faisal is going to take the throne himself?" said the president.

"The royal family is worried about another Arab Spring–type revolution. The first one cost them $130 billion in social-welfare programs to placate the population and they don't have that kind of cash lying around anymore. They're already running a $60 billion budget deficit. Faisal and his connection to the Chinese will make his ascension a done deal."

"It seems as if his plan is working," said the president.

"Most of it is," said the DCI, "but Faisal wasn't counting on Iranian meddling. They've been arming and provoking what had been mostly peaceful protesters inside the kingdom. The country is at a tipping point."

"Mr. President, you should speak with King Ali and

tell him what we've learned," said the national security adviser.

"He still isn't taking my calls."

"What about Ambassador Marek?" said the secretary of state. "Those two have a long history."

General Landgraf interrupted. "Sir, while I think the secretary is absolutely right about reaching out to King Ali, we need to assume that the Saudi communications network may be under Prince Faisal's control. Even before this recent power grab, the head of the National Guard was a formidable position. If Faisal learns we're onto him, he might initiate a coup, and that would be a bloodbath, maybe the beginning of civil war. The conversation with the king should happen face-to-face."

"There isn't time to get Marek on a plane," said the president. He looked to the secretary of state. "Can you send the deputy chief of mission?"

"Everyone is locked down inside the embassy."

The president turned to the CIA director. "Who do you have in-country?"

"About a dozen officers, including the one who recruited Faisal's chief of staff. I'd like to send him."

"Ali isn't going to like what he's hearing," said the president.

"This officer was also part of the ground team for Drifter-72," said the director. "He knows the situation and he might be our only chance to convince the king that we didn't kill those people in Mecca."

"Have Marek set it up immediately." The president looked at his chief of staff. "What's next?"

"We need to cover China, Iran, and Pakistan, plus the domestic situation."

"Let's cover the military action first." The president looked at General Landgraf.

"The Iran strike package is being assembled now, and we have live targeting data on fourteen of the twenty principals we designated, including all of the top five."

"And we're excluding the president and the foreign minister?"

"We're monitoring their movements and won't fire on any target within half a click of their locations."

The president nodded.

"We're going to hit the targets at night and in a single run," said General Landgraf. "Approximately fifteen minutes from the first impact, the Iranians will know we're out there. They'll launch everything they have at us, and every minute we loiter, the odds go up that they'll get lucky and down one of our aircraft."

"And China?" asked the president.

"For maximum tactical surprise, the event matrix dictates that the cruise missiles be launched just as the first bombs are falling on Tehran. We already have one SSGN in the South China Sea targeting the drone manufacturing facility and another one on its way to the East China Sea to target the drone control complex. Once they fire, they'll turn for blue water, where we have picket lines of attack subs waiting to intercept any pursuers."

"How many missiles are we firing?" asked the secretary of state.

"Twenty Tomahawks," said the secretary of defense from the doomsday plane. "Ten from each sub, ten for each target."

"We're operating on the assumption that fifty percent will make it through Chinese defensive counterair measures," said General Landgraf. "They have S-400 batteries along the coast."

"How many civilian casualties are we expecting?" asked the secretary of state.

"It will be after midnight there, so casualties at the UAV factory should be minimal," said the general. "The drone control center will be staffed by PLA forces."

"What about on our side?" asked the secretary of the treasury.

"Our subs will run deep as soon as they complete their fire missions, Mr. Secretary," said Landgraf. "The Chinese have some good nuclear and diesel-electric subs out there, and capable antisubmarine aircraft as well, but our subs and our crews are the best in the world. They'll be safe twenty minutes after they launch."

"What about escalation?" asked the president.

"As you know, we constantly war-game military action with other nations. Given China's nuclear capabilities, the consequences of escalation are potentially catastrophic, but it's not so much the possibility of escalation as the probability of escalation that we need to focus on. The Chinese are rational actors, but that doesn't mean they think the same way we do. Cultural differences, domestic politics, and the balance of power in nuclear and conventional forces all enter the calculus. It really depends on how they view our action. They probably had a meeting just like this one before they hijacked Drifter-72."

"So they've already accepted the possibility of retribution," said the president.

"In theory, sir, yes, but Drifter-72 did not physically target the U.S. homeland. If they perceive our cruise missile strike to be an escalation, specifically a preemptive strike on their limited nuclear arsenal, they will feel compelled to retaliate, most likely with a direct nuclear strike on the United States."

"And we still don't know what their objective was in attacking Mecca," said the secretary of state. "If they're trying to portray us as untrustworthy, then they'll deny any involvement in the hijacking and accuse us of once again attacking a peaceful nation. With the right messaging, they could use a U.S. attack on China to improve their standing and diminish ours. 'First Saudi Arabia and now China. Reluctantly, we must defend ourselves, and the rest of the world, from this unbridled American aggression.' It would be a public relations coup."

The room was quiet for several seconds.

"What do we think escalation would look like?" asked the president.

"Prior to the hijacking of Drifter-72, I would have said that we were the world leader in cyber," said General Landgraf, "but China appears to have highly capable quantum, and possibly postquantum, computers at their disposal. As I mentioned earlier, we consciously kept cyber options to a minimum on our targeting list because it's a road we don't want to go down. However, if China chooses to retaliate against our kinetic strike with cyber warfare, we could expect anything from GPS outages and power grid disruptions to a shutdown of telecommunications networks and attacks on our financial markets. The pervasiveness of technology makes the permutations almost limitless."

The president rubbed his eyes. "What else?"

"They could hit us with a limited conventional strike on a military facility, but they also have highly advanced space forces with hunter-killer satellites, and their ICBM fleet could kill fifty million Americans. It's all a question of how they view our actions and how rough they want to play."

"So if the Chinese leadership sees our strike as proportional retribution for hijacking Drifter-72, they'll accept their punishment and it's over?" asked the president.

"That's our assessment," said Landgraf.

"But if they somehow see our strike as unprovoked, we should expect an escalation."

"Yes, Mr. President, probably by an order of magnitude. Their memory of Japanese aggression in World War II is still quite vivid. China will respond aggressively to any unprovoked attack."

"And so will we," said the president. "China and Iran are about to learn that the hard way. Let's not forget who started this."

Heads nodded around the room.

"What about Pakistan?" asked the president.

"Sir," said the secretary of defense, "we had a meeting earlier with the directors of CIA and FBI and the

Joint Chiefs. Our conclusion was that we don't presently have enough information to act. We recommend bringing Colonel Turani back to the States, letting the intelligence agencies question him about his associates in AQAP, and keep drilling down until we know who within the Pakistani ISI provided the weapon to the terrorists."

"And then?" asked the president.

"If it was a rogue actor within ISI, then it'll probably be a job for JSOC or CIA," said the defense secretary. "If the order came from up the food chain, then we'll be reviewing another list of targets."

The president nodded. "I concur."

He looked at the clocks on the wall, he looked at the faces around the room, and he looked down at the target decks for Iran and China.

"Be ready to execute on my order."

## NINETY-FOUR

DESPITE JAKE'S PERSONAL animosity toward Ted Graves, the man excelled at getting things done. He'd been Jake's first call after Turani's confirmation of the nuclear weapon, and within hours the United States had gone to DEFCON-2, tripled search assets along the border with Mexico, and begun block-by-block searches of cities with radiation-detector-equipped air and ground assets.

And now it was time to call him again.

With no knowledge of Wǔ-Dīng's involvement in the attack on Mecca, China's Standing Committee would logically conclude that any U.S. military strike was the initiation of hostilities with China. They would be compelled to retaliate. It was the type of scenario that could quickly escalate into a nuclear exchange.

Jake used a secure laptop to videoconference Graves. Though it was nearly three a.m., the Special Activities chief was in his office and on-screen in four minutes. Jake ran through everything he'd been told by al-Shezza, focusing on Wǔ-Dīng's abuse of Chinese military assets and Faisal's plan to buy nuclear weapons from Pakistan. Graves fired back with a dozen questions and Jake answered them all until there was no doubt that Wǔ-Dīng had acted without the authority of the Chinese leadership.

"I need to get this to the White House," Graves said, "before we make a catastrophic mistake."

# NINETY-FIVE

GENERAL WŬ-DĪNG YŎNG was in his four-engine Y-20 transport plane, flying west over Inner Mongolia. Even in its VIP configuration, the cavernous interior was filled with nonskid flooring, tie-down straps, and cargo rails. The general had insisted that it all remain in place so the aircraft could fulfill its original role in times of war.

China's top military officer was en route to Riyadh, where he and Faisal would stand together and announce to the world the realignment of oil-rich Saudi Arabia away from the dangerous and unpredictable United States and to the People's Republic of China. It would be a significant foreign policy achievement that would further bolster China's political and military standing in the world.

But despite the cadre of aides constantly traveling with him, Wǔ-Dīng found himself essentially alone. There was no one with whom he could share his most important news. He picked up a telephone and dialed his home. His wife picked up after the third ring.

"Hello, my dear," said the general.

"Yǒng!" answered his wife. "How is your flight?"

"I am but one hour into my nine-hour journey and I miss you already."

"I am sorry we were unable to see each other this evening," she said. "I was hoping the 'chubby girl' could get serviced again before you left."

The general laughed.

"I would have liked to join you on your trip," his wife continued, "but my conscience will not allow me to travel to a country that treats its women like property."

"They are making progress, but I appreciate your feelings," said Wǔ-Dīng. "My darling, I am going to hang up and call you back on the secure telephone in my study. Please answer it."

"Is everything OK?"

"I have only good news."

The two reconnected on the secure line.

"Why the secrecy, Yǒng?" she asked.

"Do you recall how I told you that the Standing Committee was displeased with President Chéng's handling of the crisis between the Saudis and the Americans?"

"Of course."

"The committee has decided that the president will not receive a second term as general secretary."

"I will be grateful to be rid of catatonic Chéng," she said, "but the crisis doesn't even involve China. How could it topple him? Has he been lining his pockets? It would be a shocking display of hypocrisy after his endless missives about corruption in government."

"You would have made a formidable politician, my

darling wife, and Chéng has many faults, but corruption is not one of them. The situation with the U.S. and Saudi Arabia has broadened in scope rather significantly, to a point where the Americans are attempting to implicate China. Chéng is not a thief, but his inaction has most certainly put China at risk."

"Will there be war with the United States?" she asked.

"It cannot be ruled out. Chéng's idleness has emboldened them, but we are increasing our readiness now."

The general's wife was quiet for several seconds. "Will Mèng-Fù be the new general secretary?"

"Yes. He is the logical and best choice."

"Well, who will be the next premier? Not that straw bag from Discipline Inspection, I hope."

"No."

"The party secretary?" she asked.

"It will not be him either."

"I am tired of guessing, Yǒng. Whom have they chosen?"

"Me."

"But you are a military man and a low-ranking member of the committee!"

"My counsel has become much sought after among the other Politburo members. They have finally realized that there is no 'activity' in Chéng's policy of 'active defense.' "

"Congratulations, my dear. I know you will do great things for China."

Wǔ-Dīng smiled. His wife understood him perfectly. Throughout his career, his ascension was never about personal advancement. He never lorded his rank over those under his command. Increased status was desirable only as it presented a higher platform from which to guide China. His intent in hijacking the drone was never to topple President Chéng. Wǔ-Dīng sought only to present him with opportunities: the opportunity to secure China's supply of natural resources, the opportunity to diminish the standing of its chief global rival, the opportunity to ensure China's security and prosperity for centuries to come.

Opportunities that Chéng had failed to grasp.

A light flashed on the general's comms set indicating that he had an incoming call from PLA headquarters.

"You must tell no one, my darling. Though approval is just a formality, our new positions will not be official until the Presidium of the National People's Congress meets next month."

## NINETY-SIX

THREE UP-ARMORED SAUDI Humvees met Jake's cab outside the gate at Yamamah Palace. Just forty minutes earlier, Ted Graves had called and ordered Jake to brief the Saudi king on Prince Faisal's activities. Graves emphasized how critical it was that the king trust Jake, not only to restore a working relationship between the two nations, but for him to leave the palace with his head still attached to his neck.

Jake stepped out of the taxi and two muscular soldiers pinned his arms back while another wanded and frisked him. He was directed to the middle Humvee and the three vehicles drove through the rows of desert palm trees and past the fountains, through the man-made oasis in the searing heat of the city.

The small convoy stopped in front of the palace. Gone were the Royal Guards' gold-braided tunics and ceremonial swords. The twenty men who met Jake's vehicle were outfitted with black paratrooper uniforms and automatic rifles. He exited the car wearing a tan bisht over his thobe and was thrown up against the Humvee and thoroughly frisked again.

The scale of the palace was otherworldly, as if it had been built for giants. The bronze doors, marble floors, and silk-paneled walls were undeniably beautiful, but Jake was uneasy. He'd studied economics and understood global trade, but there was something about seeing firsthand how Americans' paychecks were being spent that drove the point home like never before.

*Maybe I'll buy an electric car when I get back to the States.*

The guards led him to a marble-tiled room, fifty feet wide by a hundred feet long, where another group of guards waited. He was frisked a third time before the guards parted to reveal His Majesty King Ali bin Abdul-Aziz al Saud, Custodian of the Two Holy Mosques. The king was seated on a dais, with three additional guards on each side. Jake approached to within thirty feet and was told to stop.

"I have known Anthony Marek for twenty years," said the king. "And throughout the complex machinations of international affairs and delicate matters of diplomacy, he has never lied to me. After what your country did to the Masjid al-Haram, that personal trust is the only reason you are here. You have ten minutes."

Jake looked around. There must have been thirty guards in the room. "What I have to discuss is extremely sensitive, a matter of life and death."

"I trust these men with my life every day," said the king.

"There is a highly placed traitor—"

The king raised his hand, commanding Jake to stop.

The king squinted, his thick eyebrows angled into a wedge of skepticism. After a moment, he dismissed all but the six guards on the dais.

Jake spent the next ten minutes detailing Prince Faisal's long history with General Wǔ-Dīng. He explained the men's repeated trips to Libya, the Chinese hardware that Jake had discovered, and Faisal's idea to attack Mecca during the Hajj. Jake described how communications intercepts and satellite technology had definitively proved Chinese involvement in the hijacking.

Twenty minutes later, Jake had explained the rest of Faisal's treachery, including how the prince had privately encouraged the king to support the U.S. while promoting unrest inside Saudi Arabia. Finally, Jake revealed Faisal's plan to depose the king and eventually the crown prince.

The king stared at Jake for a very long minute.

"There are not five men in the kingdom who could know the details of what you have just told me," said the king. "I have deduced your source and I have a question: Why did he go to you?"

"Your Majesty, his loyalty to you and the kingdom is his only motivation. The individual feared that if he asked for a private audience with you, and Prince Faisal learned of it, he would be killed."

The king nodded. It was a reasonable assumption.

Jake continued. "The prince's actions have allowed Iranian agents to foment the riots that are consuming your country. The pistols, the rifles, the explosives for the car bombs—they were all smuggled up from Yemen, courtesy of Iran's Qods Force."

"Tell al-Shezza that he is to be rewarded for his loyalty," said the king as he rose from his seat. "Tell him also that he need no longer worry about Prince Faisal, for I am going to cut off the traitor's head with my own sword."

## NINETY-SEVEN

THOUGH IT WAS well past the dinner hour, President Chéng Minsheng of the People's Republic of China did not feel much like eating. Lingering anxiety over the American accusations and dissent within the Communist Party occupied nearly all his time, yet accomplished nothing. Everywhere he turned he faced calls to do more, but the problems he was fighting were amorphous. Strategies and solutions proved elusive.

The president was in his office with several advisers, discussing a planned city into which the government had already sunk the equivalent of $19 billion. Completed twenty-three months earlier, it was less than 10 percent occupied. The provincial government had overborrowed to help finance construction, efforts to encourage private industry to relocate there had failed, and the national government either needed to double down and relocate state-run enterprises to the city or raze it to the ground. Despite the crisis with the Saudis and the Americans, it was a problem that could not wait. The interest expense and the maintenance costs would bankrupt the provincial government within a few weeks.

A knock at the door interrupted the conversation.

"Mr. President," said one of Chéng's assistants. "General Xiang is here to see you."

The president squinted. "Was he on the schedule?"

"No, sir, but he said it's urgent."

"Yes, of course," said Chéng. He dismissed the others from the room.

The head of the Ministry for State Security entered alone and closed the door behind him.

"I am sorry to disturb you, Mr. President, but I thought it best to speak in person."

The president gestured to several upholstered chairs and a coffee table from the Han dynasty.

"I looked into the items you requested," said General Xiang.

"Have you discovered the Americans' motive for accusing us of the strike?"

"No, sir."

"Is there evidence of a foreign power attempting to cause a Sino-American rift?"

"We have found no such connection."

President Chéng leaned forward. "Then why are you here?"

"You also asked me if it was possible for someone to commandeer the American aircraft."

The president folded his arms across his chest. "And?"

"One of my officers visited GSD Third Department, Second Bureau, to see if it was feasible to hijack a tactically encrypted unmanned aerial system. The bureau's commander indicated that he could not discuss the matter without proper clearance, so I called him myself. He told me that several months ago they made a breakthrough in penetrating tactical encryption using a new quantum computer."

"I am familiar with Second Bureau's work," said the president, "but they are gatherers of intelligence, not exploiters. This is outside their area of expertise."

"That is what their commander said, but he also suggested that Unit 7474–505B in Shanghai would be able to help with the investigation. However, the man I believe to be the unit's commander refused to even acknowledge its existence, much less provide any information."

President Chéng picked up the phone. "We do not have time for such bureaucracy, General. Who is the commander's superior officer?"

"I'm sorry, sir?" asked Xiang.

"Who does this commander report to?"

"I apologize for my confusion, sir, but I was told it reports directly to the Central Military Commission. That's why I came here. I was hoping you could grant me access."

The president's eyes narrowed as he replaced the telephone in its cradle.

"Then we have another problem, General. Because I am chairman of the CMC, and I've never heard of it."

## NINETY-EIGHT

SPECULATION RAN RAMPANT among the Royal Guards who'd been dismissed from the king's meeting with the American. Most concluded that he was an agent provocateur, sent with a story about a traitor to provoke a witch hunt and further divide the royal family.

But instinct was a powerful force, and one of the guards could not completely dismiss the possibility that the American might be telling the truth. The king certainly had not. The two men had spent nearly an hour behind closed doors.

Concluding that the revelation of a high-ranking traitor might tip the already fractured nation into civil war, the guard called his older brother, a brigadier general in the Saudi Arabian National Guard. The general respected his brother's judgment and, given the possibility that the National Guard might be called in at any moment to repel a coup attempt, the colonel did what any good soldier would do. He escalated it—straight to the head of the National Guard.

Prince Faisal hung up the telephone, but kept his

hand on the receiver, like a child afraid to end his turn at a board game.

*Perhaps the Americans have learned the existence of a traitor, but not his identity,* he thought.

After a moment he reconsidered.

*Ridiculous . . . Prince Sahib must have betrayed me. He was probably conspiring with the king to test my loyalty.*

The prince reconsidered again.

*No, I forced Sahib to take the first step. His overtures were genuine. It's more likely that the American intelligence services traced the Chinese satellite hardware back to Wŭ-Dīng and then to me. The king will have me executed, but the citizens will tear me limb from limb if they learn that I was responsible for the deaths of their brothers in Mecca.*

Faisal made two more calls and exited to a waiting car. If he acted decisively, his choices would not be limited to death by beheading or death by dismemberment. There was a third option.

His wives and children would suffer, of course, but there was no time to gather them. They would be stripped of their wealth and titles, ostracized by their friends and family, and forced to live as pariahs. Their future at the hands of the Mabahith would be distinctly unpleasant, but this did not trouble Faisal. They had become lazy and complacent. Perhaps a taste of the real world would do them good.

One engine was already turning on the Boeing 767 by the time he arrived at the airport's royal terminal. A warm breeze blew across the tarmac as Faisal walked to the plane. He turned at the top of the stairs and looked to the desert beyond, to the sky and the stars above. He breathed in the air, the smell of sand and sage, and closed his eyes. There was no turning back. Leaving the country without his staff and family, without notifying the king, would be a tacit admission of guilt.

*So be it.*

Faisal stepped inside the aircraft. In ten minutes, they were headed northwest, climbing through sixteen thousand feet. The Costa del Sol had long been a retreat for the Saudi royals. For decades they'd built extravagant homes on the bluffs overlooking the Mediterranean and traveled with servants and staff numbering in the hundreds. Faisal's residence was forty thousand square feet, with formal gardens and a subterranean garage filled with custom-built English and Italian cars.

The prince stared at the moving-map display, counting down the minutes until they were clear of Saudi airspace. He knew that as soon as King Ali discovered his absence, the king would launch a flight of his F-15SA fighters, booming through the air at Mach 2 while their phased-array radars and infrared search pods scoured the sky for the big 767.

The fighter planes would not warn the prince. They would not force his plane to land.

They would launch their missiles and fire their cannons.

And the flaming wreckage on the ground would be blamed on a tragic mechanical malfunction.

—"

## NINETY-NINE

W
Ǔ-DĪNG WAS ELEVEN thousand meters over
western China, looking through the window of his Y-20 transport. For as far as the
eye could see, the moonlight cast long, rippling shadows on the ground below. He lifted his secure phone
and reached Faisal on the third try.

"I am flying over the great Taklamakan Desert," said
Wú-Dīng. "Two thousand years ago, the Silk Road
trade route ran through its dunes, connecting China
and the Middle East. I thought you would appreciate
the parallel."

"I seem to recall that the Silk Road also carried the
plague west from China," said Faisal, "and perhaps that
is more fitting under the circumstances. Where are you
headed?"

"To Riyadh, of course. You sound distressed, Faisal.
What's troubling you?"

"You have heard nothing from your government?"
asked the prince, wondering if maybe he'd overreacted.

"Faisal, you're making no sense. What's wrong?"

"King Ali has discovered the presence of a 'high-ranking traitor' inside the government. I am on my way to Marbella until I can purchase a suitable residence further from the Saudi sphere of influence. I have a great deal of money offshore, in Switzerland mostly, and—"

"Are you certain it's you?" interrupted Wǔ-Dīng. "There must be many senior officials looking to distance themselves from the king. It could be the crown prince. It could be the minister of the interior. It could be anyone on the Allegiance Council."

"It could be, but it is not. The information came from an envoy of the U.S. president. We haven't admitted a single American into the country since the attack, and all of their diplomats are bottled up inside the embassy, so the envoy is most likely an intelligence operative who was already here."

"How does that exclude the others?" asked Wǔ-Dīng.

"Because, General, no Saudi would reveal a traitor through the Americans. He would tell the king directly to be rewarded for his loyalty. The Americans learned of my involvement because of your carelessness. They discovered your equipment in Libya. They uncovered Chinese involvement in the hijacking and connected me to you."

"Perhaps," he said, "but not everyone seeks a reward for his actions. I find it odd that I have heard nothing from Beijing if our affiliation precipitated the American outreach to Ali."

The general spent forty minutes trying to alleviate Faisal's fears, walking him through a dozen alternative scenarios for the American's meeting with the king. Wǔ-Dīng, by virtue of his tenacity and shrewd reasoning, had nearly convinced Faisal to return to Riyadh, when the general looked up. His pilot, a lieutenant colonel in the PLA air force, was walking aft along the hundred-foot-long cargo bay, his head down, his eyes averted.

Wǔ-Dīng hung up the phone in midsentence.

"Pardon me, General," said the pilot, still looking at the floor. "We have received orders to return to Beijing at once."

"Who issued the order, Colonel?"

"By order of the party, sir, direct from the Standing Committee. The CMC has moved to the joint battle command center and all PLA forces are now at Readiness Condition One. The strategic rocket forces in eastern Qinghai province are being relocated and readied for launch."

Wǔ-Dīng glanced out the window. To the south was a snowcapped mountain peak awash in moonlight, reaching up almost to the altitude of the airplane. It was the Kongur Tagh, the tallest mountain in the Pamir mountain range, and it was fifty miles inside the Chinese border from Tajikistan.

Wǔ-Dīng removed a pad of paper from the nylon briefcase on the seat next to him. He wrote a few sentences and signed it conspicuously before handing it to the pilot.

"Colonel, we cannot be sure that the unusual order you received is authentic. In your hand is a written order from me acknowledging receipt of the return order, but instructing you to continue on to Riyadh until we can verify the instructions you have received. I will speak with Beijing." He nodded to the colonel.

"Yes, General." The pilot saluted and walked back to the cockpit. There wasn't a soldier in the PLA who wouldn't lay down his life for the general, but there was no point in making him do so unnecessarily. Wǔ-Dīng's note would be the pilot's get-out-of-jail-free card upon his return to the capital.

The general looked out the window. A few minutes later, the Y-20 crossed into Tajik airspace and Wǔ-Dīng dialed Faisal once again.

"I was correct. Wasn't I?" asked the prince.

"We were ordered back to Beijing," conceded Wǔ-Dīng, "but the flight crew is loyal to me. We are continuing on."

"Chéng is showing his teeth at last," said Faisal. "You can't go to Riyadh. The king will have you detained the moment you step off the plane."

The general was silent. He preferred thinking to Faisal's endless talking.

"Of course, you must have some money abroad," said the prince. "Where will you go?"

"I have no assets outside China. The trappings of my position belong to the office, not to me personally. I am but a civil servant."

"That is a shame," said Faisal without a hint of sincerity. "Perhaps you could call Nafusa. Even a bankrupt Chinese general could probably live well in Libya."

"Be careful, Faisal. It is not just King Ali who will be after you. The Americans and the Chinese will also seek justice, and they are formidable hunters. There will be very few places for you to hide."

Faisal pounded his fist on the table, spilling a glass of ice water onto his lap. He cursed and began to blot it with his napkin. A moment later, his pilot came over the intercom.

"Your Highness, we are being ordered to turn around and land in Cairo."

"Ordered by whom?" snapped the prince.

"There is an American fighter aircraft on our left side, sir."

"Where are we now?" asked Faisal.

"In Algerian airspace, sir. Just past Tunis."

Faisal doused his reading light. A hundred feet from his wingtip was an F/A-18 Super Hornet with "US NAVY" stenciled on the side. Several air-to-air missiles hung beneath its wings.

"Turn south," said Faisal.

"I'm sorry, sir?" said his pilot.

"Turn south now!" Faisal snapped.

"Sir, there is probably another fighter behind us. That's standard protocol for an interception."

"Colonel, if you turn south now, there is perhaps a fifty percent chance that the Americans will fire and you will die a relatively quick and painless death. If you disobey my order, there is a one hundred percent chance that you will die a very slow and eminently painful death."

The 767 banked slowly to the south. The fighter accelerated and turned sharply in front of the larger jet.

"Are you still there, Wǔ-Dīng?" Faisal asked, but the line was dead.

# ONE HUNDRED

J AKE RETURNED TO the safe house after his meeting with King Ali. Youssef was in the basement, running Turani through another round of questioning before his rendition to the United States.

Fadi was waiting in the kitchen. "Graves called for you," he said. "Twice."

Jake nodded and took the laptop upstairs. In six minutes, he had Graves on a secure videoconference.

"King Ali said he'll normalize relations," Jake said, "but he needs a few days to clean house before going public."

"He's got a lot of cleaning to do. Faisal is as good as dead, Crown Prince Mohammad will be lucky to end up in prison, and if I'm on the Allegiance Council, I'm probably expecting someone to crash in my door in the middle of the night."

"What about Wǔ-Dīng?" Jake asked.

"I took it to the director and he took it to the White House, but the president is sticking with the assumption that the Chinese government was behind the hijacking. He's unwilling to stand down solely on al-Shezza's testimony."

"King Ali believed him."

"King Ali had the pieces of the puzzle in front of him already," Graves said. "Al-Shezza just put them in the right places. It's a different dynamic with President Day. He doesn't know the players. He only sees the physical evidence: the cyber task force's work and the hardware you brought back from Libya. Both point to a sanctioned Chinese military operation."

"This could spiral out of control very quickly," Jake said.

"POTUS isn't calling off the strike on China without corroboration. We've got twelve hours to figure out a solution."

"Where is Wǔ-Dīng now?"

"It appears that both he and Faisal are airborne with their transponders off."

"Faisal left Saudi?" Jake said.

"Less than an hour ago," said Graves. "He filed a flight plan to Jeddah, but canceled it once they were aloft. We intercepted his plane in Algerian airspace, but he turned south overland and the fighters broke off the intercept."

"Who ordered that? He's the most wanted man on earth right now."

"The navy wasn't going to shoot him down over a populated area, and an Algerian S-300 surface-to-air missile battery was already painting our aircraft with its engagement radar."

"So where is he now?"

"At this point we have no idea of his destination or Wǔ-Dīng's."

Jake swore in frustration. Without Faisal or Wǔ-Dīng, the president would launch the attack on China and likely start a war.

Jake stared at the screen as an idea formed in his head.

"Libya," he said softly. "They're going back to Libya."

## ONE HUNDRED ONE

GRAVES CALLED BACK an hour later. "I've been pressing your theory that Faisal and Wǔ-Dīng are bugging out to Libya and the president has agreed to stop the attack on China—but only if we can find the two of them together. The current evidence is just too circumstantial."

"We have to try, Ted," Jake said.

"We are trying, Jake," Graves said. "A Delta troop is leaving Djibouti in an hour. They're going to rendezvous with the Bush carrier group in the Mediterranean, then wait for approval."

"Approval? We're about to attack China and we can't green-light the mission?"

"We're wrestling with JSOC over who has legal authority to go after two senior foreign leaders."

"Shouldn't the president make that decision?"

"The president has made his decision," Graves said, "and it's to not make a decision. He doesn't want to be wrong about this in case it goes south. The plan is to hit the ruins a couple hours before dawn if we can settle the Title 10/Title 50 issue."

"What size force?"

"Twenty men."

"We need to send more," Jake said.

"It's all that's available. The Unit is in high demand right now. You might have noticed that we're at DEFCON-2."

"They're going to be slaughtered."

"It's Delta, Jake. I think they can handle a couple of middle-aged guys and a squad of Libyan militia."

"I'm not questioning their ability, Ted. That amphitheater is a maze of hidden rooms and hallways. There are a dozen sightlines to every approach. Twenty defenders could hold off a hundred assaulters."

"I'm sure they've trained for action over open ground."

"It's not the exterior that I'm worried about. Each of the three levels is laid out differently. The arena is a killing field with only two staircases up to the next level, both by the podium and easily defended. The second level has collapsed walls and easily a hundred columns to provide cover for the Libyans, and most of the upper-level staircases were wooden. They rotted away a thousand years ago, which means the Delta troop is going to have to find the few remaining stone ones. The Libyans will know this place inside and out. Our guys will be massacred."

"And we still won't have Wǔ-Dīng."

"You are one cold sonofabitch."

"Look, Keller, I don't want to see our soldiers die any more than you do, but it's a risk we have to take. Do you think Eisenhower launched Overlord thinking every one of those boys would be going home to his family? Grow up. Leadership isn't a reward; it's a responsibility."

"They won't make it past the first floor."

"So what do you suggest?"

"Send me," Jake said.

"You just said it was a suicide mission."

"They'll have a fighting chance if they know the layout."

"Delta will laugh you out of the building."

"Not once they see the place. I don't want to run the show, Ted. I just want to stop World War III before it has a chance to start."

Graves sat back in his chair and clasped his hands under his chin.

"It's your funeral," he said.

"Then so be it."

---

T HE LIBYAN SOLDIERS got to their feet as the sound of jet engines broke the early morning stillness. A few minutes later, the enormous Chinese transport plane landed and taxied to the apron with its lights off. General Nafusa's Land Cruiser drove out to meet it.

General Wǔ-Dīng emerged from the loading ramp and the two men exchanged greetings over the noise of the idling engines.

"Prince Faisal has arrived already?" shouted Wǔ-Dīng.

"A few hours ago," said Nafusa. "My men took him south to the ruins."

"I would have thought the base in Tobruk would be more secure."

"There are too many eyes in Tobruk. You'll be safer outside the city."

Wǔ-Dīng frowned. "What about his plane?"

Nafusa pointed to the 767, parked inconspicuously among several commercial aircraft.

"Keep it guarded and fueled," said Wǔ-Dīng. "We may need it on a moment's notice."

The Chinese general faced the ramp of his own aircraft, where the pilot stood at attention in the dim light of the interior. The pilot snapped off a salute, which Wǔ-Dīng returned. In ten minutes, the "Chubby Girl" had made a hot turnaround and was on her way back to Beijing.

"There will be a lot of people looking for that plane soon, if they aren't already," Wǔ-Dīng said to Nafusa.

"The prince said there were complications," Nafusa said as he opened the SUV's door for his guest.

"An understatement, to be sure," said Wǔ-Dīng. "We may soon have visitors with hostile intent."

Nafusa climbed into the passenger seat. "Do not fret, General. I have not forgotten what you have done for us. You will not fight alone while a single one of us is alive."

Wǔ-Dīng took stock of the convoy of old SUVs, dented cars, and armed pickup trucks as it pulled out of the airport.

Sand blew across the road as they headed south, deep into a desert where not a drop of rain had fallen in three years. The vehicles rode with their windows lowered as the sun rose above the horizon. Rocket launchers and rifle barrels protruded from every opening.

It was late morning when the convoy stopped in front of the oval amphitheater. The ruins were just as Wǔ-Dīng remembered. Two thousand years of strong winds and blowing sand had worn down every surface that wasn't covered in limestone stucco. He exited the SUV, still wearing his leather boots and uniform jacket in the hundred-degree heat.

Nafusa spoke. "General Wǔ-Dīng, I fear that all these soldiers and the vehicles, especially the technicals, will attract the attention of American surveillance. I will reposition them to a nearby town where they will not arouse suspicion."

"Perhaps we could shelter them under the larger arches," said Wǔ-Dīng, but Nafusa was already giving orders to his lieutenants.

"It's too perilous," said Nafusa. "Fifty of my best men will remain here to provide security."

"I would prefer a larger force to hold such a sizable, open structure," said Wǔ-Dīng.

"Their tribe has lived here for hundreds of years. These men know the land better than anyone," said Nafusa. "However, the residents of the town will not be receptive to the arrival of Libyan National Army troops, so I will need to travel there myself to smooth things over. My men will be able to reach me if you require our assistance tonight; otherwise, I will return in the morning."

"How far is the town?" asked Wǔ-Dīng.

"One hour south of here, on the edge of the Great Sand Sea," said Nafusa.

Wǔ-Dīng scowled. A quick reaction force that was an hour distant was useless.

In a few minutes, Nafusa had rounded up his fighters and departed. The remaining men were scattered about. Most sat half-asleep in the shade of the amphitheater's arches, their weapons lying on the sandy ground. The veterans had left with the general. The men he'd left behind were barely old enough to shave.

Faisal emerged from the hundred-foot-long colonnade on the south side of the amphitheater, the corners of his mouth turned sharply down. Wǔ-Dīng regarded the prince and could not help but smile. Faisal's hand-tailored suit, crocodile shoes, and enormous gold watch were all covered in dust.

Wǔ-Dīng knew a little Arabic. "Good morning, my desert-dwelling friend! You didn't think to pack a thobe and some sandals?"

A few of Nafusa's men chuckled. Faisal did not.

Wǔ-Dīng continued. "You shall soon see how you'd be living if Ibn al Saud hadn't pitched his tent atop an ocean of oil."

"We would not be here at all, if not for your recklessness."

"We will probably never know, will we?"

Faisal began walking back to the colonnade. Wǔ-Dīng walked alongside.

"I trust your quarters meet with your satisfaction," said the general. "Did they remember the fresh dates for your pillow?" He reached out to pat the prince on the back, but Faisal slapped his hand away. He did not welcome the general's attempt to lighten the mood.

"You are a fool, Wǔ-Dīng. I agreed to your terms only so the Allegiance Council would replace the king. After Mohammad was gone, I was going to sell our oil on the open market to the highest bidder."

"You can't be serious, Faisal. You would have been another failed Middle Eastern state within a year, with anarchy in the streets and at the mercy of Iran."

Faisal stepped forward until he was inches from Wǔ-Dīng.

"Not with an arsenal of nuclear weapons purchased from Pakistan."

"I am afraid it is you who has been foolish, Faisal. Do you really think Pakistan would sell you weapons just because they are fellow Sunnis? Was ISI stringing you along? What did you offer, one hundred million dollars? Five hundred million dollars? Alienating China and the United States would cost Pakistan *billions* in aid alone."

Faisal trembled with anger.

"They can barely maintain control over their own stockpile," Wǔ-Dīng continued, "and they need those weapons to compensate for their conventional-forces deficit with India. What do you think would happen to the balance of power in the Middle East if Saudi Arabia had its own nuclear arsenal? Do you think Iran would stand idly by? How would Egypt react if Iran's nuclear weapons program was accelerated? Might Jordan and the UAE decide that it is in their best interest to have their own nuclear forces? Israeli jets would be flying laps around the region, dropping their atomic weapons. You are impetuous, like a small child. Always acting, never thinking. Pakistan would *never* sell you a nuclear weapon."

Faisal spit on the general's chest.

"Be careful, Faisal. I am not a prideful person, but this uniform represents more than just a man."

The prince raised his chin and spat again.

Wǔ-Dīng knocked him effortlessly to the ground. The prince wiped blood from his jaw.

"This mess is of your own making, Faisal. Islam is rooted in teachings from the seventh century, and now you have returned to that era, a time when food, shelter, and survival were a man's primary needs." Wǔ-Dīng gestured around him. "Forgetting the lessons of your father and his father before him, you have come back to the desert, where your title and your money count for nothing. You have no motorcade, no bodyguards, and no army. Let's see how you survive here on your own. Let's see what kind of man you truly are."

Wǔ-Dīng turned his back on the prince and proceeded into the amphitheater alone.

Faisal wiped more blood from his face as he walked to the end of the colonnade. A Libyan soldier was sitting alone under the grand entrance. Faisal removed the gold watch from his wrist. Two months earlier the prince had paid $250,000 for it in Geneva.

He showed it to the guard and traded it for a pistol.

# ONE HUNDRED THREE

A CORPORATE JET WHISKED Jake to the Greek island of Crete, where he transitioned to a civilian helicopter. The twin-engine EC-225 lifted into the night sky and turned out to sea. It was nearly midnight when the CIA pilots landed on the aircraft carrier USS *George H. W. Bush*.

A helmeted sailor in a white jersey opened the helicopter's side door.

"The old man wants to see you," the sailor shouted over the roar of the flight deck.

Jake stepped onto the steel deck. The wind was blowing thirty knots over the port bow as the carrier steamed east-southeast. In two hours, the strike group would be fifty miles off the coast of Tobruk.

The sailor led Jake across the deck. Slivers of moonlight between the clouds revealed a black sea and white-capped waves. Half a dozen MH-60M Black Hawk helicopters were tied down in the corral just forward of the island. Even from one hundred feet away, their matte-black paint made them nearly invisible.

The two men entered the carrier's narrow superstructure, ducking and weaving through hatches and around other personnel as they made their way to the upper deck of the island. The strike group commander was speaking with the air boss when Jake entered.

"Admiral Vogel, the VIP is here, sir," said the sailor.

The admiral motioned for Jake to follow him to another room. An F/A-18 Super Hornet emerged from the darkness over the stern and was recovered to the flight deck as it snagged the third arresting cable.

The admiral looked out over the flight deck as he spoke. "This command is one of the ten most powerful fighting forces in the world. I've got eighty-one hundred sailors, ninety-six aircraft, ten ships, and an attack submarine," said the admiral. "It's a responsibility I shoulder with pride, but we've never been to DEFCON-2 before and don't exactly know what to expect, so we're ready for anything."

He turned to face Jake.

"Frankly, I'm glad to see that we're finally going on the offensive. I know the attack on Mecca wasn't ordered by the United States of America. It's not what this country stands for."

The steam-driven catapult launched another heavily armed Super Hornet into the air. Its afterburners illuminated small vapor trails in its wake.

A man dressed in combat fatigues entered the room.

"Major Smith," said Admiral Vogel, "this is Jake. He's going to accompany you into the target."

"*To* the target or *into* the target, sir?" asked the major.

"*Into* the target. It looks as if this is going down as a

Title 50 mission," said the admiral, "which means CIA owns it. They're entitled to have a man inside."

"I'm not comfortable with that, Admiral," said Smith.

"I'm not looking to put anyone at risk, Major," Jake said. "And for what it's worth, I just spent six months training with a couple of former H Squadron guys."

"I'm sure you're totally switched on, sir, and I'm an ex–H Squadron guy myself, but I would have the same concerns with any of those men, some of whom probably had a lot longer in the building than I do. The soldiers going on target tonight train together as a team. They can read each other's minds. To have an outsider in the stack is going to add a variable that might get someone killed when a split-second decision has to be made."

"I won't get in your way. I just want to make sure the mission is successful and your men don't get slaughtered in the process."

The admiral turned to Jake. "Make no mistake, the Agency may own this mission, but Major Smith is ground force commander. His word is law."

"Roger that, sir," Jake said.

"I understand this is a time-sensitive target, so I'll let you two get to it." The admiral dismissed the two men and they headed toward the mission's tactical operations center.

"I get it, Major," Jake said. "A troop is a troop. I'm not looking to step on anyone's toes."

"It's nothing personal," Smith said as the two men shook hands. "Hell, I usually stay out on perimeter until after the initial breach. You should be prepared for a little pushback from the troop sergeant major, though. Jeff's been rude from time to time."

Inside the tactical operations center were a dozen men in their mid to late thirties wearing camouflage pants and long-sleeve T-shirts. Most were standing around a table with a model of the ruins on it; others were studying a video monitor with a large topographical map of the area. Behind them was a group of pilots from the army's 160th Special Operations Aviation Regiment, studying detailed slides of the ingress route and diagrams of the objective. On the wall were more monitors, including one that displayed a slow-moving infrared feed of the site.

"We put a UAV overhead a couple of hours ago," said an intelligence analyst upon seeing Jake and Smith. She gestured to the screens. "There's some low-power radio traffic and a few military-age males, but not much activity."

Smith introduced Jake to the room. "Jake is going to accompany the assault force inside."

The troop sergeant major, a rock of a man with unruly hair and flecks of gray in his beard, gave Jake a hard stare. "It might be safer for everyone if you were out on cordon until the site exploitation."

"There isn't going to be any site exploitation if your men can't secure the objective," Jake said. "I walked every inch of it two days ago and it's like a maze, with a huge advantage to the defenders. They'll have the high ground, good cover, and long sightlines on all the approaches. You'll be funneled into ambushes and strong points. It's just the way it's laid out."

"What's your background?"

"I was an analyst before I joined Special Activities—"

The troop sergeant major grimaced.

"Then I spent six months training with former Unit guys who work with us now and the last four weeks running low-vis ops in Yemen. I know I'm nowhere near your standards, and I'll stay out on cordon if you insist, but twenty seconds after the initial breach it's going to get ugly in there and you're going to wish I was with you. We should be assaulting this place with a force three times this size."

Jeff looked down at the model, then back up at Jake. "What do you know about the opposition?"

"Most likely Libyan National Army. The targets have partnered with General Nafusa in the past," Jake said.

"He usually travels with fifty to a hundred men," said the intel analyst. "They'll have technicals, heavy machine guns, and maybe some antiaircraft weapons."

The sergeant major looked up at Major Smith. "We're going to be outgunned, boss."

The MH-60M helicopters were fast, tough, and armed, but the weapons were mostly for self-defense.

Major Smith approached the Night Stalker flight lead, a solidly built man in his mid-forties who looked as if he could stare down a statue.

"Any DAPs in the package?" Smith said, referring to the aviation unit's Black Hawk gunships. With rockets, miniguns, cannons, and laser-guided missiles, they were formidable platforms.

"Two," said the Night Stalker pilot, "plus a stack of fixed-wing support at echelon."

"A-10s?" said Smith, referring to the close-air-support plane respected for its lethality and its fearless pilots.

"None in theater, but we requested an AC-130 fixed-wing gunship from Aviano and we'll have Super Hornets off the boat."

"We're going to need it all," said the troop sergeant major.

The intel analyst spoke again. "Keep in mind that Daesh and Ansar-al-Sharia are also active in eastern Libya. The threat we encounter might not be the one we're expecting."

"This is getting worse by the minute," Smith said. "Couldn't we just drop a couple JDAMs on your targets?"

"We need positive ID," Jake said.

"Is this a kill mission?" the troop sergeant major asked Jake, "or does your organization want these two alive?"

"Capturing the prince and the general would be an intelligence windfall," Jake said, "but no one up the command chain seems to want to make that decision, so we may have to launch without it."

"Just so we're clear," said the troop sergeant major, "if one of these sons of bitches reaches for a weapon, it's over."

"I'll pull the trigger myself," Jake said.

"What about enemy quick reaction forces?" asked Smith.

"Nafusa has a battalion based in Tobruk," said the

intel analyst. "They have heavy weapons, multiple-launch rocket systems, and antiaircraft capability, mostly man-portable missiles and 20mm cannons, but they're two and a half hours out, so they shouldn't be a factor unless they move to the ruins before time-on-target."

"In which case we scrub," said Smith. It wasn't a question.

The intel analyst continued. "There are also a half dozen towns, camps, and compounds within an hour's drive that could hold light-infantry fighters. We'll be watching the ISR, and there's a Global Hawk comms node orbiting the target, so you'll see any threats in real time."

"What do we have on cordon?" Smith asked.

"Two squads of Rangers puts us at our weight limit," said the Night Stalker flight lead. "We'll log some ground time to save fuel, but it's a long hop overwater and we need loiter time at the objective."

The group was quiet for a minute. They needed more of everything, but the math was the math.

A dozen eight-by-ten-inch photographs of Faisal and Wǔ-Dīng were taped to a wall. It was a welcome contrast to many missions, where the subjects were poorly known and teams went into the field with only a dated, grainy photograph for comparison. Jake stared at a picture of Wǔ-Dīng reviewing a line of troops.

"This man ran the People's Liberation Army. He isn't going to make this easy," Jake said. He walked over to the video wall and gazed at the live feed from the ruins. "If we miss him tonight, he's gone."

"It'll be damn quiet out there in the middle of the night," said the troop sergeant major, "and the wind is from the north, so we'll do an offset infil from the southwest and a five-click patrol to the objective."

"We're going to need to keep an eye on those winds," said the flight lead. He pointed to the map on the wall. "There's an unstable air mass the size of Texas out there. If it starts blowing from the east, the front will kick up a dust storm from the Great Sand Sea."

"How will that affect us getting on target?" Jake asked.

"We'll get you there if it's physically possible, but a violent weather system en route will make this mission a no-go. That wall of dust and wind will fuck our shit up."

Jake examined the model of the amphitheater. It was four feet long and highly detailed, right down to the missing stairways and fallen columns on the top level.

"This is incredible," he said.

The intel analyst smiled. "The UAV scanned the site with radar and lasers during its first few orbits and we used a 3-D printer to make the model."

"What can you tell us about the interior?" said Smith.

Jake spent twenty minutes describing the layout, talking them through each of the three tiers and drawing half a dozen diagrams on a nearby whiteboard.

The sheer volume of information, combined with Jake's detailed recall and his insightful analysis of the tactical challenges and opportunities presented by the two-thousand-year-old structure, gave the two Delta leaders pause. The design of the amphitheater would indeed give the defenders an enormous advantage.

Jake was right, they needed him in the stack.

And he was right about something else too.

It was going to be ugly.

F AISAL CLUTCHED THE pistol in his hand as the
moon rose into the sky.

Much of the fragile sandstone had collapsed over the past two millennia, leaving his room without most of its roof or exterior walls. The howling wind scattered sand everywhere: across the floor, in the corners, in his hair. But the prince had not chosen his quarters for protection from nature, he'd chosen them for protection from man. It was the farthest point from the main entrance, with a fallen column across its entry.

Faisal lowered himself into a corner and faced the doorway. The prince racked the slide on his pistol, a Soviet-era Tokarev 7.62, and an unfired round popped out amid the swirling sand. Faisal carefully placed it back in the chamber and held the gun in his lap, flinching at every shadow and unfamiliar sound.

GENERAL WŬ-DĪNG HAD suspected Nafusa was giving them the brush-off when they'd driven to the ruins instead of the base in Tobruk. Though the Libyan warlord had vowed to protect his former benefactors, it appeared that he had abandoned them once they were no longer of value to him. His departure with his seasoned soldiers had merely confirmed it.

Wǔ-Dīng surveyed the amphitheater, walking through the colonnade, under the arches, and over the rows of seats. He noted the sightlines and the natural obstacles, the places that would be easy to defend and those that would be more challenging. The remaining Libyan troops were scattered around the perimeter. Most were sitting under the arches; several were smoking. All looked bored.

The general passed a statue of a Roman centurion and approached one of the fighters, a wiry man in his early twenties. Wǔ-Dīng stood next to the young man, looking out over the moonlit desert.

"A difficult place to defend," the general noted pleasantly.

The man squared himself away, adjusting his mismatched uniform and the cloth *shemagh* around his neck.

"Yes, sir."

"If we were attacked tonight," asked the general, "where would they come from?"

It was the first time an officer, much less a general, had ever asked the soldier for his opinion.

"From the north, sir, so the sand will be in our faces."

"But sound carries far on the desert wind. Might they not come from the south?"

"They will come with the sand at their backs," the soldier said confidently. "As the desert tribes have always done."

The general pointed. "Then we won't see them coming over that ridge until they're on top of us."

"We could move higher," offered the young man.

"An excellent idea," said Wǔ-Dīng. "Why don't you round up half the men and take them to the top floor. Be sure each has a roof over his head to hide him from aerial surveillance."

"Yes, sir!" said the young man. He saluted the four-star general and disappeared through the outer ring of the building.

Wǔ-Dīng continued with his tour of the defenses, setting up fire teams, establishing communications, and repositioning men for overlapping fields of fire. They had limited ammunition and he emphasized the importance of using aimed fire instead of simply pointing in the general direction of the enemy and holding down the trigger.

Around and around the general walked, until he knew each floor, each room, each patch of crumbling floor. He knew the bottlenecks and the blind spots. He pointed out avenues of approach and identified kill zones where the invaders would have to cross open ground. He turned the Libyan radios to low power settings and explained the capabilities and the limitations of the thermal and night vision technologies the soldiers might be up against. The Libyan fighters started asking questions.

By midnight, every weapon had been cleaned and inspected and not a single Libyan soldier was smoking or sitting down. They were watching and listening, preparing physically and mentally for what would soon be a fight for their lives.

## ONE HUNDRED FIVE

THE THREE BLACK Hawks handling the lift cranked their engines in unison at 01:15:00, their passengers loaded for bear. At 01:35:24, the aircraft simultaneously pulled pitch and departed from the deck.

With their interior and exterior lights doused, the matte-black helicopters quickly disappeared from view, lost among the murky silhouettes of the ships in the carrier task force. Wind gusts buffeted the aircraft as they flew south toward the coast, three hundred feet above the waves.

The aircraft carrier *George H. W. Bush* had been running combat air patrols over the southern Mediterranean for the past six hours while American E-2D Hawkeye aircraft and unarmed navy and air force UAVs orbited the battlespace, sending real-time intelligence and infrared video back to the carrier, the helicopters, and a smattering of interested parties in the intelligence and military chains of command.

Wearing night vision goggles and face masks, the Night Stalker pilots chose an ingress route that avoided populated areas and Libyan radar. At the same time, formations of F/A-18 Super Hornets performed fighter sweeps up and down the coast to dull the senses of Libyan shore-based radar operators and discourage any Libyan aircraft from taking to the sky.

Inside the lead Black Hawk, call sign Owl-61, the aircraft was packed tight. With the side doors locked open, three men sat on each side of the cabin with their legs dangling outside the helicopter; another four sat front to back down the centerline.

Some of the men checked their kit, some racked out, and some just stared out over the Mediterranean Sea, but Smith was doing everything he could to ensure the success of the mission and the safe return of the men under his command. Jacked into the aircraft's intercom system and the command and fires communications networks, he monitored the intelligence, surveillance, and reconnaissance assets for any updates since they'd launched. Several times, he wrote notes on strips of fluorescent tape or a small whiteboard and passed them around.

On either side of the cabin, the two crew chiefs scanned the outside world, their hands resting on the electrically powered miniguns in front of them. Each weapon could spit out three thousand rounds per minute if the need arose.

Jake was on the left side with his legs dangling outside. A crescent moon illuminated a sandy beach as they crossed into Libya, twenty miles east of Tobruk. The formation flew south between a Daesh camp to the west and the Libyan National Army's main base to the east.

The crew chiefs shouted over the noise of the wind and engines as they reached the target approach point.

*Two minutes!*

Jake looked around. The trip from the carrier had felt like ten seconds. Around him, the Delta operators echoed the two-minute call down the line, adjusted their kit, and prepared to release the snap links holding them to the floor.

*One minute!*

The Black Hawks were powerful and fast, but loud. To maintain the element of surprise, they flew to a landing zone far from roads or anything else. It was unfamiliar territory filled with unknown dangers. Something as simple as a power line or an unmarked antenna could take down one of the helicopters, kill everyone aboard, and scuttle the mission. It had happened before.

The workload in the cockpit became so intense that the pilots split the duties between flying and navigating. In a well-practiced partnership, the pilot navigating kept up a steady stream of staccato calls, identifying landmarks, distance, and heading. The pilot on the controls repeated it all back, knowing that even a slight misunderstanding could mean disaster.

The crew chiefs leaned aggressively out of their windows, scanning for threats, confirming landmarks, and looking for the landing zone. They rattled off a series of terse prelanding checks so quickly that anyone listening would have thought it was gibberish.

The aircraft slowed and pitched its nose down a few degrees.

"LZ in sight. I have the field, wadi to the south," said the pilot on the controls.

"Roger, LZ in sight," acknowledged the other. "Altitude good, one hundred feet. Fifty knots forward speed. Zero point three nautical miles to the LZ."

"Roger."

"Winds steady at twenty-two knots from your ten o'clock."

"Copy."

"Before landing checks complete. Pax secure?"

"Pax secure," answered the two crew chiefs.

"You're point one out. Thirty knots. Eighty feet," said the pilot navigating.

"Touchdown point in sight."

"Heavy dust at the tail," said one of the crew chiefs.

"Dust at my window," said the other.

"In the cloud," said the pilot flying.

And the dust cloud wasn't just outside. With the cockpit doors removed and the rear doors locked back, airborne sand swirled throughout the interior.

"Twenty knots. Fifty feet," said the pilot navigating.

The pilot at the controls finessed the twenty-two-thousand-pound helicopter like it was an extension of his body.

"I'm on the cues," he said.

The crew chiefs were leaning almost entirely out of the bird, searching for the ground through their NVGs.

"Left has the ground," said one over the IC.

"Right has the ground," said the other. "Tail on in five . . . three . . . one . . ."

The aft section of the aircraft touched down.

"Mains down in two . . . one . . ."

"On the brakes," said the pilot flying.

"We're good," confirmed the other.

The aircraft settled to the earth as hydraulic struts absorbed its weight. Jake could make out the other Black Hawks as they descended through the growing cloud and set down diagonally at hundred-foot intervals.

The passengers hustled out the side doors. The Rangers established a security perimeter around the three birds while the SOAR crews started shutting down the aircraft. With enough warning from the UAVs, the crews would spool up the engines and reposition the helicopters if they were compromised, but the Rangers and the aircrews would defend the aircraft with their lives if they had to. The partnership between the 160th and its customers was unbreakable.

The Delta troop assembled outside the rotor wash. All were wearing advanced fusion goggles that combined low-light and thermal sensors to give the men the ability to see in almost any conditions. Jake and the troop sergeant major were reviewing the assault plan when one of Owl-61's crew chiefs walked over.

"I tested your video feeds," he said. The two men were wearing helmet-mounted cameras that would send live video back to DoD and CIA command centers. "You're good to go."

Jake looked up as the helicopters' rotors stopped turning and the dust began to clear. The only sound was from the wind. The only light was from the moon. A complex mix of excitement and anxiety swept through him. He'd volunteered for the mission and he was ready for it, but it suddenly became very real.

He took a deep breath. They were three miles from the ruins.

"Troop sergeant major?" Jake said.

"Name's Jeff."

"Ready when you are."

The ground underfoot varied from jagged stone to soft sand as the team patrolled to a staging area southwest of the objective. The featureless landscape made it impossible to navigate by terrestrial reference points, so the men mostly oriented themselves to the moon, glancing only occasionally at the GPS receivers on their wrists to compensate for the moon's movement across the sky.

Major Smith spoke over the assault net, which each operator monitored through the radio headset he wore under his helmet.

*"This is Echo-1. ISR has two military-age males patrolling clockwise around the perimeter, presently one hundred meters west of building one."*

Jake looked to the northeast, hoping to catch a glimpse of the ruins, but the wind was blowing sand in his face. He adjusted the shemagh covering his nose and mouth and approached Smith.

"The wind is shifting," Jake said.

Smith nodded. "We might want to circle around and approach from the northeast."

"I don't know how much you've been told," Jake said, "but if we don't locate Wǔ-Dīng within ninety minutes, the United States is going to attack mainland China."

Streams of sand blew over the ground like ghostly

serpents, rising and falling along the contours of the dunes. All was quiet except for the howling wind.

The major checked a small tablet with the ISR feeds. The two MAMs had returned to the interior of the ruins. He waved over the troop sergeant major and filled him in.

"What do you want to do?" Smith said to the senior NCO.

"We go east half a click and hit it," Jeff answered.

Smith nodded and the troop set off at a brisk pace.

The top level of the amphitheater soon came into view. Heated hours before by the midday sun, its columns and arches and sandstone walls were cooling more slowly than the surrounding air, giving crisp detail to the thermal sensors on the team's night optical devices. A few minutes later the soldier on point came over the assault net.

*"This is Echo-12. Visual contact, two MAMs, weapons in sight, third floor."*

The raiding party continued its advance and it soon became clear that the Libyan soldiers had successfully avoided the overhead surveillance. At least eighteen of them were placed strategically along the eastern side, probably that number again on the western side, and undoubtedly more in the interior. The Americans were heavily outnumbered.

A gust of wind sounded like a low-flying jet as it blew by, covering every exposed surface with dust. The men brushed the sand off of their uniforms and shook it out of their kit.

Jake flipped a three-power magnifier into position

behind the red dot sight on his rifle. A lone man came into view on the second level, speaking to two of the sentries. The man lingered for a few moments before moving on to the next group. The guards seemed alert despite the late hour and poor conditions. The assault team would not be catching anyone sleeping tonight.

Smith came over the radio again. *"This is Echo-1. ISR update: crickets. Execute in five."*

Everyone acknowledged, including the fixed-wing aircraft and the three lift helos of Owl Flight, who started spooling up their engines. The two DAP gunships had launched from the carrier thirty-eight minutes after the others and would be overhead ten seconds after the initial breach.

A pair of two-man sniper teams moved into overwatch positions one hundred meters to the north and south of the amphitheater. Each was equipped with a Delta Level Defense M110 semiautomatic sniper rifle chambered in 6.5 Creedmoor. The teams would provide precision fire and an exterior cordon for the men who'd be assaulting the building. Major Smith stayed with one of the sniper teams to coordinate ISR and air support and give every possible advantage to the men who'd be kicking down the door.

The fifteen assaulters advanced on the objective, grateful for the swirling sand that covered their approach. Each one moved deliberately over the uneven ground, scanning a discrete arc, his rifle moving in lockstep with his eyes to minimize reaction time and maximize accuracy.

The major's voice came over the assault net again when they were twenty yards out.

*"Echo-1 to snipers, stand by."*

The marksmen on the ground would hold their fire until the assaulters had lost the element of surprise.

The troop stacked up outside the hundred-foot-long colonnade on the south side. Each carried a suppressed Heckler & Koch 5.56mm rifle and a .45-caliber handgun for backup. The pistol was a favorite of the Unit. Aside from packing a serious punch, the .45 also sent a message.

*America was here . . .*

The troop started checking in over the assault net.

*"Echo-1, set."*

*"Echo-2, set."*

Jake's senses sharpened as each member of the team confirmed that he was ready to go. Time seemed to slow.

*"Echo-11, set."*

*"Echo-12, set."*

As soon as the last man in the stack checked in, Smith gave the order to initiate the assault.

Two hundred fifty yards to the north of the amphitheater, a Unit sniper was prone on the back of a dune with only his head and rifle visible. He flicked off the safety on his DLD-M110 and stroked the single-stage trigger. A 142-grain bullet leapt from the 20-inch Kreiger barrel at 2,600 feet per second and impacted the first Libyan sentry in the center of his heart. The sniper to the south did the same and more sentries went down.

The lead assaulter swung inside the colonnade and moved to his right against the low wall that provided a base for the columns. The number two man followed but turned left. The two men advanced down the sides as the rest of the troop swept inside.

The team's rifles were mounted with infrared lasers. The beams of light, invisible to the naked eye, sparkled in their night vision goggles as they reflected off the swirling sand. In only a few seconds, the fifteen men expertly divided the colonnade into cones of responsibility. Fallen columns and scattered rubble made for odd shapes and shadows. At one point or another, half the team drew a bead on the statue of the centurion with the drawn sword, but no one pulled the trigger.

No threats were found and not a shot was fired. The fifteen men exited the colonnade and stacked up at the grand entrance to the amphitheater.

They flowed through the gate and seamlessly split into three five-man teams. Team one went left and team two went right. They started clearing the ground-level archways and more Libyans went down.

The troop sergeant major had taken Jake into the third team along with Mike, Kevin, and Lou, three veteran Delta operators. They advanced directly into the central arena.

The arena was ringed with dozens of columns and fifteen-foot-high sculptures of man and beast. Jeff, Jake, and Mike stayed to the right and walked toward the far side along the high wall. They searched 180 degrees to their left, scanning the seats over the heads of Kevin and Lou, who stayed left and scanned 180 degrees to their right. The moonlight, swirling dust, and soft sand underfoot made the experience almost surreal. Largely devoid of rubble, it was as it had been two thousand years earlier, when other men had fought to the death within its walls.

The team reached the end of the arena. The podium where the Roman governors once sat was in the center, twenty feet above the floor. Thick iron gates, long since rusted away, had once blocked the staircases on either side. The assaulters cleared both staircases and linked up on the second level.

Steady gunfire could be heard throughout the ruins as status reports from the various teams came over the radio.

*"Echo-7, two enemy killed in action, first floor, southwest side, look like Libyan National Army."*

*"Echo-12, four EKIA, first floor, southeast, confirm LNA."*

Jake looked at Jeff. "Faisal and Wǔ-Dīng are here."

The troop sergeant major nodded.

Jake motioned to the left, and the five-man team entered an aisle in front of the stadium seats. Four men covered the front and flanks while the fifth provided rear security. The open layout and sheer volume of the amphitheater demanded that each man aggressively scan his sector. Fallen columns, broken walls, and loose ceiling tiles provided constant distractions.

"Contact left," Mike said as he fired four shots from his suppressed rifle. Muzzle flashes and the distinctive sound of an AK-47 came from across the arena on the third level. Jake swung left and fired twice, but the two Libyan soldiers were already falling to the ground.

More gunfire and an occasional grenade echoed throughout the stadium. Reports came over the assault net of well-organized defenders waiting in ambush. The usual Middle Eastern "spray and pray" shooting style was nowhere to be seen. The enemy was using controlled bursts and coordinated attacks, and the defenders' superior numbers were starting to take their toll. Two operators had already been wounded.

Smith was on the radio networks, directing one of the sniper teams into the amphitheater to assist with the assault and coordinating air support. The DAP helicopter gunships and the AC-130 were overhead and waiting for targets, but the fighting was going on inside the amphitheater, where the aircraft's weapons were useless.

Jake led the team through a narrow hallway under the seats, to the place where a modern stadium would house its concessions. He aimed his rifle through a large hole in the ceiling as they passed under where a wooden stairway had once stood.

They advanced another twenty yards through a narrow passage and stacked up outside an open doorway. Beyond it lay the labyrinth of hallways and rooms that comprised the southern end of the floor. It was the exact place Jake had envisioned an ambush when he'd asked to join the assault team. He quickly described the layout to his teammates.

He and Jeff swung around the corner and into a long hallway. Mike and Kevin came in on their heels and turned into the first room on the right. Lou was behind them, covering the rear. Doorways on both sides of the hall provided half a dozen lethal sightlines to the men's position. They moved quickly, always in motion, spending just a second or two in each room before moving on to the next. The wind howled through the crumbling exterior walls.

The rooms were empty.

The team held short at the end of the hall. To their left was the eastern side of the floor. They swung around the corner just as a gust of wind sent a cloud of sand swirling through the air around them.

Twenty feet away, crouching behind a stone wall, an LNA soldier squeezed the trigger on his AK-47.

And Jake went down.

# ONE HUNDRED SIX

THE PUMPS ABOARD *El Nuevo Constante* had been working since the first wave crashed over her side and were finally pumping out more water than the ship was taking on. The tramp freighter was riding higher and moving faster than she had in days. The late afternoon sun, blazing through the clear skies that followed Beulah, was drying her out nicely.

*The captain would be pleased,* thought Carlos. *If the sharks hadn't finished him off already . . .*

Carlos struggled to find a comfortable seating position. He looked at the gauze covering his abdomen. It was saturated with blood. There had been times over the past few days when he'd wished his cargo had simply been smuggled aboard the narco-sub with the rest of the team's gear, but American law enforcement made that too great a risk. Conventional weapons were replaceable. His cargo was not. It required a shepherd.

Despite his suffering, Carlos was grateful that Allah, in His infinite wisdom, had chosen Carlos to be that shepherd.

He winced as he craned his neck to look out the

window. *El Nuevo Constante* had just rounded Galveston Island. In two more hours, his mission would be complete, his suffering would be over, and he would ascend to Paradise.

MARINE TRAFFIC FROM across the globe converged on the Port of Houston. As the second-busiest port in the United States, over one hundred billion dollars' worth of goods passed over its docks each year. It was a gateway for critical components of the American economy, from petroleum products and heavy machinery to passenger cars and imported liquor.

Before they'd left Mexico, Carlos had mounted a slim GPS receiver to the roof of the container. It was wired to a circuit board, a truck battery, and a relay. Once the GPS determined that it had reached 29.705 degrees north latitude, it would trigger the weapon. Carlos had even programmed the autopilot to take the ship there, north of the Fred Hartman Bridge near Houston, in case he succumbed to his injuries before *El Nuevo Constante* reached its final destination.

Not only would the explosion vaporize the bridge, but it would generate a radioactive tsunami that would flood the eastern part of the city. The enormous port, the fourth-largest city in the United States, and an additional 25 percent of U.S. refining capacity would forever be unusable. The radioactive half-life of uranium was measured in hundreds of millions of years.

But there was always the possibility that the authorities might try to stop him. Though he was delirious from blood loss, Carlos resolved with a fanatical clarity of purpose that if the American Coast Guard attempted to board *El Nuevo Constante*, he would use the remote detonator he'd brought to trigger the weapon and take as many unbelievers with him as possible.

The ship traffic became more pronounced as he neared the bay. A massive container ship, nearly nine hundred feet long, was anchored to the west. Up ahead, an even larger crude oil tanker was heading into port. Carlos stared at the giant ship. It was twice as wide as *El Nuevo Constante* was long.

*It would be a nice bonus if one of those were alongside when the weapon detonates,* he thought.

The terrorist was neither a physicist nor a chemist, but he assumed that vaporizing and igniting a million gallons of oil inside the blast radius would add considerably to its destructive power.

He returned to the wheelhouse as *El Nuevo Constante* pulled abreast of the container ship, anchored half a mile away. Nearly two hundred feet tall, its brightly painted containers formed a colorful mosaic on deck. His eyes were drifting over the containers when he heard a sound that was familiar, yet strangely out of place.

It had imprinted itself on his memory, somewhere in the rough desert climate of the Mideast, yet he couldn't place it. It seemed out of context on the ship, surrounded by the tranquility of the sea.

He searched for the source. It wasn't the constant hum of the old diesel engine beneath him. It wasn't the distant noise of a passenger jet overhead. It wasn't even the mechanical whine of the two white speedboats racing each other on his starboard side. It was more of a flutter.

*What was it?*

Carlos lifted the remote detonator from the nav table and staggered out of the wheelhouse.

Half a mile away, two helicopters emerged from the bright sunlight and passed over the container ship. They were flying fast and in tight formation.

Carlos recognized them immediately. Apache gunships. The Longbow radar domes above their main rotors made them unmistakable. He had seen them before in the Bekaa Valley, when their arrival had presaged death and destruction. Rockets and missiles had leapt from their sides, destroying the vehicles and weapons of his fellow soldiers. Then the Israeli pilots had switched to their cannons and slaughtered the survivors.

The attack helicopters dove for the wave tops, but their 30mm chain guns remained trained on *El Nuevo Constante.*

Carlos realized that the success of his mission was at risk. Every significant event in his life had led to this moment. All of the training, all of the sacrifice. It was time to show his true devotion. He lifted the remote detonator and began to enter the ten-digit code. Each number was an exercise in agony as he held the detonator in his good hand and entered the digits with the one Miguel had shattered with the hammer.

The quad-engined speedboats turned toward the tramp steamer and accelerated to over fifty knots.

Puffs of smoke appeared in front of the helicopters as their chain guns fired.

The Apaches fired several fifty-round bursts up opposite sides of the deck, their shallow angle of attack designed to kill anyone on board without penetrating the hull. The helicopters circled the tramp freighter as it continued on autopilot. Thermal sensors scanned the ship's deck for movement, but there was only one heat source, and it was down.

The two white speedboats pulled to either side of the ship. Eight men with compact rifles leapt onto its deck. Half of the Customs and Border Protection Special Response Team went forward, the other half aft. In two minutes they'd cleared the ship, turned for the open sea, and radioed the helicopter pilots, requesting that they stay on station until a Nuclear Emergency Support Team could come aboard and disarm the weapon. One of the customs officers walked up to Carlos's body and removed the remote detonator from his hand.

There were nine numbers on the display.

# ONE HUNDRED SEVEN

PRESIDENT J. WILLIAM Day was in the Oval Office, preparing to depart the White House for Joint Base Andrews and Air Force One. The increasing likelihood of a nuclear exchange with China had finally convinced him to relocate.

The remaining staffers had departed earlier in a motorcade of black vans and SUVs. Only the chairman of the Joint Chiefs of Staff was still with the president, reviewing final plans for the attacks on China and Iran.

Landgraf looked out over the Rose Garden while the president made a call to the leader of Taiwan. The island nation would pay a heavy price in any conflict between the U.S. and China. President Day, while not disclosing the impending military action, informed the Taiwanese president that two U.S. aircraft carrier battle groups were steaming into waters outside the First Island Chain, fully prepared to honor the United States' legal obligation to come to Taiwan's aid if it were ever attacked by China . . .

\* \* \*

DESPITE WIDESPREAD ANXIETY surrounding the recent terror attacks, a few dozen spectators still lined the fence along the South Lawn of the White House. A Hispanic-looking man wearing sunglasses and a baseball hat smiled at the small children next to him as a murmur of excitement rippled through the crowd. The president's iconic "white-top" helicopter was approaching from the south, banking gently in front of the Washington Monument as it descended.

GENERAL LANDGRAF WATCHED the helicopter fly over the Ellipse before touching down. The pilots shut down the engines, the rotor blades stopped turning, and the marine guards prepared for embarkation.

President Day finished his call with the Taiwanese president. The Asian leader had asked his American counterpart point-blank if he should be preparing for hostilities with China, and President Day responded, *You should always be prepared* . . .

A Secret Service agent opened the exterior door to the Oval Office. "The helicopter is ready, sir."

The president and the general walked outside under a cloudless blue sky. Neither of them had felt the sun on his face since the attack on Mecca.

A FEW BLOCKS north of the White House, a black Sprinter van was parked on 16th Street. Identical vans were parked to the west and east. With triple-tinted windows and the logo of a limousine company on their sides, the vans were nothing more than pieces of the Washington landscape, their utterly common appearance unnoticed by everyone who passed by. It wasn't until their teammate at the South Lawn sent a text message that the men inside the vans sprang into action, sliding the rooftop air-conditioning units back to reveal the sky.

"JAY," SAID THE president as they walked toward the helicopter. "We need to find a way to de-escalate the situation with Iran after this is over. If we throw too much support behind the president and the foreign minister, the hard-liners and the remaining Revolutionary Guard leadership will label them as puppets of the U.S. and they'll lose their standing with the people."

"Sir, I think if we move our carrier group out of the Persian Gulf for a while and let the Iranian president take credit for negotiating it, it will give him credibility and calm some nerves."

"What if the hard-liners come out on top?"

"Then those aircraft will be eight minutes from the coast."

The president nodded. "We'll need to set up back-channel communications with the new leadership," said the president. "As soon as things settle down, I want to press for reforms to their nuclear programs."

"That genie isn't going back in the bottle, sir, but

what will bring about lasting stability is the country's evolution from a disruptive, extremist theocracy to a—"

The two men were fifteen feet from Marine One when a high-pitched siren wailed across the White House grounds. Though he knew it to be a bad omen, the president had no idea what it meant, but General Landgraf had heard it before.

Too many times.

He pointed at the marine guard standing at attention at the foot of the helicopter stairs and shouted, "Incoming! Get everyone off the helo, now!"

The general grabbed the president's arm and turned toward the West Wing.

Concealed in a nondescript structure atop the White House Executive Residence, a counterbattery radar system had detected an incoming mortar attack. In less than a second, its cover retracted and its 20mm rotary cannon started spinning. The cannon's automated fire-control system adjusted its azimuth and elevation to intercept the incoming mortar shell and fired a thousand rounds in less than two seconds. A flash in the eastern sky confirmed that the incoming mortar had been destroyed. The remaining cannon rounds self-destructed, sounding like fireworks as they exploded harmlessly in the air.

But the siren was still wailing.

The helicopter crew was out and sprinting for safety. Landgraf and the president ran toward the Oval Office while two Secret Service agents rushed to meet them.

The 20mm cannon spun to the west and fired again,

sending shells arcing across the sky above the Eisenhower Executive Office Building as it neutralized a second attack.

When General Landgraf heard the CRAM firing a third time, he knew from experience that the cannon wouldn't have time to intercept the next incoming round. The mortar shell would detonate before the president could make it into the building.

"Get down!" he screamed to the Secret Service agents as he tackled President Day from behind and drove him to the grass. The general covered him with his body and crossed his ankles just as a third mortar round exploded on the far side of the helicopter.

The high-explosive shell detonated ten feet above the ground, sending shrapnel flying through the air at five thousand feet per second. The helicopter was aflame and on its side, its windows shattered and its tail boom broken, but the fuselage had absorbed much of the blast, saving the lives of its crew. They were bloodied and concussed, but they'd live. The siren stopped and the all clear sounded a few seconds later.

The president dusted himself off and looked at the burning helicopter. "When will it end, Jay?" he said.

General Landgraf sat on the grass and pried a half-inch piece of shrapnel out of the sole of his boot.

"When the jihadis realize that the real struggle is inside their minds."

## ONE HUNDRED EIGHT

JAKE WAS LYING back on his elbows, gasping for breath. "I'm hit," he said.

Jeff and the others fired at the shooter, but the Libyan soldier had taken cover behind a thick stone column.

"Frag out!" Kevin shouted. He pulled the pin on a grenade and rolled it behind the column.

The explosion killed the Libyan, but the blast also took a chunk out of the sandstone column. It broke in two and collapsed. Thick stone tiles started falling from the ceiling and shattering on the floor.

Mike reached down and pulled Jake to safety a fraction of a second before a three-hundred-pound section of ceiling crashed to the ground. Jeff dropped to his kneepads and searched Jake's sides and legs for the gunshot wound.

"Where're you hit?" Jeff said.

"Chest . . ." Jake said weakly. "Hard to breathe . . ."

Mike and Kevin fired inches away from each other as they engaged another Libyan. The man went down with four rounds where the bridge of his nose had once been.

Jeff found the hole. The incoming round had hit Jake's ceramic body armor. It was only the kinetic energy dump that he'd felt. The bullet had been stopped.

"You took one in the plate," Jeff said with a crooked smile. "Shake it off."

Jake stood and caught his breath. "It feels like I got kicked by a horse."

The five Americans made their way to a stone staircase. An LNA soldier leaned over the top of the stairs and Jake fired two rounds from eight feet away. The soldier tumbled onto the steps. The team climbed around him, but a hailstorm of lead was waiting for them on the next level. They retreated down the steps for cover.

There was steady gunfire in other parts of the ruins as well. The Libyans, emplaced by General Wǔ-Dīng, were fighting from fortified positions. The U.S. forces found themselves channeled into kill zones and forced to cross preplanned fields of fire. A stalemate ensued, with the highly trained Americans heavily outnumbered.

Jeff was listening to his headset, in comms with Major Smith on the command net. Jeff spoke to his teammates as the five men hunkered in the stairway.

"ISR's got vehicles inbound from the east, including gun trucks. Light-company strength. ETA fifteen to twenty."

"Libyan National Army?" Lou asked.

"Could be LNA, Daesh, or some fucking militia

we've never heard of," Jeff said. "But it really doesn't matter because the AC-130 should have them in ten."

The gunfire intensified, with the Libyans firing blindly over the team's heads.

"There's a low stone wall at the top of the steps, five or six feet to the right," Jake said as he changed magazines, "but it's only wide enough for two men."

"Go," said Jeff. "I got your six."

Mike took a flash-bang from his vest and pulled the pin.

"Banger!" he shouted as he lobbed it up the stairway.

Six loud blasts and flashes of light disoriented the Libyans as Jake and Jeff hustled up the steps and neutralized the threat from behind the stone wall.

The rest of the team linked up with the first two. Just a few feet to their right, a crumbling stone balustrade was all that separated them from the ground, sixty feet below. Ahead was the narrow upper level that had been the seating tier for the lower classes. Dozens of walls marked where wooden grandstands had rotted away centuries ago, leaving most of the space open to the night sky. As they had been on the second level, the northern and southern ends were warrens of small rooms.

"Flight lead just radioed that Owl-62 had trouble starting an engine," Jeff said. "It's turning now, but visibility is going to hell. A weather front is kicking up a dust storm so big that they're tracking it on radar."

"What does that mean for us?" Jake asked.

"It means our mission window just got shorter. The

helos can't fly through the storm or they're going back to the taxpayers. The fixed-wing aircraft can fly above it, but they can't see the targets."

Jeff listened to his headset again.

"ISR just lost the enemy convoy in the dust," he relayed to the team. "The AC-130 never got a shot off."

"How much time do we have?" Jake asked.

"Twenty minutes," said Jeff. "If we're not out of here by then, the helos won't be able to take off."

"Which means we'll have to fight it out with the convoy," said Mike.

The men heard steady gunfire on the lower levels.

"We've already got six wounded," Jeff said. "With the AC-130 out of the fight and the helos grounded, we're fucked."

"Let's clear north first," Jake said. "That'll put us above the main entrance when we exfil."

Jeff nodded and the five men moved quickly toward the cluster of rooms at the north end. Gusts of wind howled through the ruins. Swirls of sand blew across the floor.

"Contact rear," Lou said.

Two Libyan soldiers had heard the shooting and run up the steps.

Lou put them both down. One of the Libyans fired a wild shot into the night sky as he fell. Another Libyan soldier popped up from behind a stone wall and started spraying bullets. Jake fired three rounds into his chest.

"Troop sar'nt major," Kevin said. His rifle was in his left hand, his right arm dangling at his side. "I caught one in the arm."

Mike cut away Kevin's sleeve. The wound was in his

triceps and bleeding heavily. Mike tore open a hemo-
static bandage and taped it tightly into place.

Jeff looked at Kevin. "What do you want—"

"Go!" he said as he slung his rifle behind his back
and switched to the pistol strapped to his thigh.

The northern end of the floor was blocked by a
hundred-foot-wide wall with entrances on the left and
right. Jake and the others stacked up outside the archway on the right.

"It's a different layout than the ground floor," Jake
said. "Smaller rooms, rooms within rooms, more places
to hide. It's going to be fast."

Jake went in first and turned left, with Jeff on his
heels. They held the hallway while the others instantly
cleared a small alcove to the right. The space was a
maze of rooms off a main hall. Everywhere the team
went, they were visible from at least three other rooms,
presenting dozens of possibilities for ambush. It was a
nightmare, fraught with risk, but they never stopped
moving. They advanced down the hall clearing both
sides at lightning speed.

A Libyan soldier popped out from a room on the left
and Mike hit him with three rounds. The team heard
Major Smith on the assault net. He'd joined the fight
inside the building and was asking for reinforcements
on the second floor, but the rest of the troop was either
engaged or out of the fight with casualties. There was
more traffic on the radio.

"*Spooky-41, available,*" said the AC-130's fire control
officer. The air directly above the ruins was still clear
enough to acquire targets.

*"Negative, Spooky, we're fighting room to room,"* Smith responded. *"Cover the primary extraction point for casualty evacuation."*

The flight lead aboard Owl-61 followed, *"Echo troop, this weather is forcing our hand. You've got nine and a half minutes."*

Heavy gunfire sounded from outside the amphitheater as the enemy convoy arrived. The much smaller Delta team was ready for them, but severely outnumbered. The best they could hope for was to hold the enemy off for a while. A burst from the AC-130's 25mm cannon destroyed the first vehicle but the leading edge of the sandstorm rolled in and obscured the others. The two DAP gunships were orbiting the extraction point to cover the troop as it moved into exfil posture.

Jake and the others kept advancing down the hallway, knees bent, upper bodies steady, propelled forward by the mission clock. The weather had further shortened their already tight timetable.

Jake and Jeff turned into the first room on the right while the others cleared the room on the left. Both were vacant. The five men linked up in the hallway and cleared two more rooms, popping into each for no more than a second before moving on. Jake was in front because he knew the layout, but the Delta operators moved like athletes who'd practiced their plays for years. Fast, efficient, precise.

*"Owl Flight at extraction point,"* said the flight lead over the radio.

The helicopters' rotors were sheathed in halos of faint

light as they sliced through the leading edge of the sand-storm. The DAPs circled above, scanning for targets, but the degraded visibility forced them to keep their heavy weapons tight, firing only occasional bursts from their 7.62mm miniguns when they caught glimpses of the enemy convoy.

Jake and Jeff came to the last room on the right. From the hallway they could see only a sliver of the interior. Its ceiling and outside wall had collapsed long ago, leaving only the floor and the side walls. Behind it was a light show of muzzle flashes, tracers, and exploding grenades that played havoc with their night optical devices. Sand whirled through the open space.

Jake swung inside and turned left. Jeff followed behind and swung to the right, but he stumbled on a fallen column that was hidden by the blowing sand.

A gunshot rang out.

Faisal was cowering in the corner, clutching the pistol with both hands. He pulled the trigger a second time, but sand had jammed the action. Jeff shot him twice in the face and Jake put two more rounds into the prince's chest. Mike was in the room a second later.

Jeff cursed as he fell to the ground. "I'm hit in the thigh."

Jake popped into the hallway to check for more hostiles, but the area was clear.

Mike was on his knees examining Jeff's wound. "It's bleeding pretty good, but it missed the femoral," he shouted over the din of battle. "Let's get a tourniquet on it and get him to the helo."

Owl-61's pilot was on the radio, warning that the sandstorm was moving in faster than expected. *"This shit is chewing up our engines. You've got five minutes!"*

Jake looked at his watch, then to Mike and Lou. "The Tomahawks are launching any second. Can you two handle Jeff?"

"We got him. Find Wǔ-Dīng!"

Jake exploded through the doorway, his rifle moving from side to side like a metronome. He pushed to the southern end of the amphitheater, his senses in overdrive.

Bullets crashed into the wall next to him. A Libyan soldier was prone on the nearest stairway. Jake fired a pair of 77-grain bullets into the man's head.

Jake seated a fresh magazine and took two deep breaths outside the southern cluster of rooms. He popped into the hallway for a fraction of a second. The right side was empty. He popped back out. He lowered himself onto one knee and scanned left. Also empty. Jake rose to his feet and cleared the first room on the left in under two seconds. He did the same in the second and third rooms.

There was constant chatter on the assault net. Most of the casualties had been loaded aboard Owl-62, but the three helicopters were still on the ground in a close-proximity firefight. Departure time was four minutes and not a second later.

Jake swung into the next room. His rifle came to rest on General Wǔ-Dīng, standing in full uniform under an exterior arch. The general's hands were empty and at his sides.

"Turn around and get on your knees!" Jake shouted over the howling wind and the din of battle. He pulled a set of flex-cuffs from his vest.

Wǔ-Dīng snapped to attention. The crescent moon behind him glowed red through the blowing sand.

"Everything I have done," he said, "I have done for China."

The general turned to face the night sky and took one step forward.

He landed headfirst on the stone colonnade, sixty feet below.

"Dammit!" Jake screamed. He'd just lost his last chance to stop a war.

He glanced at his watch. Three minutes till the helicopters were gone.

Jake ran for the stairs, but half a dozen enemy soldiers were closing in from the other direction and he started taking fire immediately. He spun around, but three more Libyans cut off his escape. He was trapped in the middle, but the Libyans were firing cautiously, wary of accidentally hitting their teammates on the opposite end of the hallway.

Jake sprinted for a gap in the floor where a wooden stairway had once been. Wearing forty pounds of gear, he leapt into the hole and fell fifteen feet through the air, rolling onto his side and coming back up on his feet. He ran toward a set of stone steps at the end of the hall.

There was more gunfire up ahead, including muffled bursts from the suppressed American weapons.

*Two minutes.*

He came around a downed column and spotted Jeff and the rest of the team, pinned behind a low stone wall. Bullets zipped overhead as he crawled to their position.

"Where's Wǔ-Dīng?" Mike said.

"He took a swan dive from the top floor," Jake said.

"Shit! We need postmort ID."

"No time," Lou said.

Five Libyans were at the end of the hall with a stone wall in front of them and an open archway behind. Mike lobbed a hand grenade over the wall, but it flew through the archway and exploded outside.

"We can't get past them," Lou shouted, "and the only stairway is right there!" He indicated a spot twenty feet in front of the Libyans. The Americans would be slaughtered if they tried to reach it.

"There's a gap in the floor behind me," Jake said. He pointed back toward the direction from which he'd come. "We can jump."

Mike glanced at his teammates. Lou had taken down two of the Libyans already and Jeff was laying down fire, but he was pale and the bandage around his leg was soaked with blood despite the tourniquet. Kevin was awkwardly reloading his pistol with his good hand. If they didn't jump, they'd die where they were.

"Do it!" Mike said.

"I've got Jeff," Jake shouted. "Go!"

Mike laid down a blizzard of suppressive fire and forced the Libyans behind cover. Jake pulled the troop sergeant major's arm across his shoulders and the two men hobbled toward the hole where another wooden staircase had once stood. Kevin jumped down with the pistol in his hand. He executed a parachute-landing fall, rolled onto one knee, and came up firing, engaging a threat on the ground floor.

Jake yelled to Mike, "Take Jeff's wrist."

The two men lowered the troop sergeant major into the hole until he was five feet from the ground.

Jake caught sight of his watch.

*One minute.*

"Let go on two!" Jake shouted. "One, two!"

Jeff fell to his good side with a shock wave of pain exploding through his body but no additional injuries. Jake and Mike leapt down after him and the team started moving again.

Owl-61 was on the ground just outside. A hundred Kalashnikov rifles and a dozen RPD light machine guns were shooting from inside the cloud of airborne sand. The airborne DAPs were firing bursts from their miniguns and even the occasional rocket, but visibility was so poor, and the enemy fighters were so close to the U.S. soldiers, that the gunships couldn't fully engage.

"Owl-61," Mike shouted into the radio. "Friendlies coming out at your five o'clock, five men!"

The helicopter's right-side crew chief shifted his aim away from the amphitheater. Sparks flew off its fuselage and its spinning blades as enemy rounds found their mark. An RPG flew ten feet over Owl-63 before disappearing into the night sky.

A heavy machine gun opened up from the back of an enemy vehicle, spraying rounds blindly through the dust cloud toward the sound of the American helicopter. The bullets chewed up the ground between the amphitheater and the helicopter's ramp. One of the DAPs spotted the muzzle flashes and a pair of 2.75-inch rockets blew the truck to pieces.

The dust kicked up by the storm and the helo's rotors hit Jake and the team like a sandblaster as they emerged from the ruins. Lou lifted the troop sergeant major onto his shoulder and ran for Owl-61. Two more Delta operators pulled Jeff inside and Lou and Kevin climbed in behind them.

Jake and Mike were the last two Americans on the ground, sixty feet back, firing at a group of Libyans and covering the others' escape.

Another RPG soared into the sky, splitting the air between Owl-62 and Owl-63 just as the two helos went airborne.

Jake was ten yards from the door of Owl-61, when enemy gunfire erupted from the second floor of the ruins. One of the DAPs fired its 30mm chain guns and the enemy position was obliterated.

Jake turned for the helicopter, only to see Mike stumble and fall to the ground with a gunshot wound. Jake reached down and dragged him to Owl-61, where two of his teammates hauled him into the cabin. Jake was the last to snap in, with his legs hanging over the side.

The pilots pulled pitch immediately, but the sandstorm tumbled down on top of them like a breaking wave, pushing the helicopter toward the ground. Owl-61 gained altitude slowly, its twin-turbine engines struggling to generate power amid all the airborne dust. With sand swirling through the cabin and enemy gunfire ripping through the air, the Night Stalker pilots focused on their instruments and turned the Black Hawk for home.

Jake scrambled through the packed cabin and jacked into the intercom system. A moment later he was patched through to Ted Graves at CIA headquarters.

"Ted! We found Wǔ-Dīng. He and Faisal—"

"We saw the video," said Graves.

Jake had forgotten about the helmet camera he'd been wearing the entire time.

"The Tomahawks just self-destructed over a Chinese mountain range," Graves said. "President Day is on the phone now with President Chéng."

Jake lowered himself to the floor and looked down the length of the cabin. Nearly half the troop had been wounded in the assault, but it appeared that they would all survive. Jeff had an IV drip in his arm and was speaking to a medic. Mike had been grazed in the ass and was already absorbing vulgar jokes from his teammates.

"Everyone is standing down," Graves said. "Great work, Keller."

## ONE HUNDRED NINE

PRESIDENT DAY AND President Chéng made a joint statement conceding both countries' culpability in the attack on Mecca. They acknowledged that the increased deployment of unmanned combat systems, in the air, on the ground, and at sea, was greatly increasing the likelihood of more incidents like the one in Saudi Arabia. The two leaders vowed to add additional safeguards to reduce the chance that World War III would be started by a hacker.

The raid on Tehran had gone down as planned, with twelve of the top twenty leaders killed in their beds, but Major General Shirizani had survived and was now supporting an ambitious ayatollah who opposed the reform-minded president and foreign minister. It was still very much a situation in flux.

Eight senior members of Pakistan's Inter-Services Intelligence Agency disappeared from the streets of Karachi and eleven more vanished from foreign posts. Each had had a hand in the transfer of the nuclear weapon to Mullah Muktar and his al-Qaeda forces in Yemen. There was more housecleaning to be done, but

CIA and U.S. special operations forces were sending a clear message that a line had been crossed and a price would be paid.

The Delta Force troop sergeant major spent two days at Landstuhl Regional Medical Center in Germany before being transferred to Walter Reed in Maryland to continue his recovery. Despite their initial friction, he and Jake had formed a close bond during their time in Libya and Jake had taken to visiting him between debriefing sessions at CIA headquarters.

JAKE HAD BARELY stopped his old Jeep Gladiator in front of the hospital when Jeff bounded through the front door and tossed his crutches in the bed.

"Any problems?" Jake said as he pulled away.

Jeff was recovering well, and his pregnant wife and three-year-old daughter were arriving from Wyoming late the next day, but he wasn't due to be released for another seventy-two hours.

"Negative," Jeff said. "I'm sure the nurses will bark some when they figure out I'm gone, but Smitty's got a slow-mover badge of his own. He gets the drill."

Jake turned east into heavy traffic on the Beltway.

"How's your wife handling it?" he said.

Jeff grimaced. "She's working on a list of stuff for me to do around the house before the baby's born."

Jake laughed. "No rest for the weary."

"Amen, brother."

It was nearly sunset when they turned onto a two-lane country road and rolled down the windows. The mud tires on the pickup truck hummed as they passed sweet-smelling fields of corn tinted orange by the fading daylight. Jake eased around a farm tractor with an American flag flying from its cab.

The farmer waved.

Jake turned down an unmarked gravel road that dead-ended at a large farm situated on Chesapeake Bay. Scattered white clouds contrasted with a sky painted in brilliant shades of pink and blue.

Jake grabbed Jeff's crutches from the bed of the truck and the two men walked to the barn. A serious-looking man met them at the door. His high-and-tight haircut and "Semper Fi" T-shirt left no question about his affiliation. He gave the new arrivals the once-over.

"Help you?" he said.

"We're here to get drunk," Jake said.

The man nodded and led them inside to meet the rest of Roach's friends.

_____

T WAS SAID that seawater ran through his veins.

The scion of a Greek shipping dynasty, the young man cared not for the wheeling and dealing of the industry, or the megayachts and private jets that came with it. He loved his family, but its enormous wealth brought him neither pride nor shame—it simply did not define his existence. When he graduated school and the time came for him to enter the family business, he chose instead—as he would for the rest of his life—to chart his own course.

The young man ventured fourteen hundred miles to the northwest, to the Dutch port city of Rotterdam, where he found work at a competing line as an ordinary seaman. He signed on under an alias—eager to prove to himself that he had earned his position and not inherited it—and was soon scraping paint, cleaning heads, and scrubbing decks on everything from 150-foot-long tramp freighters to twelve-hundred-foot-long oil tankers. He worked hard, learned quickly, and moved rapidly through the ranks. Soon there wasn't a crewman's job aboard any ship anywhere that he couldn't handle and he left the industry.

But he wasn't finished.

He was just getting started.

He moved to Belgium and attended maritime college, spending four years studying navigation, load handling, and engineering before returning to the sea with his degree in hand—as a ship's officer.

Strikingly handsome, with a square jaw and wavy dark hair, his resemblance to his father grew as he aged until, by his late-twenties, even strangers would comment on the similarity. Once he'd attained the rank of ship's master, he resumed using the family name. No one he'd served with would dispute that he knew his crew, his ships, and the sea, as well as anyone who'd ever commanded a merchant vessel.

In short order he was hired by the largest shipping company in the world to drive fourteen-hundred-foot supertankers across the seas, navigating his way through storms that would frighten a statue and across oceans so vast that the crews often spent days without sighting another ship.

But as years passed and ships became more automated, crews became smaller and satellite telemetry made him feel less like a master and commander and more like a bus driver. By the time he was in his late thirties, he moved back to his family's shipping line where he could once again manage the voyage and not simply optimize fuel consumption based on computer models and satellite predictions of weather and current.

With Asia to his north and Africa to his south, Captain Romanos was at the helm of the 860-foot M/V *Lindos* as it steamed east into the turquoise waters of the Gulf of Aden.

Sixty feet wide and fifteen feet deep, the oil tanker's glassed-in bridge offered a spectacular 360-degree view of the world as the sun fell through scattered clouds and disappeared below the horizon. The ship's officers watched the sky and sea meld into blackness, interrupted only by the stars above and their reflections on the water below. Though they'd seen it a thousand times before, its mystical beauty never failed to reinforce their calling to the sea.

It was five past midnight when Captain Romanos turned the bridge over to his second-in-command and prepared to retire to his stateroom. He was halfway to the portside door when the navigator spoke up.

"I've never seen that before."

Romanos stopped short.

The navigator and most of the other officers had come with the captain from the larger shipping company where they'd worked together for nearly a decade. They'd become fast friends, spending more time with each other than they did with their own families, and they'd learned to trust each other's judgment and anticipate each other's thoughts. Together they'd survived typhoons, been boarded by unfriendly navies, and had more barroom fistfights than he could count.

As far as the captain was concerned, the navigator had seen everything.

Romanos turned around.

"All three radars are full of static," said the navigator. "Lost our GPS position fix, too."

"Radio?" said the captain, nodding toward the single-sideband.

Another officer turned up the volume.

"Nothing but noise. Same with the VHF."

The captain looked at the chief engineer. "It could be electrical interference, but—"

The doors on both sides of the bridge burst open.

Six men in black and gray uniforms stormed in, three on each side, with rifles snugged in tight against their shoulders.

For as long as the captain could remember, ships' crews had been instructed to cooperate when boarded. They would be threatened, they might even be abused, but their value as hostages decreased by one hundred percent if they were dead. It had been the same with the airlines. The pilots had been told to accommodate hijackers because they were looking only to make a political statement or maybe take a free ride to a forbidden destination. More often than not, all of the hostages were safely released.

Cooperate and live.

It had worked for most of modern history.

But piracy was experiencing its 9/11 moment.

The captain squared off against the gunman closest to him. The tall man's blue eyes locked on like a hawk tracking its prey, but the captain stared right back.

"I'm the captain. What is it—"

The pirate fired three rounds into his heart, and Captain Romanos was dead before he hit the ground.

* * *

IT WAS SIX days later and a thousand miles to the north when the guard met the three trucks. Covered in dust from their long journey through the desert, he escorted the small convoy through the seaport's high-security gate to a darkened warehouse. The guard parked out by the door while the trucks drove inside.

A lieutenant colonel from Iran's Revolutionary Guards stepped down from the lead vehicle and began issuing orders to the forklift operator who'd been collecting overtime for the past four hours, waiting for the shipment to arrive. The forklift had already unloaded a dozen crates of rifles and rocket-propelled grenades from the first truck's bed when two soldiers grabbed the warehouse's sliding metal doors and shut them in the guard's face.

Four soldiers climbed into the bed of the second truck. Though it was midsummer on the Persian Gulf, each man shivered as the group took hold of a sturdy plastic case the size of a footlocker. It wasn't heavy, but the men moved the sealed container slowly and deliberately as they lowered it from the truck and placed it inside an empty wooden crate. Another solider packed the empty space with blocks of dry ice and placed the wooden lid on top.

A bead of sweat formed on the soldier's brow as the colonel handed him a hammer and a dozen nails. The soldier had seen the bio-hazard symbols painted on the plastic container and had no desire to disturb whatever was inside, but the colonel's gaze was unyielding.

The solider carefully aligned the hammer and gently tapped each nail into place.

An hour after they'd arrived, the three trucks emerged from the warehouse and were escorted back to the main gate by the waiting guard. The entire operation had been shrouded in secrecy—from the civilian trucks to the late hour—and the guard's name had been deleted from the roster, with explicit orders from his supervisor to forget everything he'd seen.

The guard turned in the keys for his pickup and went to the employee locker room to change out of his uniform. He sat on a worn wooden bench and rubbed his eyes. It had been a long day, and his shift was finally over, but he still had a phone call to make before his work was finished.

**FALLEN PATRIOTS** ®

**COLLEGE FOR THEIR CHILDREN**

A portion of my royalties from each copy of *Rogue Strike* sold goes directly to Children of Fallen Patriots Foundation, a 501(c)(3) charity whose mission is to provide college scholarships and educational counseling to military children who have lost a parent in the line of duty. The organization is dedicated to serving the families of service members who have died as a result of combat casualties, military training accidents, and other duty-related deaths.

If you have lost a parent in the line of duty, or would like to help those who have, please visit FallenPatriots.org.

Ready to find
your next great read?

Let us help.

**Visit prh.com/nextread**